LOVING THE AMISH QUILTMAKER

He wanted to kiss that jelly off her bottom lip so badly, he thought he might go crazy. His heart beat a wild rhythm as he stared at her mouth. She stopped breathing and stared at his. He curled his hands around her upper arms and lowered his face to hers.

And got a ruler right in the eyebrow.

Esther gasped and then giggled.

Levi pulled back and rubbed the spot on his eyebrow where Esther's ruler had gotten him. "Ow."

"Oh, dear," she said, pulling the ruler from behind her ear. "I'm sorry. I was measuring stitches and forgot it was even there."

"Am I bleeding?"

"There's a little scratch, but you won't have a scar."

"*Gute*, because I wouldn't want to tell our children about how I got it."

Her eyes glistened with hope and promise. "Our children?"

Levi wrapped his arms around Esther and pulled her close. "Will you marry me, my dear, darling quiltmaker? I love you more than you will ever know . . ."

Books by Jennifer Beckstrand

The Matchmakers of Huckleberry Hill
HUCKLEBERRY HILL
HUCKLEBERRY SUMMER
HUCKLEBERRY CHRISTMAS
HUCKLEBERRY SPRING
HUCKLEBERRY HARVEST
HUCKLEBERRY HEARTS
RETURN TO HUCKLEBERRY HILL
A COURTSHIP ON HUCKLEBERRY HILL
HOME ON HUCKLEBERRY HILL

The Honeybee Sisters
SWEET AS HONEY
A BEE IN HER BONNET
LIKE A BEE TO HONEY

The Petersheim Brothers
ANDREW
ABRAHAM

Amish Quiltmakers
THE AMISH QUILTMAKER'S UNEXPECTED BABY

Anthologies
AN AMISH CHRISTMAS QUILT
THE AMISH CHRISTMAS KITCHEN
AMISH BRIDES
THE AMISH CHRISTMAS LETTERS
THE AMISH CHRISTMAS CANDLE

Published by Kensington Publishing Corp.

The Amish Quiltmaker's Unexpected Baby

JENNIFER BECKSTRAND

ZEBRA BOOKS
KENSINGTON PUBLISHING CORP.
www.kensingtonbooks.com

ZEBRA BOOKS are published by

Kensington Publishing Corp.
119 West 40th Street
New York, NY 10018

All Kensington titles, imprints, and distributed lines are available at special quantity discounts for bulk purchases for sales promotion, premiums, fund-raising, educational, or institutional use.

Special book excerpts or customized printings can also be created to fit specific needs. For details, write or phone the office of the Kensington Sales Manager: Attn.: Sales Department. Kensington Publishing Corp., 119 West 40th Street, New York, NY 10018. Phone: 1-800-221-2647.

Zebra and the Z logo Reg. U.S. Pat. & TM Off.
BOUQUET Reg. U.S. Pat. & TM Off.

First Printing: March 2021
ISBN-13: 978-1-4201-5199-2
ISBN-10: 1-4201-5199-1

ISBN-13: 978-1-4201-5200-5 (eBook)
ISBN-10: 1-4201-5200-9 (eBook)

10 9 8 7 6 5 4 3 2 1

Printed in the United States of America

Chapter One

Esther Zook had four hundred and thirty-five reasons to run screaming from the house and never come back.

But she wasn't really a screamer, and she'd certainly never been much of a runner. She found it completely incomprehensible that people actually ran for fun. But most of them were *Englischers*, and she'd never been able to understand much of what *Englischers* did, so her confusion was expected.

Instead of screaming or banging her head against the refrigerator, Esther stood in the middle of her tiny kitchen and read Ivy's letter over and over again. After all Esther had done for her sister, this was how Ivy repaid her? The world had turned upside down, topsy-turvy in a matter of seconds.

And then the *buplie*, the baby, started crying.

Esther was going to throw up.

And Esther wasn't a thrower-upper. She'd never thrown up in her life, even that time Grossmater made her try cow's tongue at the state fair.

Esther growled and tore Ivy's letter in half, then in half again. Then in half again and again. Then she scrunched all the pieces together in her fist, made a raggedy paper ball, and with a great heave, threw the ball across the kitchen. It landed in the only potted plant in the house, caught in the long, feathery leaves of her fern like a bug in a spider's web.

A strong knock at the front door startled Esther out of her thoughts and sent a wave of relief crashing over her. Ivy had changed her mind and decided to come back, which was just what Esther would have expected from Ivy. That girl couldn't make up her mind about what to wear every morning. She was as flighty as a sparrow.

Esther rushed to the door and threw it open. Instead of Ivy on the other side, a tall, handsome Amish stranger with wavy brown hair and a deep cleft in his chin stood on her porch. He wasn't Ivy, but he'd have to do. Esther grabbed a fistful of his shirt and pulled him into the house. "Do you know how to change a diaper?" she said, because that was her immediate need, and she wasn't going to waste time with unnecessary chitchat.

Surprise and shock popped all over his face. "I'm sorry, what?"

"Can you change a diaper? Because I can't, and my *schwester* has run off."

He took a step back and looked as if he was going to bolt like a skittish horse. She tightened her hold on his shirt. She couldn't let him get away, not when she needed him so desperately.

He raised his hands as if stopping traffic and slowly looked down at her fist balled around the fabric of his shirt. Hopefully, he wasn't fussy about wrinkles. "Um. My *mammi* sent me to look at your bathroom. She says it needs work. There must be some mistake."

Esther clenched her teeth as the wails from the other room got louder. "We can sort out the mistakes later. Can you change a diaper or not?"

"I can," he said tentatively. He was wise to be suspicious. She was about to draft him. "But I don't especially like it."

She pulled him into the baby's temporary room and pointed to the portable crib. "The baby is in there. Her diapers are in that suitcase."

He drew his brows together and gazed at her, his expression a mixture of confusion and panic. "This is a little . . . I don't know what to say . . . my *mammi* said to come look at your bathroom."

Esther huffed out a short and impatient breath. "Enough about the bathroom. I need you to change the baby's diaper. Then we can talk about the bathroom. Is that good enough for you?"

He must have sensed her frustration, or maybe he thought it was best to just agree with the crazy Amish woman. "I suppose so."

"*Gute.* I'll get a diaper."

The stranger looked into the crib as if its contents would jump out and bite him. His mouth immediately relaxed into a dazzling smile. "Well, aren't you sweet?" he said, and it took Esther a fraction of a second to realize he was talking to the *buplie* and not to her. He reached down and picked up Ivy's baby and cradled her in his arms like Esther had seen *gute* mothers do. The baby immediately stopped crying. Esther caught her bottom lip between her teeth. She probably should have tried that.

The stranger cooed and bounced the baby like he knew what he was doing. Did he have his own children? He didn't have a beard, so he probably wasn't married, but for sure and certain, he seemed like the fatherly type.

He laid the baby on the twin bed next to the crib. The baby kicked and grinned at him as if he had a whole bag of lollipops in his pocket. "What's her name?"

Esther clenched her teeth again as she felt her face get warm. "Winter." It was embarrassing just saying it.

The stranger raised an eyebrow. "Winter?"

"I don't know what my *schwester* was thinking." But that was nothing new. Esther was never sure what her sister was thinking. She handed him the diaper.

He smiled at the baby and talked to her in that soft little voice people always used with *buplies*. "Well, Winnie, you sure are a beautiful baby."

"Winnie?" Esther said. "That's much better."

The stranger glanced at Esther as if she was a distraction, as if she'd been the one to barge into *his* house and not the other way around. He slipped the wet diaper off Winter—Winnie—making a crackling sound as he pulled the tabs on each side of the diaper. Then he wrapped his fingers around Winter's ankles and lifted her bottom so he could slide the clean diaper under her. In a lightning-quick motion, he fastened the diaper around Winnie and onto itself. It happened too fast. "Could you do that again? I'll watch more closely." Not that she was planning on changing any more diapers. For sure and certain, Ivy was bound to walk back through that door within the hour.

He frowned. "How have you managed this long? Your baby must be at least three or four months old."

Esther pushed a long and frustrated sigh from her throat. "She's not my baby."

He picked up Winter, being careful of her floppy head, and bobbled her up and down on his hip. "She's cute."

Esther glanced at Winter. She had a shock of fine black hair that floated around her head like a patch of ragweed. And even at four months, she had dark, well-defined eyebrows that made her look older than she was. "Of course she's cute. That doesn't mean I know how to change her diaper."

The stranger smoothed his thumb down Winter's soft cheek. The baby studied his face as if he was the most interesting thing she'd seen in her short life. He was definitely the most interesting thing Esther had seen since she'd come to Colorado. "She looks like you," he said.

Was that a compliment? Winter was cute and all, but her head was unusually big for her body. Did the stranger think Esther had a big head? "*Jah.* I guess she looks like me." Esther's temper flared at the thought of her *schwester*'s betrayal. "My *schwester* showed up last night with Winter. She asked if she could stay for a few days. What could I do? You don't turn away family."

"Of course not."

Winter was done being fascinated with the stranger. She squirmed in his arms, made a face, and started crying in earnest. "Do you think she needs another diaper change?" Esther said, because out of the two of them, the stranger was the expert.

One side of his mouth twitched upward. "I expect she's hungry."

"Hungry? She can't be hungry. I don't have anything to feed her."

The stranger held Winter close and patted her back

gently. It was a sweet gesture, but it did nothing to quiet the crying. "Is there formula in the suitcase?"

Formula! Esther had watched Ivy make a bottle last night. She knelt down and stirred the contents of the suitcase until she found a white and blue plastic container with a picture of a baby on the front. "This is it. And there's a bottle on the dish drainer in the kitchen. Ivy washed it last night." How nice of her. Esther nearly growled out loud. Ivy had abandoned her baby and left Esther with a very serious problem, but at least she'd been thoughtful enough to wash the baby's bottle before she left. Esther was going to explode with the injustice of it all.

Since his hands were busy, Esther placed the tub of formula in the crook of the stranger's elbow. "Do you know how to make a bottle?"

"You'll have to hold the baby."

Esther never did anything unless she was confident in her ability to do it perfectly, and she wasn't about to mess up with the baby, especially not with a stranger watching. She snatched the formula from its place on his elbow. "You hold the baby. Tell me how to make the formula." It couldn't be that hard.

The stranger bounced the baby more zealously. Winter cried fiercely. "You just have to read the directions."

Directions. Esther knew how to read directions. She made intricate quilts that required concentration and strict following of directions. She could make formula. She read the directions twice, just in case she missed something the first time. "How warm does the water need to be? I have a cooking thermometer."

"I don't think the cooking thermometer will help."

"Why not?"

The baby was getting hysterical, but the stranger stayed as calm as a summer's morning. How did he do that? "You just have to guess."

"Guess? You can't guess with a baby."

Still patting Winter's back, he strolled into the kitchen and turned on the tap water. "You wait for it to get pleasantly warm, then you fill your bottle."

Esther frowned. "Shouldn't you use purified water? I think we're supposed to use purified water."

That quirky little smile appeared again. "Tap water is fine, and Winnie is too hungry to be picky."

Esther sidled up to the sink as if it would bite her and put her hand under the running water. It was a good thing she had a solar-powered water heater. She had all the warm water she wanted.

"Is it warm?" he said.

"I can't decide if it's lukewarm, pleasantly warm, or unseasonably warm."

"Good enough," he said.

"Good enough? For someone who claims to know a lot about babies, you seem to be quite irresponsible about bottle temperatures." Esther opened her gadget drawer and started searching for her cooking thermometer.

"I never claimed to know anything about babies."

"Well, maybe you should have told me that before you barged in here and changed Winnie's diaper."

He lifted an eyebrow. "As I remember it, I didn't barge. You dragged me in."

Okay. He had a point, but that in no way excused the tap water idea. "We don't have time to argue about it now." No time at all. Winnie's high-pitched screams would soon break all the windows in Esther's house. Esther didn't need any extra house repairs. She'd only just moved in.

The stranger glanced up at the ceiling and expelled a puff of air from between his lips. He cradled Winnie in one arm, tested the water temperature for himself, and grabbed the bottle from the dish drainer. "Good enough," he repeated, and at that point, Esther had to agree. It was either tap water or new windows. He filled the bottle with water and handed it to Esther. "Now put the formula in."

"How much?"

A glance up at the ceiling again. "Read the instructions."

A little embarrassed that she was so flustered, Esther read the instructions two more times, pulled out the little scoop, and poured three scoops of formula into the bottle. She spilled quite a bit on the floor, but cleaning up would have to wait. Poor Winnie was out of her head with hunger, and she couldn't have been looking forward to a bottle tainted with tap water.

Esther screwed the nipple onto the bottle and started to shake it up, just like the directions said. She shook vigorously, as instructed, and tiny droplets of milk flew from the hole in the nipple. Esther squeaked as formula splattered her nose and cheeks. She glanced at the stranger. A solitary drop of milk hung precariously from a strand of the curly hair that fell over his forehead, and four more drops trickled down his cheek.

"You have to cover the hole," he said, calmly wiping the milk from his face. The big drop slipped from his hair and plopped onto Winnie's cheek. Winnie momentarily stopped wailing.

For some inexplicable reason, the look on the man's

face struck Esther's funny bone. She couldn't keep a smile off her face. "It doesn't say *that* anywhere in the directions."

He laughed. "They probably should have mentioned it." He reached out and dabbed at Esther's cheek with his thumb. Something sweet and warm trickled down her spine. She ignored the sensation and the surprise that followed. She hadn't allowed a man to break through her defenses in a very long time.

"Okay, cover the hole," she said, gathering her scattered wits. She placed her finger over the hole on the nipple and shook the bottle hard.

Winnie's face was red, and she took great halting breaths in between screams. Bless his heart, the stranger was doing his best to quiet her, though nothing was working. "That's probably enough shaking," he said, wincing at a piercing scream directed into his ear.

"*Ach.* Okay."

Esther handed him the bottle, and he stuffed it into Winnie's mouth while she was still upright. Winnie sucked ravenously on the bottle, and the stranger slowly maneuvered her into a supine position in his arms. Carefully, he sat down at the table in one of Esther's four kitchen chairs and shot a grin in Esther's direction, flashing his extra-white teeth. "Success," he whispered.

Esther sighed and wiped her hands on a dish towel. First crisis averted. Lord willing, there would never be a second crisis. Unfortunately, she had an inkling her life was going to be one crisis after another until Ivy came back. "I'm sorry I got *griddlich*."

His smile made her feel better. "It's okay you got cranky. The sound of a baby crying is the most stressful noise in the world. People will do just about anything to stop it."

"How do you know so much about babies?" She cleared her throat. "Do you have children?" She didn't want him to have children, because that would mean he was married, but why she cared about that, she couldn't really say.

"*Nae.* I'm not married." Esther worked very hard to refrain from clapping her hands. "I have eleven *bruderen* and *schwesteren*," he said. "I'm the oldest, and my youngest sister, Lydiann, is two. The good news is she was potty trained last month, so no more diapers for either of us. I've changed plenty of diapers in my life, though I've always tried to get out of it. My sister Mary Jane is much better at diapers and children. She has two of her own."

Winnie reached up and wrapped her fingers around one of the stranger's suspenders. She kicked her tiny feet and gazed at him as if she hadn't recently been a total emotional wreck. She really was a darling little thing. Too bad her mother was a ninny.

The stranger glanced at Esther as if he didn't want to pry but felt compelled to anyway. "So Winnie is living out of a suitcase, you've never changed a diaper before, and you have a piece of chalk behind your ear."

Esther pursed her lips. Her life sounded quite strange when he put it like that. "*Ach.* You never know when you're going to need a piece of chalk."

His grin overspread his whole face. "I mostly never think about chalk."

"I always put chalk or a pencil behind my ear just in case I need to mark a pattern or a piece of fabric. Then I don't have to stop what I'm doing to search for something to write with." A quilter always needed chalk. Sometimes Esther walked around town with chalk dust on her cheek and got strange looks from her neighbors.

He nodded. "That's right. You're a quilter."

How did he know that? "The suitcase and diaper problem came last night." She walked around the table and retrieved Ivy's letter from her potted plant. She sat across the table from the stranger and unwrapped the letter. It crumbled to shreds when she pulled at it. He raised his eyebrows. She smiled sheepishly. Maybe she shouldn't have been so enthusiastic about tearing it up. "It's from my *schwester.*"

"She sent you a ball of confetti?"

Her face got warm. Why had she let her temper run away with her? "It used to be a letter. She left it for me this morning."

"It looks as if you didn't like what it said."

"My *schwester* hasn't been in my life for many years."

He pulled the bottle from Winnie's mouth and set it on the table. Then he lifted Winnie to his shoulder and patted her back. Winnie smacked her lips and let out a half-hearted whimper. "About halfway through feeding a baby, you need to burp them."

"Good to know." Esther fingered the pieces of Ivy's letter. "My sister probably found out I had money. She was extra motivated to find me."

"Okay?" he said.

She shook her head. "I don't have a lot of money. But my sister is destitute, so to her, I'm rich. None of my *bruderen* would have taken her in, though I'm sure she wouldn't have wanted to live with any of them."

He scrunched his lips to one side of his face. "I really have no idea what you're talking about."

"I'm sorry. I'm just so angry I could spit, but I won't, because it's rude." She smoothed out all the pieces of her sister's letter and laid them in order like she was putting together a puzzle. "I have four older *bruderen*. I am the oldest daughter, and Ivy is the youngest in the family. She is four years younger than I am, and my parents spoiled her rotten." Esther glanced at Winnie. "I'm not blaming them for how she turned out. From what I've seen this morning, being a parent must be well-nigh impossible."

His lips twitched. She'd seen that expression several times already—a mixture of amusement and lighthearted-ness that she found quite attractive, as if nothing ever upset him or made him lose his temper. He'd probably never tear up a letter from his sister, let alone throw it across the room. "Maybe you should save your judgment until you've had a little more time to settle in," he said.

"I don't think so."

Winnie let out a *gute* burp, and the stranger moved her to his other shoulder. He obviously knew what he was doing. If Esther had enough money, she'd hire him as a full-time mother's helper. Esther took a deep breath. She wouldn't need to do that, because Ivy was definitely coming back. Soon.

Esther looked at the shreds of Ivy's letter. Maybe she should try to put it back together to look for clues to Ivy's return. She retrieved the tape from the gadget drawer and sat back down at the table. "When Ivy was eighteen, she jumped the fence and ran away with an *Englisch* boy."

"That must have been hard for your family."

Esther squared her shoulders so the weight of her

memories wouldn't knock her over. She tried never to think about the months before and after Ivy left home. Ivy had hurt Esther and Mamm and Dat in so many ways it was hard to count them all. In the last eight years, it had been easier to forget Ivy even existed.

Esther pulled a short piece of tape from the roll and taped the first two strips of paper together. The stranger watched her with interest. "I've seen Ivy twice in the last eight years. We rarely heard from her. She didn't even know Mamm had died until six months after the funeral."

"I'm sorry about your *mamm*."

Esther nodded. "*Denki*."

"Maybe your *schwester* was ashamed to come home. That happens sometimes."

Esther shrugged. "Maybe. But last night she showed up on my porch as if she'd never been gone. I don't know how she got here, but it was just her and Winter, with no blanket for the baby and no coat for herself. I don't know what she was thinking. April is still cold in Colorado."

"Maybe she came from somewhere warm."

There he went again, giving Ivy the benefit of the doubt, even though she didn't deserve it. Esther pressed her lips together, a little ashamed of herself. Maybe she was too determined to think badly of Ivy. "She had a black eye and a bruise on her wrist."

"*Ach.*"

"Poor Ivy. She never thought she deserved better."

"So you let her stay the night," he said.

Esther nodded, the anger bubbling up again like a pot of caramel on the stove. "I woke up this morning and found this note on the kitchen counter." She finished taping the last piece and smoothed the creases. "*Dear*

Esther," she read, glancing at him in irritation. "*Jordan texted me last night, and he is really, really sorry. I don't think I've given our love enough of a chance. I need to know if this is going to work, and I can't work on our relationship if there's always a baby between us. I just need to leave Winter here for a few months while I figure it out. Jordan loves me. This is real, Esther.*"

The stranger's eyes were as round as pincushions. "*Ach, du lieva,*" he said.

Esther huffed out a breath. "*Jah.* That's what I said." Along with some other bad words she'd learned from the TV in the hospital waiting room. She had spent a lot of time there when Dat was sick. "It gets worse," she said. She scanned the letter to find where she'd left off and continued reading. "*I knew you'd say no, so I left without telling you. You're going to be mad, but please try to think about my feelings and what's best for me instead of always thinking about yourself.*"

"*Ach, du lieva,*" he repeated.

Esther couldn't stand it anymore. She ripped up the letter again, wadded it into a ball, and threw it across the kitchen. It landed in the sink. There were just so many reasons to be mad, and there wasn't enough paper in the whole world to make her feel better.

"What are you going to do?" he said quietly.

"How long can you stay?" she said, only half joking. Well, maybe more than half. He could never really stay, and she would never really ask him. But for sure and certain it was a tempting thought.

He laughed but then stopped himself and studied her face as if to determine if she was serious. "I have another appointment in twenty minutes."

THE AMISH QUILTMAKER'S UNEXPECTED BABY   15

"Don't worry. I would never actually ask such a thing of anyone. But I truly have no idea what to do. Maybe my *schwester* will come to her senses and be back before supper." Esther groaned, draped herself across the table, and thumped her forehead against the wood. "Or maybe she'll be gone for another eight years."

"It won't be that bad. This Jordan guy doesn't sound like he's going to last very long."

"You'd be surprised how dedicated my *schwester* is to a lost cause. She once had a pet worm that she fed for weeks after it died. Mamm finally made her throw it away."

The stranger pulled the bottle from Winter's mouth, set it on the table, and stood up. "I'm wonderful sorry, but I have to go."

"Of . . . of course. I understand." With a look of regret and maybe a little doubt, he gave Winter a few more pats on the back and handed her to Esther. Esther cradled Winter against her chest like she'd seen him do, but it didn't feel natural.

"Give her a few more burps. In an hour or so she'll need to go down for a nap. Then she'll want another bottle and a diaper change. If all else fails, feed her. Babies need to eat a lot."

Esther nodded as the panic rose like bile in her throat, but she wasn't going to beg him to stay. It wouldn't be dignified.

Winnie drooled all over Esther's shoulder.

Nope. She wasn't going to ask him to stay, not even with drool dripping down her sleeve. He walked to the entry-way and glanced in the front room. "Nice quilt," he said.

Esther gazed longingly at the small quilt she had on

frames in the front room. It was a special order from someone over the Internet, the long neck of a mother giraffe going from the top of the quilt to almost the bottom, where she licked the top of her baby's head. It was a darling quilt, and she'd finished the top just yesterday. Now it was highly unlikely she'd ever finish quilting it. She couldn't give anything but her full attention to the baby.

The stranger gave Esther a very sorry look. "There's nothing to worry about. You'll do just fine."

That was a bald-faced lie, but Esther was too polite to accuse him. He'd already changed a diaper and fed Winter. She could at least give him a pleasant send-off. "*Denki* for your help. I couldn't have done it without you." She managed to say it without bursting into tears.

"Maybe Ivy is already on her way back."

"Maybe," she said, not believing it for one minute, and annoyed with him for trying to make her feel better right before he abandoned her. If she hadn't had her hands full of baby, she would have pulled her chalk from behind her ear and chucked it at him. You never knew when you were going to need a piece of chalk.

With one last awkward nod, he escaped. Only after he shut the door behind him did Esther realize she had no idea how she was supposed to "put the baby down for a nap." She could have kicked herself for not asking him before he left.

And . . . why had he come? She had no clue about that either. She hadn't even asked him his name, and he hadn't offered it. Maybe he hadn't wanted her to know who he was. He'd be a lot harder to track down that way. If she couldn't find him, she wouldn't be able to rope him into changing more diapers.

Esther ground her teeth together. She should have at least asked his name.

Winter immediately started fussing, as if she realized just whom she'd been left with. Esther bounced her up and down the way she'd seen every mother deal with a baby when it got squirmy. "Hush now," she said. "It's going to be okay, Winnie. Do you mind if I call you Winnie? It's so much less embarrassing than Winter."

Winnie pursed her little lips and squinted like she was thinking about it very hard. Then she opened her mouth as if she was about to cry and threw up all over Esther.

Chapter Two

Winnie squeaked in her sleep, and Esther woke with a start. She looked at the clock with blurry eyes and tried to make it come into focus by sheer force of will. She finally gave up trying to determine the time. It was light outside, so it must have been morning, but for all she knew, it could have been anywhere between six and ten a.m.

Winnie hadn't taken a nap yesterday, and more than once Esther had scolded herself for forgetting to ask the stranger how to give a baby a nap. After Winnie threw up all over Esther's dress, Esther laid Winnie on her bed, changed clothes, and put her soiled dress in her bathroom sink to soak. As she was filling the sink with water, Winnie rolled off the bed, bonked her head, and screamed as if someone had stolen all her toys. Esther felt horrible about it, but how was she supposed to know that Winnie had learned how to roll over? Babies weren't supposed to roll over until they were like a year old or something, right? She needed some sort of chart to tell her all the things Winnie could and could not do so she'd be prepared for next time.

Poor Winnie got a red mark on her head, and Esther spent half an hour mopping up water because she'd been so upset about Winnie that she'd forgotten to turn off the faucet and the water had overflowed all over her bathroom floor. After turning off the water, Esther had pulled the beautiful, intricate quilt off her bed, laid it on the floor, and sat Winnie on top of it. Unfortunately, Winnie did not know how to sit yet. Fortunately, Esther caught her before she face-planted into the quilt and broke her nose. She laid Winnie on her back and kept one eye on her as she mopped up the floor, all the while feeling bad about Winnie's head and ferociously angry at Ivy.

When Winnie started crying again, Esther made her another bottle and fed her until she fell asleep. But when she tried to lay Winnie in her portable crib, she woke up immediately. Seven times Winnie nodded off to sleep as Esther fed her but woke up as soon as Esther tried to lay her down.

Esther ended up holding the bottle in Winnie's mouth while Winnie slept on her lap for a total of twenty minutes. It had to be the shortest nap in the history of naps. Winnie spent most of the rest of the day crying and fussing and occasionally nodding off to sleep in Esther's arms, and Esther spent most of the rest of the day holding Winnie and wishing that nice stranger with the curly hair and interesting eyes would come back and save her.

Unfortunately, he didn't return to save her from the "diaper incident." At about three in the afternoon, Winnie flared her nostrils, crinkled her lips, and made some sort of suspicious noise in her pants. At 3:05, she started to stink. At 3:10, Esther couldn't ignore it any longer.

It took her ten minutes and the entire package of

baby wipes, and the quilt on the bed in the extra room would have to be washed, but at the end of it, the baby was freshly diapered and actually seemed happier that her bowels were empty.

Late last night, Winnie had finally fallen asleep out of sheer exhaustion. She hadn't even stirred when Esther put her in her portable crib. Esther had walked out of the room, extinguished her propane lantern, and fallen into bed in her clothes. And her apron. And her *kapp*. She'd never gone to bed in her *kapp* before.

In the other room, Winnie squeaked again, and Esther rolled over and slid the pillow over her head. Every muscle in her body ached, and there was a sharp pain right between her shoulder blades. She had never hated her sister so much as she did in that moment.

That was an uncharitable thought. She didn't hate her sister. She could never hate the person who had played dolls with her and held her hand when they walked to church. She could never hate the girl who had sneaked a flashlight under the covers so they could talk and giggle late into the night while her parents were asleep. Esther didn't hate Ivy, but she was sure going to give Ivy what for when she came back. *If* she came back. Esther couldn't bear the thought, but it was a real possibility she'd seen the last of her sister.

She took a deep breath and sat up in bed. Winnie might have been awake, but she wasn't crying yet. Maybe Esther would have time to go to the bathroom. The bathroom! That was what that stranger had come for yesterday. But how did he know the toilet in the spare bathroom wasn't working? It was just another mystery to add to his coming. Maybe he was an angel sent by Derr Herr to help Esther out. In her sleep-deprived state, she could almost believe it. He was handsome and kind enough to be an angel. But did angels know how to change diapers? It seemed like angels would be concerned with more important things. Of course, to a baby, a clean diaper might be the most important thing in the world. It was all about perspective.

Esther used the bathroom and splashed her face with cold water. She didn't think she could survive another day like yesterday. Dread grew in her chest like mold. How many more days of this did she have? She took a peek into the spare bedroom. Winnie squirmed in her portable crib, but she wasn't crying. It was best to leave her there until absolutely necessary. What was that saying about not borrowing trouble?

Esther jumped out of her skin when someone knocked loudly and repeatedly on the door. Winnie let out a startled screech and began crying. Esther marched to the door. If it wasn't that stranger here to save her, she was going to give the loud knocker a piece of her mind. Didn't they know a baby was trying to sleep?

Esther opened the door so forcefully she fanned up a breeze. It wasn't the stranger and it wasn't an angel, but it looked to be something just as good. Or better. Three smiling Amish women stood on her porch with their arms full of what looked like supplies. Baby supplies. Maybe she was dreaming. Maybe she'd died last night and gone to heaven.

"Esther Zook?" the first woman said, with an utterly happy smile on her face. She looked to be in her late sixties, with very short salt-and-pepper gray hair under her *kapp* and laugh lines around her mouth. An Amish *fraa* with short hair? It was unheard-of.

"*Jah*, that's me," Esther said, ignoring the hair in her joy that these women hadn't accidentally come to the wrong house.

"Well, isn't this *wunderbarr*?" said the short-haired Amish woman. "I thought you'd be much older. I'm Nanna Kiem. This is my daughter-in-law Hannah and her daughter Mary Jane. Levi said you might could use some help."

Nanna's daughter-in-law Hannah wore a warm smile and looked like someone who knew how to take care of babies. "We brought diapers," she said, holding her bag open so Esther could look inside. Esther nearly burst into tears of relief.

The youngest woman, Mary Jane, couldn't have been more than twenty-two or -three, with curly brown hair and lively eyes that reminded Esther of yesterday's stranger. Her eyes sparkled with delight as she showed Esther her basket. "Levi said the *buplie* needs some clothes. Rosie has grown out of these."

Levi? Who was Levi? At that point, it didn't matter. Esther was so happy, she could have hugged all three of them.

Nanna motioned in the direction of all the noise. "Would you like some help?"

"*Ach, jah*, of course," Esther blurted out. She'd been standing in the doorway grinning like a cat when there was a *buplie* to tend to. She was just so gloriously happy. Gotte answered prayers after all.

Nanna walked in the house and set the bin she'd been carrying in the entryway. Hannah put her bag on top of the bin. They both immediately headed to the spare bedroom, where Winnie was making quite a racket. Nanna bent down, picked up Winnie, and planted a kiss on her wet cheek. "Well, aren't you sweet."

That's exactly what that stranger had said yesterday. Esther was obviously missing something. The baby was cute, but not necessarily sweet. She smelled like sour milk and had snot bubbling from her nose.

"Careful. She throws up." Esther held up her hand as if to halt any notion Winnie might have of getting Nanna's dress dirty.

Neither Nanna or Hannah seemed the least bit repulsed. "That's what *buplies* do," Hannah said.

Mary Jane laughed. "Spit-up doesn't scare Mamm. She has twelve children."

Esther's eyes nearly popped out of her head. "Twelve? I'm completely bewildered with one."

Winnie had calmed down considerably, but she still fussed in Nanna's arms. Nanna smoothed Winnie's unruly black hair. "Mary Jane, will you make a bottle?"

Mary Jane glanced at Esther, who pointed her toward the kitchen. "Her bottle is in the sink. But I was too tired to wash it. There's formula on the counter."

Mary Jane smiled, and the expression was so familiar, Esther immediately knew where she'd seen it. "Are you related to the boy who came to my house yesterday?"

"*Jah*," Mary Jane said on her way out of the room. "My older *bruder*. He's the one who sent us over. He said you looked like you could use some help."

At that moment, Esther could have kissed Mary Jane's *bruder*, which would have been completely inappropriate, so it was a *gute* thing he wasn't there. "Your *bruder* sent you? Well, bless him. He changed Winnie's diaper and fed her a bottle. I was very grateful."

Hannah nodded. "My Levi. He's a *gute* boy." She handed Nanna a diaper and Nanna set Winnie down on the bed. Esther watched very closely as Nanna changed Winnie's diaper, just in case she could pick up any tips. "She's got a little diaper rash," Nanna said. "Hannah, will you get the cream from my bag?"

Hannah went into the hall and soon returned with a white tube.

"What is that?" Esther asked. Tips. She needed tips.

"Diaper rash cream," Nanna said. "You should put it on every night when the *buplie* goes to bed."

Hannah and Nanna both cooed at the baby while Nanna finished changing her. They were obviously "baby people." Esther was not. Ivy should have left Winnie with a baby person, the kind of person who gushed over babies and didn't mind stinky diapers. Nanna lifted Winnie into her arms. "Now, let's see about breakfast."

Nanna was talking to Winnie, but Esther's stomach growled. She'd eaten three potato chips and a granola bar for dinner last night. And nothing for breakfast or lunch yesterday. They paraded into the kitchen, where Mary Jane had a bottle ready for Winnie. Esther was fairly certain Mary Jane hadn't used the cooking thermometer to check the temperature of the water. It was like she just instinctively knew how warm to make it. How was Esther ever going to learn to do that?

Mary Jane sat down at the table, and Nanna handed her the baby. Mary Jane talked to Winnie like all *gute* mothers talk to babies. "You're a skinny little thing. We're going to fatten you right up." Winnie settled naturally into Mary Jane's arms, as if she knew Mary Jane could be trusted. A lump settled in Esther's throat. Winnie was nothing but suspicious of Esther.

Nanna propped her hands on her hips. "Now, let's see about breakfast for the rest of us."

"*Ach*, you don't have to do that," Esther said. She didn't mean it, but it seemed like the polite thing to say.

"Nonsense," Nanna said. "You had a hard night."

How did Nanna know Esther had a hard night? She put her hand to her head. Her *kapp* was still there, but her hair stuck out all around the edges. There were four dots of spit-up on her right shoulder and a whole line of spit-up down the front of her dress. *Jah*. She'd had a hard night.

Nanna opened Esther's fridge. It was nearly empty. "It's a good thing we got here when we did."

Esther bit her bottom lip. "I'd planned on doing some shopping yesterday."

"Not to worry," Hannah said. "We brought our own supplies." She retrieved the bin from the hall. "Do you like pancakes?"

"I love pancakes."

Hannah nodded in satisfaction. "*Gute*. Pancakes with peach syrup. And bacon." She pulled an apron from the bin.

"You brought bacon?"

Mary Jane laughed. "*Ach*, Mamm comes prepared."

"I can help," Esther said.

Nanna shook her head. "You're going to sit right there by Mary Jane. You've had a hard night."

Esther didn't argue, because it *had* been a hard night, and Nanna had mentioned it twice now. Esther must have looked like she'd been through the wringer washer. She sat next to Mary Jane and watched Winnie eat her bottle. Winnie hadn't eaten that well for Esther yesterday. She was sort of jealous. "Why did Levi come over yesterday? He said he needed to look at my bathroom."

"Levi's wonderful *gute* with plumbing and tile," Nanna said. "I sent him over because that toilet in your second bathroom hasn't worked well for years."

"How do you know about the bathroom? I only just bought the house."

"Well, I'm the one who said you should buy it. I feel responsible."

Esther's mouth fell open. She pointed at Nanna. "You're Hannah Kiem?" She shook her head and pointed at Hannah. "*Nae. You're* Hannah Kiem. I'm confused."

Hannah and Nanna laughed. "We're both Hannah Kiem," Hannah said. "Nanna's real name is Hannah, but when I married her son, it was too confusing to have two Hannahs in the family. We started calling her Nanna, and I kept Hannah."

Nanna nodded. "It worked out quite well when Hannah and Jacob started having children. 'Nanna' is a nickname for *mammi*."

Esther furrowed her brow. "So which one of you is Hannah Kiem, famous quilt blogger?"

The older Hannah with the short hair raised her hand. "I'm not that famous, but it's always thrilling to meet someone who has heard of me. I'm Nanna at home, but I use 'Hannah Kiem' when I blog. That's how people know me."

Esther couldn't hold herself back from standing and

giving the older Hannah a hug. Nanna hugged her right back. "I . . . I can't believe you're standing in my kitchen."

Nanna waved her hand in the air. "No need for that. We're old friends."

Nanna was the reason Esther was in Colorado. Five years ago, Esther had discovered Nanna's quilting blog while she was on the computer at the library. She'd started writing letters to Nanna, and they'd exchanged quilting tips and techniques, recipes, and news about their families. They had never met, and since the Amish believed photographs were graven images, they had never seen photos of each other.

When Esther's *dat* died, Esther told Hannah—or rather Nanna—in a letter that she needed a fresh start, and Nanna suggested Esther move to Colorado. There was a house that had been built by one of the first Amish families to settle in Byler. The family had moved to Montana and were having trouble selling the house because it wasn't wired for electricity. No *Englischers* wanted it, but it was perfect for Esther. She bought the house without even seeing it.

Nanna pulled a pan from the cupboard and opened the bacon she'd retrieved from the bin. "I was going to pay a visit this week anyway, but when Levi said you were in trouble, I knew we had to come right quick."

"You came just in time. I have no idea what to do with a baby."

Nanna grinned. "Here I was hoping to talk about quilting, and the first thing I find is an unexpected baby at your house. But I like talking about babies even more than

I like talking about quilts, so we should have a wonderful *gute* time together."

Esther slumped her shoulders. "I can't do much talking. The only thing I know about babies is the standard size of a baby quilt."

"That's why we're here," Mary Jane said. "We're going to teach you."

Esther smiled wryly. "I was hoping you'd say you were going to move in and take care of Winnie for me."

Mary Jane laughed. "I would love to do that, I really would, but I have little ones of my own, and Tyler can only be patient for twenty minutes at a time."

Hannah stirred water into the pancake batter. "Levi is my oldest child, but my youngest is two years old, so I can't be much help either."

"Levi's had a lot of practice," Esther said. "I could tell." He was also very handsome, but Esther didn't need to state the obvious.

Hannah tested the batter to see if it was the right thickness. "Levi's not afraid to get his hands dirty, and he's not one of those boys who thinks he's too important for housework or caring for children."

"I saw that right off," Esther said.

The bacon smelled heavenly. Esther sighed. There wasn't much in the world that couldn't be made right with a crispy piece of bacon. Nanna turned the slices with a fork. "I wish I could help more, but I've got three quilts to make in April alone, plus I have to get a start on my quilts for the wedding season." She tapped the fork against the pan. "Maybe we should send Levi over to help."

"*Ach*, no, Mamm," Hannah said. "He's got more than enough work in the valley. He doesn't have time to spare."

Hannah smiled at Esther. "He's saving his money to get married."

Esther's heart dropped to her toes. *Ach.* Levi was engaged. It shouldn't have disappointed her like it did. She had long ago resigned herself to being an old maid, and after what had happened with Menno, she didn't want to marry anyway. She was much happier single than she'd ever be married, especially to a skunk like Menno Hertzler or a widower like Yost Lapp, who just wanted a live-in babysitter for his four children. She needed that kind of heartache like she needed a hole in the head. Better by far to live alone. "Oh, how nice," she managed to push from between her lips. "When . . . is Levi getting married?"

Mary Jane propped the baby on her shoulder and patted her on the back. "Levi doesn't even have a girlfriend. That's just Mamm wishing out loud."

"Well, he's going to get married sometime," Hannah protested. "And he should save up for it." Hannah looked at Esther, and her lips twitched upward. "Jacob is sending him to Ohio in October to stay with our cousins and look for a wife. There just aren't enough families in Colorado yet. He's got to go to where the girls are."

So Levi was going to Ohio in search of a wife. Esther didn't need to think any further on him. She didn't want to anyway. "I would never ask Levi or any of you to re-arrange your lives to save me, but for sure and certain, I could use all the help I can get. I'm wonderful grateful you're here this morning. I was at the end of my rope."

"Don't you worry," Nanna said. "We're going to help you all we can."

Winnie burped, and Mary Jane laid her back and put the bottle in her mouth again. "My Rosie is one year old and into everything. You are welcome to come any day and let Rosie and Winnie play together. Though at this age, neither of them really play with other children. They mostly play by themselves."

Hannah poured some batter into the pan. "You are also welcome at our house any time you want to come. The twins will be thrilled. They like playing dress-up with Lydiann, but now that Lydi is two, she's not as cooperative as she used to be. Winnie's too young to protest."

"*Denki,*" Esther said. "I would like that very much."

Hannah flipped the first pancake. "But I have to warn you, with ten children still at home, it's never quiet and it's never clean and sometimes the boys try to kill each other."

Esther laughed. "I have four *bruderen*. I know how they can be."

Mary Jane reached across the table and patted Esther's wrist. "You've found yourself in a very hard situation, and we're going to help you."

Nanna nodded. "And I'm making Levi come back over here to fix your toilet."

Esther felt her face get warm, whether from embarrassment at her finances or the thought of seeing Levi again, she wasn't sure. "I don't know if I can afford that. I'm living on a very tight budget."

With her back to Esther, Nanna waved her fork in the air. "I heard that toilet sputtering before the Yoders even left. I knew it was going to die, and I knew you'd be moving in. I want you to be happy here, and it's impossible to be happy if you only have one working toilet in your home. I know. I once had a crush on a Swartzentruber boy.

One experience in his outhouse, and that was it. I broke up with him before you can say 'raw sewage.'"

Esther, Hannah, and Mary Jane all laughed at that. The Swartzentrubers were one of the strictest sects of Amish. They didn't believe in indoor plumbing. Esther admired them for their piety but not their hygiene habits.

Nanna turned and smiled at Esther. "I shouldn't be talking about raw sewage right before breakfast. I hope you still have an appetite."

"Not to worry," Esther said. "I'm famished."

"Anyway, Levi's coming to fix that toilet and put new tile in your bathroom, and I'm paying for it."

"*Ach*, please don't pay for it, Nanna. I can manage."

Hannah set a plate on the table, and Nanna slid four perfect pieces of bacon onto it. "I insist. I feel responsible, and as you can see, I have bathroom issues. We've sent so many letters back and forth, you feel like a daughter. Or granddaughter. You're young enough."

"Not that young," Esther said. "I'm thirty, and you can't be more than sixty."

"What a *wunderbarr* thing to say," Nanna said. "But I'm sixty-nine. It's the weight lifting. Keeps you young."

"Weight lifting?"

Nanna nodded. "My *Englisch* friends at the quilters club talked me into it. It keeps you from getting old lady arms."

Esther drew her brows together. "Is that allowed?"

"There isn't anything in the Ordnung that says we can't exercise. Besides, the bishop gave me permission."

Hannah's lips curled upward. "My husband."

"My son," Nanna said. "He's not going to say no to his

own mother. And lifting weights is better than dying of a heart attack or arthritis."

Mary Jane sat Winnie up on her lap and patted her back. "I don't think you can die of arthritis, Mammi."

"I'd rather not find out."

It was probably rude to ask, but Esther was just too curious not to. "Did the bishop . . . I mean, your son, give you permission to cut your hair short like that?"

Yep. She shouldn't have asked. Hannah looked at her in surprise—or maybe it was indignant shock. She turned to Nanna. "You never told her? I thought she was like a daughter to you."

Esther's gaze flicked from Hannah to Nanna. "I'm . . . I'm sorry if that was a rude question. It's probably none of my business."

Nanna laughed. "Don't fuss about it, Esther. I had cancer last year." She leaned closer and lowered her voice as if it was a big secret. "I had a double mastectomy, and it was horrible."

"*Ach.* I'm so sorry."

Nanna waved off her concern. "I didn't tell you because you were going through all that with your *dat*, and I didn't want to make you sadder than you already were. I probably should have shared it with you. It took over my life for a whole year."

"I would have liked to know about it, but you're right, it would have made me wonderful sad."

Nanna nodded. "They told me the chemotherapy was going to take my hair, so I went to a salon for the first time in my life and donated my hair. You can do that. They make it into a wig, and it goes to poor people who need it."

Esther wasn't sure why poor people needed hair, but she wasn't going to ask. "So they cut all your hair off?"

"Most of it. Then the rest of it fell out." Nanna fingered the hair poking from her *kapp* at the base of her neck. "This is about six months' growth."

"It looks nice," Esther said, because there was nothing else to say. It was just so odd to see an Amish woman with short hair under her *kapp*.

Nanna flipped a strip of bacon. "I kind of like it short." She winked at Esther. "I don't think I can convince the bishop to let me keep it this way, but it will probably never grow as long as it was. For now, I have short hair and no breasts."

Esther's laughter exploded from her lips, then she clapped her lips together. This was no laughing matter. "I'm sorry."

"Don't be sorry. There are advantages to not having breasts."

Hannah smiled wryly and propped her hand on her hip. "Less strain on your back."

"Exactly," Nanna said. "Dresses fit better. Crumbs don't collect on my chest. I can sleep on my stomach."

Nanna was joking, so Esther let herself laugh. "Lots of advantages."

"The best part is that I'm alive, and the doctor says I probably have many years left, Lord willing, which is *gute* because I need to make a lot of quilts before my hospital bills are paid off."

Esther frowned. "Oh, dear."

"The church is helping," Mary Jane said. "And a card shower brought in almost four thousand dollars."

"People are so kind," Nanna said. "My blog also brings in some money. I'll be okay, Lord willing."

Winnie cooed and opened her eyes wide, as if she was perfectly full and perfectly happy on Mary Jane's lap. "Oh," Hannah sighed. "Look at that little face."

When she wasn't fussing or crying or throwing up, Winnie really was a beautiful baby. She had big round eyes and an angelic face and fat round cheeks that just asked to be squeezed. But she was definitely cuter sitting on someone else's lap.

Mary Jane caught Esther looking at the baby. Esther must have had a relatively pleasant look on her face. "Do you want to hold her?" Mary Jane said.

Hannah handed Esther a plate of pancakes. "Let her eat first. She'll handle everything better on a full stomach."

Esther wanted to argue that she would never handle the baby better, not even on a full stomach, but it definitely couldn't hurt. Her quilting was always better after a cup of *kaffee* and a hot breakfast.

Esther ate pancake after pancake with the amazing peach syrup Hannah had brought in her bin. She was already wondering what other surprises they would pull out of that bin. Bacon, for sure and certain. Nanna had brought four—four!—packages of bacon. She cooked them all and told Esther to eat all she wanted. Esther did, even if her new friends thought she was greedy. All-you-can-eat bacon was a luxury she would probably never experience again.

After breakfast, Esther held the baby while Mary Jane and the others did the dishes. Mary Jane said that Esther needed to get used to holding Winnie, and Winnie needed to get used to Esther. She said Winnie needed to bond, which sounded like something that only happened in books.

After the dishes, Mary Jane showed Esther how to put Winnie down for a nap, which turned out to be very traumatic. No wonder Levi hadn't stayed yesterday to help put the baby down. He probably hadn't wanted the emotional distress. After watching Esther change Winnie's diaper, Mary Jane directed Esther to hold Winnie close to her chest and rock her back and forth while singing something soothing and peaceful. Esther couldn't sing, so none of her songs sounded peaceful or soothing, even "Das Loblied," which they sang in church.

Winnie wouldn't stop squirming, and Esther wanted to skip the singing, but Mary Jane insisted it would help Winnie fall asleep. Esther wasn't convinced. After that ordeal, they laid Winnie in her portable crib, where she immediately began to scream.

"Did your *schwester* bring this crib," Mary Jane said, "or did you have it?"

"It came with the baby."

"That's very nice of her to think of it."

More nice words about Ivy. Esther gritted her teeth against them. She wasn't going to think well of Ivy, no matter how hard the Kiems tried to see the good.

They tiptoed out of the room and shut the door. Winnie's cries grew louder. Mary Jane held up a finger. "Now we wait five minutes."

"Wait for what?"

"It's what we do." Esther couldn't argue with that. She wasn't a mother, and if the whole motherhood club did it this way, then who was she to argue?

For the longest five minutes of Esther's life, they stood

outside the room and listened to Winnie cry. "How do you stand this?" Esther said.

"You just have to tell yourself that the sound of a baby crying is the most distressing sound in the world. It's Gotte's way of making sure we don't ignore our babies."

"But then, doesn't Gotte want us to go in and get her?"

"Just a little more time," she said.

At the end of five minutes, they went back into the room, and Mary Jane directed Esther to pat Winnie's back and say sweet things to her. Esther couldn't think of anything sweet to say so she just chose the things that would comfort her if she were lying in bed bawling her eyes out. "Winnie, Winnie. It's okay. I found some very nice fabric at the store, and I'm going to make you a quilt. How about that? Would you like a nine patch or a log cabin? Wild goose chase would make a nice baby quilt."

Mary Jane nodded and nudged Esther to leave the room. Winnie started crying all over again. "That didn't work," Esther said.

"We do it again in six minutes, then seven, then eight, so Winnie can see you'll always come back. It makes her feel confident enough to go to sleep."

Esther didn't know if a baby could feel confidence in anything, but Mary Jane had two children and Esther had none. They'd do it Mary Jane's way. Sure enough, after the third time going in, patting Winnie's back, and talking about quilts, Winnie wound down and fell asleep. Esther was ecstatic. She now knew how to put Winnie down for a nap. She clapped her hands silently and beamed at Mary Jane. "We did it!"

Mary Jane smiled like any teacher would smile when

her pupil finally learned the lesson. "I knew you could do it."

They walked quietly back into the kitchen, where Hannah and Nanna were making sandwiches. "How did it go?"

"She's asleep," Esther said, unable to keep the pride from her voice.

Hannah cut a tuna sandwich in half. "Mary Jane is a wonderful *gute* sleep trainer."

"I learned all I know from you, Mamm," Mary Jane said.

Nanna stuffed a tuna sandwich into a zipper bag. "Is that quilter's chalk?"

Esther fingered the chalk piece behind her ear. It hadn't even fallen out when she'd gone to bed. "You never know when you're going to need something to write with."

"What an excellent idea," Nanna said. "I'm going to try that."

Esther's heart beat a little faster. Hannah Kiem, famous quilter, was going to try Esther's chalk trick. The day was just getting better and better.

Hannah pointed to the pile of six sandwiches on the counter. "Now, we've made you some sandwiches for when you get busy with Winnie. You can always eat a sandwich while you're feeding her, so at least you won't starve."

"Oh, *denki*. You've been more than kind." Esther pressed her lips together. They were getting ready to leave, and she wanted so badly to ask them to stay. But they'd done enough for her already. She could fall to pieces after they left.

They gathered up their supplies and put them in the

bin of wonders but left the diapers, the extra formula, and four packages of baby wipes. That should at least get her through the weekend. All three gave her big hugs before they left. She held on extra tight to Nanna until it got awkward.

Nanna patted her cheek. "What a blessing to have a beautiful baby to love."

Esther couldn't see any part of this as a blessing. "It feels like Gotte is playing a joke on me."

Nanna smiled. "Gotte can make all things beautiful if we let Him. I like to think of Him as the master quilter, taking plain scraps of fabric and bringing them together to make a beautiful pattern. You'll see. And after things settle down, you and I can start quilting."

Esther tried to smile. In her present situation, she couldn't imagine ever quilting again. "I'd like that."

Nanna pointed to the chalk behind Esther's ear. "That tells me you are a girl who's ready for anything. Even a baby."

Esther wasn't going to argue with her, but she would never be equipped to care for a baby. It was why Gotte had never given her a husband.

"We'll be back," Mary Jane said. "Just remember about the sleeping."

Esther waved goodbye. She *had* learned how to put the baby down for a nap. Considering what had happened yesterday, it was a stunning accomplishment. Maybe things weren't so helpless after all. Maybe Gotte could make a quilt out of the torn scraps of her life.

She shut the door.

The baby started screaming.

Chapter Three

Levi pulled up in front of the house with his horse and wagon. Esther's house was small, with not even enough room to hold *gmay* there, but the Yoders had done a lot of work on the yard. Evergreen bushes grew up against the house, and a row of cheery yellow daffodils stood in the beds in front of the bushes. The grass was that early spring yellowish-green, but once Esther put some water to the lawn, this would really be a nice little place for her.

Levi didn't have any objection to going a second time to Esther Zook's house. She was funny and honest and wonderful pretty to look at, but he was really just here to do her bathroom. Seeing Esther again was a bonus, but his only reason for coming back was because Mammi had asked him to fix Esther's toilet and redo the tile.

Levi had set the brake, jumped out of the wagon, and pulled his backpack from the wagon bed when he heard an unusual, rhythmic squeaking noise coming from the side of the house. Each squeak was followed by a thud and a grunt. Either Esther was behaving very strangely or an animal was dying on her property.

Levi strolled across the yard and peeked around the

corner of the house. Esther stood in the side yard holding a rag rug in her fists. Sweat beaded on her face as she let out an angry squeak and slapped the rug against the house. Then she grunted, lifted the rug above her head, and hit the house again.

Levi tried very hard not to laugh. "If there was any dirt on that rug, you've scared it away."

Esther halted mid-swing. She turned and glanced at Levi, her lips twitching sheepishly at the sight of him. "*Ach*, Levi Kiem. I didn't hear you drive up. Your buggy wheels must be well greased."

"Having a bad day?"

Esther held up the rug. "Not as bad a day as this rug."

"Did it make you mad?"

She scrunched her lips. "*Nae*. This poor rug just happened to be the first thing I saw to grab. But it has never been cleaner."

"I don't wonder that it hasn't." He leaned against the side of the house. "Anything I can do?" His heart lurched. "Where's Winnie?"

"*Ach*. She's in her crib. It took two hours, but I think she's asleep. I thought I was doing so *gute* yesterday when your sister was here, but Winnie barely slept a wink last night, and that five-minute, six-minute, seven-minute trick Mary Jane taught me didn't work this morning."

Levi rubbed his hand down his jawline. "That usually works."

"Not for me. If there was any person less suited for taking care of a baby, I'd surely like to meet her."

"It's not that bad. You got Winnie to go down for a nap this morning. That's something, no matter how long it took."

Esther snorted with cynical laughter. "I think she finally collapsed from sheer exhaustion. But I'm just assuming she's asleep. She might be sitting in her crib plotting ways to keep me awake tonight. You never know with babies."

It was obvious Esther hadn't gotten much sleep last night. She was still as pretty as a picture, but wisps of hair stuck out from her *kapp*, and there was a dull, glassy look in her eyes that signaled her fatigue. Levi had lived with his *mamm* and sisters long enough to know you never tell a woman she looks tired. To her that means you think she looks bad, and no woman wants to hear that. He stifled a grin. The chalk was gone, but Esther had a bright orange carrot stick tucked behind her ear.

"So you're upset that Winnie didn't sleep last night, and you're taking it out on a rug that never did you any harm?"

She raised an eyebrow. "It tripped me once."

"And never apologized?"

Esther folded the rug in half, tucked it under her arm, and joined Levi at the corner of the house. "I'm discouraged about Winnie, but that's not why I'm upset. Who could be mad at Winnie? She has no control over her mother's bad choices."

"You're mad at your sister."

"*Jah.* The three hundred dollars I hid in my fridge is gone. Ivy left the baby and took my money. I'm so mad I could spit. But I'm not going to spit, because it's rude."

"You hide your money in the fridge?" Levi said.

"Of course. Robbers don't think to look in the fridge."

"Ivy did."

Esther growled. "Because she knows the secret. Dat always hid money in the fridge. I suppose I should have moved it when she came, but I never thought my own sister would steal from me."

"That's too bad. I'm sorry she did that."

"Me too. And so is this rug."

"Do you hide your money next to the carrots?" he said.

Her expression popped with surprise. "How did you know?"

Laughter burst from his mouth as he pointed to her ear.

She formed her lips into an O and touched the carrot on the side of her head. "I was moving vegetables around looking for my money. I must have put this here without thinking." She pulled the carrot from behind her ear and examined it. "You never know when you're going to need a carrot."

"You might want a mid-morning snack."

"I'll pass," she said, tossing the carrot on the ground. "I wash behind my ears regularly, but there's been a lot of dust flying this morning. My sister is going to pay me back for every last carrot. That's for sure and certain."

Levi showed her his backpack. "I brought something that might cheer you up."

Esther puckered her lips skeptically. "Unless it's a full-time mother's helper, it's not going to cheer me up."

He pretended to deflate. "No mother's helper. Just tile samples for the bathroom."

She shrugged and gave him an enchanting smile. "It's not what I wanted, but it's something. Who isn't in a better mood after looking at tile samples?"

"Exactly what I think. *Ach*, I also brought a present for Winnie."

"A present? How nice. What did you bring her?"

He shook his head and gave her a teasing smile. "I can't tell you. It's Winnie's present. Let's let her open it."

She rolled her eyes, then led him into the house. The minute they entered, he heard Winnie crying. Esther sighed heavily. "What did I tell you? I don't think she ever went to sleep. I've only been outside for ten minutes."

Levi opened the door to Winnie's room. "Let's see what we can do." The spare bedroom in Esther's house contained a twin bed covered in a stunning quilt, a small dresser with two drawers, and Winnie's portable crib, plus the suitcase that held all of Winnie's things. There wasn't much in it. The minute he stepped into the room, Levi knew what was wrong. A pungent smell hung in the air.

"Oy, anyhow," Esther said, waving her hand in front of her nose. "I'll never get used to that."

Levi picked up Winnie and held her close even though she stunk like a barn full of chickens. "It's hard to sleep with a full diaper."

Esther grabbed a diaper and some wipes from the suitcase. "All right, then. Let's get this over with." She held out her arms for the baby.

"I can change her if you want," Levi said. He didn't really enjoy changing diapers, but it was better for Winnie if he did it instead of Esther.

To his surprise, she shook her head. "That's a wonderful kind offer, but I need the practice. Besides, I want you to come back sometime. I'll never get that bathroom done if you stay away because you're expected to change a diaper every time you come."

He chuckled. "Okay. I'll watch you, then."

"Please do. I'm not good at it yet. I need all the advice I can get."

Esther was in a very sorry state to have to get baby advice from a twenty-four-year-old Amish plumber. But she sure was funny and fun to be with. He wasn't going to mind returning again and again, even if he had to change a diaper now and then. It wasn't as if he was even mildly interested in Esther as a potential *fraa*—not one bit, even though girls in Byler were scarce and he liked Esther quite a lot.

When she had talked about her sister that first day, Levi had done the math. Her sister jumped the fence when she was eighteen and had been gone for eight years. Ivy was four years younger than Esther. That meant Esther was thirty. Way too old for Levi, who was twenty-four. He had no interest in desperate old maids who hadn't been able to convince anyone to marry them. And Esther was in Mammi's quilting club. He most certainly wouldn't date a girl who was in an old ladies' quilting club. He'd never live that down with his friends.

Besides, he didn't want a girl who already had a baby. If Winnie was a temporary problem, Levi didn't want to risk getting attached. If she was a permanent problem, Levi didn't want a child complicating his life. Of course, Winnie wasn't really the problem. She was darling, and Levi liked babies. Mamm always said he was a baby person. But Winnie was an obstacle that made everything harder. He wasn't interested in unnecessary complications in his life.

Dat was sending him to Ohio in the fall, and according to his cousin Peter, Ohio was teeming with pretty Amish girls who were eager to find a husband. That was the kind of *fraa* Levi wanted: young, pretty, and unencumbered. That was the kind of *fraa* he deserved.

Esther changed Winnie's diaper, using about seven

baby wipes, and even though her efforts were clumsy, Winnie's bottom was clean and dry at the end of it. That's probably all that mattered, even if Esther was going to be spending a lot of money on baby wipes.

Winnie fussed when Esther picked her up. Esther drew her brows together. "Do you think she's hungry?"

"When was the last time she ate?"

"Two hours ago before I put her down for her nap."

Levi nodded. "She's probably hungry."

Esther seemed to brace herself, as if feeding the baby sounded like the hardest thing in the world. "Okay. Can you hold her while I fix a bottle?"

Levi suddenly felt very sorry for Esther. She'd been thrown into something she hadn't asked for and certainly wasn't prepared to handle. That's why he'd asked his *mammi*, *mamm*, and *schwester* to come yesterday. "Why don't you let me feed Winnie while you look at tile samples."

She acted as if he'd offered to donate one of his kidneys. "*Ach*, would you mind? That would be *wunderbarr*."

"Not at all." He set his backpack on the floor and took the baby from Esther's arms. "You make the bottle, and I'll feed. And burp. You can concentrate on picking tile."

Esther tried to pick up his backpack, but she couldn't lift it. "What's in this thing?"

"I told you. Tile samples."

"Your *mammi* is right. I'm getting old lady arms. I'll carry the baby into the kitchen if you carry that backpack."

Levi chuckled. "Okay. I'll put it on the table."

"Don't set it down too hard. I don't want my table to collapse, though the way my day is going, it wouldn't surprise me if it did."

They went into the kitchen, where Levi deposited the backpack on the table and took Winnie from Esther's arms. Esther washed the baby bottle and filled it with water, then pulled a cooking thermometer out of the drawer and stuck it in the water. Levi smiled to himself. Even though she hadn't asked for a baby and she was furious with her sister, she was trying very hard to do the best she could for Winnie. Warmth radiated through Levi's chest. Mothering obviously didn't come naturally to Esther, but she seemed to care very deeply. All the skill in the world was no substitute for a *gute* and honest heart.

When she seemed satisfied with the water temperature, Esther dried the thermometer on a towel, slid it behind her ear, and finished measuring out the formula. She turned to Levi, and it looked as if she had some sort of pressure gauge attached to her head. He didn't say a word. You never knew when you were going to need a cooking thermometer.

She shook the bottle, being careful to put her finger over the hole in the nipple, then smiled and handed the bottle to Levi. That smile, a mixture of gratitude, friendship, and delight, set Levi's heart thumping against his chest. It was a *gute* thing he wasn't interested in Esther. That smile could make any man's knees weak.

Why had she never married?

Levi couldn't understand it.

He cradled Winnie in his arms and stuck the bottle in her mouth. She ate as if she hadn't been fed in days— another reason she hadn't fallen asleep. A hungry baby didn't sleep.

Esther noticed. "Honestly, I fed her before I put her down."

"I believe you. Babies are funny that way. Sometimes

you can't get them to eat a thing. Other times they can't get enough."

She smiled again. "You're very kind. I'm doing it all wrong, and you still try to be nice about it."

"Not at all, Esther," he said, pinning her with a stern gaze. "You're doing just fine. This whole situation is not of your doing, but you're trying to make the best of it."

An attractive blush reddened her cheeks, and the cooking thermometer rattled when she shook her head. "By beating rugs against the house."

He widened his eyes in mock innocence. "I don't know what you're talking about. How else are you going to clean the rugs?"

"I'm afraid I'm going to need more rugs to beat on. I don't think my sister is coming back anytime soon. I might not hear from her ever again. When she jumped the fence, it took two years before she contacted us. Then she sent some pictures with a letter telling us she was in Canada. That was a comfort to Mamm, knowing that Ivy seemed healthy and happy. Six months after Mamm died, Ivy sent us another letter with a cell phone number where we could reach her. I called and told her about Mamm."

"Was she sad?"

"She was wonderful upset, but she'd been away a long time, and we had no way to reach her. I can't help but think that if she truly loved Mamm, she wouldn't have stayed away so long. My *dat* died last November. Ivy came to his funeral, but she didn't look good. She was pregnant and too skinny, with black circles under her eyes. Her boyfriend waited in his car while we stood at the graveside. She had convinced him to bring her to the funeral, which is something, I guess."

Levi slipped his finger into Winnie's little hand. "So you moved here after your *dat* died."

She nodded. "Dat left everything he owned to me. I sold the house and the farm and bought this property because your *mammi* invited me to Colorado."

Levi tilted his head. "I thought you had older brothers."

"*Jah.* My *bruderen* were wonderful upset they didn't get any money, but my *dat* wanted me to have my independence. An Amish old maid can't have her own life without money."

Levi knew exactly what she meant. Old *maedels* usually ended up living with one of their *bruderen* or married *schwesteren* and taking care of the nieces and nephews. Levi couldn't imagine Esther happy as a visitor in someone else's home, caring for someone else's children, having nothing of her own.

"I'm *froh* your *dat* did that for you."

"Dat wanted me to be able to take care of myself, but he wanted me to look after Ivy too, though at the time, we didn't even know where she was. I was a *dumkoff.* I actually saw her return as a *gute* thing. I thought I would have a chance to take care of her like Dat wanted. But Ivy only thinks about herself."

"You could count that three hundred dollars as Ivy's inheritance. For how she's treated you, you don't have to feel like you owe her anything else."

"That is a *wunderbarr* idea. I feel better about the money already."

"Your rugs are saved," Levi said, as if he was very relieved.

She laughed. "Oh, don't be so certain. Something else is sure to come up to try my patience." She unzipped

Levi's backpack. "Now let's see about these tile samples you're so excited about."

"I'm not that excited. They're just tile samples."

Esther pulled them out of his backpack one by one, lining them up in rows across her table.

"I brought the six-inch squares," Levi said. "But we can get them in eight- and twelve-inch. Just about any size. It's a small bathroom, so I thought six-inch might look nice. You can also get them in rectangles."

"I don't want to spend a lot of money."

"My *mammi* is paying, and she said not to tell you how much it costs. Pick whatever you want."

Esther frowned. "That's wonderful nice of her, but I feel like I'm taking advantage of her kindness. And she still has hospital bills."

"You didn't ask her to pay. She feels bad because she's the one who found the house for you." He pointed to the peeling wallpaper. "It needs some repairs, and the bathroom needs to be completely redone. She wants it to be nice. She wants you to be happy here."

Esther sighed. "*Ach*, the house is fine. It's my sister who's ruined Colorado for me. I never should have given her my address."

He leaned forward. "Still, wouldn't it be nice to have two working bathrooms?"

"*Jah*. It would." She smiled. "You're very kind to fix my bathroom."

"If it makes you feel better, I can show you the tiles that are least expensive."

"Please."

Levi pointed out the three or four tiles that cost the least amount of money. "We have a case of these left over from another job, and a half a case of this light brown one. Too bad we can't just lay all our leftover tiles on the floor. They'd cost next to nothing."

Esther suddenly got very excited. "Why not? I use scraps of fabric to make patchwork quilts. What if we used leftover tiles to make a patchwork bathroom floor? Or even better, a watercolor bathroom floor." She caught her breath as delight spread over her face. "We could use different sizes and colors. It would be beautiful."

"You want to paint the bathroom floor with watercolors? That won't last long."

"*Nae.* Watercolor is a type of quilt design. Your *mammi* is one of the most famous quilters in the world, and you don't know what a watercolor quilt is?"

Levi raised an eyebrow. "I love my *mammi*, but we don't talk about quilting so much. It's boring."

"Boring? How can you think quilting is boring? I get heart palpitations just walking into a fabric store."

Levi couldn't see the appeal. "Is my *mammi* really that famous?"

Esther nodded. "She's got her own blog. She makes all the quilts, and her *Englisch* friend Allison takes all the pictures and posts them online. She's got twenty thousand followers on Instagram."

"I don't know what that is."

"It's okay. It's not an Amish thing. I happened upon her blog when I was looking for quilt patterns online at the library. I started writing letters to her, and she personally answered every one. We became friends. Your *mammi* has never been too famous to connect with her fans."

"Fans? Mammi has fans?"

"Thousands of them."

Levi couldn't believe it. Maybe he should start paying more attention to his *mammi*, even if she was an old lady. "Does my *dat* know about this?"

Esther nodded. "He's the bishop, so she has to get permission from him for everything she does."

Levi curled one side of his mouth. "I can't imagine my *dat* would ever say *nae* to his own *mater*."

"I don't know why he'd say *nae*. She makes the quilts, which is a very acceptable activity for an Amish woman. Allison takes all the pictures and posts all the blogs and answers all the emails. There's not a photo of your *mammi* anywhere online."

Even though the Ordnung said they were supposed to stay separate from the world, it didn't seem like there was much harm in Mammi's making quilts, especially if Mammi was never shown in any photos. Mammi needed the money.

Grateful he wasn't the bishop, Levi pulled the bottle from Winnie's mouth, draped her over his shoulder, and patted her back. "She's nearly asleep," he said. "I'm going to put her down for a nap."

Esther pulled a face. "*Gute* luck with that."

"Then I'll pull the linoleum off the floor in that bathroom while you pick tile." Levi stood up, carried Winnie into the spare bedroom, and softly laid her in her crib. She stirred slightly, then seemed to settle in for a long rest. Since she hadn't really slept all morning, she was ready to give up the fight.

He closed the door behind him and went back into the kitchen, where Esther was rearranging tiles on the kitchen table. "Did she go to sleep?"

"I think so."

Esther smiled at him. "You're a natural."

He shrugged, ignoring the way his heart sort of tripped all over itself when she smiled. "Not really. She seemed pretty beat."

"Poor baby. I'm sure Ivy dragged her all over the place with no consideration of her sleeping or eating. I wonder if Ivy even remembered to feed her most days. What present did you bring for Winnie?" Her lips curled upward. "Or would you rather wait until she wakes up so she can open it?"

Levi reached clear to the bottom of his backpack and pulled out a pacifier still in its package. "I thought this might help her sleep."

Smiling, Esther took it from him and fell silent as she read the entire package. "It says, 'Do not tie pacifier around a child's neck, as it presents a strangulation hazard.' That's good to know." She glanced up at him. "Do you think it will help?"

Levi shrugged. "I don't know. A pacifier always helped Lydiann, but Mamm used it from the day she was born. Winnie might not like it, but if she does, it might help her sleep."

Esther studied his face. "*Denki.* This is a very thoughtful gift. Do they have such a thing as a pacifier for adults? I need one of those every time I think of Ivy."

Levi laughed. "I think it's called chocolate."

"Chocolate? I don't like chocolate."

"You don't like chocolate? Who ever heard of someone not liking chocolate?" That was *gute* to know. Her not liking chocolate gave him another reason to positively, absolutely *not* be interested in Esther, especially since he found himself drawn in by those fascinating greenish-blue eyes.

Levi looked away and made a list in his head.

She is old.

She is in my mammi's quilting group.

She doesn't like chocolate.

Her smile makes my pulse race, which will likely lead to high blood pressure.

It was the start of a pretty *gute* list of reasons not to be interested in Esther Zook.

Esther pointed to a blue-tinted tile Levi had used on a bathroom two weeks ago. "Do you have more of this one?"

He cleared his throat, tried not to be pulled into her gaze, and thought hard about how much he loved chocolate fudge. "*Jah.* Probably half a case."

"Wonderful *gute*. This will be the most beautiful bathroom floor ever. Too bad only a handful of people will see it."

Levi picked up the tile and smoothed his fingers over the top of it. He grinned. "You could have a bathroom party and invite the whole district."

She looked up at the ceiling as if she was considering it. "Yes, because no one would think I was a strange old *maedel* if I invited them over for a bathroom party."

He laughed. "Well, you could serve cookies. They might come." He cocked his head to the side and fell silent. In the other room, Winnie started wailing. Levi smiled wryly at Esther. "See? You're not a bad *mater*. Winnie is just a bad baby."

"Levi Kiem, there is no such thing as a bad baby," Esther scolded. "Every baby is a perfect and beautiful gift from Derr Herr."

He raised his hands in surrender. "Okay, okay. I didn't mean it."

She cracked a smile. "At least that's what my *mamm* used to say, even though my nephew Raymond didn't stop screaming for three months. My other nephew John threw up every time he ate. My sister-in-law was fit to be tied."

"Your *mamm* was right. A baby doesn't choose to misbehave. Poor Winnie has had a hard go of things. As soon as she settles into a routine, she'll do much better."

Esther gazed at him doubtfully. "How long does it take to settle into a routine?"

"Two, three years," he said, winking so she knew he was teasing.

She groaned loudly. "You're a plumber. What do you know?"

He laughed softly at the look on her face. "Not a lot." He stood up, went back into the spare room, and took Winnie out of her crib. She burped loudly, then almost immediately burrowed her little face into his neck and fell asleep. He walked back into the kitchen. "Umm. It must be the crib."

Esther held five tile samples between her fingers and rearranged the rest into a pattern on her table. She took a look at Winnie in his arms and burst into laughter. "*Ach.* That's so cute. And so frustrating."

Levi shook his head. "At this rate, I'll never get that bathroom finished. I'll try laying her down again."

"Oh, no you don't. For sure and certain, she'll wake up." Esther set down the tile samples. "She needs her sleep, and she's going to get it. You hold her, and I'll pull up the linoleum." She stood and slid the cooking thermometer from behind her ear. "Show me what to do."

Levi couldn't help but smile. Esther had surprised him again. "It's kind of hard."

"I can do it. I don't have old lady arms yet."

"*Nae*," Levi said. "You don't have old lady arms, but my *mammi* wouldn't like it if she knew I let you pull up the linoleum."

Esther folded her arms. "She never has to know. Besides, you're holding Winnie as a favor to me. I want to help you. You can sit right outside the bathroom and tell me what to do."

Levi sighed. There was no use arguing with her. That much was plain to see. She'd soon figure out she wasn't strong enough to pull linoleum, and she'd give up. As long as she didn't cut her finger off or put out an eye, there was probably no harm in it. *As long as she didn't cut her finger off?* Levi frowned. "This is a bad idea."

She pulled a pencil out of the drawer and slid it behind her ear. "It's going to be fine." She carried a chair from the table down the hall to the bathroom and set it right outside the door. "You can sit here, hold Winnie, and give me instructions."

Surrendering to the inevitable, Levi eased into the chair and talked softly so he wouldn't wake Winnie. "First, you need the utility knife and pry bar from my backpack. And the safety glasses. And you better get the hammer too."

She propped her hands on her hips. "No wonder that pack was so heavy." She disappeared down the hall. Levi peered into the bathroom. He'd need to take out the toilet, but Esther could remove most of the linoleum before that. Or rather, *he* could remove most of the linoleum when Esther gave up. The bathroom had a shower, sink, and toilet, but it wasn't that big, and it wouldn't take him but two hours to take care of the linoleum.

While he sat there, Levi's back tightened up right

between his shoulder blades. He shifted Winnie so he could hold her in the crook of his elbow. She didn't even flinch.

Esther returned, looking especially cute wearing his safety glasses. Even with the glasses, the pencil stayed firmly planted behind her ear. How did she do that? It must have been a special talent of hers. From what Levi had seen, Esther had dozens of special talents, one of them being the ability to draw his full attention whenever she smiled. He definitely needed to get to Ohio to meet some eligible girls. He was obviously starved for female attention if a thirty-year-old spinster could make his pulse race like a teenager's.

She held up the pry bar in one fist and the utility knife and hammer in the other. "Okay. What should I do first?"

"Do you have a pair of work gloves? Mine are too big for you."

"Do I need work gloves?"

Levi nodded. "If the utility knife slips while you're cutting linoleum, you could lose a finger."

She drew her brows together. "Would garden gloves work?"

"Good enough."

Once again she marched down the hall and returned a few minutes later, this time wearing the glasses and a bright pink pair of garden gloves.

"You should put on your shoes," he said.

"What?"

"If the utility knife slips while you're cutting linoleum, you could cut your toe off."

She gave him a crooked grin. "So I am possibly going to lose my fingers and my toes pulling out the linoleum?"

"*Jah,*" he said. Hopefully the thought of losing her limbs would make her less eager to help with the bathroom remodel.

Esther thought about that for a minute. "I need some steel-toed boots."

"It's going to be wonderful hard for you to do this. Let me do it after Winnie wakes up."

She shook her head adamantly. "You're doing me a huge favor. And you can't be here all day just because Winnie won't sleep like a normal baby. I'm going to help, and if I lose a toe, it would just make me a more interesting person. Everybody would want to meet the woman who cut off her own toe."

It would also be a *gute* thing to add to his list of reasons he wasn't interested. Who wanted a *fraa* with only nine toes?

"Okay. It's your foot. I guess you can do what you want. When's the last time you had a tetanus shot?"

"I can't remember, but we'll cross that bridge if we come to it. I'll go get some shoes." She strolled down the hall in her glasses and gardening gloves. She'd have to take the gloves off to put on her shoes. Levi chuckled to himself. By the time she was ready to pull linoleum, for sure and certain, Winnie would be awake. Then Levi could take over.

Esther would be finished before she ever began.

Chapter Four

It was wonderful hard to quilt with three bandaged fingers and a sore elbow, but Esther was determined to keep up with the other four women in the room. They were all at least thirty years older than she was, and maybe she felt like she had something to prove. Maybe it was her pride, but she wanted to convince them and herself that even though she was completely inept at caring for a baby, she was a *gute* quilter.

"Oh dear, Esther," Allison said. "What happened to your fingers? Did you cut yourself?"

"I cut myself on Sunday," Cathy Larsen said, holding up her left thumb with a bright pink Band-Aid on it. "My grandson sold me one of those really sharp and expensive knives, and I sliced right through my thumbnail."

Esther glanced at Nanna, Levi's *mammi*. Levi had said Nanna would be annoyed if she found out Esther was remodeling her own bathroom while Levi held the baby. "I cut myself doing some work around the house."

"I injure myself with the vegetable peeler at least once a week," Cathy said.

Rita Alvarez looked up from the quilt and pinned Cathy

with an exasperated look. "Maybe you should stop peeling your vegetables."

Esther smiled, but she had her face turned down to the quilt, so Cathy didn't see it. Esther had known Cathy all of fifteen minutes, and she'd already heard about Cathy's gall bladder surgery, a hangnail she'd had ripped out by the doctor, and her precancerous moles that the dermatologist was keeping an eye on. Cathy was obviously not shy about sharing all of her business with strangers.

Of course, maybe Cathy wasn't in the habit of sharing with strangers. Maybe she already considered Esther a friend. Warmth spread up Esther's arms. What a nice thought. Cathy had already made Esther a part of her circle of friends. Esther didn't mind hearing about Cathy's colonoscopy.

Allison threaded a needle. "Esther, if it hurts too much to quilt, we don't mind if you just watch and visit. We don't want any blood on the fabric."

Where Cathy seemed ready to accept Esther into their group, Allison was more tentative. Esther tried not to feel bad that Allison was less than eager to let her quilt. Allison wasn't completely convinced Esther belonged in the quilting group, and she was just being protective of her quilt. She'd made a stunning quilt top, king size, and for sure and certain, she didn't want an amateur ruining it. The quilt truly was one of the most breathtaking tops Esther had ever seen. It was a Lone Star quilt pattern in browns and yellows and dusky oranges, and the star looked as if it moved toward you if you stared at it long enough. No wonder Allison didn't want just anybody working on it.

The five of them sat around Allison's quilt, and the frames took up one entire room in Allison's basement.

Before Esther had moved to Colorado, Nanna had invited her to join the quilters group after she got settled into her new house. Of course, Esther would never be settled in now that she had Winnie, but her fingers ached to quilt, and her heart longed to talk quilting with women who really knew what they were doing. Levi's *mamm*, Hannah, bless her, had offered to take Winnie for a couple of hours so Esther could finally meet with Nanna's quilting group. Levi had picked her and Winnie up, dropped Esther off at Allison's, and taken Winnie to Hannah's house.

Esther's heart danced an uneven rhythm when she thought of Levi. *Ach.* She really liked him, and that thought made her want to go outside and beat a rug against the house. Liking a boy had only gotten her into trouble. She certainly didn't want to feel that pain ever again. Levi was handsome and kind and so patient with Winnie, but he was also a male and six years younger than she was. It would never work out. Aside from the fact that Esther didn't trust men in general, Levi was young. Why would he ever be interested in an old maid?

"Allison, are you sure you want a stitch in the ditch?" Cathy said. "Stitching on top would be so charming."

Allison nodded. "I'm sure. It's already busy enough."

"It's not busy," Nanna said. "It's *wunderbarr*. The colors are so bright."

"I used vintage fabric. The woman I'm making the quilt for had drawers and drawers of old fabric from her mother. It's an heirloom piece as much as it is a quilt."

Esther couldn't have been more delighted to be included in Nanna's quilting group. Where else would she find women who got excited about vintage fabric and keepsake quilts? It was like no quilting group Esther had ever seen before. Amish women got together all the time for quilting frolics, but Nanna's quilting group was serious business. Allison was Nanna's blog partner. Cathy looked to be in her eighties, but Esther had been able to tell right off that she was as comfortable with a needle as she was with her own fingers. Rita was a cute little Hispanic woman who talked to herself in Spanish when she quilted. Nanna and Esther were the only Amish in the group.

Each of the women had a quilting blog. Rita had a website where she sold quilt patterns and did quilting tutorials in both Spanish and English. She also owned a quilting machine for quilts she didn't want to quilt by hand, and according to Nanna, she'd built quite a business doing machine quilting for other people. Cathy taught quilting classes at the library and gave lectures on the history of quilting all over the state. All the women sold their quilts for outrageous prices. Nanna said when you called it "folk art," you could charge three or four hundred dollars extra.

Sometimes the quilters met at Allison's, sometimes at Nanna's. Theirs were the only two places with rooms big enough to accommodate a king-size quilt on frames.

Esther cleared her throat and tried to sound more confident than she felt. "Lord willing, no one will bleed on your beautiful quilt, Allison. I've never seen anything like it."

The praise seemed to allay Allison's fears. She smiled and tucked some imaginary hair behind her ear. "It's for their cabin in Aspen. I think they're going to be pleased."

Nanna poked her needle into the fabric. "Don't worry about Esther," she said. "She's a better quilter than I am."

Esther felt her face get warm. How sweet of Nanna to say such a thing, considering that one of Nanna's quilts hung in a museum in Ohio. "That's not true. I'm the least successful quilter here." She looked around the room. "But my stitches won't embarrass any of your quilts, even with three bandaged fingers."

"I once stitched and bound a quilt with a double hernia," Cathy said.

Esther almost asked if the *quilt* or *Cathy* had a double hernia but decided she was too young and too new to be making jokes yet.

"We're glad you're here," Nanna said.

So was Esther. It was the first time she'd left the house in two weeks except to go to the market to pick up things so she and Winnie wouldn't starve. And Winnie always had to have diapers. The cost of diapers alone might break Esther's bank account before Winnie was potty trained.

Was a baby this hard for everyone?

Esther truly didn't mind caring for Winnie, but she hated not being *gute* at something. And she was definitely not *gute* at babies. Levi was much better. Still, she was trying hard, and Winnie was so adorable when she wasn't crying. Esther was actually starting to enjoy their time together. Winnie's toothless smile never failed to melt Esther's heart. Winnie loved books, and Levi had given them three picture books that Esther read to Winnie often. Levi brought a gift for Winnie every time he came, but they were usually really gifts for Esther to make taking care of Winnie easier.

Esther willed her heart to slow to a normal pace. She needed to stop thinking about Levi Kiem. He'd been wonderful kind, but he was just helping her remodel her bathroom.

Esther stifled a smile so no one would ask what she

was thinking about. She was the one who was remodeling the bathroom. Levi sat on a chair in the hall and held Winnie while he gave her directions. She'd scraped her arm on a jagged edge of linoleum and cut her finger with the utility knife, but considering the effort it took to tear out the linoleum, her injuries were minor.

After she'd torn up what she could of the linoleum, Levi had come back the next day, taken out the toilet, and fed Winnie while Esther had cleared the area under the toilet. A good portion of the particleboard on the subfloor was warped with water damage. A week ago, Esther didn't even know what particleboard and subfloors were. She was getting smarter by the day. Next week, Levi was bringing his circular saw, and while he hadn't promised she could use it, she was certain she could talk him into it.

They made a *gute* team. Winnie never cried when Levi held her, and her favorite place to sleep was in his arms. Esther liked working on the bathroom, and she really liked that concerned look Levi got on his face when he gave her instructions for her next task. He obviously feared she was going to hurt herself with one of his tools. It was sweet that he was concerned for her safety, but she was *gute* with her hands, and she liked learning new skills. Amish spinsters who lived alone and wanted to be independent should learn everything they could so they didn't have to rely on the kindness of handsome strangers with attractive smiles, because those handsome strangers would for sure and certain move on when they met someone younger and prettier and more interesting.

It was just the way men were, especially handsome men. Rita cut her thread and smoothed her hand over her finished stitches. "Nanna tells us you're taking care of your sister's baby, Esther. How is that going?"

"Nanna's been a big help," Esther said. "She and Hannah and Mary Jane have been to my house four or five times in the last three weeks."

Nanna waved away any praise. "We just come to visit. She's doing an excellent job. It isn't easy taking care of a baby."

"My three babies had colic," Cathy said. "They screamed for three months straight."

"At the same time?" Rita said, with just a hint of tease in her voice.

"No. But it wouldn't have surprised me."

Allison cut a length of thread. "Nanna says your sister abandoned the baby."

Nanna's gaze flicked in Esther's direction. "I hope you don't mind that I told. These women are like my family. I don't keep secrets from family, and I certainly don't keep anything from my quilting group."

Rita nodded. "Quilting friends are the dearest kind because we bind our hearts together with real thread."

Esther gave them a genuine smile. "I don't mind. In my experience, quilters are the most loyal, trustworthy group of women in the world."

Cathy pointed her needle at Esther. "But we don't gossip." She poked her needle into the fabric. "Unless it's absolutely necessary."

Nanna laughed. "Gossip is using words to hurt somebody. We don't gossip. We *share*."

Allison brushed a piece of thread from the quilt top. "Nanna *shared* with us that your sister brought the baby to your house and then disappeared."

"We think the baby has suffered some neglect," Nanna said. "She's a skinny little thing."

"What's her name?"

Esther would always dread that question. "My sister named her Winter, but Levi thought of Winnie, which I think is much better."

Rita raised her eyebrows. "Levi is very clever. How old is the baby?"

"Five months, I think," Esther said. Almost a month had passed since she'd gotten Winnie, and Ivy had told Esther that Winnie was four months old. Of course, Ivy was so flighty, she might not have remembered exactly when Winnie was born.

Rita gave Esther a motherly smile. "You could start her on solid foods. That will help her gain weight."

Solid foods?

"The doctor said rice cereal first, but I wouldn't bother," Cathy said. "Rice causes colic. Start with the fruit."

Rita frowned. "That's not true, Cathy. I'd start with green beans. If you can get them used to green beans, they'll eat anything."

Esther felt her face get warm. "I haven't even thought about solid foods." All of a sudden, her eyes stung with tears. She didn't know why the very mention of solid foods had her so upset—probably because she had so much to learn and had no idea what she didn't know. What if something she did made Winnie sick? What if something she didn't do stunted Winnie's growth? She hated being so ignorant.

Nanna reached over and patted Esther's hand. "No need to panic. Hannah and I will come over next week and help you get started."

"Okay," Esther said, doing her best to keep her voice from shaking. She was not a crier. She was not weak. Maybe the strain of having sole responsibility for another human being was wearing on her.

"And you know Levi will do anything he can for you," Nanna said. "He's wonderful *gute* with babies, and he doesn't mind helping."

Esther took a deep breath. Nanna and Hannah and Mary Jane were mere minutes away by buggy, and Levi came over more than any of the others. Levi would be there.

"It was a horrible thing for your sister to do," Cathy said.

Now *this* was safer ground. Esther shoved down her misgivings and reminded herself how angry she was with her sister. Anger was so much safer than sadness. Sadness made her vulnerable, and she couldn't afford such an unpleasant emotion.

"Now, Cathy," Rita scolded. "That's gossip."

Cathy puckered her lips. "I can't see that it is."

"I'm with Cathy on this one," Nanna said, scooting her chair a fraction of an inch closer to Esther's. "It was a horrible thing to do to Esther, not to mention that poor little baby, and if her sister were here, I'd tell her that to her face."

Rita sighed. "Oh, very well. I agree with Cathy. It was a very mean thing your sister did to you." She leaned toward Esther and whispered, "I suppose I can just spend two extra minutes in confession this week."

Esther felt the tears pooling again. She quickly blinked them away. It felt so *gute* to have someone on her side. On nights when Winnie didn't sleep, she felt so guilty for resenting the baby. Ivy didn't deserve much consideration, but Winnie was innocent and helpless. She'd done nothing to deserve such a hopeless aunt. And yet Esther resented her just the same. Resented that she had no time to finish her latest quilt. Resented that she couldn't curl up and read Jane Austen every night. Resented that she didn't even have time to shower most days. Resented that she hadn't had a *gute* night's sleep in three weeks.

"It's been hard," was all she could muster.

"Of course it's been hard," Rita said. "Having your own baby is hard enough, and you get nine months to prepare for it."

"My first pregnancy lasted ten months," Cathy added.

Esther slumped her shoulders. "I'm just not *gute* with babies."

Allison tapped her thimble on the quilt frame. "I'm not good with babies either, but I still had seven of my own. I don't know what I was thinking except I sure had a lot of fun with them when they got older. My husband loves babies. He is more of a natural than I am. He changed a lot of diapers in those early years."

Allison's husband was probably a lot like Levi. Levi seemed to instinctively know what Winnie needed and how to get it for her. And he didn't seem to mind just sitting and holding the baby. He actually enjoyed it. He'd probably gladly let Esther finish the entire bathroom if he wasn't so concerned for her safety. Esther's heart did that skipping thing again. Levi would make a wonderful *gute fater* and husband—for whatever girl he married.

Cathy pinned Esther with a serious gaze. "Don't be hard on yourself. Ever. That's how people get ulcers. You just do your best, and God will look after the rest."

"Always good advice," Nanna said.

Easier said than done.

Cathy leaned back in her chair. "What you need is to get out of the house more. What do you know about pickle-ball, Esther?"

Esther raised her brows. "Nothing."

Rita nodded so hard she fanned up a breeze. "That's an excellent idea, Cathy. And she could bring the baby."

"Where am I taking the baby?"

Cathy got so excited, she stood up. "Pickleball is a game you play with a paddle and a whiffle ball. It's a cross between tennis and Ping-Pong."

"Oh," Esther said. "I don't know if I could do that."

Cathy waved her hand in the air. "Of course you can. I'm eighty-two, and I play three days a week. If I can play it, anybody can play it."

Esther glanced at Nanna. "I mean, I don't know if I'm allowed to play it." She was positive the Ordnung didn't say anything about pickleball or sports in general.

Nanna laughed. "You're allowed. I play two days a week. I got permission from the bishop."

Esther grinned. "You mean your son?"

"He's afraid to tell me no."

"But maybe he'd tell me no."

Nanna shook her head. "When I wanted to play, I simply pointed out to him that his brother runs five-Ks and our minister in Wisconsin rode horses. Pickleball is just another sport, and it's so easy you can play in your dress. I just put sweatpants underneath."

Esther couldn't quite picture sixty-nine-year-old Nanna in sweatpants, but she was beginning to feel that maybe she'd like to see that. She couldn't help but think her bishop in Pennsylvania never would have approved of *fraaen* playing pickleball, but she was in Colorado now, and if the bishop approved, there was no reason not to. That's probably why they called it the Wild West.

"I suppose it wouldn't hurt to try and see if I like it."

"Wonderful," Cathy said, with as much enthusiasm as she'd used when talking about her moles. "What time is Winnie's morning nap?"

Winnie only took a morning nap when Levi was around. "Umm, from about ten to noon." At least that was the time when Esther wished she'd take a nap.

"I'll pick you and Nanna up on Tuesday at eight forty-five. Will that work?"

Esther tried to muster some excitement. Maybe it would be fun. "I think so."

"I have an extra car seat for when my great-grandbaby comes to visit, and I'll bring you an extra paddle."

Rita clapped her hands. "It's going to be so fun. Who knew we'd get a new quilting friend and a pickleball player all in the same day?"

A knock pulled Allison to the front door. Esther caught her breath when she opened it and Levi Kiem stood on the porch holding Winnie in his arms. He had such a nice smile. It always took her breath away. Winnie was in a pink dress and white bonnet that Hannah had donated from her collection of hand-me-downs. Winnie and Levi were an adorable pair.

"Hello, Levi," Allison said.

"Oh, look at that baby," Rita said, gushing like a garden hose. She stood and quickly made her way around the quilt, then took Winnie from Levi without even asking. Rita cooed and cuddled Winnie, and Winnie smiled as if she and Rita were long-lost friends. Esther felt a twinge of longing in her chest. Rita was definitely a baby person, and Esther loved that Rita made such a fuss.

"I'm sorry to interrupt," Levi said, stepping into the house. "But my *mamm* asked me to take Esther home, and I had to come early because I've got to tile a shower in Monte Vista at one o'clock."

"Of course," Esther said, jumping from her seat.

"But she's only been here half an hour," Rita said.

"I know. I'm sorry. We didn't coordinate our schedules very well today."

Esther was disappointed, but she hated to be an inconvenience to anyone. She quickly dropped her thimbles into her little quilting bag and pushed her chair under the quilt. "*Denki* for having me," she said. "It's been so fun."

Allison leaned against the door as if she was settling in for a long visit with Levi. "I hear you're a great help with the baby."

He actually turned a slight shade of red. "Winnie's cute, and Esther has her hands full. We all want to help."

Rita bounced the baby. It seemed that was a requirement when anyone held a baby—just keep moving. "We love Esther. She's playing pickleball with us next week."

Levi's gaze traveled from quilter to quilter and lit on Esther. For some reason, his smile faded. "It looks like you're going to fit right in, Esther."

Esther drew her brows together. What was Levi thinking just now? And why did it steal his smile?

Rita got sort of a sly, I-know-something-you-don't-know look on her face. "So, Levi, do you have a girlfriend? I mean, are you dating anyone? Is that what the Amish call it? Dating? Esther could use a pickleball partner on Tuesday."

Esther nearly groaned out loud as Levi seemed to retreat further into himself without moving a muscle. "Pickleball," he said, as if the thought of knitting made him more excited. "I don't think I could keep up with the older folks when it comes to pickleball. I'll stick to volleyball with *die youngie*."

"What is *die youngie*?" Rita said.

"It means the young people in the district," Nanna said. "And there aren't very many of them."

Cathy shook her head. "Volleyball isn't near as fun as pickleball."

Levi's smile didn't quite reach his eyes. "I'm sure I wouldn't be able to keep up. But thanks for the invitation. Are you ready, Esther?"

"I'm ready," she said, trying to tamp down the disquiet that had suddenly overtaken her. Levi was simply having a bad day. She shouldn't read too much into his sudden withdrawal, as if he would rather be anywhere else in the world. She didn't know him well enough to know why his mood had shifted instantaneously, so she wouldn't let it upset her, even though she couldn't help but feel it had something to do with her.

She picked up her bag and took Winnie from Rita's arms. "See you next week, then."

Levi took the baby from her before she even walked out of the house. He closed the door behind him and smiled. His smile seemed more natural to his face this time. "I found more tile for you."

"You did?"

"There's a supplier in Pueblo who has odds and ends of every size, from one inch by one inch to eighteen by eighteen. He gave them to me just so he could get rid of them."

"*Ach*, Levi, that's *wunderbarr*."

"I guess, but it's going to take forever to lay if you want to be artistic about it."

She gave Winnie a kiss on the cheek. Her skin was so irresistibly soft. "Putting tiles together to create something beautiful is the fun of it. It doesn't matter if it takes longer."

He shook his head and tried to stifle a grin. "I hate to be the bearer of bad news, but laying tile isn't fun."

"That's because you haven't looked at it the right way. I'll help you, or you can simply watch, if you want, but I think doing my bathroom is going to be the funnest tiling job you've ever had."

He opened the buggy door for her. "That isn't saying much. I haven't had any fun before."

"*Ach*, it's going to be fun, especially since you'll be entertaining Winnie and bossing me around at the same time."

"Sounds like the best time I've ever had." Esther tightened her hold on Winnie as Levi snapped the reins, and the horse moved forward. "Can I come by on Tuesday?" he said.

Esther nibbled on her bottom lip. "We're playing pickleball Tuesday morning."

He focused his gaze outside and acted as if he didn't want to talk anymore. "Sounds like fun. I'll plan on coming Wednesday."

There it was again. An instant change of mood when someone mentioned pickleball. What did he have against pickleball? Maybe he wasn't a very *gute* player, and he was embarrassed. He didn't have to be embarrassed in front of her. She'd never played before. But something about pickleball made him unhappy. When she knew him better, she'd find out what it was.

He glanced in her direction. "For five minutes, I've been trying to figure out what that thing behind your ear is. I give up."

Esther put her hand to the side of her head and slid out a seam ripper—with a lid, because she didn't want to stab herself. She held it up so he could get a closer look. "This is a seam ripper. When you make a mistake sewing, you use it to rip out stitches you've already put in."

Another shadow passed across his face. "I can see how that would come in handy. We all make mistakes that need to be fixed. The best idea is never to make them."

"I don't think it's possible *not* to make mistakes."

"I guess we all make mistakes, but it's better to pull back before you get too far into making a mistake."

She nodded. "Always easier to rip out fewer stitches than to have to tear out the whole seam."

He sat up straighter. "One of Nanna's friends asked if I was dating anyone."

"Okay?"

"I just wanted to say that there's no one here in Byler I'm interested in. Dat is sending me to Ohio in October to find a *fraa*. I just thought you'd want to know."

She felt the heat travel up her neck. "Why would I want

to know?" Or, the better question: why did he want her to know?

He seemed to chew on his answer before he let it out of his mouth. "I don't want you to get your feelings hurt."

"You . . . what?" she stuttered.

"I don't want you to get your feelings hurt or your hopes up about us—or, I mean, me. I'm going to Ohio to find someone closer to my own age." He grimaced. She was sure the expression was meant to come out like a friendly smile.

She gritted her teeth. "Why would you think I'd get my feelings hurt?"

He shifted in the seat as if she'd asked him a really personal question, like "Is that mole on your neck melanoma?" or "Are you feeling constipated?"

"*Ach*, well, we've been spending a lot of time together, and I've helped a lot with Winnie. I know you're grateful, but good deeds can get misinterpreted. You're too old for me, but it's only natural that someone like you might be *ferhoodled* by someone like me." He glanced at her and must have been alarmed by her steely glare because he stammered to a stop. *Gute* thing. He was about to put his entire leg in his mouth along with his foot.

Esther wasn't one to temper her temper, and Levi was going to hear exactly what she thought of his little speech. "Of all the presumptuous, arrogant, idiotic things to say!"

He drew back as if terrified of the crazy elderly woman. "What . . . what does presumptuous mean?"

"You can just go home and look that up in a dictionary, kiddo," she said, with emphasis on "kiddo" so he knew she didn't appreciate the implication that she was an old lady. Sure, she was an old maid, but that was just an expression. She was only thirty. She still had a lot of life left to live. "If you weren't so full of yourself, you'd know that I'm not interested in you in the least."

He rolled his eyes. "Now, come on, Esther. Every time you look at me, you smile. And you can't tell me it wasn't you who put Rita up to asking me if I was dating anybody and inviting me to play pickleball."

This was getting ridiculous. "I smile because I'm grateful for your help with Winnie. If you take a simple smile as a sign of love, then you're going to spend a lot of energy worrying about how many girls are in love with you. And I didn't put Rita up to anything. She's friendly. She's interested in your life, and I'm not that desperate." Esther wanted to yank the seam ripper from behind her ear, take off the lid, and score the black vinyl seat between them.

Okay, she didn't really want to do it, but she wanted to imagine the look on Levi's face if she did.

Levi frowned. "I didn't say you were desperate."

"You didn't have to." Winnie must have been able to feel her agitation. She fussed and fidgeted in Esther's arms. "I'm a thirty-year-old unmarried woman. Of course you think I'm desperate. You don't have to worry. I don't plan on ever letting myself get attached to a man. It's not worth the trouble or the heartache. Believe me, I'm as far from interested in you as I can get. Men are inconstant, unfaithful creatures, and I'm much better off alone."

"Now wait a minute. No matter what you think of me, I read the Bible every day, I'm very *gute* to my *mamm* and *schwesteren*, and I've changed Winnie's diaper almost as many times as you have."

She took a deep breath and willed herself to calm down. It wasn't easy. She needed a rug and a brick wall.

She closed her eyes, pressed her lips together, and thought of bread pudding with extra raisins. "You're right. I'm making a generalization I shouldn't make. Be that as it may, I don't want to marry anyone. At this point, the only man who would be interested in me would be interested in my money, as meager as it is, and I can spot a money grubber from a mile away."

"That's not true."

"*Jah*, it is. I know greed when I see it."

"*Nae.* I mean, it's not true that men could only be interested in you for your money. You're very pretty, Esther."

She snorted her displeasure. "Pretty for my age is what you meant to say."

"I mean it. You are very pretty. I just . . . it wonders me why you're not married yet."

She snorted again. "There are plenty of *wunderbarr*, pretty girls who aren't married. They're not willing to settle for just anybody."

"But why aren't you married? Did you ever have a boyfriend? Did you ever have a crush on someone?"

She peered at him through hooded eyes. He certainly didn't deserve any such information, and she wasn't going to spill her guts to someone as arrogant as Levi Kiem. Let him make up any story he wanted to in his head. He'd get nothing from her. "Don't try to justify yourself, Levi. I owe you nothing, especially not an explanation. I'm happy the way I am, and I really don't care what you think of me."

She had never been so *froh* to arrive at a destination as she was at the moment when he stopped the buggy in front of her house. "I'm sorry, Esther," he said weakly, as if he wasn't quite sure what had just hit him.

She wasn't in the mood for an apology. "*Denki* for the ride," she said, not really sure if she meant it but determined to be polite all the same. She jumped out of the buggy with Winnie securely in her arms and marched resolutely toward the house, not looking back, even when she heard him drive away.

She was so mad, she could have spit, but she wasn't going to do that, because it was very rude to spit. What made her even angrier was that some of what Levi had said was just a teensy-tinsy bit true. His handsome face and exceptional kindness had piqued her interest in a way that hadn't happened for a very long time. She did sort of like him. She had even fooled herself into thinking that maybe he was just a little bit interested in her. Oy, anyhow, she felt like the biggest fool in the world.

Before she walked into the house, she pulled the seam ripper from behind her ear, took off the lid with her teeth, and stabbed the pointy part of the seam ripper into the doorjamb just outside the door. The handle broke and clattered to the ground, leaving the pointy metal part sticking out of the wood. *Gute.* Just how she wanted it.

You never knew when you were going to need a seam ripper.

Chapter Five

With growing dread, Levi pulled up to Esther's house with his wagon loaded with plywood and tools. Today he was going to pull out the subfloor and get everything ready to put in a new one. He planned on doing it himself because Esther didn't know how to use a circular saw, and he wasn't about to let her use his. She probably wouldn't even ask. Esther wasn't likely to want to have anything to do with Levi ever again. He'd seen her mad before—she would have beaten that rug to death if he hadn't interrupted her—but he'd never seen her as mad as the day he'd accused her of being interested in him.

He hooked his hand around the back of his neck and pressed his fingers into his tight muscles. He'd made some wrong assumptions about her feelings, and she'd jumped down his throat. Not that he hadn't deserved it, but what was he supposed to think when Rita had asked him to be Esther's pickleball partner? Any reasonable man would have assumed Esther had put Rita up to it. Any reasonable man would have suspected Esther was interested in him. What single young man in Levi's shoes wouldn't have been cautious? What old maid wasn't looking for a handsome husband?

Apparently Esther. She claimed she never wanted to marry. Well, she'd never find anyone willing to marry her with a temper like that.

It felt like a pile of stones weighed down Levi's gut. He could blame it on Esther all day long, but he'd said some things he shouldn't have, and Esther had used her anger to cover up her hurt feelings. He'd hurt her feelings because he had called her old and maybe made her feel undesirable—like no man would ever be interested in her. What woman wanted to hear that?

She'd protested so adamantly against marriage in general and marriage to him in particular that he began to wonder if maybe he was a little too sure of himself. Mamm and Mary Jane told him he was handsome, but maybe they were just being nice. Maybe he'd overestimated his own appeal. Way overestimated. Would he be able to find a girl in Ohio who would have him? If a thirty-year-old spinster wasn't interested in him, who would be? Of course, Esther wasn't just any thirty-year-old. She was wonderful pretty, smarter than he was, and determined in ways he'd never seen before. She was far from desperate.

Even with the baby, Esther didn't sit around waiting for someone to rescue her. She asked for help when she needed it, then set out to do it herself. The bathroom floor was the perfect example of that. How many other women would don garden gloves and safety goggles to do a job they didn't need to do? It wasn't likely she'd ever install another subfloor again in her life, but she wanted to learn how to do it just in case.

She needed her bathroom floor done, especially since the toilet was sitting in the hall and the linoleum was gone, but she wasn't going to be happy to see him. Maybe it was better if things were icy between them. He'd get the bathroom done much faster if she wasn't such a distraction. Still, he regretted how he'd behaved. He was going to miss her smile. It always made his day a little more pleasant.

Levi jumped from the wagon and strode across the lawn to the porch. At about eye level, there was a small piece of silver metal protruding from the doorjamb just outside the front door. He didn't know what it was, but somebody could snag their bonnet or hat on it if they weren't careful. He knocked softly on the door and made a mental note to get some pliers later and pull it out.

Nobody answered the door, so Levi knocked again, a little louder this time. He didn't want to wake the baby if she was asleep, but it wasn't her naptime, so he thought he was safe. Still no answer. He opened the door, stuck his head inside the house, and listened. No baby crying. No movement in the kitchen. Was Esther away? Had she forgotten he was coming? More likely she had purposefully left home so she wouldn't have to be here when he came. His disappointment surprised him. Was she really that mad at him?

Okay then. He'd just do the work while she was gone. Much easier that way. He wouldn't have to talk her out of using the circular saw, he could knock out plywood without worrying about scaring the baby, and he wouldn't have to feel guilty about being so arrogant.

The bright and colorful quilt on the frames in the front room caught his eye. The quilt was alive with all the colors of the rainbow in a pattern of small and big rectangles. It was really quite beautiful. How did Esther manage to make quilts and care for Winnie? She was a wonder.

Calling Esther's name, he wandered into the kitchen.

She wasn't there. The breakfast dishes were drying on the rack next to the sink, along with three baby bottles and two pink plastic spoons. It looked as if Esther had been trying Winnie with some baby food. Was Winnie that old already?

Plop! Something thudded against the kitchen window. Levi drew his brows together and pulled the curtains open. Esther stood under her apricot tree at the edge of her yard. Winnie sat next to her on a quilt, bundled in her jacket and propped up with two pillows. Esther's face was as dark as a thunderstorm. She reached out, pulled a tiny green apricot from the tree, then threw it as hard as she could at the house. It bounced off the brick four feet from the kitchen window.

Oh, *sis yuscht*! Where did she learn to throw like that, and how mad at him was she?

Levi opened the window just as she was about to heave another apricot. "Getting ready for softball season?"

She frowned in annoyance and lowered her fist to her side. "Just thinning the apricot tree. You get bigger apricots in the summer that way."

The thought that she might still be angry with him kept him from laughing. "I've never seen that method of thinning apricots."

She dropped the little apricot and brushed her hands together. "All the farmers are doing it this way now. And Winnie needed a little sunshine."

"She's sitting up by herself."

Esther bent down and picked Winnie up, giving her a kiss on the cheek as she secured the baby in her arms. "She's close, but she still needs the pillows so she doesn't do a head dive into the quilt."

She stood there staring through the screen at him with no indication that she wanted to continue the conversation. Levi decided he'd rather not have a serious discussion from behind a window screen. "I'll come out."

He went out the back door just down the hall from the torn-up bathroom. At least thirty little green apricots dotted the lawn next to the house. Esther had been throwing fruit for several minutes. She must have been livid. Esther had put Winnie down again and was sitting next to her on the quilt. She didn't even look up when he approached. "It looks like you've done a *gute* job culling the tree," he said.

She still wouldn't look at him. Winnie was cute, but Esther had always been able to tear her gaze from the baby before. "What I've done is made more work for myself. I'll be picking up green apricots at naptime when I could have been quilting."

Levi had convinced himself it was better if Esther gave him the cold shoulder, but truth be told, he couldn't stand the tension between them. He sat next to Winnie and her pillows. "I'm sorry, Esther."

She looked up. "Sorry about what?"

"You know what, and I don't blame you for being mad at me."

Her laugh came out more like a snort. "At least you're smart enough to know you should apologize." She picked up an errant apricot and tossed it off the quilt. "But don't be too concerned. An old *maedel* like me isn't worth getting worked up about."

He growled. "Esther, you know that's not how I feel."

She sighed. "You're right. I'm being unfair, and it's not

even about you. The apricots are because of my *schwester*. I'm even madder at her than I am at you."

"That doesn't make me feel better. Your *schwester*'s done some vile things." He tilted his head to look her in the eye. "I really am sorry. You're not old, and it was arrogant of me to think you might be interested."

She nodded. "*Jah*, it was, but it didn't surprise me. *Buwe* your age are an arrogant group in general."

"I didn't mean to offend or upset you."

"I wasn't offended or upset."

"I was there, Esther. I saw the whole thing. For sure and certain you were offended and upset."

She gave him the stink eye. "I wasn't offended. I was mad. And embarrassed. Do you know how humiliating it is to have a man of your age call me old? How embarrassed I was that you thought I asked Rita to invite you to play pickleball with me? I'm mortified that you think I'm desperate, that you think I could hope for a boy like you to ever look at a woman like me. I was embarrassed, and my embarrassment gave way to anger."

"I don't think you're desperate."

She rolled her eyes. "Of course you don't."

"I just . . . look, Esther. We've spent a lot of time together. I like you. I thought maybe a woman like you would want more than friendship from a man like me. I jumped to some conclusions I shouldn't have."

She picked up Winnie and set her on her lap as if the baby was another layer of protection between them. "A woman like me."

He gritted his teeth. "I'm sorry. I'm not saying it right. I was wrong, utterly and completely wrong, but I had good intentions, if that counts for anything. I was just trying to be honest with you. I find that honesty is much less painful in the long run than sparing someone's feelings in the short run."

She played with Winnie's fingers. "I don't mind honesty. I do mind arrogance and thickheaded assumptions."

"I understand. And believe it or not, I agree. I won't make any more assumptions, and you'll always get my full honesty, no matter how hard it is to say."

She curled one side of her mouth. "I don't know that I want your full honesty. If you think I'm old or ugly or desperate, keep it to yourself."

He smiled. "You're none of those things, and I'm being perfectly honest about that."

She acted as if she didn't believe him, but she smiled anyway, making him feel a little better about himself. He couldn't be completely satisfied, because he had been quite ungenerous and had probably hurt their relationship. He wished he had thought of that before he had let his mouth and his imagination run away from him.

"So," he said, giving Winnie's little leg a squeeze, "what did Ivy do this time?"

Esther fisted some of the quilt in her hand. "*Ach.* I got a letter this morning. Ivy wants me to take Winnie to the library this afternoon and get on the computer to do something called 'Skype.' It's where you can talk face-to-face with someone anywhere in the world."

"She wants to see Winnie."

Esther frowned and put her hands over Winnie's ears. Winnie struggled and fussed at having her head trapped like that. "I don't know what she wants," she whispered. "If she truly wanted to see Winnie, she never would have abandoned her."

Levi couldn't help but smile. "I don't think Winnie can understand what you're saying."

"She will someday, and I don't want her ever thinking she isn't wanted." She removed her hands from Winnie's ears. "What Ivy wants is to soothe her conscience and to make sure I know who still has control. If she reminds me how selfish I am, she knows I'll come running to do her bidding."

"You're not selfish, Esther."

"I'm resentful and angry. In my heart, I want to punish Ivy for"—she glanced at Winnie—"what she did. But that is an uncharitable feeling, and Ivy knows how to make me feel guilty."

Winnie reached for Levi. He held out his arms, and Esther handed the baby to him. "Then don't go. There's nothing that says you have to keep that date at the library. If Ivy's letter had arrived a day later, you would have missed it anyway. You can blame it on her for not giving you enough warning."

"I could."

Levi bounced Winnie on his knee. She giggled.

Esther smiled. "I've never heard her laugh before."

"Anyone in your situation would be very angry at Ivy. It's completely understandable. Try not to feel guilty. I can't help but think it was Gotte's will that brought Winnie here. Can you imagine what would happen to her if she was still with Ivy?"

Esther thought about that for a second. "Do you think Gotte put it into Ivy's heart to leave her baby with me?"

"*Jah.*"

"But how could that be? I'm the last person Gotte would trust to take care of a baby."

"*Ach, vell,* Ivy might be the last person. You're only the second-to-last person."

She cuffed him on the shoulder.

"Esther, you think you're a bad mother, but you're wrong. You don't know anything about babies, but you care for Winnie as if she was your own. You test the water temperature every time you fix her a bottle. You put diaper rash ointment on her bottom every time you change her. You buy that organic formula for sensitive stomachs. You learned how to crochet so you could make her a blanket to have something soft to cuddle. Esther, you are more of a mother than Ivy ever was."

"That's a pretty low bar."

He shrugged. "A *mater* doesn't have to know everything. She just has to be willing to try and have the love in her heart to always want what is best for her child. That's what you do with Winnie every day."

"That's a very nice thing for you to say."

"You probably don't believe I know how to say nice things."

"*Nae.* I've heard you say nice things before. They're just outweighed by the *dumm* things you say."

He laughed. "I'll try not to say any more *dumm* things."

"I won't hold my breath."

Levi ran his finger along the silky-soft skin of Winnie's cheek. "So what are you going to do about the library?"

Esther pulled a little green apricot from her apron pocket and tossed it toward the house. "I'll go. No matter how neglectful Ivy is, she's still Winnie's mother. She doesn't deserve to see Winnie, but maybe it will prick her conscience. She did send a letter. It proves she cares, if even just a little."

"Do you want me to come with you?"

Esther thought about it for a minute. "*Jah*. But you're not going to get the bathroom done sitting at the library. I shouldn't even ask."

"You didn't ask. I did. I want to help. Besides, I've heard so much about Ivy, I'd like to get a good look at her."

Esther seemed doubtful. "Not much to see. She's a younger version of me. Much younger."

"Not that much younger, and I've already told you, Esther—you're not old."

She threw back her head. "Ha! I don't believe you."

He grinned. "I always try to tell the honest truth. You're not old." He cleared his throat. "Just too old for me." He probably shouldn't have said that, but if he didn't explain himself, she was going to think he was a liar every time he opened his mouth.

She seemed to be deciding if she should be offended. "Fair enough. Then I suppose I can tell you that you're handsome. Just not handsome enough for me."

He winced. "That hurt," he said, pressing his hand to his heart and coaxing a smile from her lips.

"You deserved it."

"I suppose I did." He slumped his shoulders in mock dejection and made her laugh, but she'd hit a little harder than he wanted to admit. She didn't think he was handsome enough? Why not? Would any girls in Ohio be interested in a slightly handsome Amish boy? He tried to brush off her words. She was only teasing. He was plenty handsome for anyone, even Esther Zook. Levi stood with Winnie in his arms. "What time is Ivy calling?"

She got up, folded the quilt, and picked up the pillows.

"At three. We can go after Winnie's nap. That will give us some time to work on the bathroom."

He shook his head. "Maybe not. It's going to be loud. Winnie won't be able to sleep through it."

"We can get a little done before she goes to bed. You can feed her the bottle and show me what to do."

"*Nae.* It's tear-out-the-floor day, and you are not going near my cordless circular saw."

Esther drove the buggy around behind the library and glanced at Levi. Was it a lie to tell him he wasn't handsome enough for her? Probably not. Levi was wonderful handsome, but Esther didn't want to marry anyone, so no one was handsome enough for her. Absolutely true.

Why was she even thinking about whether Levi was handsome or not when she had bigger things to worry about? She was going to talk to Ivy, and she had no idea what to say to her.

Esther set the brake and glanced at Levi. He gave her an encouraging smile. "You okay?"

"*Nae.* I'm unsure, and I hate being unsure. Part of me wants to scold her. Part of me wants to tell her how worried I am about her. I still love her very much."

"I'm sure you do."

"My parents would be disappointed in me. They asked me to watch out for my *schwester.*"

Levi secured one of Winnie's booties, which had been slipping off her foot. "Your parents couldn't help Ivy. They certainly wouldn't ask any more of you than they could do themselves. We both know you'd do everything you could to help her if she asked. It's not your fault she won't let you help. You're taking *gute* care of her daughter, and that's really the biggest help she needs, even if she would never see it as help. I don't wonder but your parents are grateful you're taking care of their granddaughter."

"I suppose so, even if I have been a bit resentful about it."

"Who wouldn't be?"

"I'm back to the problem of what to say to Ivy. I'm tempted to give her a sermon about the evils of abandoning a baby, but I don't want Winnie to hear it. What would you say?"

"I don't know," he said, sliding the door open and stepping down from the buggy with Winnie in his arms. "I've never met your *schwester*."

Esther grabbed the diaper bag and sighed out her frustration. "Do you think Winnie will be upset to see her mother?"

"*Nae*. It's sad for Ivy, but Winnie doesn't know who her mother is."

Esther's lips curled upward. "She probably thinks you're her mother."

"I wouldn't be surprised."

They strolled across the tiny parking lot. "I'm not sure if I should ask Ivy to come back and take responsibility for her baby or tell her to never return again."

"I can't believe it was just by chance that Ivy brought Winnie to you," Levi said. "Gotte had a hand in it. Until Ivy settles down and quits running, Winnie is much better off with you."

Esther stopped walking. Levi halted too. She covered Winnie's ears with the palms of her hands. "I'm not the best mother in the world, but I'm a far sight better than

Ivy, who is never in one place for very long. What kind of life is that for Winnie, living out of a suitcase, dragged from place to place by a mother who changes boyfriends as often as she changes her stockings?"

Levi frowned and nodded. "You told me Ivy had a black eye when she came to your house."

"What if Ivy showed up at my house with a boyfriend?" Esther lowered her voice even further. Winnie didn't need to hear any of this. "What if that boyfriend hurt Winnie the way he hurt Ivy?"

Levi's expression turned deadly serious. "I wouldn't stand for it."

"I wouldn't either," Esther said, shuddering at the thought of someone harming a child. Winnie squirmed until Esther pulled her hands from Winnie's ears.

Levi squared his shoulders. "Okay then. Tell her, 'Ivy, don't come back. We're doing just fine without you.'"

Esther's heart sank like a rock in the lake. "That won't work. Ivy likes to upset me. If she thinks I don't want her to come back, she'll come back just to spite me."

He hooked his fingers around the back of his neck. "*Ach, du lieva.*"

"I've got to make her think I want her to come back without actually talking her into it."

"Sounds like a real trick."

"The trickiest." Esther opened the library door. "I don't want Ivy to see you. I don't know how she'll react."

Levi acted as if he didn't know whether to be offended or amused. "I'm not *that* homely. Do you think she'll start throwing things at the screen?"

Esther rolled her eyes and nudged him toward the nearest computer. "Just the opposite. When she was a teenager, Ivy was always giddy over one handsome Amish boy or another." She shouldn't have said that. Levi's head didn't need to swell any bigger than it already was.

He exploded into a smile and sat down. "Do you think she'll see how handsome I am and rush to Colorado to meet me?"

"I don't know what Ivy will do. It's better to be safe. Ivy was boy crazy as a teenager, and she got wonderful excited about handsome *Englisch* boys and handsome Amish boys." Especially if Esther was interested in one of them or one of them was interested in Esther. Esther had learned the hard way never to show interest in any boy, or Ivy would try to steal him. Esther sat next to Levi and took Winnie from his arms. "Don't look so pleased with yourself. Ivy's just as likely to throw things at the screen if she thinks you're homely or handsome."

Levi scooted his chair away from the computer so Ivy wouldn't be able to see him when she called. Or was Esther the one who was supposed to call? She looked at the computer. They had a different kind at the library in Pennsylvania, and Esther didn't even know how to turn this one on. Levi turned it on for her, but then he had to ask the nice lady at the reference desk how to do the Skype thing.

With her heart pounding fiercely in her ears, Esther pulled Ivy's letter from her bag and found the number she needed to call. The computer made a strange ringing noise, but no one answered on the other end. Was there anyone at the other end? Esther glanced at Levi, who seemed even more tense than she was. "I'll check the number," she said.

Winnie tried to grab the keyboard and pushed some button that made the computer screen go blank. Oh, *sis yuscht*. Levi strolled back to the reference desk and asked the nice lady to come fix the computer. The librarian navigated back to the Skype page and keyed in the number for Esther. That metallic ringing noise again and again, but nobody appeared on the screen. Esther checked her letter again. She was there at the right time using the right number. Where was Ivy?

Levi handed Winnie her teething ring, and she shoved it into her mouth, but after a few seconds she dropped it and pounded on the keys again. Levi chuckled and took Winnie from Esther's arms. "Winnie," he cooed, "you're not making this easy for Aendi Esther. *Cum.* Let's go find some books."

Esther smiled her thanks and tried her call again. Maybe she had the wrong number, or maybe something was wrong with the computer, but Ivy didn't appear on the screen, and Esther had already tried three times. She looked up from her computer. Levi was sitting in a soft chair with Winnie on his lap patiently reading her a book. Eyes wide, Winnie tapped her hand on each page as if she wanted to play with the book instead of read it. Levi had to time it just right to even turn the pages.

Something like affection caught in Esther's throat, and she had to swallow hard to dislodge it. She was too old for Levi, and he was too big for his britches, but for sure and certain no one had ever looked more attractive than Levi Kiem cradling her niece in his arms and trying to read her a book. He didn't seem to care that Winnie was drooling on his sleeve or that he had to read the same sentence over and over because Winnie wouldn't let him turn the pages. It was the sweetest, most adorable thing Esther had ever seen.

Levi glanced up and caught Esther staring at him. If he noticed her misty eyes or bemused expression, he didn't show it. He raised his eyebrows expectantly, and she shook her head. Still no Ivy.

Esther waited another minute and tried again. No response on the other end. She examined Ivy's letter again. She had the right date, the right time, and the right phone number. She called again, waited five minutes, and called again.

Ivy wasn't there, wasn't wherever she was supposed to be to get Esther's call. Esther shouldn't have been surprised. This was typical Ivy behavior. *Of course* Ivy had missed the call, and Esther was most irritated she'd made the effort to come to the library at all. Maybe Ivy had never had any intention of showing up. The letter was just another way to throw Esther into a tizzy and control her emotions from a distance. Ivy was determined to make Esther's life miserable in every way. Would she get tossed out of the library if she started throwing books at the window?

Esther took a deep breath and let her gaze travel across the room to Levi and Winnie. Levi had given Winnie his tube of lip balm, probably so she wouldn't try to eat the book. With the book laid across his lap and his arm securely around Winnie, he was fast asleep. Esther cracked a smile. She was angry with Ivy, but she should probably count her blessings before she started throwing books. Winnie was gaining weight and actually slept through the night most nights. Levi and Mary Jane and the Hannahs had been Esther's lifelines. Gotte had sent them at exactly the right time. And even though Esther was frustrated with her *schwester*, she loved Ivy fiercely. It was nice to have someone you loved that much, even if she drove you crazy. Ivy had lost her way, but at least she was alive. And she'd had sense and love enough to bring her baby to a place where someone would take care of her.

To own the truth, Esther was more relieved than she was annoyed. She hadn't been forced to talk to Ivy and hadn't had to figure out what to say to make her stay away. Esther wasn't good at being devious like that. That was Ivy's talent.

Esther ambled over to the soft chair where Levi was resting while Winnie played happily on his lap. She gave Levi a nudge, and he opened his eyes and caught his breath as if he'd had a sudden shock. His arm tightened around Winnie. "I'm awake. I'm awake," he said, running his hand across his eyes and smiling like a boy who's just been caught stealing cookies from the cookie jar.

She laughed. "Have an early morning?"

"Just as early as usual, but I had to wrestle my circular saw away from a very stubborn Amish woman earlier today. It took all the energy out of me."

"There was no need to wrestle that saw away. You should have shown me how to use it."

"You're not using my saw. I told you, I'll cut. You can pop out the old floor sections with the sledgehammer."

She glared at him. "I can't even lift the sledgehammer."

"Hmm. Too bad." He patted Winnie's head and closed the book. "That was a short call—or have I been asleep longer than I thought?"

"I tried six times. Ivy didn't answer."

He studied her face. "I'm sorry."

She shook her head. "I shouldn't admit it, but I'm *froh*. Now I don't have to figure out what to say."

"I'm just glad she didn't catch a glimpse of me in the background. We don't know what could have happened."

She rolled her eyes. "For sure and certain, there would have been trouble."

Levi laid the book on the table next to his chair and stood up with Winnie in his arms. "Should we go, then?"

"Not yet," Esther said. "Now that we're here, I want to show you something on the computer."

"Show me what?"

"It's about time you learned what a famous person your *mammi* is. We're going to look at her quilting website."

Chapter Six

Mammi was the dearest soul in the world, but she was completely incapable of leaving the house on time for any occasion, even when the family went to church. Levi sat in the buggy waiting for her to find her bag and her bonnet and her glasses. She had come out once, then had to go back into the house for a pot of soup she'd made for Esther. After another ten minutes, she finally bustled out the side door and settled herself into the buggy. "Sorry that took so long. I realized I hadn't put any onions in the soup, so I chopped some right quick. Soup just isn't soup without onions."

Levi forced a smile. He'd been sitting out here for ten minutes while Mammi chopped onions? *Ach, vell.* He'd learned many years ago that with Mammi, patience was not only a virtue, but a necessity. He should start keeping a book in his buggy for times when Mammi decided she just needed to run into the house to bake up some cookies for a sick neighbor. "That's okay, Mammi. I'm just *froh* to be driving a famous person around town in my buggy."

Mammi made that little noise she always made when she thought you were being frivolous. It was something halfway between a grunt and a squeak. "Famous person? What famous person?"

"Esther showed me your quilting blog on the computer. She says people all over the world have seen your quilts."

That little squeak again. "My quilts are famous. No one knows me from Adam."

"Or Eve," Levi said.

"Eve?"

"If someone met you and Adam on the street, they'd know you from Adam because he was a man."

Mammi laughed, and her shoulders shook and her eyes all but disappeared into slits on her face. Levi liked that when Mammi laughed, she did it with her whole heart and her whole body. She'd told Levi that was what cancer did to you. It taught you to enjoy every minute of your life because none of it was disposable. "So Esther showed you my website. That was nice of her."

"It's wonderful *gute*, Mammi. The photos and the instructions and the comments from women who like your designs."

"I mostly make the quilts. Allison does all the computer stuff."

"Esther showed me your watercolor quilt. She wants to do something like that on the bathroom floor. It will take too much time, but it will be pretty when she's done. Or when I'm done." He'd almost let slip the secret that Esther was the one fixing up the bathroom.

"Esther is truly an artist. She's already a better quilter than I'll ever be. For sure and certain, there will never be a nicer bathroom floor." She glanced at Levi and smiled. "This is the first time you've shown any interest in my quilts."

"It's not that I wasn't interested. It's just that I wasn't aware."

"That describes just about every boy your age, so I don't see as it's anything to be ashamed of," Mammi said.

Levi chuckled. "Me neither, but I'm *froh* Esther showed me. Now I'm not so unaware."

Mammi's eyes sparkled. "Esther's a dear girl. Very thoughtful."

Levi nodded. "She takes very *gute* care of Winnie, even though she doesn't know much about babies."

"What she doesn't know, she's eager to learn."

Mammi was a keen observer, and she was right. Anything Esther didn't know, she was willing to learn. Levi loved that about her. She wasn't content to just do the best she could with Winnie. She checked out parenting books from the library, asked Levi lots of questions, and practiced over and over again. And with the way Winnie went through diapers, Esther got a lot of practice. Esther didn't seem embarrassed to ask a twenty-four-year-old boy about feeding or naptime, and she acted as if she sincerely thought he knew what he was talking about. With the bathroom project, she was even more attentive to his instructions. She absorbed information and was grateful for it, grateful to him. He was always glad he could be of help. "Esther is smart as a whip too. We measured the bathroom floor, and she calculated in her head how many square feet of particleboard I'd need. And when I brought her tiles for the floor, she said, 'I need two more of this gray four-inch tile,' without even having to lay it out first. She has a head for numbers."

Mammi seemed pleased. "Esther has too many talents to count. I'm *froh* you've noticed." She adjusted the *kapp* over her short hair. The *kapp* must have been harder to keep in place now that she couldn't anchor it to her bun. "What a nice day for an outing."

Levi cocked his eyebrow. "An outing? Since when did this turn into an outing? I thought you wanted me to take you to inspect the progress on Esther's bathroom."

Mammi grinned and shrugged. "Who says a bathroom inspection can't be an outing? Maybe after I look at the bathroom, we can have a picnic on Esther's lawn."

Levi pressed his lips together to mask any emotion that might betray him. He'd like nothing better than to have a picnic with Esther and Winnie, but he was trying to be practical, and spending more time with either of them wasn't a *gute* idea. Depending on how quickly Esther laid the tile, the bathroom would be finished in another month or two, and Levi was already too attached to Winnie. What would he do when he didn't see her every week? Esther needed him. She was up to her neck in diapers and bottles and jars of baby food. What would she do without Levi to help her?

Levi could tell that Esther really enjoyed the time he spent at her house. He played with Winnie in the hall outside the bathroom while Esther installed the subfloor, and they talked and laughed. He loved how he could talk to Esther about anything—his group of friends, his plans for improving his father's business, his frustration at his younger brother. She always listened and never offered unwanted advice. He loved her determination to remodel her own bathroom and even her stubbornness when she wanted to use a tool he refused to let her touch. He liked how she carefully followed directions and was cautious with the power tools. He liked how she could make him laugh without even trying. It was going to leave a big hole in Esther's life when he finished the bathroom and didn't come around anymore.

A very big hole.

"I don't know if I'll have time for a picnic, Mammi."

"Oh, stuff and nonsense. Of course you have time. What's so important you can't stay and eat lunch? You can spend an hour for lunch."

"One less hour to work on the bathroom," he said.

"And that's another thing. That bathroom isn't that big. Why haven't you finished it yet?"

Levi wasn't about to tell Mammi that the work went slower because Esther was doing most of it. Esther did quality work and she was thorough, but she was just learning, so of course she'd take her time. "It's harder with the baby. Winnie likes me to hold her, and she's so cute, I can't resist."

Mammi seemed satisfied with that answer. "You always did love babies. I've told Hannah a dozen times how blessed she is to have you as her eldest. You've been a great help to her, and you're a great help to Esther. *Denki.*"

"It is my pleasure," Levi said, and he meant it. He was enchanted with Winnie, and Esther surprised him every minute. He wasn't sure how he'd managed to have any fun in his life before he'd met Esther. That was why it was going to be so hard when he finished the bathroom. That was why he needed to start distancing himself from Winnie and Esther and start thinking about finding a *fraa* in Ohio. He couldn't be Esther's friend forever.

Levi pulled the buggy in front of Esther's house and jumped out. He carried Mammi's pot of soup, and Mammi carried the bag of fabric scraps that she took everywhere.

She said the fabric was in case she needed to match something, but it seemed to Levi that she'd only need to match something if she was at the fabric store. He couldn't see the sense of carrying the bag everywhere. But if it made Mammi feel more secure, he didn't see any harm in her carrying a bag of fabric to Esther's house or to pickleball or even to church. Maybe a quilter like Mammi just felt happier having her fabric with her at all times. It was much like Levi and his crescent wrench. He would have liked to take it everywhere with him, but it might look odd if he started carrying a toolbox to *gmay*.

He knocked softly on Esther's door because it was Winnie's naptime. When Esther didn't answer, Levi opened the door and walked into the house. Mammi cocked her head and raised her eyebrows. "Esther doesn't mind if you let yourself in?"

Winnie's room was immediately to the left. Levi pointed to her door and whispered. "Sometimes she's got her hands full with the baby or a quilt. I usually just knock and then walk in."

"But Esther wouldn't like it if just anybody strolled into her house," Mammi said, lowering her voice.

"For sure and certain she wouldn't. But she doesn't care if I come in."

Mammi nodded as if she'd just learned how to spell "chrysanthemum," as if she thought she was pretty smart. "I see."

Levi frowned at her. "It's not rude if Esther says it's okay."

Mammi seemed about ready to laugh. "*Ach*, I never said it was."

The quilt set on frames in the front room was made of

small rectangles in many different shades of purple. When Levi squinted at the quilt, the pattern seemed to move and swirl before his eyes. It was a trick Esther had taught him. He was starting to appreciate what a talent quilt making was, and Esther was wonderful *gute* at it.

They tiptoed into the kitchen, but Esther wasn't there. Levi set the pot of soup on the stove. Mammi drew her brows together and pointed down the hall. Someone was in the new bathroom sniffling and whimpering softly. Levi didn't like the sound of that. He strode down the hall with Mammi close behind him. Esther sat on the new subfloor with her face buried in her hands and a full roll of toilet paper at her feet. A piece of red licorice was tucked behind her ear.

Levi's heart fell to his toes. He'd seen Esther ferociously mad often enough. The anger never bothered him. But her sadness absolutely tore him apart. He knelt down next to her and laid his hand on her arm. "Esther? What's the matter? How can I help?"

A tiny sob escaped her lips, and she turned her face away from him. "Oh, *sis yuscht*. I was going to be done before you got here."

"Can we help?" Mammi said, pressing her fingers to Levi's shoulder.

"I'm a terrible mother," Esther said, with a mournful note to her voice. "I'm just a terrible mother."

Levi grabbed her hand. "That's a big lie. You're a *wunderbarr mater*. Winnie loves you."

Esther unrolled a long strand of toilet paper and dabbed at her eyes. "I tried to clip her fingernails this morning, and I cut her pinky finger. She started to bleed, and I don't have a single Band-Aid in the house. What kind of mother doesn't have a supply of Band-Aids? She looked at me like I'd betrayed her."

"It's for sure she doesn't think you've betrayed her," Levi said, trying not to smile. Now that he was assured Esther wasn't seriously injured or someone hadn't died, he felt a thousand times better.

"I didn't have a Band-Aid, so she got blood on her dress, and I had to put her to bed in just a diaper, because there isn't one clean outfit in her drawer, and now there's blood on her sheets."

"A lot of blood?" Levi said doubtfully. Just how badly had Winnie been cut?

"Two spots," Esther said, "but nobody likes blood on their sheets. And when am I supposed to do laundry? If I'm not taking care of Winnie, I'm washing dishes or mopping the floor or trying to work on a quilt. I thought I could wash some clothes when I put her down for a nap, but all her dirty clothes are in the basket in her room and I'll wake her if I go in to fetch them. When I realized I had time to do the laundry but the clothes were out of reach, I sort of fell apart."

She couldn't have been comfortable on that unfinished bathroom floor. "*Cum,*" Levi said. He slid one arm under her knees and the other around her back and lifted her off the floor. Instead of resisting, she slipped her arms around his neck and sort of melted into his embrace as he carried her to the kitchen and set her down in a chair. Mammi followed with the toilet paper, which she gave to Levi as soon as his hands were free. He unrolled another long piece and handed it to Esther. She took it gratefully and blew her nose.

"First of all," Mammi said, "you did the right thing with

the Band-Aid. You never put a Band-Aid on a six-month-old. She'll work it off her finger and swallow it. Or worse, choke on it."

Esther sniffed into her toilet paper. "I never thought of that."

"Your instincts are better than you realize." Mammi set her bag of fabric next to the chair and sat down. "Every mother has cut her baby's skin at least once while trying to cut fingernails. I usually snipped fingernails while my babies were asleep. Then at least they didn't wiggle. Some mothers chew their babies' fingernails down to size."

"She kept scratching herself."

"You did the right thing." Mammi patted Esther's arm. "Now, Levi is going to sneak into Winnie's room and snatch up her laundry."

Levi scrunched his lips together and gave his *mammi* the stink eye. "How am I supposed to do that?"

Mammi wasn't impressed with his expression. "You're young and cocky. You're supposed to be able to do everything."

Esther was feeling better enough to giggle.

Levi should have been offended, but he was one of Mammi's favorites, so he knew she was teasing. "You're lucky I greased the hinges on Winnie's door last week. She kept waking up every time I put her down for a nap and shut the door."

"Well then, get to it. I'd like to get a tour of the bathroom and a *gute* start on Esther's laundry before we leave."

Levi always tried to do as he was told. He tiptoed to Winnie's room, opened the door, and managed to drag out

Winnie's clothes basket without making a sound, or at least without waking Winnie.

Mammi was brewing a pot of *kaffee* when he returned to the kitchen. "I did it," he said.

She smiled at him. "*Denki*. Don't get a big head."

Esther pressed her hand to her forehead, and her fingers found the licorice. She pulled it from behind her ear and curled one side of her mouth. "My breakfast. Winnie started crying, and I forgot to eat it."

"You never know when you're going to need a Twizzler," Levi said.

Mammi clucked her tongue. "You're going to blow away with the wind if you don't eat better than that."

"There's no time," Esther said. "And I'm just so tired."

Mammi stirred the *kaffee* and studied Esther's face. "How long has it been since you've had a break from this *haus*?"

Esther shrugged. "I've played pickleball twice, and Levi took me to the library last week."

Mammi shook her head. "That doesn't count. You need to get out of the house without the baby."

"Hannah babysat when I went to quilters group."

"Not *gute* enough," Mammi said. "You need to go have fun with *die youngie*, and I'm a very *gute* babysitter."

Esther laughed. "I don't wonder but you're the best babysitter there is, but an old maid doesn't fit in with *die youngie*." She glanced at Levi when she said "old," and Levi's face warmed with his own embarrassment.

Only six short weeks ago he'd made it very clear to Esther that she was too old for him, that he wasn't so desperate as to be interested in a spinster who had been passed over by other boys. If Esther and Mammi hadn't been in the room, he would have kicked himself.

Of course Esther belonged with *die youngie*. She belonged with the quilting ladies and the pickleball team and the volleyball players at the gathering. Esther had that rare ability to fit in everywhere, to be young and mature, smart and capable in any group. Or maybe she just had a special ability to fit in with Levi. He was only beginning to realize how well she fit. She wasn't a fresh-faced schoolgirl, silly and preoccupied with boys, but Levi didn't mind that. Adoration from girls fed his pride, but unbridled gushing got old after a while. Would he find more of the same in Ohio? What he needed was a girl like Esther: smart, feisty, determined, and teachable, eager to learn, with a bad temper and a *gute* throwing arm.

Mammi poured all three of them some *kaffee* and slid the mugs onto the table. "I'm sixty-nine years old, Esther. I can truthfully and happily say I don't fit in with *die youngie*. But you're a spring chicken and too young to be spending your life sitting on the bathroom floor crying your eyes out."

Esther waved her licorice in Levi's direction. "*Ach.* You caught me in a moment of weakness. I'm fine. When I realized I shut the laundry in the only room I couldn't go in, I sort of snapped. Under normal circumstances I'd throw a chair or something to make myself feel better. It won't happen again. I'm not usually a crier."

A chair? Levi had never seen Esther throw a chair. That was something he'd pay money to see.

"I know your behavior isn't normal," Mammi said. "That's why you need a break. You snapped like a piece of dried-out licorice. There's a gathering tonight, and you're going." Mammi took a sip of *kaffee* and peered at Levi over the rim of her cup. "I'll be here at six to babysit, and Ben will drive you to the gathering."

Ben? What was Mammi thinking? Ben was Levi's younger *bruder* and a completely unsuitable choice to take Esther anywhere. Levi loved his brother, but Ben wasn't especially responsible when it came to buggies or girls or life.

"Ben?" Esther asked, glancing at Levi doubtfully. She was wise to be wary. "You mean Levi's brother Ben?"

Mammi was obviously thrilled with the prospect of Ben driving Esther to the gathering. "Have you met him?"

"*Nae,*" Esther said. "But Levi has told me a lot about him."

Mammi seemed to love that bit of information. "Really? You've spent enough time together to hear about Levi's family? How nice."

Levi pressed his lips into a hard line. Mammi wouldn't think it was so nice if she knew he'd told Esther about the chickens that mysteriously got trapped in the school. Eight years ago, Ben and some friends had locked a flock of chickens in the school over the weekend. The mess on Monday morning was disgusting. Levi cleared his throat. "Ben doesn't like gatherings. He wasn't planning to go."

Mammi didn't seem to care that Ben was a horrible choice. "*Ach*, he'll go if I ask him, especially if he has a chance to drive a pretty girl. Besides, he can't make trouble if he's at the gathering." She gave Esther a reassuring smile, and it was completely fake. "I'm not saying he'll make trouble. Ben is a *gute* boy, and I'm sure Levi told you how nice-looking he is. He'll get you to the gathering in one piece."

Esther tied her strand of licorice into a knot. "Really, Nanna. I don't need to go to the gathering. I'll feel out of place, like a dandelion in a field of clover. I won't have a *gute* time."

Levi nodded. Esther shouldn't go to the gathering, but not because she was a dandelion. She'd be more like a rose among the ragweed.

"Stuff and nonsense," Mammi said. "Everybody loves Ben. He's friendly and funny, and he'll watch out for you. Nobody can make me laugh like Ben."

Annoyance buzzed in Levi's ear like a mosquito. He loved his *bruder*, but somebody in this room had to put his foot down. "Ben is irresponsible, unreliable, and he smokes like a chimney, Mammi. I can't let you do that to Esther. It would be better for her to stay home."

Mammi peered at Levi as if she was thinking about arithmetic and a new watercolor quilt pattern. "*Ach, vell.* Esther needs to get out of the *haus*, so I suppose you'll have to take her."

Esther lowered her eyes and took a bite of licorice. "Levi doesn't want to take me."

Of course he didn't want to take her, but not for the reasons she might have thought. She'd have a terrible time.

"Levi wouldn't mind at all. Would you, Levi?" Mammi gazed at him as if all her hopes and dreams lived in his answer.

He cleared his throat. Against his better judgment, he'd have to agree. It was either Levi or Ben. And Mammi was blind when it came to Ben's shortcomings. "I don't mind."

Esther shook her head. "I suppose I should be more blunt. I don't want Levi to take me."

Levi tried not to show his surprise. Esther didn't want

Levi to take her to the gathering? Why not? They'd been getting along so well. Was she still mad at him for calling her old? Was she embarrassed to be seen with him because she was so much more mature? What was wrong with him?

He straightened his shoulders. What was wrong with *her*? Levi was a *gute* catch, handsome and good-natured. What girl wouldn't want him to drive her to the gathering? This was definitely Esther's problem, not his.

So why was he having trouble swallowing?

Mammi seemed more perplexed than ever. "You don't want to go with Levi?"

Thank you, Mammi. He wasn't the only one who recognized how strange Esther was acting. What girl in her right mind wouldn't want to go to the gathering with Levi?

Esther gave Mammi a wry smile. "Levi shouldn't be shackled to an old maid when there are other friends he could be spending time with at the gathering. I want him to have a *gute* time."

Ach. Was that all? He didn't care if Esther's presence discouraged other girls, and she'd attract a lot of attention from his friends. He drew his brows together. He really didn't want Esther to go to that gathering. She had a *gute* life with Winnie and her quilts and her bathroom remodel. Why would Mammi want to mess up such a well-ordered routine? "I don't mind going to the gathering with you, but all we do is eat and play volleyball, and most of *die youngie* aren't very good players. You won't have a *gute* time."

Mammi grunted. "Why all this talk of not having a *gute* time? Of course you'll have a *gute* time. Esther will be able to get out of the house and feel like herself again."

Esther shrugged. "I didn't get out of the house much before."

Mammi waved that observation away like a pesky fly. "Stuff and nonsense, Esther. You're going to that gathering." She turned on Levi like a cat on a mouse. "And Levi is going to take you."

Levi put his hands in the air in surrender. "Okay, Mammi. Okay." His heart beat faster. Was it with excitement or dread? He didn't want to know.

Esther wasn't so compliant. "Nanna, I can't impose on you or Levi like that. When Winnie goes down to bed, I'll go outside and thin apricots."

Levi nearly spoke up. He'd seen Esther thin apricots. Her method wasn't good for the lawn, the apricots, or the kitchen window.

Thank Derr Herr, Mammi had enough sense to say something. "That is not getting away. That's just going outside. Levi is coming to pick you up, and I'll be here to babysit. You're going to have fun." When Mammi said it like that, everyone knew the discussion was over. Having fun was an order, and there was nothing Esther or Levi could do about it.

Esther pressed her lips together, glanced at Levi, and took a bite of licorice. "It sounds like more fun to thin apricots."

Levi tried not to take it personally.

This was a very wonderful bad idea. Esther did not want to go to a gathering. She did not want to impose on Nanna Kiem, and she certainly did not want to be more of a bother to Levi than she already was. The look on his face when Nanna ordered him to take Esther to the gathering told Esther all she needed to know about what Levi thought of that idea. He'd tried to talk Nanna out of it. Esther grunted in annoyance as she slammed her bonnet onto her head. She wouldn't be surprised if Levi thought Esther had put his *mammi* up to it.

Levi Kiem could just drive his buggy into the lake if he thought for one minute she wanted to go anywhere with him. She wasn't interested in being a burden on anyone, especially Levi, who thought she was old and desperate and who was going to Ohio to find a *fraa* because he couldn't convince anyone in Byler to marry him. Who was the desperate one now?

Winnie was sitting on the floor playing with a set of stacking cups Levi had brought for her. She was too young to stack or nest them, so she just moved them around with her hands and occasionally put one in her mouth to see what it tasted like. Esther never could understand why everything went into Winnie's mouth, except maybe babies were like goats. Her brother kept a few goats, and they liked to investigate their world by testing things with their tongues. That's how goats had gotten the reputation for eating everything, when in reality they just liked to explore their surroundings.

Winnie had a fresh diaper and a full stomach. All Nanna would have to do was put her to bed in about half an hour. Half an hour was all it was, and this whole thing was silly. Esther didn't need to escape from her life. She needed to learn how to handle the life she'd been given. She wouldn't be able to do that at a gathering where all the girls were ten years younger and all the boys were practically children. She'd much rather stay home than try to make idle conversation. She'd met most of *die youngie* at *gmay*, and while they had all been kind to her, she was too old to relate to any of them. Certainly too old to find any friends at the gathering.

She should have been perfectly miserable, but her heart skipped a beat when she thought about being with Levi— even at a gathering. Levi was pleasant and easygoing. He knew how to talk her down from a temper tantrum and make her laugh at a stupid joke. Tonight he'd try to make her feel comfortable with *die youngie* and maybe even play on her team in volleyball. Of course, he might decide his duty ended when they got to the gathering, and he'd leave her to fend for herself and run off to be with his real friends, his friends who weren't old or tied down by a baby. That could happen too.

Esther frowned. Levi was young, but he wasn't insensitive. He'd stay by her side the whole evening if she wanted him to. She sniffed in irritation. She didn't want him to stay by her side. She didn't want to impose.

She didn't want to go to a gathering with Levi.

She didn't want to go anywhere with Levi.

She didn't want to go anywhere at all.

Esther snatched the bonnet off her head, hung it on the hook, and knelt next to Winnie. "Don't you worry, *heartzley*. I've changed my mind. I'm staying in tonight." She'd much rather tear all those fragrant little berries off her red cedar bush and throw them at her mailbox. Levi would probably do a happy little jig when he found out he wouldn't have to take her after all. Nanna would just have to manage her disappointment.

She steeled her resolve when she heard the knock on the door, only sorry Levi and Nanna had made the trip over for nothing. She opened the door. Nanna and Levi stood on the porch, Nanna with the tote bag she carried everywhere and Levi with a bouquet of flowers and a pair of pliers. *Ach*. Not flowers! How was she supposed to cling to her iron resolve when he brought her flowers? She pretended not to see them. "Nanna, I've decided I'm not going tonight. It's been a long day with Winnie, and I'm wonderful tired." That was all true and reasonable. Nanna knew what it was like to care for a *buplie* all day.

Nanna didn't even acknowledge Esther's hard life. She stepped cheerfully over the threshold. "Levi brought you flowers."

Levi seemed almost embarrassed. He held up the flowers in one hand and the pliers in the other. "They're from the side of the road," he said, as if he was apologizing.

Maybe he didn't need to apologize. Maybe Esther liked the thought of a bouquet of wildflowers.

"And there's a stray piece of metal sticking out of your doorjamb right here. I brought my pliers to pull it out so no one will snag their bonnets or hats."

Stray piece of metal?

Ach.

Her fallen seam ripper.

She really must learn how to control her temper, or at least take her anger out on things that wouldn't leave a permanent mark. "You didn't need to bring me flowers. No one ever has."

Levi didn't answer. He handed Esther the bouquet and got to work on that piece of her seam ripper stuck in the wood. Esther lowered her head and smelled the flowers. Honeysuckle. Delicious. No wonder the bees loved it.

Nanna grinned. "Hasn't a boy ever brought you flowers?"

Esther shook her head. Menno had never given her flowers, not even when he'd proposed. Esther hadn't expected him to. It wasn't something the Amish did. "Amish men don't give flowers."

Nanna picked Winnie up from the floor. "We definitely need to start a new tradition. Women love getting flowers."

Esther turned to Levi. "*Denki* for the flowers, but like I said, I'm wonderful tired. I'm staying in tonight."

Holding Winnie in one arm, Nanna took the bouquet from Esther's hand. "You can sleep when you're dead. Levi, have you finished with that door yet?"

"*Jah*, Mammi." Levi showed them his pair of pliers with the pointy end of her seam ripper between its jaws. "It wasn't no trouble to pull it out. Do you want to keep it, Esther?"

Did she want to keep it? Maybe to remind herself why her seam ripper got stabbed into the doorjamb in the first place. Maybe to remember how Levi thought she was old. She should carry it in her apron pocket and press it between her finger and thumb whenever she got the notion that Levi Kiem might be the least bit interested in her. That seam ripper would remind her how mortified she'd been that day and that she would never let herself be taken in by a handsome face again. She held out her hand. "*Jah*. I think I'll keep it. *Denki*."

"Be careful," he said, dropping it into her palm. "It's sharp."

Nanna held Esther's flowers and bounced Winnie on her hip. "All right then. Get going before the gathering ends." She snatched Esther's bonnet from the hook and sort of smashed it onto her head. Esther opened her mouth to protest, but Nanna cut her off. "I won't hear any excuses. Go have a *wunderbarr* time."

Resigned to her fate, Esther straightened the bonnet and tied it under her chin. "Winnie can go down at about seven. If you feed her a bottle right before—"

"I know," Nanna said, shooing Esther out the door like a stray cat.

Esther sighed, then left as if she was going to her own funeral. Levi led the way to his buggy, acting almost cheerful at the thought of having to take Esther to the gathering. Maybe he was just pretending, but when he turned around and winked at her, Esther wasn't so sure about that.

She almost tripped on her own feet as her heart began to race. What did he think he was doing, acting all charming and enthusiastic like he was really looking forward to this evening? Wasn't he dreading this as much as she was? Of course he was dreading it. He didn't want to be seen with Esther at the gathering. She was dreading it because it was a huge imposition on Levi, and she hated the thought of being an annoyance, like a cocklebur stuck to your stocking. Men! She just couldn't figure them out.

He opened the door for her, then jumped in on his side. There was a single purple wildflower lying on the seat between them. He picked it up. "May I?" he said.

Esther frowned at him. "May you what?"

"Put this behind your ear. I noticed you don't have anything there today, and I thought a flower might look nice."

Esther's heart palpitated wildly. Maybe she really was as old as Levi thought, because she was definitely having a heart attack. "Okay," she murmured. The word came out more like a question. Did she want Levi to get close enough to slide a flower behind her ear? Did she need a flower behind her ear? Was it inappropriate to show up to a gathering with a flower behind her ear? Did she look good in purple?

Levi didn't seem worried about any of those things. He sort of caressed the side of her head with his left hand while sliding the wildflower behind her ear with the other. It wasn't any big to-do. His fingers barely grazed the curve of her cheek. She still felt her face get warm and her breath go shallow. She was definitely having a heart attack.

Levi drew back, studied her face, and gave her a wide smile. "There. You look more like yourself with some-thing behind your ear, and that purple brings out the blue in your eyes."

Ach, vell. That answered the purple question.

Levi jiggled the reins, prodding the horse to a trot. "This is going to be so much fun."

Esther eyed him suspiciously. "You seem unusually excited to get to that gathering."

He laughed as if he'd been holding it in for hours. "Esther, I don't want to go to the gathering."

Esther's heart sank, even though she had known that was how Levi was really feeling all along. For goodness' sake, it was how she was feeling too. Why did the thought of not going make her sort of sad all of a sudden? "*Ach,*" she said, waiting for some appropriate reply to fall out of her mouth, but she couldn't think of anything. Did he want to go somewhere else to be with his friends? Did he want to drive around in the buggy until a certain amount of time had passed and Nanna would be satisfied? She'd rather not waste her time. There was a half-finished quilt waiting for her at home. "If you drop me off here, I can just walk home."

He raised his eyebrows. "Don't even joke about that. Mammi would feed me to the ants."

"Well . . . then . . . what? What do you want me to do?" He'd personally tucked a flower behind her ear. Did he have some sort of plan?

He laughed again. The joke was on her somehow. She wanted to rip his hat in two. "I knew you wouldn't have fun at the gathering, but Mammi never listens to me. But she's right that you needed to get away from the *haus*. I don't want you to go crazy. You might start throwing my power tools."

"You won't let me touch your power tools."

"That's what I mean. Crazy people don't follow rules. So I thought of something that we'd both enjoy more than a gathering."

Esther cocked an eyebrow. "*Ach*, *vell*. That doesn't seem like a very hard thing to find." She shifted in her seat and smoothed an imaginary crease from her dress. "*Denki* for the flowers. I love honeysuckle."

"Me too. It smells so *gute*."

"Where did you find it? I hope you didn't steal it from someone's yard."

He chuckled. "I told you, I got it from the side of the road."

"That doesn't mean it wasn't in someone's yard."

His smile only got wider. "If you must know, Mary Jane has a huge bush on the east side of her house. I nearly got stung. There are about a thousand bees buzzing around that bush this time of year."

"*Denki* for risking your life. And I'm glad to know you didn't steal someone's honeysuckle."

He gave her a strange, slightly bemused look. "It would have been worth it." Levi pulled up to his own house, drove the buggy around to the barn, and set the brake. "Okay. Let's go," he said, opening the door and jumping out.

"Your house?"

He shrugged. "Mamm needs us to clean bathrooms."

"Uh. Okay." She didn't want to go to the gathering, but cleaning bathrooms was not her idea of a night away, especially with a flower tucked behind her ear. The presence of the flower made her feel like she needed to do something fancy.

Levi laughed harder. He was really starting to annoy her. She looked for a pile of manure to throw at him. "I'm teasing, Esther. The driver should be here any minute."

"Driver?"

He nodded. "You've only been here a couple of months. I want to show you the most exciting place in the valley, and it's too far to go by buggy."

Esther couldn't keep a smile from taking over her face. "That sounds interesting. What is the most exciting place in the valley?"

"You'll see."

Esther scrunched her lips together. "I'm not going to have to jump out of an airplane, am I?"

"*Nae*, but that sounds like another fun activity."

"What are the chances of me dying or getting seriously injured on this exciting adventure?"

His enthusiasm didn't dampen one little bit. He looked up at the sky as if he was thinking about it very hard. "There's maybe a little chance. That's all I'm going to say."

She rolled her eyes. "I feel so much better."

They walked around to the front of Levi's house just as a car pulled up. Two women sat in the front seat. "Hi, Levi," the driver said.

"*Hallo*, Mrs. Kemp. This is Esther."

Both Mrs. Kemp and the woman in the passenger seat turned around as Esther and Levi slid into the back. "Hi, Esther," Mrs. Kemp said. "I'm Colleen, and this is my sister, Marie. We sometimes drive the Amish around when we have some free time, and I was really excited when Levi said we were going up to Alamosa."

"What's in Alamosa?" Esther asked.

"Well, lots of things, but I promised Levi I wouldn't tell where we're going until we get there. I guess he didn't want you jumping out of the car when you found out."

Esther wasn't the timid type, and the thought of doing something that might make other girls jump out of the car and run for their lives got her pulse racing. She buckled her seat belt and looked at Levi. "You've got my full attention."

Levi just laughed, but this time Esther wasn't annoyed. Maybe the joke wasn't on her after all.

About half an hour later, Colleen pulled off the highway and turned down what looked like a deserted road. Up ahead, there was a huge truck trailer on the side of the road that was impossible to miss. It was painted bright lemon yellow and had green lettering on the side. COLORADO GATORS REPTILE PARK, it said.

Esther looked at Levi. "Umm. Where are we going?"

Levi pointed out the window at a wooden alligator standing upright on a fence post. His smile was so big, Esther could have counted all his fillings if he'd had any, which he didn't. "To see the biggest alligators west of the Mississippi."

Esther nearly squealed with delight, except she wasn't a squealer, so she kept her mouth shut and simply smiled. She didn't know what she had been expecting, but the Colorado Gators Reptile Park was not it. Levi was a genius. "I've never even seen the biggest alligators *east* of the Mississippi."

His eyes flashed with excitement. "Then you're going to love it. I brought extra money in case you want to take alligator wrestling lessons."

Esther's heart all but leaped out of her chest. "How likely am I to get my hand chewed off? I can't change diapers with one hand."

Levi shrugged. "Ben changes diapers with one hand. With practice, you'd get pretty *gute* at it. Wrestling alligators is probably a lot like getting Lydi to hold still long enough to change her diaper. You kind of need two people."

Colleen parked the car in the makeshift parking lot, and all four of them got out. "You're staying?" Esther asked.

Colleen nodded. "We love this place. They let you hold a baby alligator. Our dad loved it too." She leaned closer and lowered her voice. "Last year we scattered our dad's ashes in the garden here. But don't tell anybody. I think it's illegal."

Marie shook her head. "It's only illegal in Disneyland."

They walked down a little dirt path, where they encountered a gorgeous lilac bush and a huge green sign that Marie read out loud. Maybe she wasn't sure Esther and Levi could read English. "'Colorado Gators is not responsible for accidents, theft, injuries, death, or damage to personal items. This is a dangerous place. Please be careful.'" Marie glanced at Colleen. "People die here all the time. I'm sure they didn't mind Dad's ashes in their azaleas."

Esther didn't really believe people died here all the time, but the sign was impressive. For sure and certain, it added to the excitement of the outing. Another sign greeted them outside the fence. CAUTION. THIS IS A WORKING FARM. IT DOES SMELL. Esther pointed it out to Levi, and they both laughed. The Amish were well aware of the realities of smelly animals. They lived with smells every day.

Levi kindly paid the entrance fee for both of them. Esther would have paid, but she hadn't brought any money with her, and Levi wouldn't have let her anyway. He was thoughtful like that. Esther liked that about him. Her brothers were notoriously stingy. It was nice when someone didn't purse his lips and make a sour face over the cost of a pound of apples or a gallon of milk. Frugality was a *gute* quality. Stinginess was nothing but unpleasant.

Colleen and Marie went in one direction, saying something about emus and snakes. Levi and Esther followed the signs straight to the alligators.

"Are you scared?" Levi asked.

Esther snorted. "*Nae.* Are you?"

"Terrified."

The look on his face made Esther laugh. "I'm sure you are."

He winked at her again. Boys should not wink at girls like that. Alligators didn't make her legs turn to jelly, but apparently a little attention from Levi Kiem did. "I'm just trying to make you feel better. I know you're just pretending to be brave because you don't want to embarrass yourself."

"*Ach*, we both know I have no trouble embarrassing myself no matter who's watching. You don't have to spare my feelings."

He put an extra spring in his step. "*Ach, vell* then. I'm *froh* I no longer have to worry about your feelings." He stopped short and slumped his shoulders in mock dejection. "But I still have to worry about you throwing things at my head. Or stabbing me with your seam ripper."

Esther widened her eyes. "You know about the seam ripper?"

"You were wearing it behind your ear that day at the quilting group. After I pulled it out of your doorjamb, I realized where it had come from and who had skewered it into the wood. At least you didn't stab it into my arm. Or my face."

Esther giggled. "I was tempted. You were aggravating and arrogant and said some *dumm* things."

He motioned to her ear. "That's why I gave you the flower. If you stab me with that, you probably won't draw blood."

"You needn't worry. I don't take my temper out on people or animals. But I make no such promise with apricots or brick walls."

He grinned and nodded. "That is very *gute* news, unless you're an apricot."

"The *gute* news is that you never have to guess. I'll always tell you when I'm angry. I'm not a pouter."

"I can't stand a pouter."

Esther had never seen anything like the gator farm. There were several pens surrounded by chain-link fencing where the gators sunned on the sand or floated about in the water like submerged logs. It was an unusual place to take a girl who'd been expecting to go to a gathering, but a wonderful *gute* place to take a girl who needed some time away from her hard life. Of course, in a world full of problems, Esther had to admit that her life wasn't all that hard. She hadn't had cancer like Nanna Kiem or liver disease like her *dat*. She hadn't lost a child like her cousin Perry or been paralyzed in a buggy accident like her neighbor Marta in Pennsylvania. She didn't have an abusive boyfriend like Ivy or any kind of the life like the one Ivy must be living. And she had a beautiful little baby who was fussy and kept her up at night but was also cuddly and innocent and lovable. Esther couldn't complain, but it was still nice to get a break.

Levi bought some alligator food, and they fed the alligators. Then they strolled among the tortoises and petted their rock-hard shells. Esther loved the tortoises. They didn't seem to be ruffled by anything, including people, and the pattern on their shells could have been made into an interesting geometric quilt. Levi and Esther saw too many snakes, lizards, and birds to count. Levi's favorite was the emus. They were huge birds, so big they couldn't fly, with long legs and brownish-gray feathers that were so fine they looked like fur, especially on the tops of their heads.

When they got hot, Levi suggested they go inside. They sat on a bench while they looked at the snakes. "I'm afraid we're not going to be able to wrestle alligators today. It costs a hundred dollars for a class, and the man said it would be really hard to do in your dress."

"Kind of like pickleball," Esther said. Pickleball was

not impossible in a dress, but it was a little hard to dive for a ball, though that didn't stop her from trying. Esther was the only one in her pickleball group who dived for balls. Sometimes she fell down. Sometimes she made spectacular saves. The other women didn't play that hard by choice. Cathy didn't want to break a hip. Allison said winning wasn't near as important as being able to get out of bed the next day. Esther watched as a bright yellow snake slowly coiled around itself and closed its eyes for a nap. "I would love to learn how to wrestle alligators, but a hundred dollars would be better spent on fabric, I think."

Levi studied her face and smiled. "You're the most unexpected girl I've ever met."

"What is that supposed to mean?"

"Snakes don't scare you. Or spiders."

Jah. She'd seen plenty of spiders when she pulled up that subfloor, even a black widow, which she had promptly squashed with her thumb. Levi had been astounded, but she'd been wearing her gloves, so she hadn't seen it as anything to make a fuss about. Of course, black widow spiders were all gooey when you squished them, so she had to clean off her glove before getting back to tearing out the floor. "Spiders are helpful critters. Haven't you ever read *Charlotte's Web*?"

"*Nae.*"

"I don't see how killing spiders makes me unexpected. Is that the word you used?"

He chuckled. "It's just that . . . you always surprise me. You think alligator wrestling would be fun and you want to spend extra time laying fancy tile on your bathroom floor, but you also have a practical side that measures the temperature of Winnie's bottles and prefers to spend money on fabric. And you have a very *gute* arm for throwing things."

"Three years of softball on a city team. Mamm wasn't happy about it, but Dat said girls had just as much right to have fun as boys."

"Your *dat* was right. And those years of softball weren't wasted. You can thin apricots with the best of them."

Esther made a face at his teasing. "*Jah*, I can, and don't you forget it."

A man with an alligator tooth hanging around his neck stood in the doorway and clapped his hands. "Ladies and gentlemen, we'll be closing in ten minutes. Say one last goodbye to your favorite snake."

Levi glanced at Esther. "Would you like to say one last goodbye to anything?"

"Let's go find a tortoise."

By the time they'd finished petting the tortoises, Esther was wishing she'd brought a notepad. She would have liked to sketch the pattern from a tortoise shell. She and Levi strolled to Colleen's car and waited for Colleen and Marie to return.

"That was a better time than being at the gathering," Levi said. "Don't you think?"

Esther nodded enthusiastically. "I like the sense of danger in the air. There's not much danger at a gathering."

"Unless you happen to eat one of Mayne Lapp's cookies." They both laughed. It had been a long time since Esther had gotten so much attention or had so much fun.

Unfortunately, the best part of the evening was being with Levi. He would only agree to let her hold the baby alligator after he'd held it to make sure it was safe. His concern was irritating and endearing at the same time.

He'd exercised the same concern when she used the crowbar on the stubborn particleboard of her bathroom floor or the power drill to secure screws into place. She'd seen the careful way he played with Winnie and even how attentive he was to his *mammi*. He was much more nurturing than Esther was, but he didn't make a big show of it or need constant recognition. It was just in his nature.

Esther was honest enough with herself to admit how much she enjoyed spending time with Levi. She liked him. She liked him a lot. That was the unfortunate part. Levi had made it clear he wasn't interested in Esther. As an old maid with a baby, she would be *deerich* indeed to hold out any hope for him. He was young. He wanted a young, pretty, unencumbered *fraa*, probably preferring someone who was soft and delicate and didn't throw things when she was angry. She couldn't blame him.

Besides that, she'd told him right to his face that she didn't want a husband. Levi was only being so nice because he thought he was safe—safe to show an old maid a little kindness without her building up all sorts of expectations. Esther had accepted her life and Levi's place in it, but that didn't mean she wasn't sad about the way things would inevitably turn out. Levi would finish the bathroom too soon, and she and Winnie would only see him at *gmay* from then on. He'd go to Ohio, where he'd find a hundred girls more interesting and attractive than Esther, and Esther wouldn't even be a pleasant memory by the time he got back.

Sometimes the pain of knowing she would lose Levi took her breath away, which was silly because she'd never "had" him to begin with. He'd just be absent where he once was there. She should probably cut him out of her life immediately. She could figure out how to tile the bathroom by herself, and he would never need to return. It would be less painful for Winnie and her if they didn't have a chance to get more attached. But she wasn't ready for Levi to be gone yet. She would enjoy every minute she had with him, even knowing how much more it would hurt when he finally left. The pain then was part of the happiness now.

And she was happy. Winnie had turned out to be a great blessing in her life. Esther wasn't a natural *mater*, but she was learning. She wouldn't trade the lessons Winnie was teaching her about love and sacrifice for a thousand quilts—lessons she might never have learned, especially since she wasn't planning to marry and would never have the chance to bear a child of her own. With the blessing of Winnie in her life, her cup was already overflowing, but because of Winnie, Levi, Nanna, Hannah, and Mary Jane had all come into her life. She truly had so much to be grateful for.

Colleen and Marie strolled out to the car about five minutes later. Marie carried a plastic bag with something swimming around in it. She held it up for Esther to see. "Mosquito fish," she said. "I'm putting him in my bathtub until I can build a pond."

Could somebody build a pond?

Colleen unlocked the car doors. "When all is said and done, you'll have fewer mosquitoes if you get rid of the fish and scrap the pond idea. Ponds are breeding grounds for millions of mosquitoes."

Marie drew her brows together. "You're right. Maybe we can find a pond that already exists and just throw my mosquito fish in there."

"Good idea."

Levi opened his door and slid into the back seat. "If you need someone with a good throwing arm, Esther can do it. She used to play softball, and she's really good at throwing apricots."

Esther cuffed him on the arm. Nobody needed to know about her little fit the other day.

Marie turned around in her seat. "Apricots? I used to be good at throwing apricots until I got bursitis. I had to give it up."

When Marie turned around again, Levi smiled and winked at Esther. She had to clamp her mouth shut and turn and look out the window so she wouldn't burst into laughter. *Jah*. It was going to hurt something wonderful when she and Levi finally finished that bathroom. How would she ever be happy without him? Had she ever been happy before?

Chapter Seven

Levi had to hold himself back from jogging across Esther's lawn. A nice, calm stroll would get him to her porch in plenty of time. He was just so excited to see her today. He'd been at a flea market yesterday and had found three of the most interesting tiles he'd ever seen. He couldn't wait to see Esther's face when he showed them to her. She was going to be thrilled. Her bathroom floor was turning into a work of art.

Before he knocked on the door, he pulled a small jar of putty from his pocket, unscrewed the lid, and scooped up a small glob with his finger. Then he smoothed it over the tiny hole in Esther's doorjamb. The doorjamb was white and the putty was white, so he shouldn't even have to paint it. Nobody would know anything violent had happened there.

He smiled to himself. He liked Esther's fiery temper, even when it was directed at him. Her eyes were an even deeper blue when they flashed with anger, so pretty he couldn't look away.

And when he was with her, he never wanted to look away.

He put the lid on the putty and slid it back into his

pocket, but before he could even knock on the door, Esther threw it open. Winnie was propped on her hip, her cheeks red and moist, and she was screaming like a wounded animal. Esther didn't look much better. Her face was pale and drawn, and it looked as if she might burst into tears any second.

"*Cum reu,*" she said, grabbing his arm and pulling him into the house. She handed him the baby. "Something's wrong with Winnie, and you need to drive us to the hospital."

Levi took Winnie and immediately bounced up and down in an effort to calm her. "What happened?"

"She cried all day yesterday and just wanted me to hold her. This morning she's been worse, and she's got a fever." Esther pulled a baby thermometer from behind her ear. "I took her temperature. Ninety-nine point two."

Levi cradled Winnie in his arms and pressed his palm to her forehead. "She does feel warm, but ninety-nine point two isn't that high. Maybe she's teething."

"It's not that," Esther said. "I thought of that." As if she didn't like his reasoning, she took Winnie from his arms and hugged her tightly. "I gave her some Tylenol, but it doesn't seem to help. And now look." She lifted Winnie's dress to reveal a single red blister on the small of her back.

Levi got closer to take a look. "Did she get bit by a spider?"

"I don't know," Esther said, the words escaping her lips with a sob. "I need your help. We need to go to the hospital."

"Okay," Levi said. "But we should call a driver. It's over an hour by buggy. Let's go to my house. My *bruder* Ben has a cell phone."

Esther bit her bottom lip, handed Levi the baby, and marched into the kitchen. He followed her. She opened her fridge, reached into the meat and cheese drawer, and pulled out a cell phone.

Levi cocked an eyebrow. "You keep a cell phone in the fridge?"

"I didn't want anybody to know, but I have a baby now. I need a quick way to get ahold of the fire department or the police. And this is one of those times."

Esther might have felt a little guilty for owning a cell phone, but to Levi, it seemed like a pretty sensible thing to have. "Good for you."

She glanced at him in surprise before flipping open the phone and dialing the number. "Hello, Cathy? Winnie is sick. Is there any way you could drive us to the hospital? Oh . . . okay. Really. That's too bad . . . Thank you so much." Esther closed her phone. "She says her estrogen's out of balance."

"Is she coming?"

"As far as I know, you can still drive with an estrogen imbalance." Esther patted Winnie's cheek. "Poor baby. Let me get you a tissue." Winnie calmed down a bit in Levi's arms. Esther wiped Winnie's nose and face, then handed Levi a bottle. "See if she'll eat anything while we wait."

Levi sat down at the kitchen table and tucked Winnie into the crook of his elbow. She took the bottle but whimpered every few seconds as if to remind them she was not feeling well.

Esther sat next to him and chewed her thumbnail. "I'm glad you're here. I didn't know what to do."

"You seem to be doing fine," he said, because she was. She just needed more faith in herself.

She shrugged. "I feel better with you here. I can worry myself sick while you hold the baby. It's harder to do both jobs at once."

Winnie let out a wail as if she'd just bitten her tongue. Levi laid her over his shoulder and patted her back. "There, there, Winter. It's okay. We'll be to the doctor soon enough, and you'll feel so much better. Unless he gives you a shot."

Esther shushed Levi. "Cover her ears if you're going to use such talk. She's upset enough as it is."

Winnie calmed down enough for Levi to feed her more of the bottle. He peered at Esther across the table. She looked exhausted. "Did you get any sleep last night?"

Esther pressed her hand to her forehead. "*Nae.* Winnie was up every few hours crying. I should have taken her into the emergency room in the middle of the night, but I didn't want to wake Cathy, and I didn't want to go by myself." Her eyebrows inched together. "I should have taken her in. What was I thinking? I should have taken her in."

"*Nae.* You did the right thing."

Esther stood and paced around the small kitchen. "I didn't want to go alone. How could I be so selfish?"

"Esther, you're not selfish. Winnie didn't sleep well, but she wouldn't have slept at all in the hospital. Babies need rest most of all when they're sick. My *mamm* wouldn't have taken her in."

Esther looked up from her pacing and stopped. "She wouldn't have?"

"Mamm has twelve *kinner*. She doesn't take them to the doctor unless there's a bone sticking out of their arm."

One side of Esther's mouth curled upward. "How many times has that happened?"

"You don't want to know."

Esther fingered the thermometer at her ear. "Do you think I gave her an alligator disease from the reptile park? I washed my hands really well after I held that baby alligator, but maybe not well enough."

"I don't think there's such a thing as an alligator disease," Levi said, trying hard not to smile. He didn't want her to think he was laughing at her. He loved how conscientious Esther was. Her concern was adorable, if a little overanxious.

"*Ach*. I'm sure there are alligator diseases. That's why they have to wrestle the alligators, to give them medicine. The man at the reptile park said so. Weren't you listening?"

In truth, Levi had been watching Esther listen and hadn't paid much attention to anything but her the whole time. But she didn't need to know that. She'd get her hopes up, and no matter what, he was going to Ohio for a young *fraa*. He swallowed past the lump in his throat. Why didn't Ohio seem as exciting as it had only a few weeks ago? It was almost as if he didn't want to go anymore, but he didn't see how that could be possible. He'd been wanting to go to Ohio for months. There was nobody for him here.

"You washed your hands," Levi said, "and if Winnie has an alligator disease, you and I and everybody else there that day should have gotten it too."

Esther thought about that for a second and nodded. "I suppose you're right. Maybe it was something I fed her. I let her try rice cereal on Monday. Do you think she's allergic?"

"Did she like it?"

"She thought it was nasty. I tasted it and thought it was nasty too. I won't feed my baby something I'm not willing to eat myself. She's never getting that again, and not just because she might be allergic."

Levi gazed at Winnie's face. Esther had called her "my baby." That was the first time he'd ever heard her say that. "Allergies don't usually cause fevers."

"So maybe it wasn't the rice cereal." She glanced at the clock on the wall. It had pictures of different quilt blocks where the numbers were supposed to be, and it said, "Time to Quilt." "I'm going to pack the diaper bag so we can leave as soon as Cathy gets here. And I'll grab the car seat."

Winnie drank about half the bottle, but she fussed more than she ate. It was plain she wasn't feeling well. A car honked in front of the house. "Esther," Levi called. "She's here."

Esther met him in the front hall with the diaper bag and the car seat. "Okay. Let's go. *Denki* for coming with me."

Levi carried Winnie out to the car, and Esther strapped the car seat in the middle of the back seat and then buckled Winnie into the seat. Esther had bought the car seat a month ago, and Mary Jane had spent half an hour one day giving Esther lessons on how to use it. Esther was very *gute* at buckling it now. Levi and Esther climbed in the back on either side of Winnie.

Cathy didn't seem any worse for wear because of her hormone imbalance. She turned and sort of smiled at both of them. "What's wrong with the little one? Do I need to speed?"

"Don't speed," Esther said, laying her hands in her lap.

"But if you wouldn't mind driving as quickly as possible, I would appreciate it."

Cathy pulled onto the road. "Has she got the flu?"

Esther shook her head. "She has a fever, and she's been crying and fussing all day. This morning I found a tiny red bump on her back, like maybe she was bitten by a spider."

Cathy pulled the car over not a hundred feet from Esther's house. "Can I see it?"

Esther's gaze flicked to Levi. "We'd . . . I'd have to take her out of her seat. I'd like to get to the hospital as soon as possible."

Cathy turned off the car, and Levi could feel Esther's annoyance along with her undercurrent of panic. "Let me take a look. I might be able to save you three hundred dollars."

"I don't care about the money," Esther said.

Cathy got out of the car. "Spoken like a true and loving mother. Good for you."

Levi felt like he needed to speak up for Esther's sake. "Can't you take us to the hospital and then we'll show you the bump?" Esther gave him a grateful smile that unexpectedly took his breath away.

Cathy opened the back door. "That's how they get your money. I once went in with a sore arm, and eight thousand dollars later, I left with a stent." She held out her arms, and Esther was obligated to unbuckle Winnie and pull her out of her car seat. The sooner Cathy was satisfied, the sooner they could go to the hospital. Esther handed the baby to Cathy, and Cathy pressed her cheek to Winnie's. "She's definitely warm. Let's take a look at this bump." She propped Winnie on her shoulder, lifted her dress, and took a look at the spot. Then she turned her around and lifted her dress away from her tummy. There were four more spots.

Esther gasped. "It's spreading. We need to get to the hospital right now."

Cathy handed Winnie back to Esther. "I'll take you wherever you want to go, honey, but you don't have to see a doctor. Winnie's got the chicken pox. All four of my children had them. I'm lucky I got my shingles shot. It gets in the air, you know."

Esther's mouth fell open. She looked from Cathy to Levi and back again. "Chicken pox? Where would she have gotten chicken pox? Not from alligators, right?"

Cathy scrunched her nose. "What about alligators?"

"We went to an alligator farm a few days ago," Levi offered.

Cathy almost smiled. "Up there past Alamosa? I love that place."

Esther clung to Winnie as if chicken pox was the worst disease ever. Winnie began to fuss again. "But where did she get chicken pox?"

Cathy leaned her hands on the top of the door and peered into the back seat. "It's hard to say. Winnie could have been exposed two or three weeks ago. That's the problem with chicken pox. You think you're okay, and then, bam, you break out in spots. Has she played with anybody who had the chicken pox?"

Esther patted Winnie on the back. "I don't think so."

Cathy nodded as if she knew everything. "I'd check with all the parents of the kids who've been around your baby. You could probably get one of them to confess."

Esther frowned. She took Winnie to *gmay* every other week, and sometimes Winnie played with Mary Jane's girls or Levi's little sister. Esther smoothed her hand down Winnie's dress over and over again. "What do we do about chicken pox?"

"Well, for one thing, you don't need to see a doctor," Cathy said. "There's nothing the doctor can do except take your money. The last time I went in for a cold, they scheduled me for a colonoscopy."

"She doesn't need a doctor?"

Cathy shut Esther's door, opened her own door, and climbed back into the car. "Children have been getting chicken pox for as long as there've been children. Just make sure she drinks a lot of liquids." She started the car. "I'll drop you two off at the house, and then I'll go to the store for some supplies. Juice and oatmeal and calamine lotion. You put oatmeal in her bath. That helps the itching. So does the calamine lotion. Keep it on those spots. Give her Tylenol. Do you have baby Tylenol?"

Esther nodded.

"Do you have baby-sized mittens?"

"No," Esther said. "Do I need mittens?"

"You don't want her to scratch the rash. She could get an infection. I'll see what I can find at the store, but I don't think they'll have mittens in June. You could always put socks on her hands, but I'm not sure she won't pull them off." Cathy turned the car around and drove the hundred feet back to Esther's house. "I suppose she'll pull mittens off just as easy as socks, so I won't look real hard for mittens."

Esther seemed to feel better, which was quite a surprise, considering Cathy's gruff manner. Cathy seemed so completely unsympathetic about anything. But maybe that was what made Esther feel better. If Cathy wasn't frantic or even all that concerned, maybe Esther figured she didn't need to be either. "Oh, thank you, Cathy," Esther said. "I'm still sad that Winnie is sick, but I don't feel like such a bad mother."

Cathy put the car in park and turned a stern eye to Esther. "Never judge your mothering skills by something you have no control over. Babies get sick. Babies get grumpy and whiny. You're a good mother if you love them and take care of them and keep your head when things get hard. You're doing fine, Esther. We all know who the bad mother is, and it's not you. Let's just hope your sister develops a mother's heart before she comes back."

To Levi's surprise, Esther's expression wilted like a daisy in the desert. "Oh. Yes. Thank you for driving us, Cathy."

"Call me anytime. I'm an old lady. I like to feel useful. I'll be back with those supplies."

Levi unbuckled the car seat and grabbed the diaper bag while Esther carried Winnie into the house. "Well," he said when they stepped into the front hall, "that was a short trip."

"I want to take her temperature again." Esther went into Winnie's room and laid Winnie on the bed. She undressed Winnie down to her diaper and took the thermometer from behind her ear. "Look," she said. "More spots."

Winnie did indeed have more spots around her neck and stomach. "That can't feel *gute*."

Esther put the end of the thermometer under Winnie's arm and held it there until it beeped. "One hundred and one," she said. "I'm going to give her some more Tylenol and then I want to give her an oatmeal bath. I have some oatmeal. We don't need to wait for Cathy."

Levi studied Esther's face, trying to discern the reason for her sudden change of mood when Cathy had dropped them off. It was plain Cathy didn't hand out compliments often, but she had reassured Esther that she was a *gute* mother. What had made Esther so upset? Levi didn't like it. Esther should always be smiling. "Do you want me to fill the tub?"

She eyed him hopefully. "You don't mind?"

"Of course not." It didn't matter that he had another job at one. He'd stay as long as Esther needed him.

"Only fill it about four inches deep. I have a ruler in the drawer by the stove. And get the kitchen thermometer and make sure the water is no warmer than one hundred degrees."

Levi chuckled. He couldn't help himself.

She cracked a smile. "Don't even think about it."

"About what?"

"About teasing me over the way I bathe my baby."

He pressed his lips together and shook his head. "I'm not even thinking about it."

Levi filled the tub and measured the temperature of the water. Ninety-nine degrees. You couldn't get much closer than that. He opted to estimate the depth of the water. It looked about right—enough to get Winnie wet but not enough to reach her mouth if she turned her head.

Esther came into the bathroom with Winnie in one arm and a tub of oatmeal in the other. She looked in the tub. "Did you test the temperature?"

Levi held up the kitchen thermometer. "I did."

"How deep is it? I don't see a ruler."

"I lay a lot of tile. I know what four inches looks like."

Esther didn't look convinced, but she must have decided

to let it go. She handed Levi the oatmeal, laid Winnie on the bath mat, and got her undressed while Levi sat on the toilet and watched. Esther lifted Winnie's arms up over her head. There were two more spots under her right arm. Esther glanced at Levi. "*Ach.* Poor little thing."

"How much oatmeal should I pour in the tub?" Levi said.

Esther squished her eyebrows together. "I have no idea. Pour a cup or so in there, and we'll see what it looks like. We don't want oatmeal soup."

Levi poured some oatmeal in the tub and stirred it around. "This looks okay, don't you think?"

"*Jah.* That should do the trick."

Levi watched while Esther gave Winnie a bath, then handed her a towel when she pulled Winnie out. Winnie fussed and whined. For sure and certain, she wasn't her usual cheerful self. And neither was Esther. Lord willing, the calamine lotion would help Winnie feel more comfortable. Levi had no idea what to do for Esther.

They took Winnie into the spare bedroom and got her dressed. Then Levi held her while Esther made her a bottle, using the kitchen thermometer, of course. Levi sat at the table and fed Winnie while Esther cleaned up the tub and bathroom. By the time she finished, Winnie had fallen asleep. Levi burped her and laid her in her portable crib.

When he came back into the kitchen, Esther was making a pot of coffee. "I hoped Cathy would be here before Winnie went down for a nap so we could put some lotion on those chicken pox."

"If she gets too uncomfortable, she'll wake up. By then Cathy should be here."

"*Denki* for being here. I know you have other places to go."

"I couldn't leave. I wanted to make sure Winnie was okay." She handed him a cup of *kaffee*, and her fingers brushed against his. The touch sent a bolt of electricity up his arm. He ignored the sensation. There were much more important things to think about. "I know it's easier said than done, but try not to worry. Cathy is right. You really are a *gute* mother, even if you don't believe it."

She sat down at the table and took a sip of *kaffee*. "*Denki,*" she said, without arguing or contradicting him. Was she even paying attention to what he said?

"Did Cathy upset you? I know Winnie gave you a scare, but you didn't seem truly upset until Cathy said something about you being a *gute* mother."

Esther sighed. "She said she hopes Ivy gets a mother's heart before she comes back."

"I suppose we all hope that. Did it offend you that Cathy said Ivy is a bad mother?"

"*Nae.* Ivy is a very bad mother. We can all agree on that. It upset me that she said Ivy might come back."

Levi's stomach felt as if he'd swallowed a bucket of cement. "*Ach.* I didn't think about that."

Esther set her mug on the table and wrapped her arms around herself as if trying to ward off the cold. "I'm afraid, Levi."

He'd never heard such uncertainty in her voice. "Afraid of Ivy coming back?"

She nodded. "I'm afraid, and I'm angry at Ivy for making me feel this way. A few weeks ago, I would have liked nothing better than for Ivy to take Winnie away and disappear. But now I don't want Ivy to come back. Winnie is gaining weight. She's on a schedule. She gets someone's full attention every waking hour. Winnie has a stable home." She pressed her fingers to her forehead. "You know how bad I am with babies."

"You are not."

Her lips curled slightly before drooping again. "You know how bad I am with babies, but at least I'm caring for her. I get up with her in the middle of the night. I read her books and take her on walks. I'm not the best *mater*, but I'm so much better than Ivy would be."

"Of course you are."

"But it's more than that. At first Winnie was a duty, a nuisance, a responsibility I didn't ask for and certainly didn't want. Now I can't think of life without her. It's like she's part of me. I love her like she was my own baby, Levi. What would I do if Ivy came back and took Winnie away? I wouldn't be able to bear it. The sadness would crush me."

Levi fingered the handle of his mug, and his heart grew heavier. "You called her 'my baby' today."

"I . . . I feel that she is my baby. I've lost sleep for her and cried over her and changed her diapers and done her laundry. I've been so tired I thought I might fall over and so worried I thought I might get an ulcer. But I've also never smiled harder in my life, and hearing Winnie laugh is the best part of my day."

"Maybe Ivy is gone for good," Levi said, hoping more than believing it.

"She could be gone for a very long time, but when she runs out of money or her boyfriend loses interest, she'll be back. She knows where I keep my money now. If she's in trouble, it would be too tempting to come back."

"You really should stop keeping valuables in the fridge."

Esther's lips curled sheepishly. "I wouldn't know where else to keep them."

"But if she came back, do you really think she'd take Winnie away? Ivy might need money or a place to stay, but I doubt she'd come back to get Winnie. If she was capable of leaving her baby in the first place, chances are she won't be coming back to get the baby."

Esther didn't seem convinced. "I suppose that is true. But if Ivy discovers how much I care for Winnie, she could hold it over my head and use it against me every time she needs more money or a place to stay or a favor. I'd be trapped. I'd do anything to keep Ivy from taking my baby."

Levi finished off his *kaffee* and pretended he hadn't noticed that she'd called Winnie "my baby" again. "It was bound to happen. Any person with half a heart would have grown attached to Winnie, except for her own mother, maybe."

She nodded. "It couldn't be helped. Given another chance and another choice, I'd do the same thing again, except maybe I would have bought a different diaper bag. Winnie's needs more pockets."

"Do you think if Ivy comes back she'll want to take Winnie away?"

Esther exhaled a deep breath. "I don't know. Maybe. If Ivy senses how much I love Winnie, she might take her just to spite me."

Levi furrowed his brow. "Is she really that cruel?"

Esther closed her eyes as if to shut out a painful emotion. "I . . . don't . . . I don't know Ivy anymore. She's been gone all of her adult life. Ivy was always selfish growing up. Mamm and Dat coddled her. It was almost as if they felt sorry for her, though I don't understand why. Mamm would let her stay home from school for barely any reason at all, like when she said she had a headache or a stomachache. Once she scraped her knee on the sidewalk, and Mamm let her skip school because there was blood. Ivy hated school. She wasn't *gute* at math or reading or spelling. She made up any excuse she could think of to stay home, and Mamm let her."

"My *bruder* Henry hates school. He often works himself up to a stomachache in the mornings, but Mamm makes him go anyway."

"I don't think my parents did her any favors letting her stay home. She was always behind the other *kinner* her age."

Levi curled one side of his mouth. "I'll bet you were *gute* at everything in school."

She took a sip of her *kaffee* and peered at him over the edge of her cup. "Boys don't like smart girls." She hadn't denied that she was probably the smartest one in school, but to her, it wasn't something to celebrate.

Levi propped his chin in his hand. "Esther, I know we Amish value humility, but your intelligence isn't something to be ashamed of."

She gave him a wry smile. "You're assuming I'm all that smart. I'm not."

"*Ach*, now you're teasing me. I'm pretty sure you could whip me in a spelling bee or the multiplication tables. And I'm not even going to mention how fast you learn things. Four weeks ago you didn't know how to use a power drill. Now I can't keep up."

Esther laughed. "Now who's teasing?"

He held up his hands in protest. "Not me." They smiled at each other. "So Ivy didn't like school."

"She didn't like housework either, so I did a lot of the cooking and cleaning with my *mamm*. I guess it was easier for Mamm to just let Ivy out of the work instead of listening to her whine." Esther finished her *kaffee*. "Ivy was pretty. She went to school more in seventh and eighth grade because she got lots of attention from the boys. She loved to flirt."

"It wonders me if she felt unworthy. Or unlovable, maybe. People often seek attention to fill up something they're missing on the inside."

Esther frowned and studied his face. "I've never thought of that, but it's hard to understand why she'd feel that way. She was the joy of Mamm's heart. She was Dat's little angel."

"Maybe Ivy has forgotten the power of family ties. She's been away so long."

"*Jah*. She's forgotten everything *gute* about her family and community."

Levi shook his head. "I pity her. She's fallen very far to abandon a baby who could have given her so much happiness. She doesn't have anybody to love. There isn't really anybody who loves her. It must be a very lonely existence."

"*Jah,*" Esther said, tracing her finger along the crack in the tabletop. "You're right. Lonely and hopeless. I feel sorry for her too, but I'm also afraid. Ivy hates me. She'll do anything to hurt me."

"How do you mean?"

"She left Winnie with me. Believe me, she knew that was going to hurt. But that's not the worst of it. As soon as Ivy turned sixteen and started *rumschpringe*, she tried to steal every boy I ever liked."

"What did you do?"

"Ivy was a hundred times prettier than I was. If she took an interest in any boy, he'd follow her around like a puppy and forget I existed. Then when he stopped being interested in me, she stopped being interested in him. It was like a game to her: see how many of Esther's suitors she could steal. She probably kept a tally."

"That's terrible," Levi said, suddenly ashamed at how annoyed he had always been with his brother Ben. Ben was rebellious and careless, but he'd never do anything to hurt one of his siblings. He wasn't an upstanding young man, but he was a reasonably *gute bruder*.

Esther looked stricken by the memory. "I quit going to gatherings. Ivy was like a vulture with my friends and the boys who seemed interested in me. I pretended I didn't care. I pretended I didn't have my eye on anyone."

Levi pressed his lips together. That was why Esther had never married. Ivy had made sure of it. Levi suddenly felt very ashamed of himself. When he'd first met Esther, he told himself he couldn't be interested in a girl who had been passed over by other boys. But she hadn't been passed over at all. She'd been pushed out of the way. "I'm sorry," he said. Esther didn't even suspect how many things he was apologizing for.

She sighed and studied his face. "There's more, and I'm wonderful embarrassed to admit to it. Despite all of Ivy's efforts, I found a boy who wanted to marry me."

"I don't think that would have been too hard," Levi muttered. There were probably a dozen boys who would have married Esther at the drop of a hat.

"Menno Hertzler. He actually came over to our house to court me while Ivy was at gatherings. We got published after a year. It caught Ivy completely by surprise."

"So she didn't have time to steal him," Levi said doubtfully. Esther wasn't married, so things obviously hadn't worked out with Menno.

"Three days before the wedding, I caught Ivy and Menno kissing in our barn."

Levi's heart lurched. "*Ach.*"

Esther cracked a smile. "That's what I thought. But I was glad it happened. Much better to discover Menno's unfaithfulness before the wedding than after. I suppose I should have thanked Ivy for saving me from disaster."

"Saving you?"

"I don't want a husband who can't resist temptation. If he was that weak, he wasn't worthy of me."

Levi nodded. "You're right. Ivy behaved badly, but it was how she always behaved. Menno could easily have run the other way, like Joseph of Egypt."

"That's what I thought," Esther said. "I was ferociously angry at Ivy, but I was also grateful after I had some time to think about it. Still, it stung like a thousand wasps."

"Of course it did."

Esther huffed out a breath. "When I found Menno and Ivy together, Menno didn't apologize. He tried to blame his lack of control on Ivy. I canceled the wedding, of course. Menno and I were both horribly embarrassed. I was heartbroken. Menno was angry—at me, mostly, for embarrassing him—another reason I'm glad I didn't marry him. I can't abide a man who won't take responsibility for his own actions."

"Me neither," Levi said.

"After I broke things off, Menno covered his own embarrassment by telling everyone I was cold and unfeeling, that I had laughed at him when I called off the wedding. You can imagine how many boys wanted to drive me home after that."

Levi frowned. "Why didn't you set them straight? Tell them the truth about Menno and Ivy?"

"What did it matter? People will believe what they want to believe, and I didn't care what the boys in the *gmayna* thought of me anymore. Menno broke my heart. I never wanted to feel that way again, and I wasn't about to give another boy my love. Boys are deceitful and selfish and fickle. I gave up any thoughts of marriage."

Levi cupped his fingers around his neck in frustration. "Not all boys are like that."

She looked down at her hands. "I didn't mean to offend you. It's not fair to lump you in with everyone else, but it's hard to have much faith anymore. My parents always supported and believed in me, but my *bruderen* blamed me for the broken engagement. For sure and certain they were mostly irritated because they thought they'd get stuck with taking care of me when Mamm and Dat died. But then they were angry when Dat left me the property, even though it meant I'd be able to take care of myself. I'm a constant annoyance to them."

Levi couldn't blame Esther for feeling the way she did about men. She had felt betrayed and unloved by the ones she should have been able to trust. "What did Ivy do? Was she upset you caught her?"

Esther cocked an eyebrow in his direction. "What do you think?"

Levi heaved a sigh. "She probably thought it was funny."

"She wasn't sorry. She and Menno had been meeting secretly ever since I got engaged, and she told me I should be grateful to know what kind of boy Menno was. I should have forgiven her right off, but I couldn't. I was so hurt."

"I don't think less of you for that," Levi said. "I wouldn't have been able to forgive her either."

Esther looked down at her hands again. "I shouldn't have been so . . . I was so angry, I refused to talk to her for a month. It surprised me how deeply hurt she was by my silence. But I'd had enough. She had done something to purposefully hurt me, and I never wanted to trust or confide in her again." She pressed her fingers to her forehead. "Oy, anyhow. You might as well know the rest. It's my fault she jumped the fence. Dat yelled at her after she ruined my wedding, Mamm was too sad to do anything, and I wouldn't talk to her. The other girls in the *gmayna* were mad at her too. She must have felt like she hadn't a friend in the world. She took off with some *Englischer*, and we didn't hear from her for months. We wouldn't have lost her if I'd shown her some Christian charity."

"It wasn't your fault, Esther. Ivy chose to hurt you. Ivy chose to leave."

"She was barely eighteen. Maybe she was so ashamed that she thought it would be better for everybody if she just disappeared. Maybe she didn't think she deserved my love and left to find love somewhere else."

Levi leaned forward. "Is that what she really thought?"

A tiny sob escaped her lips. "I don't know. I've thought about it so much, I just don't know anymore. All I know is that if I had been a better sister, she might not have left at all."

Levi nodded his head slowly. "You can never go back, and looking in that direction will get you nothing but a sore neck. Ivy is responsible for her own choices, and she made the choice to pout for eight years."

Esther curled one side of her mouth. "It *does* feel like an eight-year temper tantrum."

"You gave her the silent treatment for a month. She's given it to you for almost eight years."

This seemed to make Esther feel better. "Do you think she'll get over it?"

"I hope not anytime soon. Lord willing, she'll give you another eighteen years so Winnie can grow up."

Esther smiled in resignation. "Eighteen years. That's all I ask."

Levi picked up both *kaffee* cups from the table and took them to the sink. "Maybe Ivy has already come to her senses. Perhaps leaving Winnie with you was an act of unselfishness. Maybe Ivy knew Winnie needed a permanent home and someone who would take care of her."

"I wish I believed Ivy could be that unselfish."

He smiled. "We can always dream, can't we? And whatever the reason Ivy left Winnie, she's with you now, and we can be grateful for that."

Esther's eyes lit up. "I'm wonderful grateful for every day I get with her."

Levi sat down again, and his heart skipped a beat. "I think you should call the police."

Esther acted as if he'd shot a spitball at her. "The police? What for?"

"Or maybe the mayor. I don't know who to call, but if Winnie is abandoned, you might be able to adopt her."

Still that utterly puzzled look. "Adopt her? How could I—"

"If you adopted Winnie, she would legally be your daughter. Ivy couldn't take her away if she wanted to. Actually, I think you would need to call a lawyer."

Esther furrowed her brow. "It's not the Amish way to entangle ourselves in the law."

"There are times when we have to. Everybody has a birth certificate. We are required to get a Social Security card, even when we don't take out Social Security. An Amish man in Wisconsin used a lawyer to sue the state for the right to school his own children. Sometimes we need to use the law for our good. This time, you need to use the law for Winnie's good."

Esther caught her bottom lip between her teeth. "I want Winnie to be my daughter, but do you think it's possible?"

"*Jah*, I do."

"But how much would it cost?"

Levi tapped his hand on the table, convinced it was the best idea he'd ever had. "I'm going to find out. It won't hurt to get some information."

Esther didn't seem so sure. "But do you think it would work?"

"You shouldn't live your life in fear of losing Winnie. We've got to try. I can't help but believe that if Gotte wants it to happen, He will make it happen."

Esther's smile reached out and grabbed Levi by the heart. "Lord willing, He will give me such a gift."

Chapter Eight

Winnie had been asleep, *really* asleep, for nearly an hour. Usually by this time, Esther had collapsed into bed and fallen asleep before her head hit the pillow. But tonight her head was too full to make any attempt at sleep. Levi had found a lawyer who said she would help Esther without charging her any money, which was sweet of her, but Esther still felt bad she couldn't pay. The lawyer said that Ivy would have to be gone for a whole year before Esther could even think about adopting Winnie.

A whole year!

Esther rolled over and punched her pillow. A whole year of living in fear every time someone knocked on the door. A whole year of frayed nerves and trying to figure out how to outwit Ivy. A whole year of getting more and more attached to Winnie. A whole year of that feeling of dread that Ivy would come back and snatch Winnie away from her. She'd barely been able to stand the strain for three months. How could she do it for a year? What happened at the end of the year if Ivy wouldn't give her permission to let Esther adopt? The lawyer said that if Ivy couldn't be located, the adoption would be a lot easier.

Esther pressed her palm to her forehead. Part of her

wanted Ivy to find her way back to the family and the community again, but a bigger part of her wanted Ivy to stay away for good. Was she wicked for hoping they wouldn't be able to locate Ivy, at least until the adoption was final? It made Esther feel better to imagine Ivy living in Europe or Mexico, happy with a *gute* husband and a few children of her own. Maybe Ivy would have a change of heart. Maybe she would get so wrapped up in her charity work for the orphans of Mexico that she would forget about Winnie and Esther and be content in her new life. That was the dream Esther had for her sister. So maybe it wasn't wicked to hope she never came back.

Esther slid her pillow out from under her head and threw it across the room. It made a satisfying thump against the opposite wall. *Ach.* She was so angry at her selfish sister. Angry at her for leaving their family, for getting pregnant, for being cold and unfeeling enough to abandon her baby without looking back. Angry at Ivy for setting Esther up for the worst heartbreak of all—losing Winnie. How would she be able to bear it? Caring for a baby was hard, but Esther was surprisingly happy. Winnie was thriving, she seemed to like Esther better every day, and Esther had enough time to make the quilts that supported both of them.

But for sure and certain, Ivy would swoop in one day and ruin her happiness, as she had done countless times before. And Esther was powerless to do anything about it. She hated to feel powerless. She hated to be unable to control her own life. Maybe it was wicked to feel that way. Shouldn't Gotte be the one in control? Shouldn't she have enough faith to leave it in His hands? And maybe that was why Winnie had come to her: so Gotte could teach Esther who really had the control.

It didn't seem like Gotte had been doing a very *gute* job with Esther's life. If Gotte loved his children so much, why had Mamm died of a broken heart? Why had Dat suffered through liver disease? Why had Gotte let Ivy get pregnant when He knew she was not fit to be a *mater*? Sometimes it seemed Gotte had abandoned the whole world. Was there anything besides the sunrise and sunset that Gotte *did* control with any predictability?

Esther squeezed her eyes shut. It was faithless to think such thoughts. She rolled over. It was late and Esther was so tired, and now she had to get up and fetch her pillow from the other side of the room.

It was a *gute* thing the room was so tiny.

A faint sound reached Esther's ears as she got up for her pillow. Was Winnie stirring? *Nae.* Someone was tapping lightly on the front door.

Esther's heart lurched. Only one person would be knocking at this time of night, and it was the last person in the whole world she wanted to see. She hurriedly put on her robe, not wanting to rush the inevitable, but afraid the knocking would become persistently louder if she didn't.

With an immense sense of dread, Esther tiptoed into the entryway, turned on the floor lamp, and opened the door. Ivy, thin as a rail and pale as a sheet, stood on her stoop, arms wrapped around herself as if guarding against the cold, except it was July and sweat beaded on Ivy's forehead. She wore a flimsy, saggy red tank top that looked as if it hadn't been washed in weeks and blackish-gray jeans that had more holes than fabric. She had a backpack slung over one shoulder and round, bulky earrings the size of canning jar lids hanging from her ears.

Her dark brown hair hovered over her face like a cobweb, and she pushed it out of her eyes when Esther opened the door. Her smile showed no hint of embarrassment, just that aggravating confidence Ivy had always possessed.

"I'm back," she said, as if her leaving was a big joke they both thought was funny. "How did you get on without me?"

"How did I get on without you?"

For half a second, Esther wanted to give Ivy the true answer to that question. She wanted to yell and scream and throw things and slam the door in Ivy's face. She wanted to snarl and gnash her teeth and give Ivy what for.

She would have done it too, if she had thought it would have done any good. Ivy didn't have a conscience. She didn't have the capacity to feel anything so proper as shame or guilt. She didn't care that her actions had torn Esther's family apart, had hurt the people who loved her the most. She simply didn't care. All she cared about was herself, no matter if everyone else drowned in the wake of her bad choices.

Esther was not good at curbing her temper, but for weeks she had been preparing for Ivy's return. She had rehearsed this scene at the front door dozens of times. She could throw plates or apricots later. For now, all that mattered was Winnie.

She made no move to invite Ivy into the house. She wasn't going to get cold standing out on the porch in July. Instead, Esther forced a kindly smile onto her face and spoke gently, almost as if she was happy to see her sister. "Where's your boyfriend?"

Ivy's poise wilted slightly. Her smile drooped, and the lines around her eyes deepened. "If you must know, he dumped me in Des Moines." She lifted her chin. "Actually, I dumped him. I told him to take his truck and shove it."

Esther looked past Ivy into the darkness. She didn't see any cars or trucks parked on the road. No matter what, she refused to allow the boyfriend or any other male stranger in the house. Winnie's protection was the most important thing. "How did you get here?"

"Can I please come in? It's freezing out here," Ivy said, with the I'm-barely-putting-up-with-you tone Esther knew so well.

Esther kept her temper and her calm and pretended that Ivy wasn't getting on her nerves. "You need to keep your voice down. Winnie is asleep."

"Winnie? Who's Winnie?" Ivy made a face as it dawned on her. "Winnie is the stupidest name I've ever heard. It's an old lady name. Her name is Winter. Let me in. I want to see my baby."

Ivy made an attempt to come into the house, but Esther blocked the way. "I told you, she's asleep. I won't let you wake her. She's wonderful hard to get back to sleep." She folded her arms across her chest. "Who brought you here? I want to make sure Winnie's not in any danger before I let you in."

"Danger?" Ivy's disbelief would have been comical if she hadn't been so completely serious. "I'm her mother, you idiot. And don't call her Winnie again or I'll—"

"Or you'll what? Take her away? Do you think that would be some sort of punishment? You abandoned her here, remember? And I've been stuck with her for almost four months."

Esther bit down on her tongue. It felt deceitful to act like this, as if she wanted to get rid of Winnie instead of keep her, but it was the only thing that might work. If Ivy thought Esther didn't want Winnie, she might decide to leave Winnie here out of spite.

How sad that Esther had to be so calculating. How sad that Esther had such a low opinion of her own sister.

Ivy started shivering. And it wasn't fake to get Esther's sympathy. She truly looked awful. Esther pressed her lips together and remembered how mad she was at her sister. "How did you get here? Is there another man with long hair and a nose ring lurking in the bushes?"

Ivy rolled her eyes. "You're so judgmental, Esther."

Esther didn't reply. Ivy was very good at accusing everybody but herself. Esther wasn't going to fall for it this time.

"I got a ride into town with a trucker," Ivy said, huffing out a breath as if quite put out that she even had to explain. "He dropped me off at the gas station, and I walked the rest of the way."

"Four miles?"

Ivy let out a string of profanity. Esther didn't even know what most of the words meant, but she knew they were vile. Ivy had picked up some bad habits in her eight-year absence. "I don't know how far it was. I'm not an odometer."

"You can't say those words around the baby. I won't have her learning them."

"She's my baby," Ivy snapped. Then, to Esther's surprise, she seemed to soften just a bit. "Of course I won't say those words around her. Do you think I'm stupid?"

Ivy was thoughtless and insensitive and despicable, but she wasn't stupid. She was clever. Esther wouldn't forget that for a minute. Ivy obviously had nowhere else to go, or she wouldn't be here, but it was also true that Ivy would do whatever she could to control the situation. Esther would do her best not to let her. When Ivy's teeth started chattering, a twinge of pity formed at the base of Esther's throat. Ivy looked as if she would blow over with the next passing breeze. She truly did look pathetic. After all she had done and lived through, Ivy *was* pathetic. Her sorry state was her own doing, but it didn't matter. Anyone would have felt sorry for her.

"*Cum,*" Esther said, stepping back from the doorway. "I'll make you some *kaffee.*"

Esther had spent plenty of time dreading and planning for Ivy's return, and she always knew she'd take Ivy in again, unless the boyfriend came with her. Ivy was her sister, and Dat's last wish was for Ivy to be taken care of. Esther had moved her cash and phone to another hiding place, and there wasn't really anything of value for Ivy to steal other than the appliqué quilt Esther had just finished for the shop in Boulder. But Ivy never understood the true value of anything. Esther's quilts would be safe.

Still, she was reluctant to let Ivy in the house. She reeked of cigarette smoke, and her very presence filled the air with tension and discontent. Esther didn't know how long she could bear it.

If Esther was cold toward Ivy, would Ivy be more or less likely to take Winnie away? Would kindness make Ivy more or less willing to sign the adoption papers the lawyer had drawn up? Esther didn't know, but she did know that if she couldn't show her sister a little human dignity, she wasn't really fit to call herself a Christian. Of course, that didn't mean she would let Ivy use or mistreat her—Nanna had spent many pickleball games talking to her about setting boundaries and letting Ivy suffer her own consequences. Esther wasn't quite sure how to do that, but at least she was aware.

Esther took heart from the thought that Ivy wasn't likely to stay for more than a few days. As long as she didn't want to take Winnie with her when she left, everything would be all right. Esther held on to that hope like a lifeline.

"I don't want coffee," Ivy said. "I just want to sleep." She winced when she eased the backpack off her shoulder.

"What's wrong?" Esther said.

"I broke my collarbone."

"Your collarbone? How did you do that?"

"How do you think?" Ivy said, rolling her eyes as if it was the stupidest question in the world.

"How should I know?" Esther didn't mean to snap at her sister. Why did she have to be so abrasive? In Pennsylvania, Perry Lapp broke his collarbone falling off a horse. Mandy Herschberger broke her collarbone in a buggy accident. Esther's throat tightened. "Jordan hit you."

"No duh, Sherlock."

Esther clenched her teeth so hard, her jaw was likely to crack. For sure and certain Gotte had sent Ivy to teach her patience. "You need a sling."

"As long as I don't move it, it will heal on its own."

"You need a doctor."

"I don't need a doctor."

Okay then. She wasn't going to argue. Esther refused to care about Ivy more than Ivy cared about herself.

Esther's latest quilt was fixed to the frames in the front room. It was a beautiful quilt with blue flowers and green leaves appliquéd onto a cream background. The online customer was paying her eight hundred dollars to make it. Esther moved the frames to the side as far as they would go to make a path for Ivy to get to the couch. She pulled some sheets from the hall closet and made up the couch for Ivy. Ivy watched as Esther laid a blanket across the sheets. "I won't be able to stretch out my legs."

"You can't sleep in Winnie's room. You'll wake her up."

Ivy heaved a great sigh, as if it was the hardest thing she'd ever done. "Let me sleep in your bed, and you sleep on the sofa. You're shorter than I am. You'll be more comfortable here than I'll be."

"But I'm so much older than you are. An old maid needs her own bed." Esther smiled to herself. Levi would have liked that excuse—or been irritated by it.

"But my shoulder hurts bad, Esther."

Esther hesitated. Ivy really was in pain. She wasn't faking that. But if she wheedled her way into Esther's bed, Esther would never get her out. *Nae.* She had to stand firm. She pulled an extra pillow from the closet. "Use this," she said, determined to meet Ivy's pitiful gaze. "Put it under your arm. It will help."

Ivy tested Esther's resolve one more time, probably to see if she could break it. "Don't you even care how much it hurts?"

"I care very much. Use the pillow."

Ivy grunted in complaint and shuffled down the hall. "I'm going to the bathroom."

Was there anything in the bathroom worth stealing? Ivy could take the rose-scented soap if she really wanted it.

Esther wouldn't miss it terribly. Esther thought about telling Ivy there wasn't money in the fridge anymore and not to bother looking, but it would be more fun to let Ivy find out for herself. Ivy never did like getting her hands dirty. It would serve her right to get raw hamburger juice all over her fingers trying to steal Esther's money.

The only thing that truly concerned Esther was that Ivy might sneak into Winnie's room and carry her off in the night, but Ivy looked as if she was ready to collapse into a heap on the floor. She wouldn't be able to carry herself, much less a baby, out the door. Tomorrow, Winnie's crib was going in Esther's room. Then Ivy could sleep in the twin bed in Winnie's room, and Esther would hear if Ivy sneaked into her room and tried to take the baby. It spoke to how low Ivy had sunk in Esther's estimation that Esther seriously feared Ivy would kidnap her own baby.

Ivy came out of the bathroom smelling faintly of roses, but she didn't have any strange bulges in her pockets, so she'd probably left the soap where it was. With great effort and a lot of groaning—some fake and some not—Ivy lay down on the sofa, not bothering to take off her earrings. How could she sleep comfortably with those things pressing against her head all night? Esther helped her position the pillow under her arm. Ivy winced. They were going to have to find her a sling, or she'd make her arm worse by moving it. Despite her earlier protests, the only reason Ivy didn't have a sling was because she didn't have any money. That was also very likely the reason she'd come back. She truly was desperate. Esther just hoped that desperation didn't include wanting her baby back. She tucked the top sheet under Ivy's chin and spread the blanket over that. It wasn't cold, but Ivy still shivered.

"Do you need a drink?" Esther asked.

Ivy snuggled into her pillow and smiled drowsily at Esther. That smile made her look like a six-year-old again, sweet and guileless, the little sister looking to her big sister for comfort. "Remember when I got scared at night, and you used to snuggle with me under the covers and tell me stories about Miss Mary and her horses?"

A twinge of pain shot through Esther's heart. Over the years, Ivy had done a *gute* job of ruining all of Esther's pleasant memories of their lives together. "That was a long time ago."

"I wish Miss Mary was real," Ivy said, as if she could barely stay awake to say the words. "I wish Prancing Farm was a real place." She closed her eyes. "Thank you for taking care of me. I'm glad you still love me."

Did Esther love Ivy?

Tonight, she was too tired to care about the answer.

Winnie sat on the blanket under the apricot tree playing with some of Esther's measuring cups while Esther picked apricots. The fruit was plump and large and tasted sweeter than any apricots Esther had ever eaten. She'd done a *gute* job thinning them this spring, even though the thinning was only a side benefit of ripping little green apricots off the tree and throwing them at the house.

Ivy had been here for four days, and Esther had no idea if she intended to stay for another day, another year, or forever. *Oh, please, dear Father in Heaven, don't let it be forever.* But then again, forever was better than losing Winnie. Esther threw a bird-pecked apricot at the house. She didn't even know what to pray for anymore.

She glanced at Winnie sitting on a blanket under the side of the tree Esther had already picked. Winnie was playing contentedly and drooling all over the cute pink dress Mary Jane had sewn for her. Winnie was the most beautiful baby in the whole world. What would Esther do without her? What had she ever done before? And while she was forever frustrated with Ivy, she knew she should be grateful too. Winnie was what Mamm would call a blessing in disguise.

Esther stretched up as far as she could to get the last of the apricots within her reach. Ivy had spent the better part of the last four days sleeping, probably trying to catch up after years of hard living. When she wasn't sleeping, Ivy was her own defiant self, but in a subdued and quiet way, probably because she thought she'd be out on her ear if she provoked Esther. It was plain that Ivy wasn't aware of the power she had over Esther—the power to make Esther do anything she wanted her to do just by threatening to take Winnie away. Esther wasn't about to let Ivy find out. Tiptoeing around Ivy, measuring every word, trying to be firm without offending her sister was exhausting.

She took a small measure of comfort in the fact that Ivy had abandoned Winnie before. There wasn't any reason to expect she wouldn't do it again—in a heartbeat. In a way, it was sad, but Ivy's weak character was Esther's greatest hope.

Ivy trudged around the side of the house, shielding her eyes against the sun with her good hand. She wore a white T-shirt with shorts so short they looked like underwear with pockets. Maybe the shorts weren't a bad thing. Ivy needed some sun. She was so pale, she looked as if she had one foot in the grave. A healthy tan might do her good. A nondescript tattoo sat on Ivy's upper thigh, looking very much like a blue and green bruise. She'd done that to herself on purpose? Ivy was obviously fond of dangly earrings, because even though her clothes were in tatters, she seemed to have an endless supply of jewelry to put in her ears. This morning she wore a pair of earrings made of fluorescent pink and blue feathers so long they brushed the tops of her shoulders.

Ivy had refused to see a doctor, so Esther had sewn Ivy a sling out of some homely leftover brown fabric that she wasn't planning on using for anything. Ivy wore the sling, because she wasn't stupid, but she also complained about the color and the stitching and the texture of the fabric until Esther wanted to rip the thing off Ivy's arm and let her fend for herself.

Esther took a deep breath. And then another. She was getting a lot of extra oxygen these days. She reminded herself of the good things. The broken collarbone was also a blessing in disguise. Ivy couldn't help with the dishes or laundry, but she couldn't lift or hold Winnie, and Esther liked it that way. She couldn't bear the thought of Ivy cuddling Winnie or rocking her to sleep. She couldn't bear the thought of Ivy replacing Esther in Winnie's heart. Ivy didn't seem the least bit interested in Winnie. Esther could have kissed her for her coldheartedness.

"Good morning, Ivy," Esther said, giving her sister as genuine a smile as she could muster.

"There's like nothing in the fridge," Ivy said. "What can I have for breakfast?"

"You could grab yourself some apricots and have some in a bowl with milk and sugar."

The look of horror on Ivy's face made Esther laugh. Ivy cracked a smile. "Would *you* eat apricots for breakfast?"

Esther shook her head. "I don't much like apricots, except in pies and tarts."

Ivy scrunched her lips to one side of her face and raised her eyebrows. "And now you have a whole tree of them. Poor girl."

"Yep. I feel kind of sorry for myself."

Ivy eased herself down on the blanket next to Winnie and smoothed the back of her finger down Winnie's cheek. "I'll never get over how soft her skin is."

Esther tensed and tried to pretend she wasn't tense. She dropped her apricots into the bucket. "There's nothing softer than a baby's cheek."

Winnie made a sound of protest. Ivy pulled back her hand. "From the minute she was born, all she did was cry. Jordan hated it. He's got sensitive ears, and Winter's cries gave him a headache."

Poor Jordan, Esther wanted to say, with sarcasm dripping from her lips. She knew better than to say something so foolish. "Gotte made babies that way on purpose. It's hard to ignore them when they're crying."

"I suppose that's true. But it sure can wear on your nerves."

Esther wasn't certain why—maybe it was a gift from Gotte—but she suddenly felt a rush of compassion and love for her sister. The feeling nearly knocked her over. How hard it must have been for Ivy, having a new baby but no one she could turn to for help. If it hadn't been for Levi and his family, Esther would have been completely lost when Winnie first came. She dropped the last of the apricots into the bucket and knelt beside Ivy. "I'm sorry.

For sure and certain it was wonderful hard for you. Did your labor last long?"

Ivy studied Esther's face as if to decide if Esther was sincerely interested. Esther winced inwardly. Ivy had obviously sensed her resistance. "Seventeen hours," Ivy said. "They wouldn't give me anything for the pain, because I didn't have insurance. Jordan watched football while I screamed." She turned her face away. "I hated him for that. I hated him for everything."

Esther slipped her hand into Ivy's, for once not thinking of what she was doing as a strategy for handling her sister. She simply wanted Ivy to know there was someone who cared about her. "*Ach*. You must have felt so alone."

"We were living with Jordan's stepmom and dad. Jordan and his stepmom had a big fight after Christmas, and they threw us out of the house. Can you imagine that? Kicking your son and his new baby out of the house on New Year's Eve? We lived in his truck for three days and then at a homeless shelter until Jordan found work on a road crew."

Esther shuddered at the thought of Winnie in a shelter. She hated to ask, but she couldn't bear not knowing. "Did . . . was Winnie safe from Jordan?"

Ivy turned her face away. "He never touched her. I wouldn't let him touch her, even when she cried."

"You're a good mother, Ivy."

"Jordan is a jerk. He gets drunk, and he can't control himself."

Esther wrapped her arms around Ivy's shoulders. "Oh, Ivy, I love you, and you deserve so much better."

Ivy pulled away and brushed some grass off the blanket.

"Jordan took care of me. He made sure we always had something to eat."

But at what price, Ivy? Your dignity is worth more than a square meal.

"I wish you would have come here sooner. I would have helped you."

Ivy stiffened. "Oh, yeah, like you would have let Jordan sleep in the house. We were better off in the truck than living with you and your holier-than-thou attitude."

Esther sighed as her warm feelings for Ivy evaporated into the summer air. Ivy had been a sickly little girl, and Mamm, anxious for her daughter's health, had hovered and coddled and accommodated Ivy until Ivy began to expect everyone in the world to cater to her. Even after Ivy regained her health, Mamm continued to coddle her, letting her laze around the house instead of doing chores, putting up with Ivy's demands and disrespect, and treating her like a baby instead of a capable human being. Dat called her "My poor little Ivy" up until the day he died. She had been masterful at milking Mamm and Dat's sympathy. But Ivy had rarely sought sympathy from Esther, and Esther hadn't given it to her. Maybe Esther's pity made Ivy feel weak, but why she had craved pity from her parents and not from Esther was something Esther would never know.

"You're probably right," Esther said, because it was pointless to attempt to reason with Ivy. "But I am sorry Jordan's stepmom kicked you out."

Ivy sniffed and turned up her nose. "I don't need *you* feeling sorry for *me*. You're Amish. I'm the one who feels sorry for *you*—all those stupid rules you have to follow, the ugly clothes you have to wear, those hard benches you have to sit on at church."

Esther most certainly wasn't going to attempt to reason with Ivy about that. Ivy's life was testament to the consequences of bad choices. Esther chose to obey the rules. She chose to be in the church because obedience was protection. Obedience was freedom. Caring for Winnie was elevating and refining. Serving Gotte and doing her best to be a disciple of Jesus was happiness.

Nae. She wasn't going to mention any of that to Ivy.

Winnie reached out for Esther, and Esther scooped Winnie into her arms and planted a kiss on her cheek. Her heart softened toward Ivy just a little. Ivy had brought Winnie into her life. "Come inside," she said. "I'll make you some pancakes."

Ivy relaxed her posture and grinned. "With bananas?"

"Of course."

Ivy's grin widened into a delighted smile. "You used to sneak chocolate chips into the pancake batter when Mamm wasn't looking. For me. Just for me."

That was a *gute* memory. Even though Esther didn't like chocolate, Ivy adored chocolate chip pancakes, and Esther had once loved nothing better than to make her *schwester* smile. In earlier days, she and Ivy were like one soul living in two bodies. They loved each other like only sisters could. "I happen to have some chocolate chips. I could make chocolate chip banana pancakes with maple syrup and powdered sugar."

Ivy clapped her hands together. "Yes, please."

"And a glass of milk." Ivy needed calcium.

They strolled into the house, and Esther set Winnie in the high chair while she made pancakes. Ivy sat at the table and cooed at Winnie while playing with her hands and watching her pound on the high chair tray.

"Remember when you tried to teach me how to make biscuits?" Ivy said.

"I hated making biscuits. I was hoping you'd take over that job for me."

Ivy shook her head. "I couldn't learn. Fletcher always said I was too dumb."

Esther set a paper plate and a plastic fork in front of Ivy. She tucked a second plastic fork behind her ear. You never knew when you were going to need another fork. "You are not *dumm*. Our dear brother Fletcher barely paid attention to either of us. He doesn't know how smart you are, and he certainly doesn't know how to make biscuits."

"It was too much work to learn how to do it. Easier to let you do it for me."

Esther gave Ivy a wry smile. "Much easier for *you*."

Ivy giggled. "I got away with a lot when we were younger. Maybe too much." Esther glanced at her sister in surprise. Her admission was one of the most honest responses Esther had heard from her in four days.

Esther wasn't sure why, but she wanted to make Ivy feel better about it. She shrugged. "It's okay. I was annoyed about the biscuits, but I didn't stay mad."

Ivy looked down at her hands. "Mamm didn't think I was very smart either."

"You're plenty smart," Esther scolded. "Don't ever think you're not smart enough."

"Jordan told me I was smart—mostly that I have a smart mouth."

Esther flipped a pancake on the griddle. "You were smart enough to figure out how to avoid doing your chores.

Smart enough to convince Mamm or me to do them for you." She said it with a smile so Ivy knew she bore her no ill will. At least none that she wanted Ivy to see.

Ivy rested her elbow on the table and propped her chin in her hand. "You're the smart one, Esther. You knew how to do everything—make bread, milk the cow, spell hard words. That's why the boys liked you and ignored me."

Esther cocked an eyebrow. "I don't remember any boys ignoring you."

"They only talked to me to get your attention. Mamm and Dat loved you, Esther. They never expected anything from me. They thought I was helpless."

"They didn't think you were helpless."

"I'm not like you, Esther. I could never live by myself, let alone support a baby. I need a man to take care of me."

Esther bit her bottom lip. She had never known Ivy to let her guard down like this. "Ivy, you are more capable than you think. You have many talents and abilities."

Ivy gave Esther a sharp look. "Name one."

"Name one what?"

"Name one talent I have," Ivy said, daring Esther with her eyes.

Esther held her breath. For many years, she'd thought of Ivy with nothing but resentment. At the moment, she found it impossible to come up with one *gute* quality her sister possessed. Oy, anyhow. What kind of a person couldn't think of one nice thing to say about her *schwester*?

Esther dug deep and prayed for immediate wisdom. "You . . . you are a wonderful *gute* singer."

Ivy snorted her derision. "A lot of good that does me."

Esther's mind raced as she flipped two pancakes onto Ivy's plate. "You love animals. Remember when you fed those kittens in our barn? You cried when the cow got his shots. And you could skip rope more times in a row than anyone in school." Granted, these were all events that had happened before Ivy turned twelve, but it was something. In their adolescence, Esther and Ivy had been the dearest of friends. Ivy had needed Esther, and Esther had loved being the big sister Ivy could look up to.

Ivy gazed at Esther as if she truly cared what Esther had to say. Esther felt like a young girl again, hiding under the blankets and whispering stories to Ivy to keep her from being scared of the dark. Esther cleared her throat, not sure how vulnerable she wanted to be with her thoughtless sister. "You loved me no matter what." At least when she was little.

Ivy concentrated very hard on pouring syrup on her pancake. "Those aren't talents. Those are emotions. I can't support myself with emotions. I need someone to take care of me. I always have."

Esther furrowed her brow. "But why someone like Jordan?"

"Jordan doesn't care that my teeth are crooked or that I'm not smart. He loves me. He does his best to take care of me."

"He's not nice to you, Ivy." She pointed to Ivy's collarbone. "He hits you. That isn't love."

Ivy gave Esther a look that could have peeled the bright pink polish off Ivy's fingernails. "What do you know about love?"

Esther didn't back down. Ivy knew very well that Jordan's behavior was inexcusable. "I know that if you truly love someone, you would never intentionally hurt them. I know that love is kind and forgiving and humble.

I know that love never makes you feel afraid or lost or trapped."

"It's not that simple," Ivy said, as if she was trying to convince herself more than trying to persuade Esther. "Mamm and Dat used to argue with each other. Sometimes Dat slept on the sofa in the front room. Once Mamm was so mad at Dat she threw a plate across the kitchen."

"Every couple has disagreements, but it's not okay to hit or do violence to anyone."

"You just don't understand." Ivy pressed her palm against her forehead. "I ran off with Mike, then he dumped me. Julio lasted about three months. Alan was around for a while, but only because I made good tips as a waitress. Jordan was the only one who wanted me. Now I got nothing. Nobody."

Esther hated to commit herself or volunteer for something she'd later regret, but her sister needed her and she wouldn't turn her back. "Well, you've got me, and I'm going to take care of you, little sis, at least until you can get yourself into a better situation." She shook her spatula at Ivy. "And I don't mean getting back with Jordan or finding someone equally horrible. You deserve better than Jordan. Everybody deserves better than Jordan. Believe me, being alone is a hundred times better than being with that whiny baby Jordan."

Ivy took a bite of pancake and cracked a smile. "Whiny baby? You don't even know him."

Esther made her voice lower and talked through her nose. "'Oh, Ivy, the crying baby is making my head hurt. I'm going to get a nosebleed.'"

Ivy giggled. "Yep. That's about how he talks." Her smile faded. "Right before he smacks me around."

Esther pinned her with a serious look. "You don't have to do it anymore, Ivy."

Ivy pushed the last of her pancake around with her fork. "But what else can I do? I'm not fit to do anything to earn money, and I can't stay here. I've only been here four days, and I'm already going crazy with boredom. You don't even have a TV. I can barely stand it. At least Jordan could show me a good time when he had the money."

Esther wasn't offended in the least. It didn't take much to guess that Ivy's "good time" ended with her arm wrapped around a toilet bowl while she waited to throw up the contents of her stomach. "I can't believe you would say such a thing," Esther teased. "I make quilts and bottle fruit and play pickleball. I change diapers, wipe Winnie's drool, and go to church. If that's not a good time, I don't know what is." It didn't hurt to remind Ivy about the burdens of taking care of a baby.

Ivy's reaction was just what Esther had expected and hoped for. She groaned and tossed her head back. "I think I'd rather break my other collarbone."

Esther laughed. "I know you're bored, but nobody ever died of boredom."

"I'm sure I'll be the first."

"Maybe you could start thinking of ways you could earn money. You could get a job at the gas station, or maybe at the local coffee shop."

"I refuse to work fast food. The hats they make you wear are ridiculous. And I'm not doing any sort of manual labor. I'm not built for it." Ivy fingered the feathers in her ears. "I've always wanted to make earrings to sell, my own special creations, but you can't make a living selling jewelry. Everybody knows that."

"Let's not think too far into the future." Esther wasn't about to tell Ivy about her share of Mamm and Dat's money. Ivy wasn't ready to act responsibly with it. She was just as sure as Ivy was that they shouldn't live together. Esther couldn't stand the thought of Ivy in her home, destroying her peace, invading her privacy. But she couldn't broach the subject of Ivy's moving out until she was sure Ivy wouldn't take Winnie.

"I'm moving to my own place as soon as I can, some-place with electricity to plug in a DVD player." Ivy hadn't mentioned Winnie. That was *gute*. The less she thought about Winnie, the better.

"Once your collarbone is healed and you get your strength back, we can make a plan."

Ivy shook her head. "I don't need a plan. I need a man."

"You don't need a man."

"*You* don't need a man, because you've always been coldhearted like that. I need someone to love. I need some-one to love me."

Ivy didn't realize that the someone she was talking about was sitting in a high chair not three feet away from her. What would Esther do if Ivy ever figured that out?

Chapter Nine

Levi hitched the horse to the buggy, thought better of it, and unhitched the horse again. He went back into the house and tried to read the *Budget* newspaper. After five minutes of reading the same sentence eleven times, he went back to the barn and hitched up the buggy again. His indecision was ridiculous as well as time-consuming.

He shoved his hand in his pocket, pulled out her letter, and read it for the hundredth time. It was aggravatingly short and completely impossible to understand.

Dear Levi,

 Please don't come this week to work on the bathroom. Or the next week. Please stay away until I contact you again.

        Esther

Should he go to Esther's or not? Would she be mad if he showed up when she had specifically asked him not to? Or would she be grateful that he'd sensed she needed help but couldn't bring herself to ask for it?

Why didn't Esther want him to come over? Was she mad at him? Was she sick of him coming over and invading her privacy? Did she not like him anymore?

His mind went over the last time they had been to-gether. They had met with the lawyer about the adoption, and Esther had been quite discouraged about the time and the paperwork it would take to adopt Winnie, not to men-tion the fact that Ivy was unpredictable. If she wanted to take Winnie away tomorrow, she could do it, and neither Esther nor Levi would have any say in it. It was disheart-ening, and Esther seemed to be taking it harder and harder with every passing day.

Maybe she spent her days sitting on the unfinished bathroom floor crying her eyes out. Maybe she was em-barrassed to have Levi see her like that. Didn't she know that showing vulnerability made her seem human? Attain-able? Levi liked to feel needed, especially by Esther. He liked feeling like he was of use to her, like she needed him and only him.

Imagining Esther sitting on the bathroom floor, he slid the note in his pocket and climbed into the buggy. He couldn't stay away when Esther needed him so badly. And if she was mad at him, it was better to talk things through than let them fester. Besides, that bathroom wasn't going to finish itself. Maybe Esther didn't want to impose on Levi's time any more than she already had, but if she thought she could manage the bathroom without Levi, she was sorely mistaken. She was good with a hammer, but she wouldn't be able to figure out how to cut and lay tile.

And what she didn't realize was that Levi didn't mind working on her bathroom. Okay, not only did he not mind it—the time he spent at Esther's house was the happiest part of his week. Seeing Winnie was one reason, of course, but it was Esther he couldn't stop thinking about. Esther was funny and genuine. She didn't pretend to be someone she wasn't or someone other people thought she should be. She was just her delightful, quirky self. Who else would wear a carrot behind her ear or use a cooking thermometer to test the bathwater? Who else would throw little green apricots and take out her frustrations on the bathroom rug? She had a terrible, wonderful temper and a tendency to fret about the people she loved, especially Winnie.

For sure and certain she'd be mad at him for not heeding her note, but he wanted to help her, and more importantly, he wanted to be with her. Selfish or not, he was going.

His resolve weakened as the buggy approached Esther's house. Mary Jane told him he had too high an opinion of himself. Maybe Esther didn't want him around because she'd found someone else to finish her bathroom—maybe somebody she preferred over Levi. Maybe she'd met a pickleball player who talked sweet and knew all about tile and particleboard. Levi's heart sank. How could she do this to him, drop him like a hot potato, as if he didn't have feelings? As if he hadn't already spent hours working on her bathroom?

Esther's house came into view, and Levi took a deep breath. How many expert tile layers played pickleball? Probably zero. He was all worked up for nothing. Esther might find him aggravating, but she liked him well enough. She wouldn't let someone else finish her bathroom without talking to Levi first.

Would she?

And how well did Esther really like him? Maybe she

was just putting up with him for the sake of her bathroom and Winnie. His gut clenched. Was Esther just putting up with him? He didn't know if he wanted the answer to that question.

He pulled up in front of Esther's house. It didn't look as if there was another man in there working on the tile, but Levi couldn't be sure. There were no broken windows, no apricots smashed against the walls, no flowers uprooted from their beds. If Esther had gotten angry, she hadn't taken her anger out on anything in the front yard.

Ignoring his misgivings, Levi set the brake and jumped down from the buggy. He walked across the lawn and knocked on the door, ready to duck or apologize or both if need be. He needed to see Esther. He needed to be with Esther. He was willing to take the risk.

If Esther had thrown a rock at his head, he couldn't have been more shocked at the sight that met him. A young woman with feathers dangling from her ears and one arm in a sling answered the door. She was taller and had a lighter complexion than Esther, but there was no mistaking the resemblance. She and Esther had the same blue-green eyes and the same well-defined, dark eyebrows. She was impossibly skinny, and there were dark circles under her eyes, but Esther had been right. Ivy was a beauty. Not as striking as Esther, but still wonderful pretty.

Ach. Ivy was back. And this was why Esther wanted him to stay away.

She raised an eyebrow and looked Levi up and down as if he was a horse and she was thinking about buying him. "Well. How nice. How surprising. A handsome Amish boy. Esther has been holding out on me."

For a split second, Levi thought about running back to

his buggy and driving away as if he'd accidentally come to the wrong house. Esther had said she couldn't predict how Ivy would act or react to anything. Surely Esther wanted Levi to stay away just in case he made things worse. Esther was trying to control as much of the situation as she could, and he had just ruined it. "Um," he said, his mind racing for the perfect words to convince Ivy to go away, leave Winnie here, and sign the adoption papers all at the same time. Maybe he was expecting a little too much of himself, but he certainly wanted to fix things for Esther.

Ivy leaned her good shoulder against the doorjamb. "A handsome Amish guy who doesn't say much. I like you already."

Esther appeared from the kitchen with Winnie in her arms and a plastic fork behind her ear. When she caught sight of Levi, she frowned and her eyes flashed with anger, but whether she was mad at Levi or Ivy, Levi couldn't tell. Like as not, she was mad at both of them. He should have stayed away.

Ivy's back was to her, so she didn't see the turmoil on Esther's face. Levi felt lower than the dirt. What had he done? Esther pressed her lips together and closed her eyes for a brief moment. When she opened her eyes, she had made some sort of decision. She bloomed into a smile, one that looked sincere even if it might not have been, and bounced Winnie on her hip as if it was just a normal day and she was happy to see him. "Why, hello, Levi. I wasn't expecting you, but today is as good a day as any." Esther turned to Ivy. "This is Levi Kiem. He is helping me remodel that bathroom in the back hall."

"Nice to meet you," Ivy said, letting her hand linger in Levi's for a second too long.

"Nice to meet you, Ivy."

Ivy smirked. "How did you know my name?" She smiled wider, as if she'd just discovered a big secret. "Esther, I've never known you to be a gossip. You've been talking about me behind my back."

Esther stiffened, but Ivy didn't seem to notice. "You've been gone for eight years, Ivy. I've become a terrible gossip."

Levi laughed nervously. "Not at all. When I started on the bathroom, I was curious whose beautiful baby this was."

Esther's posture got even more rigid. He'd been there two minutes, and he'd already made about ten mistakes.

Ivy suddenly took notice of Winnie as if she hadn't cared very much before. She stroked Winnie's hand and laid a soft kiss on her cheek. "She is beautiful, isn't she? She has my eyes."

Levi's heart sank. Esther's greatest hope was that Ivy wouldn't care about Winnie at all, that she would gladly leave her again and disappear from her life. Ivy wouldn't disappear if she felt something for her daughter. *Ach.* He was hurting Esther just by being here. He held her gaze for a second with an unspoken apology. She nodded slightly. "I should probably go. I can come back another time."

Ivy's gaze flicked from Levi to Esther. "Are you two a thing?"

"A thing?" Levi said.

"Dating. Are you dating? Have you driven her home from a gathering yet? You know, have you participated in any of those charming little courting rituals the Amish like to do?"

"Of course not," Esther said, forcing a laugh. "Levi is helping me with the bathroom, that's all."

Ivy snorted in amusement and disbelief. "Sure he is."

Esther's face turned red, but Levi could tell she was trying to remain calm. "You can think anything you want, Ivy."

Levi nodded vigorously. Obviously Esther didn't want Ivy to think there was anything between them, not even friendship. "I'm just helping Esther with the bathroom."

Ivy scrunched her lips to one side of her face and drilled her gaze into Levi's skull. "You seem pretty comfortable with each other."

Esther rolled her eyes. "For crying out loud, Ivy, I'm six years older than he is. He thinks I'm an old lady."

Levi laughed again, and it sounded completely unnatural. "*Jah.* She's an old lady." He felt horrible saying it, even though he was pretty sure that was what Esther wanted. Esther wasn't old. She was just right. But if she wanted Ivy to believe he was just there to do tile, then he'd act as if he was just there to do tile. He'd probably done enough damage for one day. He cleared his throat. "I can see this is a bad time. I'll come back another day."

"*Nae,*" Esther said, her voice cheerful and light. "You might as well come in since you've come all this way. We can get started laying the tile."

Since it seemed that Levi had messed up Esther's first plan, which included keeping him away from the house, he would go along with whatever alternate strategy she was hatching. As sad as it was, Esther had to have a strategy when it came to Ivy. Esther's new plan seemed to be proving to Ivy that Levi was just an acquaintance, that they felt nothing for each other but indifference, and that she didn't care if Levi was here or not. He just hoped it would work on Ivy. If she was as smart as Esther, she wouldn't be fooled.

Esther smiled at Ivy. "You should come and see what Levi and I have been working on."

"Okay," Ivy said. "I like tile."

Esther seemed to wilt, as if she hadn't been expecting Ivy to be interested in bathroom tile. Maybe Ivy wasn't interested in tile. Maybe she had a strategy of her own.

Ivy smiled at Levi and touched his arm. He clenched his teeth. "I love a man who's handy around the house."

Esther had laid out all the tile, the whole bathroom floor, in her watercolor pattern. It was going to be a truly *wunderbarr* floor, like a stunning quilt or a painting. He continually marveled at Esther's many talents.

Levi knew instinctively he shouldn't gush over it. "That looks *gute*," he said, pretending he hadn't looked at it very hard.

"Oh, Esther," Ivy said, "why go to all that work? It's just a floor."

Esther shrugged, as if the floor meant nothing to her. "It was a *gute* way to save money on tile."

"Well, you were always stingy like that, just like Dat. Wouldn't spend a dime on anything pretty to save his life. Your floor is going to take hours with all those little squares. Seems like such a waste."

The true waste was Ivy's shorts. There wasn't enough fabric to cover her underwear, let alone her legs. Levi hoped Ivy hadn't paid a lot of money for them. "Let's get started, then," Levi said, sliding his backpack off his shoulders.

"Oh, Levi," Ivy said, almost tragically, "I wish I could help you, but I've only got one good arm."

Levi couldn't resist shooting a grin in Esther's direction.

"*Ach, vell.* It doesn't matter. I hold Winnie while Esther does all the work."

Ivy frowned. "I've already asked Esther not to call her that."

"What? Winnie?" Levi said. "That isn't Esther's doing. I gave the baby that nickname. It's easier to say."

Ivy pressed her lips together and sniffed exactly once. "You made it up?"

"Don't you think it's cute?"

Ivy hesitated. "I . . . I guess so, but Esther should have asked my permission first."

If only there had been some way to reach you. If only Esther hadn't sat at the library for over an hour waiting for your call.

"Well, it was my fault," Levi said. "Be mad at me, not Esther."

"Nobody should be mad at anybody," Esther said.

"You know," Ivy said, "I actually love Winnie for a nickname. You're brilliant, Levi." Ivy patted Winnie on the head and smoothed her hand down Winnie's hair. "Winnie. It fits her, don't you think?"

"Yes," Levi said, because what else was there to say?

Ivy played with one of the feathers dangling from her ear. "You take care of Winter—Winnie—while Esther works on the bathroom?"

"When Winnie naps, we work together, but Esther asked me to teach her how to do the floor, so I play with Winnie while she works."

Ivy's lips curled into a smile. "Do you change diapers too?"

"Sometimes. Esther mostly does it."

Ivy seemed to adore that answer. "An Amish boy who

changes diapers and plays with the baby? I never would have believed it. Is there anything you don't do, Superman?"

The hall seemed to shrink as Ivy walked toward him. He sidled backward until he found himself trapped against the wall. "I've got some other supplies in the wagon," he said, sliding sideways out of Ivy's reach. "I'll go get them."

Ivy didn't seem to notice his resistance. "I'll go with you, in case you need help carrying anything."

Levi gave her a polite smile. "That's nice, but it wouldn't be right if I let you carry anything, not with that injured arm."

"Then I'll keep you company."

Levi didn't need any company, but he wasn't going to try to make a run for it. Ivy might get suspicious. He walked down the hall, and Ivy followed him through the kitchen and out the front door. He tried to think of something to start up a conversation—one he wasn't really interested in having. "What did you do to your shoulder?"

Ivy blushed and paused as if trying to decide what to say. "I've only told my sister. Can you keep a secret?"

He didn't want to know any of Ivy's secrets. "I can't."

Ivy giggled. "Oh, well, it doesn't matter. You seem like a compassionate person. I'm sure I can trust you."

She seemed to be trying to get him to act or respond a certain way. He wasn't interested in playing her game. "You shouldn't trust someone you just met."

Ivy hesitated briefly, then plunged ahead, despite his discouragement. "Oh, Levi, I've had a very hard life. My boyfriend hit me and broke my collarbone."

Levi flinched. He certainly couldn't be insensitive to that. "*Ach.* I'm sorry. No man should hit a woman. It's not right."

Ivy sighed. "That's when I knew I couldn't stay with him anymore. I came straight here. I knew Esther would take care of me."

Anger bubbled in Levi's throat even as a ribbon of warmth curled down his spine. Ivy had treated Esther very poorly, and Esther had shown Ivy kindness in return. "Esther is nice like that," he said. He wanted to say more, much more, about Esther. How she took care of Winnie and how she constantly worried about Ivy. About what a *gute* friend she was to Levi's *mammi* and how she never thought about herself. He didn't dare say any of that. Ivy would suspect they were more than acquaintances.

He retrieved some cans and other supplies from his wagon. "This is all I need," he said.

Ivy reached out and touched his arm again. He resisted the urge to snatch it away from her. "I've made so many mistakes, but I'm going to change. I promise I'm going to change."

"Jesus died for our mistakes. There is always hope."

"Yes," Ivy said, getting unduly excited. "Yes. I want to be a better person. I want to live a life of service and sacrifice and faith. Maybe I'll get baptized."

Levi drew his brows together. "I wouldn't dissuade you from that. I would encourage any true seeker of faith to get baptized."

Ivy nodded in satisfaction. "Then I want to get baptized."

"But it does seem a little sudden."

Ivy looked disappointed. "You've got to believe me. I've thought about this decision for a long time. I'm tired of living out of a suitcase. I'm tired of being hungry and scared. I want to find someone who truly loves me and wants to take care of me. I want to pledge my heart to God and a good man. Will you help me?"

"My father would be the best one to help you. He is the bishop."

Ivy's eyes grew wide. "Your dad's the bishop? How nice. Are you guys rich?"

Rich? Where had she gotten that from? "*Nae.* We're not rich. We do a little farming, and my *dat* and *bruderen* and I remodel houses."

Ivy nodded so hard her earrings swayed back and forth. "I like it when a guy has a job. A good, stable job. Jordan couldn't hold down a job to save his life. He'd show up late or fail his drug test and they'd let him go. I'm just done with the uncertainty, ya know?"

Levi didn't know what to say to all that eagerness. "*Ach, vell,* my *dat* can arrange with one of the ministers to take you through the baptism classes."

"But you'll support me, won't you, Levi? I'm very determined about this. I want to make myself worthy again."

Levi nodded. "Of course. If that's what you really want, we'll all help you."

Ivy glued her gaze to Levi's face. "Yes, that is what I really want."

Levi didn't know what to think. It was hard to imagine Ivy was sincere, but if she truly wanted to change her life, he certainly couldn't discourage her. But if she got baptized, she'd likely stay in the community. Would she be happy in the Plain life? Would she expect to live with Esther forever? Would she want Winnie back?

Would Esther be glad or irritated about Ivy's change of heart, if it really was a change of heart?

Levi swallowed past the lump in his throat.

What had he done? And would Esther ever forgive him?

Ivy stood at the front door and watched while Levi put his tools in the back of his wagon, climbed into his buggy, and drove away. She waved and giggled until Levi's buggy was far down the road, then she left the front door open and walked to the edge of the lawn trying to keep his buggy in sight, as if she planned on watching it all the way to his house or his next appointment.

Esther closed the door on Ivy, because all sorts of flies and mosquitoes were going to fly into the house while Ivy was out paying a whole lot of unnecessary attention to Levi. Esther growled softly, bounced Winnie on her hip, and strolled into the kitchen to start dinner. Esther hadn't seen this much enthusiasm from Ivy since she'd arrived four days ago. Ivy was up to something, and Esther was certain she didn't want to know what it was.

Levi had shown Esther how to set the tile in the floor with special glue and little plastic X's as spacers. Esther had gotten a *gute* start on the tile while Levi sat in the hall outside the bathroom and played with Winnie, like he always did. Esther had expected Ivy to go to her room and take a nap or go outside and get some sun or stroll into the kitchen to find something to eat. Instead, Ivy sat down right next to Levi and flirted with him the whole time. Flirted with Levi!

Ivy had even pretended to be interested in Winnie and had clapped her hands and laughed with delight when Winnie had pulled herself down the hall using only her arms. Winnie hadn't quite mastered crawling yet, and the way she got around the *haus* was adorable. Before today, Ivy hadn't cared that Winnie was learning how to crawl. She'd barely acknowledged Winnie's existence. But while Esther worked on the tile, Ivy had listened with rapt attention while Levi told her about all the cute things Winnie had done in the last month.

Levi didn't seem to mind Ivy's company. She had even made him laugh with her stories of people she'd encountered in her eight years' absence, or stories about the trouble she got into when she was a little girl growing up with Esther and four older brothers. Ivy was fun and endearing and agreeable when she wanted to be. She had definitely shown Levi her best side today, and Esther's suspicions pressed like a weight on her chest. What did Ivy want from Levi? Esther couldn't bring herself to believe that Ivy was teasing and playful with Levi just to be nice. The Ivy Esther knew was calculating and manipulative.

Esther set Winnie in her high chair and put some cereal puffs on her tray. Winnie was just learning to pick up food and could entertain herself for several minutes with a pile of cereal. Esther pulled a can of tuna and some bread from the cupboard. She heard Ivy open the front door and come in the house.

Ivy practically floated into the kitchen. "What's for dinner?"

"Grilled tuna with cheese," Esther said. She just didn't have the energy for anything fancier.

To her surprise, Ivy smiled. "Oh, that's okay. You're doing your best, I guess." She sat down at the table, picked up a handful of cereal puffs from Winnie's tray, and popped them into her mouth. "Levi is wonderful nice."

Esther had her back turned to Ivy, so Ivy didn't see her expression. "*Jah*. He's nice."

"Will you teach me how to make bread pudding?"

"Bread pudding? Why?"

Ivy's eyes danced. "Levi says he loves bread pudding."

Esther pressed her lips together. She should have known that. Was she always too wrapped up in her own problems to pay any attention to Levi? Did he resent her for that? "Bread pudding is easy to make. I can teach you."

"Oh, thank you, Esther. You're the best sister ever."

Esther swallowed hard and stirred the tuna fish with added vigor. She didn't want to know and shouldn't ask. The answer would only make her ill. "Why do you want to make Levi bread pudding?"

Ivy giggled. "Mamm always said the way to a man's heart is through his stomach."

"Why do you care about that?"

"Oh, Esther, you're so naive." Ivy stood up and strolled out of the kitchen. "Let me know when dinner is ready. And do you have a dress I can borrow?"

Levi pulled up in front of Esther's house and blew a puff of air from between his lips. Yep, Esther was mad, and that bush was never going to be the same again.

Esther, looking very pretty in emerald green, was standing in the flower bed below Winnie's bedroom window smacking at an evergreen bush with her pickleball paddle. The bush seemed to be taking it well—those evergreens were hard to kill—but Esther looked as if she was losing the battle. Sweat beaded on the back of her neck, her apron was dotted with sticky evergreen needles, and a child's stocking dangled precariously from her ear. Was she now using her head as a clothesline?

Levi climbed from the buggy and wiped any hint of a smile off his face. Esther would not appreciate his amusement at a time like this. He came up behind her, but not close enough to accidentally get whacked with her makeshift weapon. "It's a hot day," he said. "Too hot to be outside trying to chop down your bushes with a paddle."

Other than a glance in Levi's direction, Esther gave no indication that she'd heard him. Instead, she doubled her efforts with the bush. After three well-placed blows to the bush's midsection, there was a soft crack, and the flat part of the paddle broke off from the handle and lodged in the bush's thick tendrils.

"*Ach*, nuts!" Esther squeaked. She spun around and chucked the handle in the direction of Levi's buggy. She had a strong arm, but the throw wasn't good enough to make it past the lawn. Breathing hard, she plopped herself down on the grass and growled in frustration. "Cheap pickleball paddle. I knew I should have bought the fifty-dollar one."

"Next time, you should go all out and buy a chain saw. That bush wouldn't be so cocky if you had come at it with a serious weapon." He sat down next to her.

She cracked a smile, then turned her face so Levi wouldn't see it. "Don't even try to cheer me up. It won't work, especially now that I've ruined my last good pickleball paddle."

"Your last paddle? What happened to the other ones?"

She folded her arms. "I chopped one with my ax. Yesterday I smashed the other one against the road."

Levi couldn't help but chuckle. She gave him a scathing

glare. He held up his hand. "I'm sorry. I'm sorry. It's just not a *gute* week to be a pickleball paddle." He would have done anything to wipe that frown off her face. Reaching out, he wrapped his fingers around hers. She shifted her weight but didn't pull away. "What's happened?" he said gently, giving her hand a warm squeeze. "Is Winnie okay?"

"She's fine. She's taking a nap."

"So what's the matter?" Levi had no doubt that Esther's bad mood had something to do with Ivy. He only hoped it didn't have something to do with Ivy wanting to take Winnie away.

Esther huffed out a breath. "You'll see. Oh. You'll see."

Levi pulled his hand away when he heard the click of the front doorknob. He stood up, because Ivy didn't need to see him sitting so close to her sister. Half a second later, Ivy came outside, and Levi nearly lost his breakfast.

He knew it was Ivy because who else would be coming out Esther's front door with a sling cradling her left arm? But she looked like a completely different person. She wore a baby pink, calf-length dress with a black apron and black, sensible shoes. Her hair was pulled into a bun at the back of her head, and she wore a crisp white *kapp*. The earrings had disappeared, as had the fingernail polish and the eye makeup. Ivy looked like the most proper of proper Amish girls. If Levi had been chewing gum, he would have swallowed it.

"Oh, Levi," Ivy said. "I've been waiting so long for you to come."

There were no words. He kind of wished he had a pickle-ball paddle. Or a tennis racket. Even a Ping-Pong paddle would do. He and Esther could take on that bush together.

Ivy stretched out her good arm and twirled, actually twirled, for him. "What do you think?"

There were still no words, even though she stood on the stoop waiting for him to speak.

"Esther let me borrow her dress and *kapp*. And, oh, well, the shoes and everything. But the shoes are too tight."

Levi didn't risk a glance at Esther. He could pretty well guess what she was thinking. "You . . . you look Amish."

Ivy clapped her hands and giggled. "I know. Don't you love it! I told you how serious I am about getting baptized and settling down in the Amish community. I'm so excited to be starting a new life and meeting new people. I'm so happy I met you, Levi. You have truly been an inspiration to me."

Levi kicked the grass at his feet. "*Ach*, *vell*, I didn't do anything." He would be mortified if Esther thought he had played any part in this. He hadn't discouraged Ivy from preparing for baptism, that was for sure and certain, but had he been too supportive? Had Ivy decided to become Amish because of his support?

Ivy seemed oblivious to Levi's shock and Esther's irritation. "And guess what?"

"What?"

"I'm going to *gmay* on Sunday and starting the baptism classes."

Esther pushed herself off the ground. Levi reached out a hand and helped her to her feet. "It's off Sunday this week," she said, brushing tiny evergreen needles from her apron. "There's no church."

Ivy wasn't discouraged. "Then I'll go the next week. I can't wait to see the bishop's eyes pop out of his head when a complete stranger asks to take baptism classes."

Ivy smiled triumphantly at Esther. "Did you know Levi's dad is the bishop?"

Levi had always felt sorry for his *dat*. Being an Amish bishop was a time-consuming headache. District members expected him to be available and at their disposal any time of the day or night. Besides that, it was a lifetime calling. The only way Dat could get out of it was if he was dead. Now, looking at Ivy with that giddy smile on her face, Levi felt doubly sorry for his *dat*, and every other Amish bishop in the world.

And he felt four times as sorry for Esther. No wonder she'd destroyed all her pickleball paddles. Levi should probably take all her spoons and spatulas to his house for their own safety. Levi reached out and pulled an evergreen needle from Esther's *kapp*. Esther gave him a sideways glance, but otherwise didn't acknowledge him. "Well then," Levi said, "it never hurts to try to get closer to Gotte. I know my *dat* will be happy to see you."

Levi felt more and more sorry for Esther. This must be what it was like to live with Ivy, on pins and needles all the time, trying to guess what she wanted to hear, trying to say the right thing, the thing that would per-suade her to leave without taking Winnie. Ivy's deciding she wanted to be Amish was a new and demoralizing wrinkle in the plan.

He glanced at Esther. "I guess we should get to that grout."

Ivy waved Levi toward the house as if she owned it and Esther and Levi were just visitors. "Come in. Come in. I'll make both of you a cup of coffee." She left the door open and disappeared into the house.

Esther was as rigid as a telephone pole. "She doesn't

know how to make *kaffee*. And she's going to wake the baby if she doesn't shut up."

"I'm sorry," he whispered, in case Ivy was standing just inside the door.

"She stole my pink dress."

"I love that pink dress."

Esther nodded slightly. "I do too. But I refuse to wear it ever again."

"The other day she was talking about wanting to be baptized. I . . . I think I might have said something to encourage her."

Esther sighed and plucked another evergreen needle from her apron. "It wasn't what you said. It was just you."

"What do you mean?"

Esther growled. "I don't want your head to grow any bigger than it already is."

Levi curled his lips. "I don't want it to grow bigger either. I wouldn't look good with a giant head. My cousin has this neighbor who has the biggest head you've ever seen. And wonderful large earlobes. You could park a buggy on those things."

Esther cracked a smile, but it was obvious she wasn't in any state of mind to laugh. "You're handsome and nice and you have a job. Ivy is looking for a man to take care of her. She's set her sights on you."

Levi's mouth fell open in horror. "But I'm Amish. That doesn't make any sense."

"Ivy's desperate, and for eight years, she did what she had to do to survive. She sees you as her best chance for survival."

"She doesn't even know me. And she's got to know she's not my type."

"There's no way she would know that."

Levi counted on his fingers. "She's not Amish, she abandoned her baby, and she's treated you very poorly. Not my type."

Esther rolled her eyes. "She's trying to make herself your type. She's decided to get baptized, she came back to her baby, and she's making bitter *kaffee* for both of us right now."

"But why me? I thought she hated everything about the Amish. That's why she left."

Esther shrugged. "You were nice to her, and I don't think a man has been kind to her for quite some time."

Levi felt sick. "What should I do? I guess I could be rude to her, but I don't especially like being rude. But if you think it will convince her to leave, I'll do whatever you want."

Esther huffed out a breath. "I don't know. If you're rude, will she be more or less likely to sign the adoption papers?" She kicked the evergreen bush, and her stocking came away with a bunch of pine needles stuck to it. "I've had this debate in my head too many times to count. I never come to an answer."

"I'm sorry," Levi said.

"I think," said Esther, "that it would be better to just be yourself. It's too hard to pretend to be someone you're not. I think that is what Gotte would want you to do. And you should probably be nice to her simply because she's my *schwester* and Winnie's *mater*."

Levi frowned. "You are Winnie's true *mater*."

Esther turned her face away. "It doesn't matter. It might make no difference in the end."

"We can't lose hope."

"I guess it's too late to tell you that I already have."

Levi took Esther's hand and pulled her around the corner of the house, where Ivy wouldn't be able to see them if she came outside again. He cupped his hands around her shoulders. "Please don't lose hope. You told me yourself that Ivy is flighty. Tomorrow she might decide that pink isn't her color. She'll start missing all her favorite TV shows, or she might get sick of the Amish life and try the Mennonites."

A smile crept onto Esther's face. "Or she might move to Mexico and help the orphans."

"Or that," Levi said. "There's no reason you shouldn't be completely hopeful."

"It's hard not to get discouraged sometimes. I'm so afraid of losing Winnie."

"It's okay to be afraid. Just don't lose hope." She nodded. Levi was constantly amazed at how strong Esther really was. "Maybe I should stay away," he said, smiling wryly, "like you wanted me to."

Esther plucked another pine needle from her apron and gave him a reassuring smile. "I did want you to stay away. That's why I wrote that note." She gave him the stink eye. "Which you ignored."

"I'm sorry. I thought you were mad at me, or that you were trying to handle things on your own, and I wanted you to know I'm here to help."

Esther's eyes got sort of misty. His chest tightened in sympathy. "You complicate things, for sure and certain," she said. "But if you stopped coming here, I think I'd go crazy. Ivy can be insufferable, and I need you to keep me from doing something rash like clawing her eyes out."

Levi cocked an eyebrow. "You wouldn't really?"

"I'd be tempted to think about it."

He laughed. "It would be better if I bought you a new set of pickleball paddles. You could take your frustrations out on the apricot tree."

"Ping-Pong paddles are better. You can get a set of four for ten dollars at Walmart."

"Ping-Pong paddles it is." Levi swiped his hand down the side of his face. "I'll come twice a week like I always do, to finish the floor and work on the rest of the bathroom. I'll be kind to Ivy. Jesus said to be kind to everyone. At the very least, I should be a good disciple. I believe Gotte will honor our efforts and make all things work together for our good. For Winnie's good too."

"Maybe your kindness will convince her to sign the adoption papers and maybe it won't. But you're right, we should be kind for kindness' sake, and Gotte will turn it to our good."

"Okay then," Levi said. "We have a strategy."

Esther huffed out a breath. "I don't know if kindness is a strategy, but I know it's the best policy."

"*Nae.* Honesty is the best policy."

Esther made a face at him. "Whatever."

He reached out and pulled the tiny stocking from behind her ear. "Did you misplace this while doing laundry?"

Grinning sheepishly, she snatched it from his hand and scrunched it in her fist. "Winnie has suddenly decided she hates getting her diaper changed. She won't stay still, and I have to sling my leg over her stomach so she won't roll over. She lost a stocking when she was trying to kick free. I just tucked it over my ear for safekeeping and forgot to put it back on her foot after I changed her."

He winked at her. "You never know when you are going to need a stocking."

"You can collect interesting pebbles in it. Or keep one ear warm."

Levi nodded teasingly. "Very practical."

Esther relaxed her fist and gazed at the sock. "It wonders me if Winnie's foot is cold."

"*Nae.* It's July. Her other foot is probably too hot."

Esther smiled at him. "Who really knows with babies?" She slipped the stocking into her apron pocket, pulled a small sprig of evergreen from the misused bush, and tucked it behind her ear. It looked very nice there. Whether it was a stocking or a piece of greenery, Esther was by far the prettiest girl in Colorado. After making sure the evergreen sprig was in place, she squared her shoulders. "Okay then, enough lollygagging. Let's get in there before Ivy sets the house on fire."

Chapter Ten

Levi's laughter carried down the hall and into the kitchen, where Esther was cleaning up supper dishes. Esther had never felt so unwanted or so unnecessary in her entire life, which was a silly sentiment, since she was obviously very necessary to Winnie. Winnie needed her. Maybe Winnie even loved her. She most certainly loved Winnie, even if Winnie's own mother didn't.

More laughter. Ivy and Levi must really be enjoying themselves. Esther growled and tried to block out the sound by running water into the sink. Lots and lots of water. Ivy had dirtied just about every pan and dish in the house in an attempt to make Levi spaghetti for lunch. Of course, Esther was left to clean the kitchen, because Ivy couldn't be troubled to clean up her mess, not when Levi needed her help so desperately in the bathroom.

Winnie was down for her afternoon nap, and Ivy and Levi were working on the bathroom plumbing.

Ach, *vell*, Levi was working on the plumbing. Ivy was working on Levi.

Three weeks ago, Esther had finished grouting the tile, and now Levi was working on the plumbing for the toilet, sink, and tub. It was truly something Esther couldn't master with a few short lessons, so Levi had taken over the bathroom remodel. That's when Ivy had pounced. As she had told Esther, with her one good arm she certainly couldn't be expected to take care of the baby or do much of anything else around the house, but she could hand Levi tools or get him drinks of water or flirt with him while he installed a new showerhead. And since there really wasn't enough room in the bathroom for Esther, Winnie, *and* Ivy, Ivy had sort of crowded Esther out and banished her and Winnie to other parts of the house. Ivy was tricky, and it seemed foolish for Esther to insist that Ivy let her be in the bathroom too, even if she missed spending time with Levi, even if Ivy was doing her best to make Levi fall in love with her.

Esther was truly happy that Ivy had neither the ability nor the desire to take care of Winnie. There was less risk of Ivy becoming attached to her own daughter if she ignored her.

Nae, Esther didn't mind Ivy's neglect at all.

But Esther missed spending time with Levi, and it stung just a little that Levi seemed to be enjoying Ivy's company, maybe even more than he had ever enjoyed Esther's. The plan was to be nice to Ivy, not fall in love with her. Maybe Esther had been fooling herself all along. Maybe Levi hadn't really enjoyed the time they had spent together. Maybe he had tried to be nice to Esther too, when all he had really wanted to do was finish the bathroom and be done with her.

Esther plunged her hands into the water and got her sleeves wet up to the elbows. She was quite irritated with herself for being envious of Ivy. She knew what Ivy was like.

Ivy liked to flirt, and the boys had always been fascinated with her. Menno had been so fascinated he'd ruined any chance he had with Esther just for a few of Ivy's kisses. Her fiancé had certainly made Esther feel like a mess of pottage that day. Esther understood Ivy's tricks. It was irritating that Ivy still had the power to unsettle her so.

Esther took a deep breath and rolled up her sleeves. What did Esther care if Levi preferred Ivy? Esther had resigned herself to the fact that Levi was going to Ohio to find a *fraa*. He wasn't interested in Esther. It shouldn't matter, but somehow it mattered very much.

A hitch in Esther's breath betrayed her. She cared about Levi. He didn't scold her for throwing apricots at the house or stabbing seam rippers into doorjambs. He taught her how to lay tile, and he played with Winnie and changed diapers and gave Esther rides to the library. The only reason she hadn't let herself love him was because he could never love her, and he'd made that perfectly clear. She was too old, every girl in Byler wanted to marry him, he was going to Ohio, end of story.

Once she had finished the dishes, Esther couldn't bring herself to tend the garden and leave Levi and Ivy alone in the house together, so she puttered around the kitchen, wiping counters that were already clean and rearranging food in the fridge just to have something to do. Then she started washing windows. She really should work on her latest quilt, but she didn't have the heart to even look at it. It was a baby quilt for one of Rita's online customers, blue and white and black with an elephant blowing bubbles in the bottom left-hand corner. Every time Esther worked on the quilt, she thought of how badly her heart ached for Winnie. And maybe, maybe just a tiny little bit for Levi.

Ach. What a fool she was.

As she reached up to wipe a window in the front room, her hand bumped the curtain rod, and the valance and rod tumbled to the ground, sending a cloud of dust into the air and knocking her on the head. She gasped and pressed her fingers to her forehead. It didn't feel like it was bleeding, but she was going to have a nasty goose egg. She scooped up the valance, pulled it off the rod, and ripped one of the panels in half with all the fury of her pent-up frustration. She picked up another panel and ripped it in half as well. The drab green fabric made a satisfying tearing sound. The valances had come with the house, and she had never liked them. They were covered with dust, and she'd never cleaned them, because before Winnie came into her life, she had been planning to replace them. Now was as good a time as any to get rid of them.

"Is everything okay?" Levi stood in the front hall, eyeing her with concern and maybe a touch of amusement. Ivy stood right behind him, looking for all the world like a concerned sister.

Esther snatched at a cobweb dangling from her *kapp.* "Just doing some redecorating."

Any amusement Levi might have been feeling vanished as his gaze flicked to her forehead. "*Ach.* You hurt your head." He was by her side in a single heartbeat.

"The rod fell on it."

He brushed his thumb lightly over the injured spot. She winced. "Do you feel dizzy?" he said.

"*Nae.* I'm fine. I was just cleaning the window and got careless." And lost her temper.

"You're going to have an impressive goose egg." He turned to Ivy. "Can you get a towel with some ice?"

Ivy shrugged. "I really can't. I only have one good arm."

Whatever was Ivy to do when her collarbone got better? She certainly wouldn't have an excuse for laziness anymore. "I don't need ice," Esther said. "It's just a little bump." Levi grabbed Esther's arm and pulled her into the kitchen. "*Cum.* Sit here. Ice will stop it from swelling and eating your brain."

She cocked her eyebrow. "Do you really think there's any danger of that?"

"Can't be too careful." He pulled a towel from the drawer and got a few cubes of ice from the freezer. After twisting the towel around itself, he handed it to her. "I've always hated those curtains," he said, giving her a half-hearted smile.

"Me too. I just couldn't stand it anymore. They had to go." She laid the towel against her forehead. It was too cold to feel good, but it felt good to think maybe Levi cared a little.

Ivy snorted. "The whole house is an interior designer's nightmare."

Levi studied Esther's face with a question in his eyes. "Are you sure you're okay?"

She looked down, because she didn't want him to get any answers from her face. "How is the bathroom coming along?"

"I'm ready to put in the toilet, and I wondered if you'd like to help."

Esther pulled the towel from her head. "Really? I'd love to." She cleared her throat and tried to wipe the smile from her face. She was going to be an old maid for at least fifty more years. She'd need to know how to install a toilet someday. That was the only reason to get excited about it.

"You don't need Esther," Ivy said. "I know what most of the tools are, and I like to think I've been a great help to you already."

Levi gave Ivy a very attractive smile that made Esther's head hurt. "You have been a great help, but I promised Esther I'd teach her how to install a toilet, and I'm going to need two extra hands and you only have one."

Ivy stuck out her bottom lip. "I want to be of use to you in any way I can."

That smile again. *Ach.* Esther's head felt worse when Levi smiled like that. "You've been a great help. I couldn't have installed that showerhead without all the tools you handed me."

How many tools did it take to install a showerhead? And just how indispensable did Levi think Ivy was?

Mollified, Ivy laid a hand on Levi's shoulder. "I'll tell you what. I'll make us all some lemonade, and we can sit outside in the shade and drink it after you put in the toilet."

"That's a wonderful *gute* idea," Levi said.

Well. Not really. Ivy would probably make another huge mess in the kitchen and leave it for Esther to clean up. But if she made lemonade, she'd at least be out of their hair, hopefully for long enough to get the toilet in without having to work around Ivy.

Esther glanced at the clock. Winnie wouldn't sleep more than another half hour. They'd better get to that toilet. She stood and set her towel of ice in the sink. "Okay. I'm ready for the toilet."

Levi nodded and headed down the hall. "Let's go do it."

"Have fun," Ivy said, with that sarcastic edge to her voice that she used when she wanted to make it very clear how important she was and how *dumm* she thought you were.

Levi didn't seem to notice her tone, or perhaps he chose to ignore it. He turned and winked at Esther. "*Ach*, we will have fun. I love watching Esther do the work."

Esther's heart skittered around her chest like a skater bug on the water. Maybe Levi didn't mind her company so much.

And maybe she shouldn't get her hopes up.

Levi picked up the toilet that had been sitting in the back hall and carried it into the bathroom. He smiled at Esther as if she was part of his close circle of friends and family. As if she mattered. "It seems a shame to put anything on this beautiful floor, even the toilet."

"*Ach*, I'm very pleased with how it came out."

"Maybe you should come with me into people's homes and design their bathroom floors. I bet I'd get more business that way. Maybe I should put that on our flyers. *Let the quilting lady design your bathroom.*"

Esther laughed. "It wonders me if that would kill your business."

"People would love it." He reached into the tub and pulled out a large brown ring. He looked at her sideways. "Do you know what this is?"

"I think so. Isn't it the wax that goes around the bottom of the toilet, like a seal?"

Levi grinned. "I've never met anyone as smart as you are." He lowered his voice. "I miss watching you work on the bathroom while I play with Winnie."

Esther's stomach fluttered. "You'll do anything to get out of work."

He laughed. "I like that you have an opinion and that

you think things through before forming that opinion. I like that you are willing to learn anything. I even like it when you set me straight."

"Somebody has to."

"Nobody actually sets me straight but you."

"So you're saying I'm the only one rude enough to tell you how I really feel?"

He shook his head. "You're the only one who thinks I need to be set straight. Everyone else adores me."

Esther sighed dramatically. "None are so empty as those who are full of themselves. I've single-handedly taken on the task of making sure you don't get a big head. You should be grateful."

His eyes flashed with amusement. "Oh, I am."

Levi talked her through all the steps to installing a toilet. Some of them she could do herself, like setting the wax ring in place. Other things Levi had to do, like lifting the toilet onto the anchor bolts and reattaching the tank to the water supply. But when they were done, Esther felt like she could maybe do it by herself the next time, even the lifting.

Just as Levi was wiping the floor around the toilet, Ivy appeared in the doorway holding a pitcher of lemonade. "Um, Esther, I think I heard Winnie fussing. Can you get her? I can't pick her up with one arm."

Esther bit down on the inside of her mouth and tried very hard for the hundredth time not to panic. For the last three weeks, Ivy had been acting as if she were the one in charge of Winnie, but only when Levi was around. When Levi wasn't there, Ivy, thankfully, ignored Winnie as always, but the minute Levi walked in the door, Ivy fussed over Winnie, pretended to love her, and gave Esther instructions about Winnie's care, as if Ivy knew better than Esther how to be a mother. And maybe she did. Maybe just the process of giving birth made Ivy a better mother than Esther. That thought made Esther's heart hurt. Would Winnie be better off with her natural mother?

But another part of Esther, the part of her with a bad temper, just got angry. How dare Ivy abandon her child, then come back three months later and think there wouldn't be consequences? Esther had been the one to get up with Winnie every night. She'd cleaned her spit-up and changed her messy diapers. She'd nursed her through chicken pox and colic, bathed and fed her. Had done her best to give Winnie a *gute* home and as much love as any baby could ever want. Ivy had no right . . .

Esther clenched her teeth. Ivy had every right. And Ivy wasn't stupid. She saw how much Levi doted on that baby, and she knew that if she wanted to make a *gute* impression on Levi, she had to make him believe she cared about Winnie. Not only that she cared about Winnie, but that she would be a *gute mater* to as many children as Levi wanted to have. It was a horrible way to try to get someone to fall in love with you, but Ivy certainly didn't look at it that way. She wanted a husband. She needed a *gute*, stable man. She knew what she had to do and who she had to be.

"I'll get her," Levi said. "It always makes me feel good that she's so happy to see me."

"Oh, she loves you, Levi," Ivy gushed. "You're a natural father. Winnie can tell."

Levi walked out of the bathroom, and Esther glanced at Ivy. "How many more children do you want?"

Ivy gave Esther a flippant grin. "You know I don't want

any more. Labor was the worst experience of my life. But Levi doesn't have to know that until after the wedding."

"That's dishonest, Ivy."

Ivy swatted away Esther's concerns. "Whatever. He never has to know anyway. He'll be so happy married to me, he won't care about more children."

Esther chose her words carefully and ignored the throbbing ache in the middle of her chest. "I don't think most men are keen on raising another man's child. If you truly want him to consider marrying you, maybe you should leave Winnie with me. Tell Levi you want a fresh start. That might make him more likely to want you."

Ivy thought about it for half a second. "It's easy to see that Levi loves Winnie. She's more of an attraction than a difficulty." *Jah.* Ivy wasn't stupid. She'd obviously thought it through. But no matter what Ivy said, Winnie would become a difficulty the day after Ivy was married. Esther had to get Ivy to sign those adoption papers. But now it seemed harder than ever.

Ivy and Esther met Levi and Winnie in the kitchen. As expected, the kitchen was a mess and Ivy unapologetic. Levi smoothed his hand down Winnie's downy-soft hair. Ivy had noticed what Esther already knew. Levi looked so natural and so content with Winnie in his arms. "Her diaper is changed, and she's ready for an afternoon snack."

Ivy bloomed into a smile. "Esther, why don't you get Winnie a snack while Levi and I go outside and drink our lemonade?"

"Let's all go together so Esther doesn't have to be alone," Levi said. "We can let Winnie crawl around on a blanket."

Esther could have kissed him just for being so thoughtful. She nearly laughed at the look on Ivy's face. Ivy was obviously torn between showing Levi how nice she was to her sister and getting her way. "Nice" Ivy won out. She probably figured she could work on getting her way after the wedding. "Okay, I guess," she said. "But Winnie isn't going to stay on the blanket. And I don't have enough arms to keep her still. She might try to eat an ant or something."

"Ants are *gute* protein," Levi said, giving Ivy his best smile.

Even Ivy couldn't resist that. "Don't even think about teasing me, Levi Kiem. If my baby gets sick eating an ant, I'm blaming you."

Esther bristled when Ivy called Winnie "my baby." She would need to grow a thicker skin, or she would be a mess of nerves and anxiety within the month. Winnie was Ivy's baby. No amount of praying or crying or wishing would ever change that. But Esther didn't know how much longer she could bear the roller coaster of emotions Ivy put her through every day.

Should she tell Levi to stay away after all? His being here just made things that much more complicated and uncertain.

Levi carried Winnie, Ivy carried the lemonade, and Esther carried everything else outside. "Your tomatoes look wonderful *gute*," Levi said, inclining his head toward Esther's little garden plot just over the fence on the far side of the apricot tree.

"*Denki*. The tomatoes did well this year. Nanna and Hannah are going to come over next week and help me can spaghetti sauce."

"I want to help," Ivy said. "We used to can all sorts of things when we were growing up."

The offer was more for Levi's benefit than anything

else. Ivy volunteered for things to impress Levi, but when canning time actually came around, she wouldn't do more than watch the pot boil. And that was okay. The spaghetti sauce would taste better if Ivy didn't help.

Esther spread the blanket under the shade of the apricot tree. They sat down, and Ivy poured lemonade for everyone. Levi took a taste. "This is delicious, Ivy. Just the perfect amount of tart." He gave Winnie a little sip, and she shuddered and made a face that had them all laughing. "It's probably a little too sour for a nine-month-old," Levi said. He glanced at Ivy. "How old is Winnie? I don't even know when her birthday is?"

Ivy looked up as if counting the days in her head. "She was born on December first, so that makes her almost nine months. Eight months and three weeks."

"December first," Levi said. "That's an easy date to remember. Does she have a birth certificate?"

Levi was a genius. A birth certificate would make the adoption process easier, and Levi had just sneaked it into the conversation without blinking an eye or, hopefully, making Ivy suspicious.

Ivy set her glass down and leaned back on her good hand. "They had me fill out a paper at the hospital, but I don't think I ever got a certificate."

"What hospital?" Levi said.

"MercyOne in Des Moines," Ivy said.

Now they had a place. The attorney said if they knew what state Winnie was born in, they might be able to request a birth certificate. This was getting better and better.

Levi was more devious than Esther could have guessed. "Does Winnie have a middle name?"

"Dinah," Ivy said. She cleared her throat and glanced at Esther.

"Oh, Ivy," Esther said. "That's very—"

Ivy tossed her head back as if she didn't care to hear Esther's opinion. "Dumb? Sentimental? Pitiful? After how she treated me, you'd think she'd be the last person I'd name my daughter after."

Esther drew her brows together. "How Mamm treated you? Ivy, Mamm adored you. She would have done anything for you."

Ivy blinked away some moisture from her eyes. "She died without telling me."

Levi reached out and patted Ivy's hand. "It caught you by surprise. That must have been hard."

Ivy sniffed back the tears. "How was I supposed to know? I was in Florida with Alan, working two jobs just to get by. Esther called me six months after it happened. Six months!" She pitched her voice lower, as if trying to mock Esther's voice. "Like, 'Oh, Mamm is dying. I guess maybe I'll get around to calling Ivy sometime after the funeral.'"

Esther was tired of biting her tongue, and Ivy's accusations were completely irrational. "That's not fair. We had no idea where you were."

Ivy wrapped her arms around her waist. "You could have tried harder to find me. And Dat didn't care one little bit."

This was too much. Was there anything Ivy didn't blame Esther for? "You have no idea how hard we tried. You left us, Ivy. We didn't know if you were dead or alive. Can you even imagine what that did to Mamm? She cried almost every day for a whole year after you left, and you couldn't even be bothered to send us a message. You broke Mamm's heart. She died of sadness. Don't blame that on me."

Ivy erupted like a geyser. "Oh, Esther, always so self-righteous. *You* stuck by Mamm and Dat like a faithful dog. *You* never would have broken their hearts. *You* were the good daughter. Believe me, I'm fully aware of who my parents loved best. I heard it every day of my life. Well, let me tell you, sister, I got sick of it. Sick of being the disappointment, sick of trying to earn my parents' love. Sick of never being good enough. I had to get out." She stood up, overturning the pitcher with her knee and sending a river of lemonade washing over Winnie's lap.

Winnie burst into tears at the shock of cold lemonade on her legs. Ivy didn't even care. She turned on her heels and marched across the lawn and into the house, slamming the door behind her.

Levi picked up Winnie and did his best to comfort her, even though she was soaking wet and his shirt was soon soaked as well. "That wasn't a very nice thing to say, Esther."

Esther drew back. "What?"

"I don't wonder but Ivy tortures herself every day for leaving and not being there for your *mamm*."

Esther's pulse raced. It was too much. Levi was supposed to be on her side, not defending Ivy. "What do you know about it? What do you know about the pain and heartache she caused our family?"

He patted Winnie on the back. "I don't know hardly anything, I truly don't. But I know that thinking she was the cause of your *mater*'s death is very painful to Ivy. Don't you see how much it hurts her?"

He said it kindly, but his words felt like a slap across

the face. "She called me a dog and accused me of being self-righteous."

"I know, and she shouldn't have said those things, but Ivy is your sister, and she is very fragile right now. She doesn't know any better, because she's been doing only one thing for the last eight years: trying to survive."

How dare he stick his nose in where it wasn't wanted? "Mamm used to make excuses for Ivy by saying she was fragile. But the excuses only made Ivy weak."

"*Jah.* Can't you see how broken she is?"

"She should still be able to behave herself and maybe show a little remorse for everything she's put me through." Esther didn't need to stand here and take a scolding from Levi Kiem. She snatched Winnie out of his arms and fled in the direction of the house.

"I'm sorry, Esther. I didn't mean to hurt your feelings. Don't be mad at me forever."

She didn't even look back. "Go stick your head in the toilet."

"Your new one?" he called.

She didn't pause. She didn't stop. She didn't even crack a smile. Let some other lovesick girl laugh at his jokes today. "Go home, Levi."

She went into the house and slammed the door, harder than Ivy had, just so Levi would know who was more upset.

The door to Ivy's room was closed. Esther took Winnie into the room they now shared and locked the door behind her. She'd installed the lock not four days ago when she woke up in the middle of the night for no reason, terrified that Ivy was going to sneak in and steal the baby. Maybe Levi needed to remember what kind of person Ivy really was. Maybe he needed to remember that Ivy ran away from home, got pregnant, then abandoned her baby. She should refresh his memory about the hour spent in the library waiting for a call that Ivy couldn't be bothered to make or the diapers Ivy refused to change or the baby Ivy chose to ignore.

If he was so enchanted with Ivy, he should marry her and see how long that lasted. After Ivy ran away with some truck driver, Esther could go to his house and say "I told you so" and "Who's broken now?"

That spiteful thought gave Esther no pleasure. She didn't want Levi to marry Ivy. She didn't want to tell anyone "I told you so." She just wanted Ivy to go away, leave Winnie behind, and keep her greedy little hands off Levi, even if Esther was ferociously mad at him. Even if she would never, ever forgive him in a hundred years. Even if he was already in love with Ivy.

Esther sat down on the bed and pulled soggy Winnie against her chest. *Ach.* She wished she'd never met Levi. She had been happy enough before he came into her life, but now her pleasant, boring, predictable existence was ruined forever. She was completely miserable, and all because she had finally admitted to herself that she was outrageously, wildly, impossibly in love with Levi Kiem.

And he didn't love her. After that miserable conversation under the apricot tree, she realized he probably didn't even like her. He thought she was mean and petty and, apparently, blind to how broken Ivy was. It had been the same way with her parents. They had always made excuses for her. "Ivy has a weak constitution. We have to take extra *gute* care of her. Ivy isn't as sure of herself as you are, Esther. We need to be kind and make allowances for her bad behavior. Ivy just wants to be loved. That's why she kissed your fiancé."

If she hadn't been so miserable, Esther would have laughed at the unfairness of it all. Ivy was the mean one, the insensitive one. Ivy had tried to steal Esther's fiancé, left the family, and abandoned her baby, but Esther was the one who got the lecture about being nice to her sister. Levi had taken her sister's side, admonished Esther for perfectly justified feelings, and made her feel like a horrible person. Was he in love with Ivy? Or just disinterested in Esther? Or both?

Once and for all, Ivy had spoiled Esther's hopes of finding love. And if she lost Winnie, Esther would never be happy again.

With one hand, she spread a blanket on the floor and laid Winnie on it. She took off Winnie's wet stockings and clothes and changed her diaper, then wiped Winnie down with three baby wipes to remove all traces of sticky lemonade. Winnie tried to wiggle away as Esther dressed her in clean clothes. She handed Winnie a plastic tablespoon she left in her bedroom for times like this when she needed to keep Winnie occupied. While Winnie quietly chewed on the tablespoon, Esther slipped stockings onto her feet. In the stillness, she heard Ivy quietly crying in her room.

Esther picked up Winnie and kissed her petal-soft cheek. Winnie needed her. She needed Winnie. It was nice to be needed. Esther pressed her lips together and hugged Winnie tighter. She didn't need Ivy, and she certainly didn't need Levi. At least, it was easier to tell herself that than to feel all this hurt.

Esther did her very, very, very best to put Levi from

her mind. If he loved Ivy, there was nothing Esther could do about it but make herself miserable. The things that made her miserable would have to be dealt with one at a time. Right now, she only had enough misery to spend on Ivy. Feeling heartbreak over Levi would have to wait.

Esther heard the back door open and close, and a herd of butterflies came to life in her stomach. Levi had come in the house. Holding her breath, she listened as he placed the lemonade pitcher on the table and walked toward Esther's bedroom. Did he want to apologize? Did he want to make sure her feelings weren't hurt?

He had hurt her feelings, but she'd smile and reassure him that she wasn't really mad. She'd told him to stick his head in the toilet, so it was quite generous of him to come check on her.

His footsteps passed the door to her room and went farther down the hall. He knocked on a door, but it wasn't Esther's. "Ivy," he said softly. "Are you okay?"

Chapter Eleven

Ivy strolled out of her bedroom and preened like a rooster. "How do I look?"

Esther's heart sank. She sort of wished she had sewn Ivy's new dress out of some drab brown fabric instead of the brilliant royal blue that brought out the intensity of Ivy's eyes. But Ivy had been very enthusiastic about the blue, and Esther had wanted to make her happy, though why she even wanted to try was a mystery. What could she have done? Besides, even though brown was a dull color, Ivy's complexion looked as silky as peaches and cream in brown. Unless she put a paper bag over her head and wore a flour sack, Ivy couldn't help but draw plenty of attention to herself. And a flour sack would also draw attention, in its strangeness. It really didn't matter what Ivy wore. "You look very pretty," Esther said. She always tried to speak the truth.

Ivy let out a little squeak of delight. "I know. It's the perfect shade, and Levi's favorite color is blue."

"He's bound to like it, then."

Ivy made a little turn in the hall. "I'm glad I finally have my own dresses. I was getting so tired of yours. And they're too short for me. Levi doesn't like dresses too short."

"He told you that?"

"*Nae*, but he's a faithful, pious Amish man. I've known enough of them to have a good idea what they want. I think Levi is already in love with me."

Esther was sick of hearing about Ivy's hopes for a future life with Levi. She was sick of Ivy's insincerity, sick of Ivy's ideas about romance, and sick of that smug look Ivy gave her whenever she talked about marrying Levi. Ivy was so satisfied with herself that she had complete confidence Levi would propose to her, and she'd only known him a few weeks.

"I've told you, Ivy. Levi is going to Ohio in October to find a *fraa*. He's not interested in you or anyone else in Byler."

This didn't seem to bother Ivy. "He might have told you that story about going to Ohio, but he hasn't mentioned it to me once. Could it be he isn't interested in you and wanted to discourage you from falling in love with him? You do sort of act like a lovesick poodle when he's around. Don't think I haven't noticed."

What was it about Esther that made Ivy compare her to a dog? Esther didn't want to let Ivy's words affect her, but they did anyway, especially since Levi had told her about going to Ohio the same day he had accused her of being interested in him. He had been trying to discourage her when he mentioned that trip, but he didn't seem inclined to discourage Ivy. Besides, he'd made his preference very clear on Friday afternoon when he'd come in the house to comfort Ivy instead of Esther. Esther couldn't have felt worse if the house had fallen down over her head. "Levi and I are just friends, and I'm very grateful to him for teaching me how to tile and grout." Truer words had never felt so painful. *Just friends.* She and Levi were just friends. And seriously, she didn't even know if that was accurate anymore. Levi thought she was mean and insensitive. Maybe he'd never speak to her again.

Ivy felt she had to make her own way in the world. It had probably been that way for eight years. Esther had underestimated Ivy. If Ivy was good at anything, it was attracting men. She could be demure and simpering, agreeable and alluring. She could make herself into anything a man wanted and seem completely sincere doing it. The worst, most heartbreaking part of all was that Levi seemed to be falling for it. Esther didn't know if she should warn him or stay out of it. A little voice in the back of her mind scolded her for being jealous. How could she begrudge her sister a small measure of happiness after all she'd been through?

Ivy talked and talked and talked, as if Esther was as excited as she was about Levi taking her to her first gathering. Esther couldn't share in her enthusiasm, though she tried for a pleasant expression.

"If Levi had any doubts before tonight, they'll be gone when he sees me in this dress," Ivy said. "What do you think, Esther? If he wasn't interested in me, do you think he would have asked me to a gathering?"

Did Ivy truly want her opinion, or was she just rubbing in the fact that Levi had never taken Esther to a gathering? Esther was trying very hard to think well of her sister, but Ivy had always taken a great deal of pleasure in Esther's unhappiness. Of course Ivy didn't want her opinion. Or maybe she did, because for sure and certain his taking Ivy to a gathering meant Levi was interested. But Esther kept her mouth shut. She wouldn't give Ivy the satisfaction.

"I wish I could wear my skin-tight jeans and my hoop earrings, but as far as Amish fashion goes, this is the best I can hope for."

Ivy didn't want to be Amish. She might be able to catch an Amish husband, but she wouldn't be content for long. *Ach*, the heartache Ivy had caused and the heartache she had yet to cause were terrible. Esther turned her back on Ivy and went into the kitchen, where she'd left Winnie in her high chair eating macaroni and cheese. She drew a sharp breath. Winnie had somehow managed to crawl out of her seat, and she was perched precariously on the tray, her knees and hands thick with smashed macaroni. Esther ran to the high chair and picked up Winnie before she fell and cracked her head open. "*Ach*, Winnie. What a mess you've made." She held Winnie at arm's length so Winnie wouldn't smear macaroni and cheese down the front of Esther's black bertha. There was nothing to do but give the little mischief maker a bath—and strap Winnie in at the next feeding time.

Esther called down the hall, "Ivy, I'm going to give Winnie a bath." She took a deep breath. Would it hurt to be charitable? "Have a *gute* time."

That was as far as her charity extended. Esther certainly didn't need to stand at the door and wave goodbye when Levi picked up Ivy. Ivy was perfectly capable of seeing herself out without any fanfare from Esther.

She took Winnie into the bathroom and ran the water while she got Winnie undressed. She had bought a new cooking thermometer specifically for the bathroom so she didn't have to retrieve the one from the kitchen every time she gave Winnie a bath, which was turning out to be two or three times a day, with all the messes Winnie got into. Of course, mealtime was always a messy event, but when she wasn't napping, Winnie crawled around the house all day long. Her knees were always filthy and her hands collected dirt in all the creases.

After double-checking the water temperature, Esther took Winnie's diaper off and set her in the tub. Winnie loved bath time, and Esther was more than happy to let her splash until Ivy was safely on her way. The less Esther saw of Ivy and Levi together, the easier it would be to pretend that nothing had changed.

She hadn't talked to Levi since that day under the apricot tree when he had scolded her for her feelings about Ivy. She hadn't heard what he'd said when he'd knocked on Ivy's door that day, and she probably didn't want to know, but the conversation hadn't lasted long, and he'd left without even a "boo" in Esther's direction. Immediately after he had left, Ivy had knocked on Esther's door with the exciting news that Levi had invited her to the next gathering and could Esther please make her a new dress? *Oh, Esther, it's so exciting, and I forgive you for everything.*

Getting a new dress was more important to Ivy than holding a grudge, or apparently more important than being upset about Mamm.

At least temporarily.

"What are you doing?" Esther jumped out of her skin as Nanna came storming into the bathroom as if she were chasing the cows out of her vegetable garden.

"I . . . um . . . I'm bathing Winnie." Esther furrowed her brows. "What are you doing?"

"I'm here to babysit, of course. Levi told you six o'clock, didn't he? And you're not even ready."

"Nanna, what are you talking about? Levi told me no such thing."

Nanna set the bag of fabric scraps she always carried with her on the bathroom counter and rolled up her sleeves. "Well, get going. I'll finish the bath."

"But . . ."

"You need to hurry. Levi and Caleb and about five of *die youngie* are waiting for you."

"Waiting for me? But why? Levi offered to drive Ivy to the gathering. Not me."

Nanna knelt down on the bath mat and crowded Esther out of the way. She snatched the washrag from Esther's hand. "That's not what Levi told me. He said last Friday he invited both you and Ivy to ride to the gathering with him. Why else would he ask me to babysit?" She frowned. "Unless he wanted to take you and leave Ivy here. I suppose he might have wanted me to babysit Ivy."

"That's just silly," Esther said.

"Not silly at all. I've met Ivy, and she needs constant supervision. You're doing her a great service, Esther."

Esther slumped her shoulders "Levi doesn't think so. He told me I wasn't being nice to Ivy."

"Ivy would be a trial to even the blessed martyrs. You're doing fine. And don't pay Levi any heed. He has a heart for the downtrodden and sometimes doesn't give the undowntrodden enough credit. Now go. It's rude to keep everyone waiting."

Esther's heart did a little jig. She was so happy that Levi had invited both of them, she wasn't even angry with

Ivy for leaving that little detail out. "But I'm too old. Women my age do not go to gatherings."

Nanna pressed her fingers and thumb together as if pinching Esther's mouth shut. "Not another word, or I'll make you Cathy's permanent pickleball partner."

Laughter burst from Esther's mouth. Cathy was truly a dear soul, but she was a wild pickleball player, frequently accidentally whacking her partner with her paddle or losing her shoe during a rally or screaming at the top of her lungs when she lost a point. "All right. Not another word, but do you mind babysitting? I mean, you have enough grandchildren of your own to babysit. You're probably sick of babysitting."

"I don't have near enough grandchildren. And you don't get out near enough." Nanna pushed at Esther's bottom until Esther felt inclined to stand up. "Hurry. They're waiting, and Ivy looks sufficiently irritated. You don't want to miss that."

Hmm. Nanna was right—she didn't want to miss Ivy's being irritated about Esther's coming. "Okay. *Denki* for babysitting. Winnie just finished her dinner. She can go down at—"

Nanna waved Esther away. "I know. I know. I raised six children of my own. I can handle it." Esther ran out of the bathroom. Nanna called her back. "You're going to change your dress, aren't you?"

Esther shook her head. "Winnie spit out her green beans on my blue one, Ivy stole my pink one, and I ripped the hem of my brown one."

Nanna shook her head. "You don't want the brown one anyway." She squinted at Esther as if that gave her a better perspective. "Someone is bound to fall in love with you no matter what you wear. You'll be fine."

Esther didn't know why, but she felt almost giddy. Her excitement couldn't be the thought of going to a gathering. She would really rather not. But Levi hadn't intentionally left her out, which meant that maybe he hadn't been offended when she'd told him to put his head in the toilet. Maybe he'd been amused. Maybe he could even forgive her.

And maybe he wasn't madly in love with Ivy yet.

Levi and Ivy stood on Esther's front stoop, waiting for Esther to come outside. It wasn't like her to be tardy, but Levi knew how to be patient, because Mammi was always late.

"Come on, Levi," Ivy whined. "Let's go. I told you, she's not coming."

Levi's mouth felt like a piece of burnt toast. Was Esther too mad at him to come? He glanced at Ivy. "Go jump in the wagon. I'll be right there."

Ivy pursed her lips. "But I want to sit by you."

"I have to drive." He pointed to his seventeen-year-old *bruder*. "And Caleb's sitting next to me. Just go get in the wagon. It will be fun."

Ivy tromped to the wagon, but instead of climbing into the back, she started talking to Caleb. Though Levi couldn't hear what she said, she was no doubt trying to talk Caleb into sitting in the wagon so she could sit next to Levi. Oy, anyhow, that girl was persistent. She wouldn't get very far with Caleb. He was young and easily led, but Levi had already told him that under no circumstances was Ivy to sit in the seat with Levi. Ivy had already made too many assumptions about her relationship with Levi. She had misinterpreted his kindness, and now it was obvious she was looking for a marriage proposal. *Ach*, Esther had warned him, and now Levi was going to have to let Ivy down gently. The problem was, he had no idea how to let her down, and he hated to make her so sad when she was so fragile, but he would rather wrestle a thousand gators than marry Ivy Zook. He'd rather be single. He'd rather eat dirt for breakfast, supper, and dinner than marry Ivy.

Levi peered into the front window but couldn't see Esther. Should he go in? Someone would come out, either Mammi or Esther. He'd wait. He knew how to be patient, but waiting was harder tonight, because he was desperate to talk to Esther. She'd been so angry with him on Friday, he hadn't known what to do but go home and give her a chance to cool down. He hoped she saw his invitation to the gathering as an olive branch instead of a punishment. She'd made it clear that she thought she was too old for gatherings, but hopefully she wouldn't mind coming. It would give them a chance to talk without Ivy looming within earshot. It would give him a chance to apologize for being a clumsy friend.

His heart jumped into his throat when Esther threw open the door. She stopped short when she saw Levi. Levi stopped short when he saw her. She was wearing her emerald green dress with her crisp white *kapp* on her head and flip-flops on her feet. The emerald green dress was Levi's favorite. The color made her eyes look as blue as the evening sky over a forest of maple trees.

"Oh," she said breathlessly. "*Hallo*, Levi."

Levi felt just as breathless and even more speechless. Five-months-ago Levi had been a fool. Esther was the prettiest, most appealing woman he had ever met. She wasn't old, and she wasn't boring, and she most certainly wasn't desperate for a husband.

She gave him a slight smile, as if she was unsure of him and unsure of herself. He hated that. She should never be unsure of him. "I'm sorry I'm late," she said. "I was giving Winnie a bath when Nanna came. I . . . I didn't know you had invited me to the gathering."

Levi frowned. "Didn't know? I asked Ivy to tell you."

"*Ach, vell.* It must have slipped her mind."

"I guess so," he said, shaking his head. They both knew nothing had slipped Ivy's mind, except maybe some human kindness.

She flinched as he reached out and pulled an orange noodle off her neck. He showed it to her, and she gave him a more genuine smile. "*Ach.* Winnie had mac and cheese for dinner. She's learned how to crawl out of her high chair. She almost fell out tonight."

"We'll have to watch her more carefully. Don't want her breaking her head."

"The high chair came with straps. I just never thought I'd need to use them."

He pointed to her ear. "Planning on doing some cutting at the gathering?"

She pulled a small pair of scissors from behind her ear. "I finished Ivy's dress right before you came."

"It's a wonderful pretty color."

Her smile faded. "It really accents her eyes."

"Your dress really brings out the blue in your eyes too."

With her fingers wrapped around the scissors, she

clasped her hands together in front of her. "*Denki,*" she said, as if she didn't believe him. "I suppose I should put the scissors in the house, but I don't know what Nanna will do if I go back in there."

"It's a little dangerous putting scissors behind your ear. What if you poked your eye out?"

Her lips twitched. "It hasn't happened yet."

Levi held out his hand. "Here. I'll put the scissors in my pocket. That way, you don't have to go back in the house, and if you need them at the gathering, you just have to say the word and I'll whip them out so fast, you won't believe your eyes."

Esther burst into a smile but then seemed to think better of laughing. "All right. But don't get any ideas about stealing my scissors. I'll expect them back at the end of the night."

"*Cum*, Levi," Caleb called. "Let's go."

Levi glanced at Esther. "You ready?"

Esther peered at the wagon full of young people. "How many girls did you ask to this gathering?"

"I just offered to give people rides. I didn't want any girl to think I'd singled her out."

Esther slumped her shoulders. "*Jah*, well. You don't have to worry about me. I know we're just friends."

Levi hated those words, "just friends." And tonight they tasted especially bitter. "Esther, that's not it at all. I was trying to cheer Ivy up, even though you're the one I really wanted to invite."

There was that slight, tentative smile again. "I prefer gator farms." She started toward the wagon.

"Me too, but we would have had to invite Ivy, and I like that the gator farm is just between us."

Esther lowered her eyes. "I like that too."

"This way, she never has to know about the gator farm, and she can get to know some of *die youngie*." And, Lord willing, lose interest in Levi. But then there was the danger of one of the other boys being pulled in by her beauty and making a huge mistake by marrying her. *Ach, vell*, he'd just have to trust that the boys here in Byler were smarter than that or that Ivy would truly have a change of heart and become the pious Amish woman she was pretending to be.

Ivy sat in the wagon next to Freeman and Sarah Sensenig. She pressed her lips together and eyed Esther resentfully. *Jah*, Levi was going to have to speak to Ivy plain and deflate her hopes gently. But the whole thing was tricky because of Winnie. If he made Ivy mad, she might just take Winnie and move to Iowa. If he wasn't forceful enough, she'd expect a marriage proposal by December.

Caleb sat up in the wagon seat, but before Esther could climb into the wagon, he jumped down and got in back. "Esther," he said. "You take the front with Levi. I've always liked riding in the back."

Ivy opened her mouth to protest, but Caleb nudged her arm and asked her a question that Levi couldn't hear, distracting her attention and leaving Esther free to climb onto the wagon seat beside Levi. Caleb noticed things and tried to be a *gute bruder*.

Esther looked a little bit surprised, but she climbed up into the seat next to Levi. She kept glancing back at Ivy, and every time she did, she unintentionally nudged her shoulder against Levi's. It wasn't a bad arrangement at all.

The gathering was held at a city park that was nothing

more than a little grass, some playground equipment, and a tiny pavilion. Since there weren't many young people, the pavilion was a sufficient size. Besides Caleb, Esther, and Ivy, Levi had brought five more of *die youngie* in the wagon. Four others joined them. Thirteen young people plus one of the ministers and his wife who had brought the eats—homemade root beer and pretzels. The minister had set up a volleyball net, and Freeman Sensenig and three girls started hitting the ball around.

Levi helped Esther down from the wagon, and the electricity when he touched her hand was palpable. She had soft hands and thin wrists and bright orange cheese smeared up her forearm. She smiled wryly, licked her finger, and rubbed the cheese off her arm. "If you see any more of that, will you warn me? It's a wonder I manage to put my shoes on the right feet every morning."

Levi chuckled. "But you sure smell *gute*. The boys will be hanging around you all night, and they won't even realize it's because you smell like melted cheese." Their eyes met and held, and Levi could have gotten lost in those blue pools of warmth.

Ivy cleared her throat loudly. She stood in the wagon with her hand outstretched. "I don't think I can get out myself with this bad arm."

Without another word, Esther strolled toward the pavilion. Levi wanted to chase after her, but it probably wouldn't be nice to leave Ivy stranded in the wagon like a beached whale. Levi took Ivy's hand and made himself a steady support while she climbed out of the wagon. "You should go play volleyball, Ivy. You'd like it."

Ivy made a sour face. "That's all they did at gatherings in Pennsylvania. And I can't play. I broke my collarbone."

In his eagerness to be rid of Ivy for a few minutes and be alone with Esther, he had forgotten that Ivy only had one good arm. "I'm sorry, Ivy. That was insensitive of me."

Ivy seemed to remember that she was trying to catch Levi, not drive him away. "It's okay. You've had enough things to think about with all the people you picked up for the gathering. I don't think I would have even been able to remember all those addresses."

He did have a lot to think about tonight, but it had nothing to do with *die youngie* or their addresses. Thoughts of Esther crowded out his brain, and he could think of little else. Levi pointed to the pavilion, where the Troyer sisters were arranging pretzels on a tray. "That's Lydia and Lily. They're in our district. They do piecework for a New York bootmaker."

"Sounds about as exciting as working at a potato processing plant."

From the sound of it, Ivy had some experience processing potatoes. "You should go meet them."

She studied his face. "Why?"

"Don't you want to make friends? That's why I wanted you to come to the gathering, to meet new people, get more involved in the district."

"I'm not really interested in meeting new people. You're the only person in Byler I care about. I was looking forward to just being with you tonight."

And Levi had been looking forward to not being with Ivy at all. "*Ach.* Well. The fun of a gathering is being with all the people. Andrew Beiler knows how to juggle, and Priscilla Mast has double-jointed elbows."

It seemed Ivy had quit listening to him altogether. "Oh,

look over there. Is it a river just over that rise in the ground?"

"Just a dry irrigation ditch."

She grabbed his hand. He pulled away, pretending he needed to adjust his hat. "I'll bet it's still pretty though. Let's go see."

"It's not pretty. It's just an old ditch."

"I want to see it. Won't you show it to me, Levi?"

Now was no time for that I'm-not-interested-in-you talk, but Ivy might plague him all night if he didn't say something now. But what to say? When he'd told Esther he wasn't interested, he'd said all the wrong things, most of which he sorely wished he could take back. Of course, he couldn't imagine wanting to take anything back from Ivy, except she'd be mad and he didn't want to hurt Esther's chances of getting Winnie. "I want you to meet all the boys in the *gmay* tonight because I'm not the right boy for you."

"How do you know that? We've only known each other for a few weeks."

Well, she was selfish and manipulative, she treated Esther very poorly, and she didn't seem to like Winnie very much, but Levi wasn't about to throw a list of her faults in her face. "I just know that we're not right for each other. You're a wonderful nice girl, but I really only want to be friends. My *fater* is sending me to Ohio to find a wife. There is nobody in Byler I have my eye on."

She frowned. "Hmm. Esther told me."

"Okay, then. You should go and enjoy yourself with the other young people. You might make some friends."

Ivy's lips curled into a sly smile. "I like you, Levi. You're sensible and careful and cautious. But you barely know me. You haven't seen all my good qualities yet. I'm not discouraged in the least."

Oy, anyhow. What was Levi supposed to do with that?

Caleb truly did try to be a *gute bruder*. He ran up to Ivy as if he had urgent news. "Ivy, come play croquet with Priscilla and Wayne and me. We need a fourth person, and you can play with one hand."

Ivy glanced at Levi and frowned. "The girl with the double-jointed arms?"

"Elbows," Levi corrected.

"I guess I can," Ivy said, "but what about Levi? I don't want him to be left out."

"Just come play," Caleb said, glancing at Levi. Levi would definitely owe Caleb a favor after this. "Levi can go eat pretzels or play volleyball. He knows how to entertain himself."

"I'm sure he does," Ivy said, "but I was planning on spending the gathering with him."

Caleb rolled his eyes. "Nobody does that. Besides, I know my brother better than anybody, and you'll get sick of him."

Ivy smiled at Levi. "Of course I won't get sick of him."

Caleb motioned to Priscilla, and she came running. She must have been in on the plan. She hooked her double-jointed elbow around Ivy's good arm and pulled her toward the game. "Come play croquet. Levi says you're fun."

Ivy couldn't very well refuse unless she wanted to yank her arm from Priscilla's grasp. That didn't seem very polite, even for Ivy. "Have fun," Levi said, not really caring if Ivy had fun, as long as she was gone for at least twenty minutes. He needed to talk to Esther.

Without turning his back on Ivy, he slowly moved

away, hoping Ivy wouldn't notice he was making a beeline for Esther. Ivy saw enough of Esther and Levi together to be suspicious of their relationship. Levi didn't want to make things worse.

When Ivy was securely engrossed in the rulebook with Caleb, Levi turned and walked quickly to the pavilion. Esther was eating a pretzel and talking to Lydia Troyer. A plastic knife was tucked behind her ear. You never knew when you were going to need a plastic knife to stab rude young men who tried to get too close.

Though Esther had never been to a gathering in Byler before, she knew most of *die youngie* from the *gmayna*. Lydia was only seventeen, and Esther did seem significantly older, but she didn't seem too old to be at a gathering. She fit right in.

Levi grabbed a pretzel from the plate. "*Hallo*, Lydia. *Vie gehts?*"

"*Ach*, nothing," Lydia said, blushing just a little. Lydia was sweet and nice, but she was way too young for Levi. He liked the maturity and sense that came with someone Esther's age. Lydia picked up the plate of pretzels and nudged it in Esther's direction. "Take another one, Esther. You didn't have any dinner."

Levi cocked an eyebrow. "You didn't have any dinner? Why not?"

"I fed Winnie while Ivy ate, then Nanna came barging in like a bull. I didn't even have time to breathe."

"Then take two," Levi said, smiling at Esther. "I'm taking you on a hike."

Her lips curled upward. "A hike? Right now?"

"It's not really a hike. There is an old irrigation ditch

just over there. It's a wonderful pretty place, and I want you to see it."

Esther studied his face as if she was trying to figure out how to tell him no. Then she shrugged. "Okay, Lydia. Give me two more pretzels. And put some of that cheese sauce on a plate. It's *appeditlich*."

Lydia giggled. "For sure and certain." She gave Esther two big scoops of cheese sauce. "Come back if you run out."

Levi took the cheese plate and grabbed a couple of napkins. Esther didn't need another cheese mishap. "This way," he said, steering Esther the long way around the croquet game and the keen eye of her sister. If Esther noticed how he tried to avoid detection, she didn't mention it.

They walked across the grass and over the rise in the ground to the bank of the irrigation ditch. It hadn't seen water for at least a month, and there were cobwebs and weed overgrowth on either side.

Esther tried to act polite. "*Ach*. Well. This is nice. *Denki* for showing me."

Levi laughed. "I know. It's not really a pretty sight, but there's a nice place to sit over there where no one will be able to see us."

She looked at him sideways. "You don't want anybody to see us? Are you planning on stealing my pretzels?"

"Maybe," he said. "Or maybe I haven't had a chance to really talk to you alone for weeks."

"We never get to talk alone. Winnie is always there."

"Winnie doesn't count. She doesn't even understand what we're saying."

Esther shook her head. "She understands all right. Just

because she doesn't talk doesn't mean she's not taking it all in and remembering it for later."

Levi led Esther to a flat patch of grass and motioned for her to sit down. "I don't mind if Winnie listens in on our conversations. Ivy is the real problem."

Esther's gaze flicked to his face. "You think Ivy's a problem?"

"You know I do."

"I know no such thing." She pressed her lips together and pretended to be very interested in something on the other side of the ditch. "I'm sorry I told you to go stick your head in the toilet. That was rude. And being angry is no excuse for being rude."

Levi chuckled. "No one has ever told me to stick my head in a toilet before. But then again, no one has tiled a bathroom for me while I watched. No one has stabbed her seam ripper into the doorjamb because of me. Every day is a new adventure with you. I never know what to expect, and I like it."

She drew her brows together. "You like it?"

"Before I met you, I had the most boring life in the whole world."

She seemed to soften like a stick of butter in a hot kitchen. "So did I." She took a bite of one of the pretzels. "I'm sorry that what I said about Ivy upset you. It's just . . . she's just so hard."

"You never have to apologize for how you feel about Ivy. She hurt you deeply, and she continues to hurt you every day, just by being here. I'm sorry I was harsh. I see how hard it is for you, but I know you can sort out any problem that comes your way. Think about how well you handled things when Ivy left Winnie."

Esther's face turned a light shade of pink. "*Ach*. I didn't handle it well at all."

"You did handle it well, no matter that you keep telling yourself otherwise. Ivy, on the other hand, can't handle anything. She depends completely on you. She has no money, no friends, no talents. There isn't one person in the world who truly wants her."

Esther looked down at her hands. "*Ach*. Not even her sister. I'm supposed to love her, and I can't even manage that. What a horrible person you must think I am."

Levi shook his head and heaved a loud and impatient sigh. "Esther, you are one of the kindest, most *wunderbarr* people I know. Ivy's choices are not your fault or your responsibility. She is now feeling the full force of the consequences of her choices over the years. Can you imagine what it must feel like to be completely unwanted, to think that nobody needs you or even cares that much, to suspect that if she leaves tomorrow, her own sister will rejoice instead of mourn?"

"It has to hurt something wonderful."

He slid closer and wrapped his fingers around hers. "She is so wretched that she thinks finding an Amish husband is her only choice." He curled his lips wryly. "She's dressing Amish and trying to learn how to cook. I'd say she's wonderful desperate."

Esther cracked a smile. "I'd say you're right." She narrowed her eyes and gave him the stink eye. "I hate it when you're right."

"Really? I love it when I'm right."

She laughed before growing more serious. "Ivy talked about finding a man almost from the first day she came to Byler, but I had no idea she would consider giving up the *Englisch* life for the Amish and the possibility of a steady husband and a secure income. It seems dire and extreme, but I can see it's how she is trying to navigate her stark circumstances. Ivy is a survivor. She'll do whatever she can to be in control."

"*Jah.* She will."

"I make her three meals a day, but she is still starving—starving for the affection I refuse to give her."

"Don't be hard on yourself. You've taken *gute* care of Ivy. Ivy can be hard to love."

A look of uneasiness traveled across her face. "Hard for some people. I've taken care of Ivy and Ivy's *dochter*, but I've also neglected her in ways that can't be measured or checked off some to-do list."

"Like I said, Ivy can be hard to love."

"You said something the other day that I pretended not to hear."

He cocked an eyebrow. "How much of what I say do you pretend not to hear?"

She pursed her lips to keep from smiling. "Most of it." She fingered the pretzel in her lap. "You said Ivy tortures herself every day for leaving us and bringing so much heartache to our *mater*. And now Mamm is gone, and Ivy can't apologize or try to make things better. She didn't even get a chance to say goodbye. I don't know, maybe Ivy blamed herself for Mamm's death. I laid too much at her feet when I told her Mamm died of a broken heart. Ivy thinks she killed our *mater*."

Levi nodded. "After a year or two of being gone, she might have felt she couldn't come back, knowing how deeply she hurt your parents. The guilt would have been very painful." He took off his hat and fingered the brim.

"She is desperate, but maybe there's a small part of her that truly wants to find her way back."

Esther frowned. "I haven't made it easy for her."

"None of this is your fault."

"It feels like it's all my fault. For sure and certain Ivy has made many mistakes, but Mamm and Dat loved her. I used to love her. She was once my best friend. Maybe I can learn to love her again too."

"Maybe you can. Deep down, I know Ivy has a *gute* heart."

Esther gave him a slight smile. "I feel sorry for her, which seems like a step in the right direction."

"It does." He stole one of Esther's pretzels and tore a piece off for himself. "I apologize for admonishing you the other day. I'd rather do anything than hurt your feelings. You have to put up with Ivy all the time. I'm just a visitor with an opinion. I shouldn't have shared it so freely. It wasn't kind."

"What you said stung my pride, but I needed to hear it. I will try my best to be more patient with Ivy and show her more love and less annoyance." Pain flashed in her eyes. "I'm still frightened I'll lose Winnie."

"Me too. But Gotte has not given us the spirit of fear."

"But of power and of love and of a sound mind," Esther said, finishing the scripture for him.

"You've got the power of your faith. You're working on loving Ivy. And you are a clear and deep thinker, when you're not mad at your pickleball paddles."

Esther laughed. "Oh, my poor paddles."

"Derr Herr will not forsake you." He wiped his hands on one of the napkins. "I feel bad for Ivy, but I hope you know I'm always on your side. I just did a bad job of showing it the other day."

She stood up and put some distance between them and looked across the ditch to the other bank. "So . . . I wanted to ask. Are you interested in Ivy?"

He shrugged. "Of course."

Esther flinched and turned her back to him.

"I'm very interested in her welfare. She's your *schwester* and one of Gotte's children."

Esther took a deep breath and slowly turned her head in his direction. "But . . . but do you like her?"

She acted as if the question made her upset. Or was it the answer she dreaded? Levi squeezed the napkin in his hand. Was she afraid he would abandon her to finish the bathroom herself if he found Ivy too irritating? Did she feel like she was imposing on him when she asked him to be nice to Ivy? She had always been very sensitive about imposing on him. That was why she had worked on the bathroom floor while he took care of Winnie. She had needed his help with Winnie, but hadn't wanted to take advantage of his good nature. She didn't need to worry about that. He was happy to help in any way he could, especially if it meant Ivy would go away and leave Winnie with Esther. That was the most important thing.

He would rather have Esther helping him in the bathroom, but the bathroom would be finished in a few more weeks. He didn't mind if Ivy wedged herself into his work. For the most part, Ivy was pleasant company, even though she was a clever manipulator. But Levi was in no danger of being deceived by her pretty blue eyes or her sudden interest in being Amish. "*Ach*, Esther. I like Ivy fine. She has many *gute* qualities. She's funny and tells entertaining stories, and I feel sorry for her. If I can make her life a little happier, I don't begrudge it at all."

"You don't?" she said, forcing the words out of her mouth as if they were stuck there.

"Don't worry about me. It's easier to say than it is to do, but try not to worry about anything. Derr Herr will provide."

"I suppose He will." She acted as if she was tired of looking at the ditch and very tired of talking to Levi. "I think I'll go play some volleyball. I haven't played volleyball for years, not since I was much younger."

"You're still young, Esther."

She glanced at him. "It depends on who you're asking." She trudged up over the rise of ground and back toward the pavilion.

Levi sat with his plate of cheese and stack of napkins puzzling out what had just happened. He had apologized for scolding Esther. She had accepted his apology but hadn't seemed thrilled about it. He was supposed to feel better, but all he felt was confused.

Maybe she still doubted him. To reassure her, he'd have to give Ivy more of his attention tonight, just to prove to Esther that he didn't mind spending time with her sister.

For sure and certain, that would make her feel better.

Chapter Twelve

Esther drizzled glaze on the hot orange rolls, and the heavenly smell made her heart hurt. Levi was going to love these.

"Esther, how do I know when the breakfast casserole is done?"

"When the timer rings, stick a knife in the center, and if it comes out clean, it's done."

Ivy huffed out a breath. "The knife never comes out clean. Can't you give me an exact time? I don't want to overbake it."

"You have to do a lot of cooking by feel," Esther said.

Ivy made a face. "By feel? But what if I'm not feeling it? What if this brunch is a complete failure?"

Esther probably should have tried to reassure Ivy that everything would be all right, but she didn't have the heart for it this morning. She had spent the better part of yesterday and this morning making rolls and breakfast casserole and fruit parfaits for a brunch she wasn't even invited to so Ivy could win the heart of the man Esther was in love with. Esther sincerely didn't care if anything turned out okay.

Ivy waved both hands in Esther's direction. "I wish you'd go. You're making me nervous." She'd quit wearing the sling this morning. She needed both hands to pull the casserole out of the oven, so the sling got thrown away. Esther certainly hoped Ivy wouldn't regret getting rid of it. "You keep sneaking bacon, and you've dripped glaze all over the table. You're supposed to be helping me, Esther, not making things worse."

Esther clenched her teeth and tried to remember how sorry she felt for Ivy. *Ivy tortures herself every day with thoughts that she killed our* mater. *She didn't get a chance to say goodbye. Ivy is very fragile right now.* Esther's teeth would crack in her mouth before she mustered any pity for Ivy today. It was well-nigh impossible to have *gute* feelings for the person who had inflicted so much pain on Esther these last few weeks. It was bad enough the way she flirted with Levi and how Levi seemed to enjoy it, but every time Levi went home for the day, Ivy would dance around the house and gush about how *wunderbarr* it would be when she got married and how it was too bad that Esther would never have a husband.

Worse yet, Levi seemed to have quit resisting Ivy's charms. He laughed and joked with her and shared funny stories and always stayed for lunch with the three of them and seemed very pleased to share Ivy's company. Esther had thought Levi knew better than to let Ivy into his heart, but apparently he'd gotten over whatever resistance he had felt early on. Esther wanted to cry.

Instead of crying, Esther set one orange roll on each plate, then put the rest in a cute little roll basket on the table.

Ivy peered into the oven anxiously and glanced at Esther. "Is your ride here yet?"

"Not yet."

"Where is she? You need to be long gone when Levi gets here. He won't propose to me if you're standing there gawking. You might have to start walking."

Esther pressed her lips together. Much as she hated to give her sister the satisfaction, she truly didn't want to be here for the special brunch Ivy had planned for Levi. The bathroom was finished, and Levi wouldn't be coming around regularly anymore. Yesterday he had taken Ivy aside and told her he had something to ask her, and she had invited him to brunch this morning. How convenient that their little meeting was on pickleball day. Was Levi going to ask Ivy to marry him? Surely he had more sense than that. Surely Esther would disintegrate into little flakes of dust and blow away with the wind.

Esther bit back the sharp reply on her tongue. She had lost. Ivy had won. Again. And there was absolutely nothing Esther could do about it, except maybe throw eggs at Levi's house in the middle of the night or toilet paper his wagon or dump all his tools into the road and watch cars run over them.

"What are you smiling about?" Ivy set three pieces of bacon on each plate and eyed Esther with something akin to concern in her eyes. "I'm sorry to be snippy. I just don't think you or Winnie should be here when Levi comes. It would be awkward."

Ivy had no idea how awkward it would be.

Esther unbuckled Winnie from her high chair and lifted her into her arms. At least she had Winnie. She thanked Derr Herr every day for the tremendous blessing of someone to love and care for. "Cathy is picking me up at nine thirty, and she is very prompt," she said, putting more kindness in her voice than she felt.

That seemed to make Ivy feel better, even as Esther felt worse. "Good. We want our privacy."

Cathy honked at precisely nine thirty. With Winnie in one arm, Esther grabbed the car seat with her other hand and headed for the car. Without being asked, Ivy carried the *kievel*, the diaper bag, out to the car. Even though it was self-serving on Ivy's part, it was still nice not to have to make a second trip back to the house. Of course, Esther had no illusions that Ivy was learning to be more thoughtful. Ivy just wanted to get rid of Esther as quickly as possible.

Esther buckled Winnie into her seat and climbed into the car. She turned to wave, but Ivy had already disappeared into the house, obviously beside herself with worry that the breakfast casserole would be dry.

On the way to pickleball, Cathy gave Esther an update on her earwax and her gout. Esther didn't even know what gout was, but it sounded unpleasant. Esther did her best to muster sympathy for Cathy's ailments, but all she could muster was a healthy dose of self-pity. Not even the prospect of slamming a pickleball over the net could cheer her up today.

Nanna and Hannah were already on the court, hitting the ball in their Plain dresses with sweatpants underneath. Esther still couldn't get over the sight of Amish women playing pickleball, even though she was one of them. Rita and Allison pulled up right behind Esther and Cathy. Esther unloaded Winnie from the car while Cathy put sweatbands on her wrists and one on her head just above her ears. Cathy seemed to have numerous health problems, but she was very serious about her pickleball. Of all of them, she was the best player, even better than Esther, who was fifty years younger.

Hannah and Cathy teamed up to play against Rita and Allison while Nanna and Esther sat on a blanket outside the fence and played with Winnie. Now that Winnie could crawl, she wasn't inclined to stay on the blanket, and Esther had to keep chasing her and bringing her back.

Nanna smoothed her finger down Winnie's cheek, then wrapped her arms around her knees. She looked at Esther, her eyes dancing with delight. "It's none of my business, but you know I don't usually care if something is my business or not. Please tell me, what is going on with Levi? This morning he was so excited and happy about something, he offered to help me organize my sewing room." She nudged Esther with her shoulder. "I'm guessing you have something to do with his good mood."

Esther grabbed a handful of Winnie's cereal puffs and started tossing them at the chain-link fence. "Why would you think I have something to do with his mood? We're just friends." *Ach.* She was going to choke if she had to say that one more time.

Nanna studied Esther's face. "Something is wrong."

Esther had to look away from those piercing blue eyes. They were so much like Levi's. "*Jah.*"

"Oy, anyhow. I think you'd better tell me all about it."

Esther threw another cereal puff. Harder this time. "It's not my story to tell."

Nanna raised her eyebrows. "Of course it's your story to tell. Things that touch your life, one way or the other, are always part of your story."

Esther threw another cereal puff. It plinked off the chain-link fence and hit Winnie in the cheek. Winnie didn't seem to feel it. She picked the puff off the ground and stuffed it into her mouth. Okay. No more throwing cereal puffs. Esther would put out somebody's eye, for sure and certain. "Levi is going to propose to Ivy this morning."

Whatever Nanna had been expecting, that wasn't it. Her mouth fell open like a largemouth bass. Esther probably could have counted all of Nanna's teeth. She was missing one in the back. "Are you sure?"

Esther pulled up some grass at her fingertips. "Yesterday he told Ivy he had something to ask her. She's home preparing a special brunch for his proposal."

Deep lines etched themselves around Nanna's mouth. "I have a very hard time believing that. Ivy doesn't know how to boil water. She wouldn't know the first thing about making brunch."

Esther couldn't keep a half smile from her face. Nanna knew Ivy too well. "I made most everything, but she's got to take the breakfast casserole out of the oven, and she felt fairly confident mixing the orange juice."

"She's going to overbake it."

"I know."

Nanna sat on her haunches and pinned Esther with a grim expression. "Why in the world would Levi propose to your sister?"

Esther sighed and ripped up more grass from the lawn. "Ivy is pretty, and she can be very charming, and she isn't old like me."

Nanna grunted her disapproval. "So Ivy only has two *gute* qualities . . ."

"I mentioned three."

"Two. Being younger than you is neither here nor there.

And you think those two *gute* qualities would ever in a million years induce my grandson to marry her?" Nanna folded her arms across her chest. "You can just put that thought out of your mind."

Esther shook her head. "But Ivy can be very persuasive, and men are unpredictable and irrational and so easily manipulated."

Nanna sniffed. "That sounds like your last fiancé, Mahlon."

"Menno."

"Menno. What a misfortune you ever got engaged to that one. But that does not sound like my Levi or any of my grandsons. Menno does not represent most men, and you know it."

Esther pulled up more grass. "I'm not sure of anything anymore."

Nanna grew more animated with every word. "Levi is a *gute* boy and smart. He would not fall in love with Ivy. He just wouldn't."

"But how can you be sure?"

"Because I know Levi. And I thought you did too."

Esther pulled Winnie back to the blanket and handed her another cereal puff. "He and Ivy have so much fun together. He likes her."

Nanna narrowed her eyes. "Didn't you ask him to be nice to her?"

"*Jah*, but there's a difference between being nice and falling in love."

"I agree, but I think you're wrong about Levi, and I'll try not to be offended that you think my grandson would be so foolish as to fall in love with your sister." She said it with a smile, so Esther knew she wasn't really offended.

"I know where Levi's heart is, and Ivy Zook doesn't have a single piece of it." She reached out and squeezed Esther's hand. "You'll see. All Ivy will get from brunch is over-baked breakfast casserole and profound disappointment. Levi would sooner eat his own hat than marry Ivy."

Esther wished, hoped, prayed that was true. Whatever happened, she'd know in a few hours. She'd hold Nanna's words in her heart and try to enjoy pickleball. As long as Cathy didn't accidentally whack her with the paddle, it might even be fun.

Nanna cupped her hand over Esther's cheek. "Lord willing, everything will turn out right. You'll see. And please stop tearing up the grass. There's a bald spot."

Levi jumped from his buggy, the manila envelope clutched tightly in his fist. His heart thumped against his rib cage, and he couldn't seem to catch his breath. Was he doing the right thing? He had been working on this plan for weeks, but it still felt hasty and maybe a little reckless. He squared his shoulders and took a deep breath to calm his nerves. Esther's bathroom was finished, and Ivy had changed. She had warmed to both Levi and Esther. For sure and certain she had seen how much work it took to care for a baby and what a *gute* job Esther was doing. Lord willing, she had warmed to the idea of letting Esther raise Winnie.

Levi had worked for weeks to earn Ivy's trust. Hope-fully she'd listen to him and give serious thought to what he had to tell her. Most importantly, the birth certificate had arrived yesterday. There wouldn't be a better time to talk Ivy into signing the adoption papers. And he could do it. He knew he could. How could Ivy refuse something that would mean so much happiness for everyone?

His heart raced. Mostly it would mean happiness for Esther, and Levi ached to see Esther happy. Having to cater to Ivy had been exhausting, and the thought of losing Winnie had been weighing on her for months. The uncertainty was beginning to take its toll. She'd been cold and distant the last few weeks, no doubt worried about losing Winnie. She barely said a word to Levi anymore when he came by to work on the bathroom. Her smile had become as rare as a blue moon, and she'd broken every wooden spoon in the house. Since the demise of the last spoon, Esther had taken to snapping toothpicks in half. That couldn't have been very satisfying.

Levi wanted to be the one to hand Esther the signed adoption papers and see the look of sheer delight on her face. But she couldn't know of his plan to ask Ivy today. If Ivy agreed to sign the papers, he would surprise Esther with the happy news. If Ivy said no, Esther wouldn't have to bear yet another disappointment.

With those adoption papers signed and filed, Esther would be happy again. Maybe she'd be able to think on other things besides losing Winnie—things like maybe giving Levi a chance to win her. He wanted to take her in his arms and tell her he'd fixed everything, and maybe she'd laugh and say, "I suppose I could consider marrying you after all."

Levi would laugh and reply, "It's all I ever wanted."

And it was. Even early on when he had told himself she was too old, he had just been making up excuses. Esther was everything to him. She was his sun and his moon and, well, the whole sky, really. He would be lost and utterly miserable without her. Did she even know what she meant to him? Probably not. She thought Ivy was prettier. She thought he was looking for someone younger. She thought she wasn't wanted. Even though she was the one who'd called off her wedding, Menno had still made her feel like a ratty sweater in a secondhand store.

Levi walked up to the door and knocked with confidence. He'd rehearsed in his mind what he was going to say to Ivy. She liked him. She'd listen. He had sensed a true change in her over the last few weeks. She wasn't selfish like she used to be. Maybe she didn't understand it yet, but he'd explain everything, and she would realize that giving up Winnie would be better for Winnie and make life much easier for herself. She'd agree to sign the papers because deep down, she really did want Esther to be happy.

Ivy opened the door as if she'd been waiting just inside. She giggled and clapped her hands. "Oh, Levi, I'm so glad you came. The breakfast casserole is amazing!"

Levi smiled. "Breakfast casserole? Sounds delicious. Is it for me?"

"I thought we could have a special brunch."

"Oh. Okay." He'd already had breakfast, but he could probably eat a little breakfast casserole. "You didn't have to go to all that trouble for me. I'm happy with coffee soup."

Ivy's mouth fell open in mock horror. "Coffee soup? I wouldn't dream of making coffee soup for such an important occasion. Come and see."

Heavenly smells greeted Levi when he walked into the house: freshly baked bread, bacon, orange juice. The scent of slightly burned eggs did nothing to ruin the other smells. Ivy led him into the kitchen. The table was set with two place settings with fancy pink napkins and a bouquet of roses in the center. "This looks real nice, Ivy. You went to a lot of trouble." A germ of doubt niggled at the back of his mind. He had just come to ask Ivy about the adoption papers. She seemed to expect some sort of special occasion.

Ivy pulled a pitcher of orange juice from the fridge and set it on the table, motioning for Levi to sit. Then she made a big show of putting on two oven mitts and taking a huge dish of something cheesy and eggy out of the oven. The edges were burned crispy, but it looked edible. She set it on the table and sat down across from Levi.

"You're not wearing your sling. Is your collarbone feeling better?"

"How nice of you to notice. Most people don't even care." With a knife, she cut two big squares from her breakfast casserole and set one square on his plate and one on hers. "Bon appétit," she said, picking up her fork and skewering her piece.

For some reason, Levi felt more and more uneasy. What was Ivy doing? And why was she so cheerful? He cleared his throat. "Should we say silent grace?"

Ivy put down her fork so fast, it clattered on the table. "Every good Amish family says silent grace."

He bowed his head and closed his eyes and prayed for guidance. Was it a mistake to try to convince Ivy to sign those papers today? But when would he have another chance like this one?

He lifted his head to find her looking at him. She smiled. "Try the breakfast casserole. I think I did it right."

He stabbed a piece of casserole with his fork and took a bite. It was a little dry but tasted surprisingly good for an Ivy recipe. "Very good. I love the cheese and potatoes."

"Thank you. Mamm used to make this at least once a week. Dat loved it."

Levi took a deep breath as his heart hammered like a bass drum. "I suppose you've been wondering why I wanted to talk to you."

She blushed. "I have been wondering."

"I'm proud of you, Ivy."

Her eyes searched his face. "Proud?"

"Think how you've blossomed since you've been here with Esther."

"Blossomed" probably wasn't the right word, but he couldn't think of a better one. Lord willing, she'd understand what he meant.

"What?" she said, smiling as if they shared a funny secret. "You didn't like my clothing choices?"

He chuckled. She *had* changed a lot. He hadn't even been thinking about the clothes. "It's not that. You've really tried to be kind to your sister and help her around the house, even though you only had one *gute* arm."

Ivy held up her hands. "Now that I have two good hands, I want to help Esther even more. She does so much around here."

"*Jah.* She does. And I know you help all you can. Thank you for that. Esther works very hard, and it's nice to know you're here to help her."

Ivy shrugged and smiled in satisfaction. "I'm her sister. Of course I want to make her burdens lighter."

"*Gute,*" Levi said. His heart now threatened to escape from his throat, but he swallowed hard and forged ahead. He showed her the manila envelope he'd been holding on his lap. "This is what I want to ask you about, and I know you will listen with your heart open."

"That's very nice of you to say."

"It's true. When you first came, you'd been through some wonderful hard things, and you didn't trust anybody.

You wanted to protect yourself, so you wrapped yourself in a hard shell."

Her lips twitched upward. "Like a turtle?"

"Yes. And I don't blame you, but I think the last few weeks I've seen the real Ivy. She's compassionate, kind, and eager to do the right thing."

Ivy batted her eyes. "I don't know what to say to all this praise. As an Amish girl, I'm supposed to be humble and modest, and you're tempting me to be proud."

"I'm only speaking the truth." He pulled the birth certificate from the envelope. "This came today." He slid it across the table to Ivy.

Doubt flitted across her face as she read it. "Winnie's birth certificate. But why did you want this?"

"Esther didn't ask you to leave Winnie here."

She pressed her lips together. "I know. But you said yourself, I've changed."

"Yes, yes, of course you've changed. It's a good change, only a change for the better."

Her smile came back full force. "You're so very forgiving, Levi."

"I'm not saying this to make you feel bad for past mistakes, but Esther was completely unprepared to take care of a baby."

Ivy folded her arms. "I couldn't take her with me. Jordan wouldn't—"

Levi held up his hand to stop her. "That doesn't matter to me." He grinned. "I was there that first morning after you left. Esther asked me to change Winnie's diaper and feed her. She had no idea what to do."

Ivy nodded. "I'm sure Esther was *ferhoodled*. She never liked children. She didn't know how to take care of a baby."

Levi chuckled. "Now she checks the temperature of Winnie's bathwater and feeds her organic baby food."

"She's always been nervous like that. I keep telling her she needs to relax and let life flow around her. I learned that in yoga."

Levi picked up the roll on his plate and peeled away a layer. "What I'm trying to say is that even though Esther was angry with you for leaving Winnie here, she has since grown to love Winnie very much. Don't you think she takes wonderful *gute* care of Winnie?"

"I suppose she does, though she fusses over her too much. She'll spoil her if she's not careful."

Levi reached across the table and laid his hand over Ivy's. Ivy stared at his hand as if it were a pile of money. "Esther only wants what is best for everyone. What would you think about letting her adopt Winnie?"

Levi withdrew his hand. Ivy didn't say anything, but she seemed to be thinking about it very hard. "Then Winnie would live here with Esther?"

Levi nodded. "She wouldn't be your daughter anymore."

She drew her brows together. "I'm a good mother."

Levi didn't want to lie, but Ivy needed reassurance, not a lecture. "Of course you're a good mother. A good mother makes the choices that are best for her child. A good mother is completely unselfish. I think deep down, that's why you left Winnie here in the first place. You knew it would be better for her to have a warm place to sleep." He glued his gaze to her face, choosing his next words carefully. "And maybe to keep her safe from Jordan."

Ivy snorted. "Jordan. What a jerk. He never liked the idea of a baby. Inconvenient."

Levi didn't want to say any more about Jordan. Ivy had picked him, and Levi didn't want her to think he was implying she had bad judgment. "If you let Esther adopt, you would be sad because you have a tender heart, but I think you can see that this would be better for everybody. You wouldn't be tied down to a child. You'd be free to live your own life. Esther would get to love and raise Winnie as her own."

Ivy stared at her plate and fiddled with one of her *kapp* strings. "I haven't really thought about what I would do with Winnie, but I think I understand what you're saying."

Levi scooted his chair from the table and stood up. "I'll be right back."

He went into Esther's room, knelt down on the floor beside her dresser, and ran his hand underneath the bottom of the drawer. This was Esther's new place for keeping money, her cell phone, and the adoption papers. Three plastic bags were taped to the bottom of the dresser. The two small ones held Esther's cell phone and some cash. Levi pulled the biggest one from the bottom of the dresser. There they were. The adoption papers. The lawyer said all he had to do was call her and she'd meet them at the courthouse as soon as Ivy was ready to sign. He took the adoption papers into the kitchen, moved his chair closer to Ivy, and sat down next to her.

She was quiet but didn't seem at all upset about letting Esther adopt her baby. "I'm a good mother, and I do love Winnie. You know that, right?"

"Of course you love her. And you want to do what's best for her." He laid the adoption papers on the table in front of her.

A smile slowly crept onto her face. "It would be better for us too."

"Um, well, yes," Levi said, not sure who "us" referred to.

Ivy nodded enthusiastically. "This is the perfect solution. I have to admit I was a little worried. Men are so prickly about raising another man's child. Giving Winnie to Esther sets me free. It sets you free too. We could start our life together and have our own children without Winnie to mess it up for us."

Levi froze as if he'd been struck by lightning. "Wait, Ivy. I don't want you to think . . . I'm not . . ."

"I don't want to go crazy and have like ten children or something. Two is a nice even number."

"I didn't say anything about getting married."

She looked at him as if he'd said something stupid. "Well, getting rid of Winnie is the first step, isn't it? That frees both of us up."

She reached out for his hand, but he pulled back before she could touch him. "No, Ivy. No. You don't understand. I don't want to marry you." It came out harsher and louder than he intended, but shock had rendered him completely undiplomatic and wildly angry—mostly at himself. How had he not seen this coming? Ivy wanted to marry him. From the looks of the special brunch on the table, Ivy had been expecting a proposal. He'd told her not three weeks ago that he did not want to marry her, but she obviously hadn't believed him, especially since he'd been extra nice since then. He had wanted to soften her up, but he'd only created expectations. Expectations he wasn't about to meet.

Ivy stared at him in disbelief. "What did you say?"

He lowered his voice. "I'm not asking you to marry

me," he said gently. "Marriage has nothing to do with it. I just want you to let Esther adopt Winnie. It would make Esther happy, and Winnie would have a good, stable home. That's all."

Ivy caught his words as if he was throwing rocks at her. "You've been flirting with me for weeks. And don't try to deny it."

Levi leaned his elbow on the table and rubbed his forehead. "I'm sorry if you thought I was flirting. I was just trying to be nice."

Her eyes flashed with resentment. "What a lie. You were being nice because you wanted to talk me into giving Winnie away. My own daughter! How could you even ask?"

"I just think Winnie—"

She stood up and moved as far away from him as she could get and still be in the kitchen. "I thought you loved me, and now to find out you were using me." She glared at Levi with all the anger of utter embarrassment. "You and Esther worked this out together, didn't you?" She pinched her face into a sneer. "'Let's be nice to Ivy and trick her into giving us her baby.' You must think I'm so stupid. Well, I'm not going to fall for it."

"Ivy, please don't be upset. This is not Esther's fault. We all just want what's best for Winnie."

"I thought Esther was glad I came back. I thought we were friends. I thought maybe she loved me. She sewed three new dresses for me. She taught me how to make breakfast casserole."

Nae, *Ivy, please don't bring Esther into this. Lash out at me, but don't do anything to hurt Esther.* He couldn't even say it out loud, because that is exactly what Ivy would do—punish Esther for his mistake. "Esther loves you with all her heart."

Ivy was beyond consolable now. She paced around the kitchen like a caged animal, moaning and panting. "Esther pretended to love me, when all she wants is my baby. *My* baby. Esther is a selfish, self-righteous, lying prig, and she's not getting her hands on Winter. Ever."

A wide, gaping wound opened up in the middle of Levi's chest. What had he done? And how could he make it right? He stood and tried to steer Ivy back to her chair. She shoved him away from her and nearly lost her balance. Not wanting Ivy to hurt herself, he quickly backed away and raised his hands. "I'm so sorry. Please, sit down. Let's just talk about it. We can work this out."

Ivy's eyes were mere slits on her face. "You want to work things out?"

"More than anything."

She picked up the adoption papers and, in one swift motion, ripped them in half. "That's how I work things out," she said, spitting the words out of her mouth like poison. "I don't let anybody tell me what to do, and I don't let anybody walk all over me. I won't be tricked into doing something I don't want."

Levi looked at the shreds of paper in Ivy's hands. That was what Ivy's spite was going to do to Esther's heart. "Ivy, please."

Ivy let the papers fall to the floor with a mocking smile on her face. "That's what I think of your adoption papers."

"Can't we talk about this?"

She pulled back her hand, and before Levi knew what was happening, she slapped him hard across the face. *Ach, du lieva.* The pain in his chest was sharp and raw. He barely felt the sting of her hand. "I'm done talking. Get out of my house."

Chapter Thirteen

After pickleball, Esther couldn't face going home, couldn't face the possibility of Ivy being engaged to Levi, so like a coward, she had Cathy drive her to the dollar store in Monte Vista, where she walked up and down the aisles and wondered how they made a profit on balloons and plates and bags of chips. Cathy bought nasal strips for sleeping, then bought lunch at Dairy Queen for all of them. After that, she drove them out to the wildlife refuge, where they looked for wildlife. It was a serene and completely unhappy day.

What would Esther do if Levi married Ivy? How could she bear it? She'd have to move to another state and start her life over again. But that would only be possible if Ivy let her keep Winnie. What would she do if Ivy wanted Winnie for herself?

After the wildlife refuge, Esther couldn't avoid it anymore. She had to go home, because Winnie would soon be hungry for dinner and then it would be time to put her down for the night. Cathy had stuck with her the whole day, bless her kind heart, and drove her home just before five o'clock. Cathy pulled in front of the house and put the car in park. "Have a good night, and tell Ivy she needs to get her act together and move out of your house. Tell her I said she shouldn't be freeloading on her sister. If she needs money, she can come to my house and pull weeds."

Esther pulled Winnie from her car seat and nodded. She wasn't going to tell Ivy any such thing, but it was nice that Cathy wanted to help. Unfortunately, nobody could help Esther but Gotte, and if He had plans, He wasn't telling her about them. There was no sign of Levi, no wagon or buggy out front. Not that Esther had expected that—she'd been gone all day—but there *was* a pile of something brown and orange and yellowish on her front step, like a thick, lumpy welcome mat.

Esther left the car seat on the grass and carried Winnie and the diaper bag to the house. She'd go back for the car seat later. As Cathy drove away, Esther paused on the step and studied whatever it was on her porch. It took her a second to realize that it was breakfast casserole, poured from its pan, with flies buzzing around it, dripping and oozing trickles of moisture.

Ivy's brunch had not gone well.

Was that *gute* news or bad news? If Levi had proposed marriage, Esther couldn't imagine Ivy dumping breakfast casserole on the porch. Esther pulled Winnie tighter as her heart did somersaults. Maybe Levi hadn't proposed after all. One thing was for certain: Ivy was ferociously angry about something. Her temper was worse than Esther's. What would Esther find behind that door? She'd be wise to prepare for anything. Something heavy and dark pressed into her chest as she opened the door. "Ivy?" she called.

"In here."

Esther marched slowly into the kitchen, wondering, hoping that maybe she'd been wrong about Levi. With all her heart she wanted Nanna to be right. The pile of breakfast casserole on the step was a disgusting mess, but it also gave her hope. And in the last few weeks, hope had become an unfamiliar feeling.

Esther gasped as she walked into the kitchen. Something very bad had happened. Either there had been a fight or Ivy's temper had gotten the better of her or both. Ivy sat at the table with her fingers laced together, her lips pressed into a hard line and a glint of fierce resentment in her eyes. Two puddles of orange juice pooled under the table, along with several strips of ripped white paper, crumbled bacon—such a waste—and shards of glass from one of the fancy plates Ivy had set on the table this morning. The table was strewn with overturned glasses, smashed orange rolls, and flower petals from the roses Esther had cut just this morning from her lone rosebush. Definitely a temper tantrum. Esther's heart galloped out of control and probably set some sort of speed record. Surely Levi hadn't proposed!

Esther scooted a piece of glass out of the way with her shoe and ventured farther into the kitchen. "What happened?" she said, trying hard to keep her voice steady and unemotional. Ivy wouldn't take kindly to any joyful exclamations on Esther's part.

Ivy's gaze flicked in Esther's direction. "You think I'm so stupid, Esther, and I'm not going to put up with it anymore."

Oy, anyhow, Ivy was mad. "I don't think you're stupid."

"Yes, you do. But just so you know, I'm not stupid and your tricks don't work on me."

"What tricks?"

"Shut up, Esther. Just shut up. I'm not some naive Amish girl you can fool easy. I've been in the real world. I've seen things, more bad things than you could ever imagine. You can't pull one over on me, no matter how hard you try."

"Pull one over on you? What does that mean?"

She turned and glared at Esther. "You see. You don't even know. Now who's the stupid one?"

"I don't think you're stupid." Ivy knew how to get what she wanted. Esther had never underestimated her. Esther picked up a petal from the table and rubbed it between her fingers. "It looks like your breakfast didn't go well."

"Too bad for you," Ivy said.

Too bad for you? What did she mean by that? Esther tried to muster some sympathy for Ivy. She'd pinned her hopes on Levi. He'd maybe even broken her heart. Esther should have felt sorry for her dear sister, but she felt nothing but relief. Levi wasn't in love with Ivy. That was the best news of her life. "Tell me what happened."

Ivy seemed to explode. She stood up and pointed at Esther. "What happened? Don't act so innocent. You know what happened. You put him up to it."

"Put him up to what?"

Ivy ripped the *kapp* off her head. "All these weeks! All these weeks I've worn this stupid *kapp* and this ugly dress because I thought he liked it. I'll bet you two had a good laugh over me in these ridiculous clothes. I thought he wanted to marry me. I made breakfast casserole because he tricked me into thinking he was going to propose. But it was all an act. He pretended to like me just so he could get me to sign your precious adoption papers."

Esther's heart stopped beating. She tightened her arms around Winnie. "What . . . what adoption papers?"

Ivy bent over, snatched a strip of paper from the floor, and waved it in Esther's face. It took Esther a split second to realize what it was. How had she found those? "Stop it, Esther. That innocent act doesn't fool me. It was your plan all along to make me think Levi loved me. You wanted to trick me into giving away my baby." She crumpled the paper into a ball and threw it across the room. "I won't do it. I'm never giving Winnie away, especially not to my two-faced sister."

Nothing but the fear of dropping Winnie kept Esther upright. Her knees locked, and her lungs refused to take in air. "Ivy, we didn't try to trick you. We just wanted you to see—"

"You're a liar. You're all liars, and I trusted you."

Unable to support herself any longer, Esther sat down at the table with Winnie firmly in her arms. She didn't understand. Why hadn't Levi said something to her? She would have told him not to do anything foolish. It seemed he'd done the most reckless thing in the entire world. Esther didn't know what to say. Was there anything she could say? It was always a nerve-racking, perilous game with Ivy. "It's not like that. I just thought you'd be happier without a baby to worry about."

"You couldn't care less about my feelings. You want my baby, and you'll say anything to get her." Ivy winced as she snatched Winnie roughly out of Esther's arms. Winnie screamed and reached out for Esther.

"Please, Ivy," Esther said. "Can't you see she's upset? Just let me feed her and get her to bed, then you can say anything you want to say to me."

"You're not her mother," Ivy screamed, wrapping both arms tightly around Winnie as if she feared Esther would try to wrestle Winnie away from her. "She'll never love you as much as she loves me."

Ivy couldn't have hurt her worse if she had slapped Esther in the face. Esther's eyes stung from the force of it.

Winnie's face turned red as she wailed at the top of her lungs. Ivy bounced her up and down as if she knew what she was doing. "Look what you've done, Esther. You've turned my own baby against me."

Ivy was completely irrational. Esther couldn't hope to reason with her. All she cared about right now was Winnie's safety and well-being. "Okay, okay, Ivy. It's going to be okay."

"Don't say that, like a few words will make everything better. You wanted to hurt me." She lifted her chin. "I'm going to do what's best for me and my baby, and that doesn't include letting a selfish, hypocritical prude be her mother. I carried Winnie for nine months. I got varicose veins and stretch marks. I went through hours and hours of labor. Don't think you can tell me anything about being a mother. You don't know anything. Anything." She made a shushing noise with her mouth in an attempt to quiet Winnie, but it did no good. Winnie screamed as if her heart were broken.

"Ivy, let me put her to bed, and we can talk."

Ivy glared at Esther. "Well, you've got one thing right. From now on, you ask my permission anytime you want to do anything with Winnie, and keep her away from lying jerks or I'll take her away so fast, it will make your head spin."

"Please don't do that. Please don't take Winnie away." It was foolish and humiliating to beg. Esther's desperation only gave Ivy more power, but the thought of losing Winnie buried her.

"I found your cash and your cell phone, and they're safely hidden for when I'm ready to take Winnie and get away. Don't think I won't do it." Ivy turned on her heels, avoided a thick piece of glass at her feet, and headed toward her room. "I'm going to spend some quality time with my baby." She slammed the door behind her, but it did nothing to muffle Winnie's cries for Esther, the woman she'd come to depend on. The woman who knew how to take care of her. But still, the woman who wasn't her mother.

Esther blinked back some useless tears, knelt down, and started picking up glass from the floor.

Levi was beside himself with worry and guilt and every other intense emotion he could put a name to. He had wanted to fix everything for Esther, to be her hero, to make her so happy that she might consider loving him, but instead he'd ruined everything. Ivy was furious. Would she take Winnie and run away? Esther's heart would break, and for sure and certain, she'd blame him—for interfering where he shouldn't have, for losing Winnie. How could he ever make it right?

He sat just down the road from Esther's house in his open-air buggy watching the sky turn orange and purple and finally a deep, sapphire blue. Winnie would be asleep, and if he sneaked around to Esther's window, he might be able to coax Esther out of the house without Ivy knowing.

This morning after the disastrous brunch, Levi had gone straight to the pickleball courts to talk to Esther. Mammi was there with Mary Jane, but she said Esther had gone into town with Cathy. Even if he'd known where they had gone, it would have been futile to chase a car around town in his buggy, so he gave up the fight and decided to go back in the evening when Winnie was asleep, Ivy had hopefully calmed down, and Esther would be available to talk.

He had to talk to Esther, had to apologize. He'd let her cry on his shoulder if she wanted to, but like as not, she'd want to beat one of her bushes to death with a tennis racket, or worse, she'd refuse to talk to him, or would even tell him she never wanted to see him again. He wouldn't blame her. If she lost Winnie, it would be no one's fault but his own.

He jumped from his buggy and walked quietly around the house to Esther's bedroom window. The blinds were shut, and the room was dark. Levi knocked softly on the window, but if Esther wasn't in her room, she'd never hear him. He held his breath and waited, but Esther didn't come to the window. He walked around to the back, got on his tiptoes, and peeked into the kitchen. It was also dark and empty. Where were they? If he wanted to talk to Esther, he'd have to go about it in a more direct way.

He walked back around to the front of the house and knocked on the front door. The sounds of movement inside the house told him someone was deliberately taking her time to answer the door, making him wait, letting him think on his sins, giving him reason to be worried.

His heart sank when Ivy answered the door. She was dressed *Englisch* again: short shorts, feather earrings, and the tattoo that looked like a bruise on her thigh. He expected her to spit at him or slam the door in his face or even sneer, but she gave him a dazzlingly fake smile that alarmed him more than anything spiteful she could have done. "Levi. I guess it's not your fault you're here. I didn't make myself clear this morning." She was all sugar and syrup and insincerity, and Levi's throat dried out like sawdust on a hot day.

"I'm sorry, Ivy. I don't mean to upset you. I just need to talk to Esther."

Ivy laughed, but there was no happiness in it. "You didn't upset me. I'm a little annoyed that I wasted my time, but I'm not upset in the least. I mean, who really, sincerely wants to marry an Amish boy?"

She was upset all right. He could see it in the set of her chin and the fire in her eyes, but he wasn't about to argue with her. She was trying to salvage her pride, and he couldn't fault her for that. "Okay. *Ach, vell*, I'm glad to hear it. I never wanted to hurt you."

"You didn't," she said, spitting the words at him like poison.

Okay. No more apologizing. Apologies obviously made Ivy feel weak and pitiful. He cleared his throat. "It wonders me if Esther is home."

"She is," Ivy said. "But that is really not your concern."

"I need to talk to her."

Esther suddenly appeared behind Ivy. Her face was pale and gaunt, her blue-green eyes dull and unfocused. Ivy glanced back. "There really isn't anything to say."

"Yes, there is," Levi said. He looked at Esther. "Could you come out and talk for a minute?"

Ivy shut the door halfway. "She really can't. We're both tired and grumpy, and we've got to clean the kitchen before bed."

Levi jumped at this opportunity. "I can help."

Ivy shook her head. "Don't you think you've done enough?"

"I just . . . please don't be mad, Ivy. I'm sorry I hurt you. I really am."

Ivy's fake smile faltered before she pasted it back in place. "You didn't hurt me." *Ach.* Why was he so stupid?

"I'm sorry you came all this way, but I can't allow you in the house. You're a bad influence, and I won't have you hanging around Winnie. As her mother, her protection is my first priority."

Levi's mouth fell open. Ivy wouldn't allow him into Esther's house? Was Ivy in charge now? He glanced in Esther's direction, and the pain in her eyes stunned him. Of course Ivy was in charge. She had something that Esther wanted more than life itself. "What would it hurt to let me talk to Esther?"

Ivy propped her arm on the doorjamb, as if barring Levi's way if he was so foolish as to try to force his way into the house. "You used me," she hissed, losing any semblance of calm cheerfulness. "You're a liar and a hypocrite, and I won't let my daughter or my sister have anything to do with you. I'm only thinking of Winnie's safety. I'm a good mother, and good mothers protect their children. If Esther does anything to endanger my child"—Ivy narrowed her eyes—"and that means associating with you, I'll take Winnie and go to California."

The pain clawed at Levi like some desperate animal wild to escape. This was worse than he had ever imagined it could be. Ivy was worse than he ever could have believed. He had to fix it. He had to fix it *now*. He pinned Ivy with a withering stare. "Not even you would be that cruel. You love Esther. Esther loves you. Don't do this."

Ivy folded her arms across her chest. "If Esther truly loves me, she'll do what's best for my daughter, and forget about you and your hurtful lies."

Levi was stunned and horrified and devastated. Esther had warned him. He hadn't realized how deftly Ivy could turn things to her advantage, how she could twist the truth to make it serve her, how she could plot the perfect revenge. He was lost on the lake without a paddle. And even if he had a paddle, he wouldn't know what side of the lake to row to. "But I don't think Esther—"

Esther pled with her eyes. "Please, Levi. Just go. Just go."

Ivy's smug smile came back. "Yes. Please go. Besides, aren't you supposed to be in Ohio looking for a wife?"

Levi could barely speak. On top of everything else, was Esther angry at him for even mentioning the adoption papers? Maybe she would never forgive him for ruining the delicate balance she had built with Ivy. "I . . . was . . . am leaving in a couple of days."

"Well, good. As far as I'm concerned, you can stay in Ohio forever. Don't you agree, Esther?"

Esther lowered her eyes. "Yes. Please just go."

There was nothing else to do. Esther was trapped by her love for Winnie, and she certainly felt deep resentment for him, or she might have tried to stand up for herself. His heart broke into a million pieces while he stood on the porch and tried to breathe normally. He gazed at Esther, hoping she saw everything he couldn't say. But maybe she didn't want to see it, and maybe a glance between them would only make things worse.

Winnie began to cry in the next room. Ivy rolled her eyes. "Look what you did now? It took her more than an hour to go to sleep. Go away, Levi, and quit hurting this family."

Since Winnie was already awake, Ivy had no reason to be quiet. With one last scowl in his direction, she slammed the door, leaving him standing on the step gasping for air.

Chapter Fourteen

Smiling, Esther wet a dish towel and wiped the smeared baby food off Winnie's face. Winnie had strange taste. She loved green beans but hated peaches. She adored carrots but wouldn't touch a banana. Esther made a beeping noise and touched Winnie's nose with the towel. Winnie giggled and reached out her arms, ready for Esther to free her from the high chair. Esther unbuckled Winnie and picked her up. Placing a tender kiss on the top of Winnie's head, Esther clutched Winnie in her arms, squeezing tighter and longer than usual. Who knew how much time they had left together? Ivy could change her mind tomorrow, leave town, and take Winnie and Esther's heart with her.

Esther vowed to do whatever she must to make sure Ivy never left, and that meant keeping Ivy happy, no matter what. After not quite a week, her plan seemed to be working. Esther's life went on much as it had before, caring for Winnie and making quilts while Winnie napped or played on the floor beside her. Ivy paid attention to Winnie when it was convenient or when she wanted to remind Esther who was in control. And Ivy was very much in control.

She did less work around the house than ever, but if Esther complained about it, Ivy would threaten to take Winnie away. *I'm not the maid, Esther. You can clean your own house. I never had to clean when I lived with Jordan's stepmom. Maybe I'll go back and take Winnie just to get you off my back.* So Esther stayed quiet about the housework.

After that first night when Ivy had snatched Winnie from Esther's arms, Ivy had let Esther deal with Winnie. Ivy didn't know how to put Winnie down for a nap or to bed. She didn't know how to give Winnie a bath or what to feed her, and she didn't have the patience to learn. Ivy was just relieved that Esther knew how to stop the crying. Ivy turned Winnie over to Esther out of impatience and sheer frustration. Esther couldn't have been happier about that. Ivy couldn't take care of Winnie by herself, and it gave Esther a small bit of power.

A small bit. But it was something.

She had in effect become Ivy's maid and nanny, but it wasn't much different than before Ivy had come back, so her life was bearable, and Winnie was still here. But Esther wasn't happy. She still had Winnie, but she'd lost Levi. Ivy had forced her to make a terrible choice, and Levi was the price she'd had to pay.

Esther pressed her lips to Winnie's forehead. She longed for Levi, ached for him like she had never ached for Menno. If she lived to be a thousand, she would never forget the look on his face when she had told him to go away. Was he hurt that she had chosen Winnie over him? Or did he simply feel bad about the way things had turned out? Was he sad he wouldn't see Winnie anymore? Would he miss Esther's friendship? Did he care for her at all?

Or did he think she was too old and too temperamental for him?

For sure and certain he felt bad about the way things had turned out. Maybe he even felt responsible for how Ivy had reacted. He should have waited. He should have consulted with Esther. But Esther hadn't spent a moment of anger on him. He had done what he thought was right, and Esther couldn't fault him for that. All she could feel was gratitude, gratitude that he had tried to help her and gratitude that he cared enough to try. And a yearning so deep, she felt the ache clear to her bones.

Because, when all was said and done, he hadn't asked Ivy to marry him. He didn't love Ivy. He probably didn't even like her. It gave Esther a small measure of comfort. She needed all the comfort and good memories she could get.

Ivy came into the kitchen. She was wearing the only blouse she owned that had sleeves and jeans that only had a few holes. She smiled that fake, taunting smile that she wore most days and stroked the back of her finger down Winnie's cheek. Winnie grimaced and turned away. "She's so cute. Isn't she cute, Esther?"

"Adorable."

"She sort of looks like Jordan around the eyes. His stepmom would love to meet her."

Just another one of Ivy's daily reminders that she had the power to upend Esther's life in a heartbeat. "I think she looks more like you. As a baby, you could have been her twin."

Ivy's smile grew in warmth. "You remember what I looked like as a baby?"

Esther nodded. "You were a pretty little thing, just like

Winnie. You had a little dimple on your cheek when you smiled. Mamm would hold you on her lap, and I would play peekaboo with you just so we could see that dimple."

"Were you jealous when I came? Some kids get jealous when a new baby comes."

"I was wonderful glad to finally have a sister," Esther said. She stifled a sigh. It had been a long time since she had been glad to have a sister.

Ivy seemed pleased with her answer. "Some kids are jealous." She studied Esther's face and played with her earrings. "Well, anyway. That was a long time ago. You're jealous enough of me now."

"I'm not jealous."

"Of course you are. Levi paid more attention to me than he ever gave to you."

Esther longed to point out that, in the end, Levi hadn't wanted Ivy, but she didn't want to provoke her sister. "For sure and certain he enjoyed your company."

"And of course you're jealous because I have Winter and you'll never be a mother."

Esther didn't know what Ivy wanted her to say. Was she deliberately trying to be cruel, or just reminding Esther of the hard truth?

Ivy sat down at the table. "What's for breakfast? Why don't you make me some of your blueberry muffins?"

"They will take some time to bake."

"Okay. How about crepes? You used to make the most delicious crepes with strawberries and whipped cream."

It took several pans and bowls to prepare crepes. "It's a lot of cleanup," she said, immediately regretting it. The more work Esther had to do on Ivy's behalf, the more Ivy liked it.

Ivy smiled indulgently. "Don't whine about it. It's not that hard to clean up, and you've got nothing better to do anyway. If Winter and I weren't here, you'd have nothing to do at all. You should thank me for being so nice and letting Winter stay, even though I could take her to California tomorrow. They have really good crepes in California."

Esther took deep breath after deep breath. She stared at Ivy and pictured this scene repeating itself for another twenty years. There was no fighting it. She had no power to fight. If she wanted to keep Winnie, she had to keep Ivy happy. And to keep Ivy happy, Esther had to give away a little piece of herself every day. She had to make all the compromises, lose all the arguments, and surrender every battle to Ivy. There was nothing else she could do. The thought of losing Winnie sucked the breath out of her and made her light-headed.

"I don't have any strawberries."

"There are frozen blueberries in the freezer."

Ivy must have recently searched for more of Esther's money. She never would have opened the freezer otherwise. "Okay," Esther said. "Blueberry crepes with whipped cream."

She set Winnie on the floor, and she immediately took off for the front room, where Esther kept a few toys for her to play with under the quilting frames that were always up. Ivy sat at the table and talked about shoes and hair dye, Mamm's bread pudding and the peeling wallpaper in the kitchen. Esther made the crepes, whipped the cream, and cooked the blueberries in a sauce, all while periodically checking on Winnie to make sure she wasn't into something she shouldn't be. When everything was ready,

Esther rolled three blueberry-filled crepes onto a plate and set them in front of Ivy.

Even though Ivy seemed to feel she was owed those crepes, she was delighted to get them. "Oh, Esther. Thank you. These look so good. First thing, you need to teach me how to make them."

"For sure and certain," Esther said, because she wasn't sure what to make of Ivy's glee and because Ivy would never actually try to make crepes. At least Esther would be spared the torture of trying to teach Ivy anything. Esther went into the front room and sat on the floor next to Winnie, who was happily sitting still and chewing on her doll's foot.

Ivy called from the kitchen, "Don't you want to keep me company while I eat?"

As it turned out, she didn't want to. Why had Ivy asked? Didn't she hate Esther as much as Esther hated her? Esther immediately chastised herself for that unkind thought. She didn't hate anybody, not even Ivy, but she certainly would be infinitely happier with Ivy out of her life. *Ach*, how she wished Ivy would go away and never come back. Then she'd never have to keep her company while she ate her breakfast crepes. Esther scooped Winnie into her arms, tromped into the kitchen, and sat down across from Ivy at the table.

Ivy was thoroughly enjoying her crepes. "You know, Esther, I was thinking. I would be so much more comfortable sleeping in your bed. I'm taller than you are and need the extra space. Will you help me move my things into that room tonight and I'll help you move your things out?"

Esther clenched her teeth. She should have been expecting this. There was nothing so alluring as a queen-size bed. "No, Ivy. It's too much work to move everything. I've got all my fabric in there and my sewing machine. Just stay where you are. Your bed is comfortable enough."

"It's too little." She took a big bite of her crepe. "Jordan's stepmom lets us sleep in a king-size bed when we stay there. I'm sure she wouldn't mind letting me and Winnie crash there."

Esther felt as if she were hanging from the edge of a cliff, barely holding on, unable to fight much longer. "Can we talk about this later? I need to finish this quilt tonight or I won't get paid. I won't have time to move any furniture."

Ivy laughed. "Don't be so dramatic. It won't take but a minute."

"Then you'll have to do it yourself."

"I can't move your sewing machine by myself. You'll just have to spare me five minutes out of your busy schedule." Ivy scooped some cream from her plate with her finger. "I need to go to Alamosa for a pair of shoes. I own one pair of flip-flops, and they're coming apart. So I need some money, and I need you to call your friend Cathy and have her drive me."

Esther bit her tongue and counted to ten. Ivy's impertinence wasn't a surprise, but the urge to lash out at her was almost overpowering. "You have my phone, and you already took what money I had in the house. You'll have to use some of that."

Ivy pursed her lips. She had four hundred dollars of Esther's money, but if she was wise, she'd be careful where she spent it. She gazed at Esther resentfully. "I have to have that money in case I need to take Winnie away and teach you a lesson."

"Then I guess you won't be buying any shoes. I don't have any more money in the house." That was true enough. She had plenty in the bank, but Ivy wasn't going to learn about the bank account if Esther could help it.

Ivy didn't like that answer. "I'll use that money, but what are you going to do when you need to buy diapers for Winnie?"

Esther planted a big kiss on Winnie's cheek to give herself some time to measure her words. "I have some money coming from a quilt I just finished. I buy Winnie's diapers with quilt money."

Ivy frowned. "You need to quilt faster. We're going to starve."

Maybe Ivy wouldn't be so cocky if she thought they were going to run out of money at any minute. Esther didn't reassure her. "I hope not."

Ivy left the kitchen and came back with Esther's phone. "So call your friend and have her come get me."

"I can't impose on Cathy that way."

"Of course you can, because if I can't even get to Walmart to buy a pair of shoes, I'll just have to take Winter and go to California. Lots of Walmarts within walking distance in California."

Ivy's ruling Esther's life was one thing, but pulling her friends into her little game was quite another. "I can't do that. Cathy is a busy lady. She can't just drop everything and drive you to Walmart."

Ivy leaned forward as if getting closer would empha-size her point. "She's like ninety years old, Esther. What does she have to do all day but watch TV and crochet baby blankets? Call her. She's probably looking for an excuse to get out of the house."

Ivy had that determined, threatening look in her eye that Esther knew all too well. It was another battle. Another surrender. And it was clear to Esther that Ivy didn't care if Cathy said yes, only that Esther did what she wanted, only that Esther submitted to her every demand.

Esther punched in the numbers on her phone. Cathy picked up after the first ring. "Hello, Esther. Is everything okay?"

"Yes. Everything is fine."

"You never call me, so I wondered. Of course, nobody calls me, not even my ungrateful children. You'd think they've all lost their phones."

Esther tried to smile, but she couldn't even muster a grimace. "Cathy," she said, her voice shaking like a flame in the wind. "Um, my sister, Ivy, was wondering if you could drive her to Walmart in Alamosa today."

There was a long pause on the other end, so long that Esther began to wonder if Cathy had fallen asleep. When she spoke, her voice was so soft Esther could barely hear her. "Is she there next to you?"

"Yes."

Another long, inexplicable pause. "For crying out loud. Tell her I'll be over in ten minutes. Wait, Esther?"

"What?"

"Better make it twenty. Don't know how long it will be to rally the troops."

"Um. I'm not sure what you mean, but Ivy can go another day if it's not convenient for you."

Cathy grunted. "Just tell her to be ready for a lecture. And if she gives me any guff, I'll make her walk home. That'll teach her." The call disconnected.

"What did she say?" Ivy asked.

"I think she thought it was rude to ask."

Ivy blew a puff of air from between her lips. "I don't care what she thinks. Is she coming?"

"In twenty minutes." If Ivy didn't care what Cathy thought, then Esther wasn't going to warn Ivy. Cathy could talk your ear off, and that was if she liked you okay. By the time Cathy got through with Ivy, Ivy would refuse to go anywhere with Cathy ever again. Ivy might be able to push Esther around, but Cathy would not be pushed.

Esther hesitated. She used to be someone Ivy couldn't push around. But Winnie had changed everything. Esther would do anything to keep hold of Winnie.

"I need you to babysit Winnie," Ivy said, almost as an afterthought. "It's a pain to take a baby shopping."

Of course it went without saying that Esther was the one to take care of Winnie, but asking Esther to babysit was Ivy's way of reminding Esther that Ivy was still in charge. And she didn't really ever ask. It was "Esther, make sure Winnie gets her bath," or "Esther, please feed Winnie. I'm going out to work on my tan."

Esther didn't mind caring for Winnie. She loved taking care of Winnie. It was what she'd been doing for six months. Ivy had a way of making her begrudge it, just the same.

Esther went back into the front room and set Winnie on the rug while she took a few stitches on her quilt. It was a single piece of black fabric that the client wanted quilted with six different colors of thick thread. It was dark and brooding and depressing, much like Esther's life. Why would anyone want a black quilt?

The pattern on the quilt was a dragon, with green eyes and blue scales. The scales were exactly the color of Levi's eyes. Esther held her breath. Maybe she should work on the purple feet. Purple did not remind her of Levi, except for maybe the purple flower he had tucked behind her ear at the park a few weeks ago. Esther looked at her selection of thick, shiny thread. It wouldn't matter what color she chose to work with—everything reminded her of Levi. Everything reminded her of what she had traded for Winnie.

Every time she went in the backyard, she thought of the day she'd thrown apricots at the house and Levi had laughed at her. She couldn't play pickleball again without remembering how he'd caught her pounding one of her paddles against an evergreen bush. She most certainly couldn't set foot in the new bathroom, because his hand was there everywhere. To help keep the pain manageable, she hadn't set foot in that bathroom since he'd finished it. Esther didn't know how to get Levi out of her heart, let alone her thoughts. Was she doomed to mourn him for the rest of her life?

Ivy went into her room and came out stuffing a wad of cash into her pocket. Esther bit her bottom lip. Her money, money that Ivy would use to take Winnie away. Esther wanted to growl. Instead, she took a stitch in the quilt and yanked the needle upward, jerking the thread up with it. Maybe this was why she had chosen to be a quilter. It was easy and harmless and productive to take your anger out on a piece of fabric. As long as her stitches were small, the quilt didn't care how angry she was when she put them in.

Ivy stood in the hall and watched Esther quilt. Didn't she have anything better to do, like wash dishes or wipe the table? "Do you remember when you helped me make a quilt for my bed?" Ivy said.

Esther remembered, but why Ivy wanted to talk about it was beyond her. "Yes. It was wonderful pretty."

"Only because you unpicked almost every stitch I made."

"It was your first time sewing. I wanted to help."

Ivy stepped into the room and ran her hand along the fabric. "I was never a good quilter."

"Of course you were. It just didn't hold your interest. You liked the outdoor chores better."

Ivy grinned. "I spent a lot of time in the haymow playing with the dog or daydreaming."

Esther pulled her thread through the fabric. "You liked to play imaginary games."

"I liked to escape." She sat down on the folding chair opposite Esther. Esther always kept two folding chairs near the quilt so Nanna could take a stitch or two when she came to visit and so Esther wouldn't have to keep moving the same chair around and around the quilt when she sewed. "Thank you for helping me make that quilt for my bed," Ivy said.

Esther hid her surprise as she glanced at Ivy. Ivy never said thank you. "I thought the colors you picked were so pretty."

"Mamm didn't like them."

"She didn't think pink and lime green would look good together, but they were beautiful."

Ivy gazed at Esther, her eyes full of an emotion Esther couldn't begin to guess at. "I loved that quilt."

Esther nodded. She and Ivy had made the quilt together when Esther was fourteen and Ivy was ten. Aside from her shoes and underwear and one dress, the quilt was the only thing Ivy had taken with her when she left home. "Whatever happened to that quilt?"

"Lost."

That one word was so full of sadness that Esther glanced up from her quilting and studied Ivy's face. What she saw made her want to weep.

Ivy flinched when they heard the car honk. She jumped to her feet as if trying to escape her past. "Be sure to give Winter her nap."

That kind of unnecessary instruction usually made Esther bristle, but maybe it was something about Ivy's tone of voice or the pain in her eyes that made it impossible for Esther to muster any righteous indignation today. All she felt was pity for her sister, herself, and what might have been. Ivy left without ceremony, and after a few seconds, Esther heard the car drive away.

She stuck her head under the quilt and looked at Winnie. "Should we put you down for a nap, sweetie?"

Winnie was chewing on a measuring spoon. She gurgled at Esther and rubbed her eyes.

"I'll take that as a yes." She crawled under the quilt, scooped Winnie up in one arm, and crawled back out. "Oh, my baby," she cooed. "Don't listen to a thing your *mamm* says about California. She's only saying that to get under my skin. You don't need to worry about it for one minute." Esther didn't want to lie, but she also didn't want Winnie to be anxious about it. There was nothing either of them could make better by worrying.

A firm and determined knock sounded at the door. For a split second, Esther thought it might be Levi. Had he waited until Ivy was away to come and see her? *Nae,* he wouldn't be that reckless. If Ivy ever found out, she'd take Winnie away for sure and certain. Levi knew enough to keep his distance.

Esther opened the door. Nanna, Mary Jane, Allison, and Rita pushed their way into her house as if they were invading. It *was* a sort of invasion, because they all talked at once, loudly, and didn't even wait to be invited in. Nanna herded the rest of the women into the house, hung her bag of fabric scraps on the hook by the door, and gave Esther the stink eye. Esther withered under her gaze. She had no energy or heart to stand up to Nanna.

"What's this?" Nanna said.

Esther's gaze flicked from face to face. "What's what?"

Nanna threw up her hands and marched into the kitchen. Esther and the rest of the women followed her. "You've got a quilt on the frame, dirty dishes in the sink, and a sister who uses one of my best friends as a chauffeur. What is this?"

It made sense that Nanna would be mad about Cathy, but Esther couldn't help the dirty dishes. She'd just made Ivy a fancy breakfast. "I . . . I don't know what you mean."

Rita pulled out a chair at the table and motioned for Esther to sit. "We're here to help you."

"And to gossip," said Allison. "I'm here for the gossip, and Cathy is wildly jealous she won't get to hear it first-hand."

Esther sat down and pulled Winnie closer. "What . . . what do you want to gossip about?"

Mary Jane held out her hands. "Is it naptime? I can take Winnie."

Esther handed Winnie to Mary Jane. "Yes. Thank you."

Nanna nodded. "*Jah*. You need your hands free to explain yourself."

Esther nearly called Mary Jane back. Winnie made a *gute* shield, and the others wouldn't dare gossip in Winnie's presence. "There's nothing to explain."

Nanna huffed out a breath, pulled a chair from the table, and sat down across from Esther. The other two sat down on either side of Nanna. Nanna peered at each of them in turn. "Now it feels like a meeting."

Allison nodded enthusiastically. "It's an intervention."

"I don't know what that means," Esther said.

Allison pulled a package of orange candies from her purse and handed one to each of them. Allison thought candy made everything better. "It means we're going to have a talk."

Nanna grunted. "It means we're going to scold you soundly."

Allison's smile froze in place. "We're going to have a talk, and you're going to listen and try to apply it to your life."

Esther wilted like a daisy in the hot sun. There were so many things Nanna could scold her about, she didn't even know which one Nanna would choose. All she knew was that she'd been beaten down and wrung out enough for three lifetimes, and she couldn't bear Nanna's displeasure. "Please, Nanna. Don't scold me."

Rita gave Esther's hand a motherly pat. "Why don't you start from the beginning."

Esther slumped her shoulders. "I'm sorry. I shouldn't have called Cathy to drive Ivy to Walmart." Maybe it was the way Nanna looked at her from across the table. Maybe it was the quilt that needed to be finished by Wednesday.

Maybe it was the thought of Ivy spending her money on a pair of high heels at Walmart. But the weight of the past week finally became too heavy to bear. She stood up, found the nearest piece of peeling wallpaper and ripped it off the wall. A strip the length of her arm came off when she yanked. It felt so *gute*, she located another peeling piece and yanked at it. This piece came off more as a chunk. It looked like Ivy's profile in silhouette. She crinkled it into a ball and threw it as hard as she could down the hall.

Rita's mouth fell open. "You . . . uh . . . you have a good throwing arm."

Allison looked completely horrified. Nanna laughed. "The Yoders were not *gute* wallpaperers. They used the wrong kind of glue. It started pulling away from the wall two weeks after they finished. Edna was wonderful annoyed."

Esther sighed. "I'm wonderful annoyed. I let Ivy talk me into calling Cathy. It was rude, and I apologize."

Nanna stood and pulled Esther back to her chair. "Esther, my dear, we're all very glad you called Cathy. I wasn't sure how to get Ivy out of the house. I've been itching to talk to you for three days. If Ivy is too speedy at Walmart, Cathy has plans to take her to the sand dunes, just to kill some time. If she gets desperate, she's assured me she'll get stuck in the sand. A tow truck could take hours."

Esther eyed Nanna in puzzlement. "You're not mad I called Cathy?"

"We're beyond grateful," Rita said. "We've been worried sick."

Mary Jane shut Winnie's door, pulled in a folding chair

from the front room, and sat next to Esther. She glanced at the wall with its missing strip of wallpaper. "Planning on redecorating?"

"Cheery yellow paint would look nice in here," Allison said.

Nanna shook her head. "It would look too much like urine." She scooted her chair closer to the table. "As devious as Cathy is, we don't have all day." She pinned Esther with a solemn and serious look. "I love my grandson, but if he has ruined his chances with you, I think I'd just as soon that he stayed in Ohio for the rest of his life."

Esther's heart suddenly felt like a thousand pounds of longing. "He's . . . he went to Ohio?"

Nanna nodded. "Three days ago and as gloomy as a minister at a dance party. He told me he ruined everything, that you would never speak to him again, that you would probably never be able to forgive him." She leaned forward to look Esther directly in the eye. "So what has he done, and how can he fix it?"

Esther's throat felt tight. "Is he looking for a *fraa* in Ohio?"

Nanna seemed to explode with displeasure. "Of course he's not looking for a *fraa*. He went to nurse his wounds."

Esther's face got warm. Nurse his wounds? What wounds did Levi have? Had she given them to him? Did he . . . ? Could he care for her? "*Ach.* I didn't know."

"You seemed to be getting along so well," said Rita. "So we want to know what happened, if you feel comfortable telling us." Rita was so kind, never wanting to upset anyone or make a fuss.

Nanna wasn't so diplomatic. Esther loved her for it, even though sometimes it made her uncomfortable. "Did you run him off because you think he's in love with your sister? Because I can tell you right now, he ain't." She glared at Esther as if everything was her doing. "He's in love with you."

Esther's heart pattered like a barrage of apricots against the window. "He's in love with me?"

Rita nodded. "We've all seen it."

It was everything Esther had wished for, longed for, thought about for months. "But, Nanna, I'm thirty years old. I've got a horrible temper, and I hardly know how to take care of a baby."

Nanna raised an eyebrow in exasperation. "Apparently, Levi likes all of those qualities."

"There's just so much about you to love," Rita said. "You're kind and conscientious, talented and enthusiastic."

Mary Jane put her arm around Esther. "You play pickleball better than anyone but Cathy, and Winnie loves you beyond anything. Levi loves you something wonderful."

Words and feelings leaped from Esther's mouth like shooting stars. "And I . . . I love him!"

Rita and Mary Jane beamed like headlights. "Isn't love the best feeling in the world?" Mary Jane said.

Nanna most certainly wasn't done with her lecture. "So why are you tearing wallpaper off the wall while Levi sits in Ohio being miserable?"

Esther took a deep shuddering breath. "It doesn't matter if I love him or he loves me. It just doesn't matter."

"Of course it matters." There was that scolding tone Nanna often used on Levi.

Esther pressed her fingers to her forehead. "Levi came over last week to convince Ivy to let me adopt Winnie. We had the papers ready and everything." She glanced at Nanna in embarrassment. "Levi had been so kind to Ivy. I thought he was going to ask her to marry him."

"I told you that is a bunch of hogwash," Nanna said.

"It wasn't just me. Ivy thought Levi was going to propose. I made breakfast casserole."

"Ivy is a ninny."

Esther agreed with Allison, but what good did it do, even if the whole world thought Ivy was a ninny? "Ivy was furious when Levi pulled out those adoption papers. She said we tricked her. She said we were only being nice to her so she would let me adopt Winnie. She called Levi a liar and a hypocrite." Esther couldn't stop her voice from shaking. "She said if I ever talked to Levi again, she'd take Winnie away from me."

The room fell silent as her dumbfounded companions stared at her.

"I was only going to scold you for letting Levi get away," Nanna said. "But this story is more like a seven-layer dip. Ivy won't let you adopt, you don't want to lose Winnie, and Levi thinks you're mad at him."

"I'm not mad at him. He thought he and Ivy were friendly enough that she would agree to sign those papers. I think he wanted to surprise me. How could he have known how Ivy would react? He shouldn't have done it without asking me, but how can I fault him for his good heart?"

Nanna fingered the wisps of hair at her neck. "So you've given up Levi to keep Ivy happy."

"I don't know," Esther said, the words escaping her lips like a sob. "I don't want to lose Levi. I can't bear to lose Winnie. Why do I have to pick?"

"You shouldn't have to."

"You're right. I shouldn't. My life is near unbearable, Nanna. All I know is that I love Winnie with my whole soul. If Ivy took her away, I would stumble around like a drunken man for the rest of my life."

Allison narrowed her eyes. "So Ivy's holding both you and Winnie hostage."

Esther pressed her lips together. "She's threatened to take Winnie away unless I do what she wants." She laughed bitterly. "This morning I made crepes because she said she'd take Winnie to California if I didn't. California! For crepes. She stole the four hundred dollars I keep underneath my dresser so that she has money in case she wants to leave with Winnie. And my cell phone. She says it's hers now."

Allison offered Esther another piece of orange candy. "That girl is a pill and a half."

Nanna leaned on her elbow, her index finger pressed to her temple. "So your love for Winnie has made you docile, afraid to sneeze in the wrong direction for fear of Ivy."

"For fear I'll lose Winnie."

"Same thing." Nanna turned to her granddaughter. "Mary Jane, will you make us all some coffee?"

"Of course, Mammi."

Nanna closed her eyes as if shutting out something very painful. When she opened them again, the compassion Esther saw there tugged at her heart like a kite in a windstorm. "Esther," she said. "You do not want to hear this, and I don't want to say it. Ivy may be bluffing. She may not. She may very well take Winnie away from you if she's mad enough." She reached across the table and grabbed

Esther's arm. "This is the part you don't want to hear. No matter how painful it will be, it is better to lose Winnie than to lose yourself."

A heavy weight pressed into Esther's chest, and she couldn't pull any air into her lungs. "You're right. I don't want to hear that."

Nanna squeezed tighter. "In the end, after all you can do, you might lose Winnie anyway. You can't live like this. Whether you get to raise Winnie or you don't, you can't surrender your life to Ivy. The cost is too high."

Rita pressed her fist to her chest. "She's right, but it hurts my heart just thinking about it."

Esther shook her head. It didn't matter what Nanna said. If it was within her power to control, she couldn't, wouldn't lose Winnie. She clasped her fingers together to keep her hands from shaking. Nothing was in her power. Very little was in her control. She might burn the pancakes tomorrow and Ivy could take Winnie away. Ivy might leave as soon as the money ran out or before the money ran out. She could decide to take Winnie on a day when she was feeling especially spiteful or profoundly depressed. And Esther would live on the highs and lows of Ivy's roller coaster for the rest of her life.

And what of Levi? *Ach*, how she loved him! Even if she held on to Winnie, hers would be half a life without Levi. He was every man she had ever wanted, would ever want. There would be no happiness if she didn't have him.

There would be no happiness if she didn't have herself.

In an effort to keep Winnie, she *would* lose herself, a small chunk every day until there was nothing left but the shell of a woman who used to be joyful and obstinate and temperamental, the woman who used to throw apricots at the house and destroy pickleball paddles and tile bathrooms and hold baby alligators for fun. She had a lot of faults, but they were her faults, her mistakes, the total of her life. And she could not give that up, even for Winnie.

What was she to do?

She didn't notice the tear trickling down her cheek until it made the smallest *plink* as it splashed onto the table.

Rita leaned over, wrapped her arm around Esther's shoulders, and made a clucking sound with her tongue. It was oddly comforting and motherly. "We must give God time to work His plan. The more we try to work it for Him, the more we fail. Trust in the Lord with all your heart and lean not to your own understanding."

Nanna nodded. "Gotte has a plan. We must trust in Him."

Esther didn't want to leave her life in the hands of a god who seemed to be messing things up badly. "If Gotte has a plan, it's not working out so well. Or if His plan is to intentionally bring me heartache and misery, how can I have faith in such a god?"

"God wants only good things for you," Rita said. "Only good things. And He wants only good things for Ivy. Though we don't especially like her, God does not see Ivy as the enemy. He loves her just as much as He loves you."

"But what if Ivy refuses to follow the plan?"

Rita looked up at the ceiling as if communicating with heaven. "God can make all things work together for the good of those people who love Him. He is a god of miracles."

"So I just sit and wait for Gotte to work His plan?"

Nanna propped her chin in her elbow. "Gotte does His

best work with someone who is already moving forward. The woman who sits and waits for Gotte to talk to her will be waiting a long time. Action is Gotte's best tool."

Mary Jane handed everybody a cup of *kaffee*.

Nanna took a sip and looked at Esther over the brim of her cup. "So, Esther, what do you think? Do you lose Winnie or lose yourself?"

The choice was agonizing. Of course it was, but with a clarity she hadn't experienced for weeks, Esther knew what she had to do. It was as if the storm clouds parted, allowing the sunlight to fall on a dark land. She would trust in Gotte and have confidence in her own choices. "I'm not going to lose myself." And she wasn't going to lose Levi.

Allison twitched her lips wryly. "Ivy is going to toss her cookies."

For the first time in weeks, Esther felt like she could breathe again, felt like being happy again. The laughter tripped from her lips. "Poor Ivy. She would be very indignant if she knew we were plotting against her."

"Oh," Allison said. "She'll suffer enough indignation with Cathy. There won't be much left to spare for us."

Nanna smiled. "Indignation is my favorite look on Ivy. She so deserves it."

Maybe Ivy deserved it. Maybe Ivy didn't. But Esther knew one thing for sure and certain: Esther deserved better. And she wasn't going to let Ivy hold her hostage anymore. And she would do everything in her power to hold on to her dignity, her happiness, and her love for Levi.

Mary Jane set Winnie's box of arrowroot cookies on the table. "We need something sweet to ease our anxiety."

"Mary Jane," Nanna said, "these are for the baby."

"There's nothing else in the cupboards, and I love these. I buy them for the children and eat them all myself."

Esther giggled and opened the box. "They're Levi's favorite too. He sneaks them when I'm not looking."

Allison took a bite and made a face. "Not worth the calories." She handed the rest of her cookie to Mary Jane. "You'll have to finish it."

"For sure and certain," Mary Jane said and stuffed the whole thing in her mouth.

Nanna finished off her *kaffee* and gazed at Esther, her eyes full of sympathy. "I'm sorry life is so hard sometimes."

"Me too."

Nanna stood and put her cup in the sink. "Well, now. We have at least an hour before Ivy and Cathy show up. Lord willing, we'll get three hours. Might as well make the most of the time. Let's go in there and finish Esther's ugly black quilt. Things will look up as soon as that's out of her house."

Chapter Fifteen

Esther knew what she had to do and she knew she was right in doing it, but her hands still shook, and beads of sweat trickled down the back of her neck. It was useless to try to quilt. Her stitches were so wide a buggy could have fit between them. She finally tied off her thread, stabbed it into the pincushion, and stood by the window watching for Cathy and Ivy.

Fortunately, Rita, Allison, Mary Jane, and Nanna had nearly finished the quilt. Esther closed her eyes and thanked Derr Herr for dear friends who knew how to quilt and would never dream of abandoning her in her time of greatest need.

"This really is a beautiful quilt," Rita said, threading her needle with a shimmering gold thread.

Nanna grunted. "It's too dark. It makes me feel nothing but gloomy."

"But the thread is stunning," Rita said. "The black brings out the beauty of the colors. Just like dark and hard times of our lives are what make the good times seem even more beautiful."

"That's true," said Nanna, "but it's not what I'd choose for my bed."

Rita smiled. "Me neither."

Esther's heart did a somersault as Cathy's car pulled in front of the house. "She's here."

Allison glanced at her watch. "Three hours and forty minutes. Cathy has gone above and beyond the call of duty today. I'll have to buy her a gluten-free dinner."

Nanna poked her needle into the quilt and stood up. "Do you need us to stay, Esther, to give you support?"

"*Nae.* I need to do this myself."

Nanna nodded. "Good for you."

Esther pulled the letter out of her pocket and handed it to Nanna. "Will you send this to Levi?"

Nanna gave Esther a swift hug. "Immediately. I'll have Cathy drive me to the post office."

Allison slung her purse over her shoulder. "She's not going to be happy about more chauffeur duty."

"Cathy is a good friend, and she cares very much about Esther. She'll probably break the speed limit just to get me there before the four o'clock mail pickup." Nanna retrieved her sewing bag and pinned Esther with a stern gaze. "Stay strong. You can do this."

Esther squared her shoulders. "I can." Even if it meant losing Winnie. Even if it meant her heart would never beat normally again.

Rita, Nanna, Mary Jane, and Allison strolled out the door as Ivy stormed across the front lawn with her flip-flops looped around her fingers and a plastic Walmart bag in her hand. Rita said something to Ivy that Esther couldn't hear, but it sounded nice, like a pleasant word of greeting. Ivy didn't acknowledge Rita or the other three women as she plowed through them like a baling machine, blew into the house, and slammed the door behind her. She caught sight of Esther and pointed toward the front yard. "That lady is crazy. I'm never getting in a car with her again."

Esther feigned innocence, which was mostly real. She had no idea what Cathy had put Ivy through today. "What happened?"

"She acted all nice and pleasant when she drove me to Walmart, like she was so happy to do me a favor. Then once I got out of the store, she told me she wanted to show me something, then she drove like a madman for like an hour until we got to some mountains of sand. It's like a state park or something. Who makes a state park out of a pile of sand? I thought I was being kidnapped. I kept telling her she'd better turn around or I'd call the police, but your phone died, and she doesn't have a charger in her car." Ivy spread her hands and raised her voice, as if Cathy not having a charger in her car was worse than murder.

"Please talk more softly. Winnie is asleep," Esther said.

Ivy lowered her voice, but she soon forgot to keep it down. "We got to the sand dunes, and Cathy wanted to look around. I told her if she didn't take me home this minute, I'd steal her keys and take myself home."

"Ivy, you didn't!"

"Oh, yes I did. But do you know what she did? She rolled down her window and threw her keys into a sand dune. It took us forty minutes to find them, and my flip-flops broke."

If Esther hadn't been so full of anxiety about the possibility of losing Winnie, she might have laughed. Hard. She would have loved to watch Ivy throw a fit. She would have loved to see the smug look on Cathy's face when she threw her keys out the window. *Ach*, life's simple pleasures. "I'm glad you finally got home," Esther said, not all that glad. *Ach*, she hoped Derr Herr would forgive her for all the lies she'd told in the last three months. "Did you find some shoes?"

Ivy held up the grocery bag. "They're ugly, but they were cheap."

Ivy was worn-out, cross, and feeling very put-upon. Esther pressed her lips together. Was this the best or the worst possible time to say what she had to say? Her courage was probably as tall as it was going to get. She didn't want to wait until tomorrow morning only to find she'd lost the nerve and the resolve. And with Ivy, there really was no good time to deliver bad news. She would react badly even if she were at a Christmas party eating pecan pie and chocolate cake.

Ivy slipped around Esther's quilt and slumped onto the couch. "What's for dinner? I'm starving. Cathy couldn't be bothered to stop at McDonald's, and she ate three protein bars right in front of me. She said she had to regulate her blood sugar. She didn't even care about my blood sugar." Ivy leaned her head back on the couch cushion.

"We're having leftovers for dinner."

"Leftovers? I refuse to eat leftovers. I want a big, juicy steak. Or how about a cheeseburger? Have you got anything like that in this horrible house?"

"We need to talk," Esther said.

Ivy lifted her head and eyed Esther suspiciously. "About what?"

"Let's go outside so we don't disturb Winnie."

"Her name is Winter."

Esther didn't respond. She held out her hand and pulled Ivy to her feet.

Ivy sort of stumbled to the front door behind Esther. "Can't this wait? I'm starving."

It might be a *gute* idea for Ivy to have something in her stomach while Esther delivered the bad news. It couldn't hurt. She ran to the fridge and grabbed three cheese sticks and an apple. If they weren't good enough for Ivy, then Ivy wasn't as hungry as she claimed.

They went outside and sat down on the porch step. Ivy unpeeled her first cheese stick. "What leftovers do we have?" she said.

Esther wrapped her arms around her waist. She was going to be sick. "Ivy, I'm not going to do this anymore."

"Do what?"

"I love Winnie very much, and I want to adopt her more than almost anything, but I'm not going to let you boss me around anymore, even if that means you take Winnie away from me."

Ivy froze in the middle of chewing her cheese. "Her name is Winter."

"You can call her whatever you want. She will always be Winnie to me. I don't care if it irritates you. I'm done being your servant. I'm not going to clean up after you or fix you blueberry crepes or give you the bigger bed. I'm not going to sew you dresses or call my friends to drive you places or give you money. You may stay here if you want, but I'm not going to let you use Winnie to control me."

Ivy stopped chewing and stood up. "Use Winter to control you? What are you talking about? I'm her mother. I want what's best for her, and you don't know how to take care of her like I do. I'm trying to help you."

"No, Ivy, you're not. You're selfish and mean, and you don't really care that much about Winnie. You don't love her or me. You only love yourself."

Ivy drew back as if Esther had spit in her face. "How dare you say I don't love my own daughter? What do you know about love? Nothing. You live in this miserable little house and work on your stupid little quilts, and your life means nothing. If it weren't for me and Winnie, you'd be nothing."

"Maybe you're right. Maybe I'm a worthless spinster who's never done anything more important than can apricots, but I'm not going to let you grind me into powder. I will allow you to stay in my house, but only if you get a job, help me with the chores, and behave yourself."

"Behave myself? You got nothing to say about how I behave."

"In my house, yes, I do. And I'm not going to let you decide who I'm friends with. I've written a letter to Levi, inviting him to come and visit us. You ruined any chance of happiness I might have had with Menno. I won't let you take Levi from me too."

Ivy laughed in derision. "You think Levi loves you? You think he'd ever look at someone like you? If Menno didn't care, Levi certainly doesn't."

Esther's heart ached. Levi was a true and loyal friend, but maybe he didn't care as much as Esther hoped. And maybe Ivy would say anything to make Esther doubt herself. "If nothing else, Levi is my friend, and you will not bar him from the house."

Ivy narrowed her eyes. "He's not allowed."

Esther stood up to face her sister. "It's not your decision. This is my house, and you are my guest."

Ivy grew angrier as she saw her control slipping away. "I will take Winter away. Don't think I won't."

"I know," Esther said, her voice cracking into a million pieces. She could feel her composure disintegrating, but it didn't matter. Let Ivy see her cry. She had to say everything before it was impossible to say anything. "I love Winnie, and I hate that you've used her as a way to get what you want from me. But taking Winnie is also your choice, and though I'll be devastated, I cannot let you steal my life from me one day at a time."

When Ivy got this worked up, there was no stopping her, no reasoning with her. "You talk like I'm some horrible person. I won't leave my child with someone who hates me so much."

"I don't hate you. I'm just not going to let you hurt me anymore." Esther's heart ached so badly, she could barely breathe. "Take Winnie away if you feel you must. Do what you have to do. Make your own choices and think only of yourself. I must think of what is best for me. I will trust Gotte to take care of Winnie."

Ivy's eyes flashed with anger and hurt. "So this is what you think of me. Well, I'll tell you something. I am a good mother. I am perfectly able to take care of my own baby, *good* care. Quit talking about God, as if you think there's no hope for Winter but through Heaven. I'm her mother. I'll give her everything a child could need."

"I'm glad to hear it," Esther choked out. It hurt to talk.

Ivy tugged her fingers through her hair. "I know when I'm not wanted. Me and Winter are getting out of here. Good riddance to this whole stupid place." Ivy pushed past Esther into the house. She nearly went into her room, where Winnie was sleeping, but must have thought better of it. Instead, she marched into Esther's room and locked the door behind her.

Esther stood on the porch and looked into the house, holding together the shreds of her self-control by sheer willpower. She shouldn't have bought a lock for her bedroom door. Ivy might stay in there for days. She would have her own private bathroom, and she could eat Winnie's stash of cereal puffs if she got hungry. Maybe Ivy's locking herself in Esther's room wasn't such a bad thing. Esther might have a little more time with Winnie, and Ivy would leave them both alone.

The slamming door woke Winnie from her afternoon nap. Esther went into Ivy's room, pulled Winnie from her crib, and clasped her tightly in her arms. Esther patted Winnie's back and rocked back and forth to calm Winnie's crying. Winnie settled onto Esther's shoulder and promptly fell back asleep. Esther cooed a lullaby and clutched Winnie to her bosom, hoping their very closeness would heal her broken heart.

Esther awoke with a lump of dread in her throat that nearly choked her. How she'd even managed to fall asleep was beyond her comprehension. She rolled over and looked at the clock. Almost eight. Her heart skipped a beat. Was Winnie still asleep, or had Ivy left already without giving either of them a chance to say goodbye?

Esther sat up with a start. Was Winnie gone?

She listened for any movement in the other room. There it was. Ivy was awake, moving around in her room, no doubt hoping she'd disturb Esther's sleep. It was the petty sort of revenge Ivy used all the time. Esther could also hear Winnie. She was making those little noises she always made when she was playing with a toy or one of Esther's measuring cups. She was probably sitting on the floor watching Ivy pack. Esther wanted to cry. Ivy was going to make good on her threat, and much sooner than Esther could have imagined.

Yesterday had possibly been the worst day of Esther's life. After she'd had that talk with Ivy, she knew in her heart that Ivy would take Winnie away from her, if only out of spite, if only because she wanted to win. Esther had understood the consequences of standing up to Ivy, but they were still more painful than a knife to the heart.

Last evening had unfolded much the same as it had for months. Esther had played with Winnie, fed her dinner, read her a story, and rocked her to sleep. Ivy had emerged from Esther's room long enough to eat a bowl of leftover Yankee bean soup and three slices of bread. She hadn't said a word to Esther and had completely ignored Winnie. After dinner, Ivy had locked herself in Esther's room again and called someone on Esther's cell phone. She'd obviously found Esther's solar charger. Ivy talked to someone for over an hour, and the conversation was in turns playful and contentious. Esther couldn't hear what Ivy was saying, but it was obvious she was looking for a ride out of Byler and maybe a place to stay when she got out.

Please, dear Heavenly Father, keep Winnie safe and healthy. She had stopped praying that Gotte would fix it so Winnie could stay. He would tell her no, and she didn't want to be any more disappointed in Him than she already was.

Ivy had finally vacated Esther's room at about ten last night. Esther quickly claimed her bedroom before Ivy had a chance to lock her out again. Ivy had pulled all the drawers from Esther's chest of drawers and dumped them out. She'd been looking for more money. It didn't take Esther but a few minutes to tidy her drawers. She didn't have much in them anyway, but it hurt that Ivy would steal from her own sister. Every time it happened, it hurt just like the first time.

Without knocking, Ivy walked into Esther's room carrying Winnie. "I need you to hold Winter while I pack," she said, an icy chill to her voice that sent a shiver down Esther's spine.

"Are you . . . are you leaving?" Esther hated how mousy she sounded. Why did she bother to ask? The answer would feel like a slap in the face.

"Of course I'm leaving, not like you care or anything. Jordan will be here in half an hour."

So soon? It wasn't enough time. Ivy should give her more time to say goodbye. "Jordan? I thought you broke up."

Ivy sneered. "He misses me. He's driving down from Fort Collins."

Esther swallowed hard. She didn't want to beg, didn't want to give Ivy the satisfaction, but she'd grovel if it meant keeping Winnie. "Jordan . . . you and Jordan would travel so much better without a baby messing things up. Why don't you leave Winnie with me? You know Jordan would like it better."

Ivy glanced at Esther's phone in her hand. "You don't respect me as a mother. I'm taking Winter."

Esther expected that answer, but it hit her right between the eyes. "Can I . . . can I help you pack?" Ivy would be too impatient. She'd probably forget Winnie's diapers or maybe her baby food. Winnie wouldn't go hungry if Esther could help it.

Ivy eyed Esther as if Esther planned to pack poison with Winnie's baby wipes. "Why?"

"I just want to make sure you get everything Winnie will need. Baby Tylenol, all her diapers, food."

Ivy glanced at the phone. "Okay. But hurry. Jordan isn't going to want to hang around waiting. And don't bother packing any of those Amish clothes you made her."

"She'll have nothing to wear."

Ivy thought about that for a minute. "Fine. Pack them. We'll get to Walmart for clothes eventually."

With her heart sitting like a stone in her chest, Esther clung tightly to Winnie with one arm as she packed up all of Winnie's things with one hand.

Esther nearly burst into tears when she heard the truck honk, but she held herself together by concentrating on how irritating it was that Jordan couldn't even come to the door like a normal person and help Ivy and Winnie and all their bags out to the truck.

Ivy pressed her lips together and grabbed her bag and Winnie's car seat. "He's here," she said, with less enthusiasm than Esther had ever heard in Ivy's voice. She tried for a smile, probably for Esther's sake, but wasn't successful. For all the fuss she'd made, she suddenly seemed reluctant to leave.

Esther followed her out the door carrying Winnie, the diaper bag, a small suitcase of Winnie's things, and the portable crib. She sincerely didn't know how she managed to stay on her feet with her world crumbling around her.

Ivy didn't know how to buckle the car seat into the truck. It had to be buckled between the driver's seat and the passenger side. How long would it be before they got sick of squishing in with the car seat and abandoned it altogether? Esther bit the inside of her mouth. Ivy would put Winnie's life in danger, and there wasn't a thing Esther could do about it.

Ivy held Winnie while Esther secured the car seat. Winnie whimpered and fussed while Esther buckled her in and gave Ivy quick instructions on how to do it next time. Not that Ivy listened, but Esther tried anyway. It wouldn't be her fault if Winnie was injured in an accident. But the thought was no comfort at all.

"Come on, babe," Jordan said. "I can't wait forever."

Ivy watched as Esther showed her how to tighten the car seat straps. "Don't make them too tight," Esther said, "or she might choke."

"I know," Ivy said, even though she didn't.

Winnie started crying in earnest. Esther tried not to panic. There were a thousand things that could go wrong. She would have to leave it in Gotte's hands. The problem was, she wanted to trust Him, but didn't know if she could. *Please, Heavenly Father. Please.*

Ivy stuffed the phone into her pocket. "Bye, sis. It's been fun," she said, tossing her hair over her shoulder as if she couldn't care less about Esther's pain. She probably couldn't.

Esther grabbed onto Ivy's arm to keep her from getting in the truck. "Ivy, listen. If you ever need to bring Winnie back here, I'll take her in a heartbeat. Don't hesitate. And I don't care where you are, if you need me to come and get her, just call Cathy. Her number's in my phone, and I've written it on a piece of paper in Winnie's diaper bag. If you and Jordan decide you don't want her complicating your life, I'll come wherever you need me and pick up Winnie. Then you and Jordan can be together, just the two of you." Something deeper than pain traveled across Ivy's face. Her features seemed to soften, and her eyes seemed to plead with Esther, but what was she pleading for? The look stunned Esther into silence.

"Come on, babe. We're wasting gas."

Ivy lifted her chin, and the unreadable emotion disappeared from her face. "I won't need you, but thanks for the offer."

Esther couldn't let her leave before she was sure Ivy understood. "Ivy, listen to me. Even if you're in Mexico or Florida or California, call me. If you can't come to me, I'll come get Winnie. Okay?" Esther had written Cathy's number on three different pieces of paper and stuffed them in three different pockets of Winnie's diaper bag. Esther wasn't going to pay the phone bill next time, and in a few weeks, her phone would be useless to Ivy. Lord willing, Ivy would find Cathy's number and use it.

Ivy rolled her eyes. "Okay. Fine. I already told you I won't need it."

Esther glanced at Winnie, who was still crying like her heart would break. "She'll need more diapers soon. I didn't have a chance to get any yesterday. And baby food. I packed a jam sandwich for her in the diaper bag. Feed her little bites at a time so she doesn't choke."

Ivy climbed into the truck. "You're so obsessed about choking, Esther. Relax. I'm Winnie's mother. She's going to be fine."

She almost smashed Esther's hand when she slammed the door. Esther stood on the grass and watched Jordan's truck bump and sputter and finally disappear down the road. She stood there for another ten minutes just staring, willing them to turn around and bring Winnie back to her.

Oppressive silence descended on Esther like a shroud. The air was still and stale. The trees were mute. Not even a bird sang. All Esther could hear was the sound of her own breathing, in and out, in and out. But how could that be? Hadn't her heart stopped beating? Hadn't the world stopped turning?

She walked around to the back of the house, sat down under the apricot tree, curled herself into a little ball, and finally allowed herself to weep.

Chapter Sixteen

Onkel Aaron strolled into the stable where Levi had just finished sweeping. "This floor has never been so clean," he said, leaning against the far post and eyeing Levi as if he was wonderful amused about something.

Levi didn't know and didn't care what Onkel Aaron was so amused about. For himself, Levi couldn't muster enough cheer to light a candle, and other people's glee was none of his concern. "I had some extra time, and the floor needed a *gute* cleaning. I think I'll spray it with the hose."

Onkel Aaron shook his head and gently pulled the broom from Levi's hands. "*Nae.* You've done plenty of work today. You've got to hurry if you want to shower before the gathering. Girls don't care how handsome you are if you stink."

Goliath, Onkel Aaron's massive Percheron horse, stuck his nose over the gate. Levi gave the horse's neck a pat. "I'm not going to the gathering, Onkel Aaron. The floor drain in the basement needs to be unclogged, and Aendi Beth wants me to help her rearrange the pantry shelves."

Onkel Aaron cocked an eyebrow, pulled up a milking

stool, and sat down. Propping his elbows on his knees, he eyed Levi as if trying to see into his skull. "We've been planning on your visit for months. Your *dat* wanted you to come to Ohio to find a *fraa*. I thought you did too."

"I did." Levi pulled a carrot out of his pocket and fed it to Goliath. He smiled to himself, remembering the time he'd found Esther beating a rug against the side of the house with a carrot tucked behind her ear. No one could wear a carrot the way Esther could.

"There it is again," Onkel Aaron said.

"What?"

"That faraway smile, like you're somewheres else. It wonders me if you really truly want to find a *fraa* in Ohio."

Levi blew a puff of air from between his lips. "I don't know. I mean, I should probably look for one. Nobody in Colorado will have me."

Onkel Aaron's eyebrow inched higher. "Nobody? A handsome boy like you? I'd think you could have your pick. Even here in Sugarcreek, where the girls can be as picky as they want, I think they'd consider you a *gute* catch."

"*Denki*, Onkel Aaron. I guess I should make the most of my time here, but I just don't have the heart for it." The thought of even trying to be polite to the girls made him tired and more than a little depressed. There was only one girl he ever wanted to talk to again, only one girl he wanted to install a toilet for, only one girl he wanted throwing apricots at him. And he'd ruined her life. He'd never forget the way she had looked at him that night when Ivy told him he wasn't allowed in the house ever again. Esther would do anything to keep Winnie. Ivy was in control now, Levi had been banished, and Esther was a prisoner in her own life.

Ach, how Esther must hate him!

"So you've come to Ohio to milk your *onkel*'s cows and do odd jobs for his *fraa*?"

Levi curled his fingers around the back of his neck. He'd come to Ohio to nurse a broken heart. He'd come to Ohio to get out of Ivy's way. Maybe if he weren't there, Ivy wouldn't take out her rage on Esther. Levi shrugged. "I could remodel your bathroom."

"You could go to the gathering. Peter has been telling *die youngie* about you for months."

"*Ach.* What did he tell them?"

Onkel Aaron chuckled. "He's built you up until you can't possibly meet their expectations."

A smile crept onto Levi's face. "Maybe I'd better shower."

Onkel Aaron's eyes sparkled. "The gathering might be fun."

Cousin Peter appeared in the doorway of the barn with a cookie in one hand and a letter in the other. "Levi, you've only been here a week and already you've done more around this farm than I've done the whole year."

Onkel Aaron shook a finger in Peter's direction. "You could learn a thing or two from your cousin."

Peter took a bite of his cookie. "Why do I need to learn anything? Levi will be here another two months. By the time he leaves, everything will be done."

Onkel Aaron growled good-naturedly. "Not by a mile, young man. Levi earns his keep, and he eats less than you do." That was true. Levi had barely been able to eat a thing since he'd gotten here. When he thought of Esther and how he'd hurt her, his stomach ached and he couldn't eat. Onkel Aaron stood and playfully punched Peter's arm. "Maybe I should send you to Onkel Jacob in Colorado and keep Levi here with me."

Peter's mouth fell open, and pieces of his cookie fell out. "But Dat, there's nobody in Colorado. I'd never get married."

Levi used to think the same thing, but he'd had a change of heart. The only girl worth having was in Colorado. But she was lost to him.

Peter took another bite of cookie. "Levi, we've got to leave for the gathering in fifteen minutes. You should shower so the girls don't faint from the smell."

Levi brushed his hands down his pants. "Girls usually faint because I'm so handsome."

"They do not."

Aendi Beth really needed help rearranging her pantry, and Levi was in no mood to talk to anybody. He was certainly in no mood to be charming for the girls. Esther had ruined him for anybody else. "I need to help your *mamm* tonight."

Peter grunted. "And then sit in your room and read your Bible for an hour, no doubt. I don't mind. It's just more girls for me to flirt with yet." He looked down at the letter in his hand. "*Ach*, I almost forgot. This came for you, Levi."

Levi's heart nearly stopped. The address was written in Esther's hasty handwriting. Esther had written to him? He snatched the letter from Peter's hand and tore it open.

Peter laughed. "I think we've figured out why Levi doesn't want to go to the gathering."

Levi glanced at Peter. "I'm sorry. I didn't mean to grab it from you like that. It's just . . ." He lost his train of thought as he unfolded Esther's letter. She had filled two pages.

Dear Levi, it started. *Please come home.*

Levi's heart hammered against his chest, and at that moment, he thought it might be possible to take flight. He folded the letter twice and stuffed it in his pocket, not needing one more speck of encouragement or a reason other than the fact that Esther wanted him back. He'd move mountains for her. All she had to do was ask.

He was definitely not going to any Ohio gatherings. "Onkel Aaron, I need to get back to Colorado immediately. Will you help me?"

Two and a half days later, Levi got off the bus at the station in town, where Cathy was waiting to take him home, except he didn't want to go home. Cathy, being a willing chauffeur, a good soul, and a hopeless romantic, drove him straight to Esther's house. Cathy gave him a sketchy update—that Esther had stood up to Ivy and Ivy had taken Winnie away in the boyfriend's truck. By the time they pulled in front of Esther's house, Levi wondered if Esther would want to see him or if she'd blame him for losing Winnie. Esther had written the letter to him before Ivy had cleared out. Maybe losing Winnie had broken Esther beyond anything Levi could repair. Maybe Esther would lay the blame squarely on Levi's shoulders and decide she could do without him in her life.

But none of this mattered. Esther needed him, and he'd be there for her. If it would make her feel better to throw him out of her house, he'd let her do it.

Cathy rolled down her window as he came around to

her side of the car. "I'll be back right before lunch in an hour," she said. "I'll take you out for tacos. You look like you could use a taco."

"That is very kind of you, Cathy, but could you give me at least three hours?" That was, if Esther would even let him in the house.

"Three?" Cathy grunted. "Nobody appreciates the sacrifices I make to drive you Amish all over kingdom come. Does nobody even care about my lumbago?"

"I care about your lumbago." He cared, but he didn't even know what that was.

"I should be home with my feet propped up watching *Poldark*. It helps my varicose veins."

Levi forced a smile. He didn't want to impose on Cathy, but he didn't want to waste any more time talking to her about her health problems. He'd grow whiskers before Cathy drew breath. "Don't worry about picking me up. When I'm done, I can walk home."

Cathy nodded. "You sure can." Her tires spit up gravel when she drove away. Must have been in a hurry to watch her show. Or go to the bathroom. She'd complained of a bladder infection all the way here.

Levi strode quickly to Esther's front door and knocked, but he didn't even wait until he'd finished knocking before he opened the door and stepped inside. He knocked three more times on the door while standing in the entry hall. "Esther?" No sign of her. He held his breath and listened and suddenly knew where she was. He hurried through the kitchen and down the hall to the new bathroom. Esther sat on the new watercolor tile floor, her head in her hands with a stick tucked behind her ear. She wasn't crying, but her posture conveyed nothing but despair.

Unable to bear the thought of the woman he loved in so much pain, he knelt down and touched her hand. *"Heartzley,"* he said, his voice shaky and weak. He loved Winnie too. Winnie was gone. There was plenty of sorrow to go around.

Startled, Esther looked up and sucked in a breath. "You came," she sobbed.

Relief washed over him in spite of the pain. She hadn't yelled at him or told him to get out of the house or chastised him for ruining things with Ivy. Maybe she could forgive him. Maybe she could love him in spite of everything he'd done wrong.

Tears streamed down her face. "I didn't know if you would come."

"Of course I came. Nothing would have kept me away." As he had once before, he reached out to her, gathered her in his arms, and lifted her off the floor. She snaked her arms around his shoulders and buried her face in his neck. "I'm here, *heartzley*. I'll never leave you again." He tightened his arms around her as great heaves of sorrow wracked her body. Standing in the hall, he cradled her in his embrace and let her cry.

After a good thirty minutes of weeping and commiserating and consoling, Levi made Esther a strong pot of *kaffee*, and they sat down at the table and gazed out the window. The autumn leaves of the apricot tree reflected the sun, glowing bright yellow at midday. The tree looked as if it was on fire. "You've never worn a branch before," Levi said, pointing to the bumpy, gnarly stick at Esther's ear.

Esther took a sip of *kaffee* and sprouted a half-hearted smile. "You never know when you're going to need a stick."

"True, like when you need to fend off the wild dogs roaming your neighborhood. Or when you meet a friendly dog and want to play fetch. Or when you want to play a quick game of pick-up sticks. Or when you happen to have more things than you can shake a stick at."

Esther's smile grew in warmth, like a sunrise on an icy day. That smile was like a balm to his heart. "I was sitting under the apricot tree, and it fell on my head. I thought it looked interesting, so I kept it."

Levi took a sip of *kaffee*. "How long has she been gone?"

Esther studied the mug wrapped in her fingers. "A week. Every day that passes takes Winnie farther and farther away from me. I'm terrified I'll never see her again."

"Me too." Levi wanted to reassure her that Winnie would come back to her somehow, but he couldn't, and he wouldn't say anything that wasn't true just to make her feel better. Empty words would only make her feel worse. "You will always be Winnie's true *mater*."

Esther blinked back some tears. "*Denki*. I . . ." She pressed her lips together.

He laid his hand over Esther's and laced his fingers between hers. "I wanted to surprise you with the signed adoption papers. I shouldn't have tried to make . . . I'm so sorry."

Esther lifted his hand to her mouth and kissed each one of his knuckles. His pulse raced at her touch. "I bear you no ill will. Neither of us could have guessed how Ivy would react. Though I wish you would have talked to me about it, I always knew that my time with Winnie would be short. Despite how unpredictable she is, Ivy is the same old Ivy, bent on taking control where she can get it." She squeezed his fingers between hers. He felt it all the way to his bones. "I love you for wanting to help. *Denki.*"

I love you? Did she mean *love* love or just the friendly love between two friends who just wanted to be friends? Because he didn't want to be just friends, and if she wanted to be just friends, he'd never be able to breathe normally again. But he'd only just gotten back and Winnie was gone and it was too soon to ask the question he'd been wanting to ask for weeks. *Do you love me, Esther? Because I love you something wonderful. Is there enough room in your heart for both Winnie and me? Is it too broken for anyone to mend? Are you too broken to ever give your heart away again?*

It was too soon. Too soon. He'd have to be patient. Being hasty was what had gotten him in trouble the last time.

"You're a *gute* friend, Levi."

Ach. "Friend." She was going to drive him insane.

"How long has it been since you've eaten something?" he said. She looked so tired. "How long has it been since you've had a *gute* night's sleep?"

"I had three carrots for dinner last night, and I haven't slept well since Ivy dropped Winnie off back in April."

He winced. "Sorry for the painful reminder."

"It hurts to talk about Winnie, but I'd rather talk about her than pretend she doesn't exist. When I feel the hurt, that's how I know it meant something. If I didn't love her, it wouldn't hurt, and I'm not going to trade that love for anything. I'd rather feel the pain."

"You're right," he croaked. He shut his mouth and swallowed hard. If he said another word, he would crack into a hundred pieces.

"I would never wish away the hurt. The pain is part of the love."

Levi cleared his throat. "I can't do much about your sleeping, but I can make you something to eat." He stood and opened Esther's fridge. There was half a gallon of milk, a jar of pickles, and a small chunk of cheddar cheese, along with a whole bag of carrots in the vegetable crisper. "This is unforgivable," he said dryly, shooting a teasing look in her direction.

Esther shrugged her shoulders. "I haven't been to the store for a few days. I'm glad when I can get out of bed in the morning."

"I'm glad too," he said. *Ach*, how he wished he could take away her pain. He hooked his thumbs under his suspenders. "*Ach, vell.* You need something to eat, and I am very *gute* at making due with what I have."

"I can help," Esther said.

"*Nae.* Let me do this for you. You rest. I'm a fair cook when I have to be. Every time Mamm has a new baby, I'm on kitchen duty. Well, me and Ben and Mary Jane. Mostly Mary Jane, but I've always watched closely."

He rummaged through her cupboards until he'd rounded up some acceptable ingredients. She watched while he boiled and poured and measured and stirred. After twenty minutes, he had made a pretty reasonable reproduction of Mamm's famous macaroni and cheese, enough for both of them. Esther was delighted. He was delighted that she was delighted. She ate three-fourths of the panful, and he ate the rest, but only after she insisted she could not eat another bite.

Esther helped him do the dishes, even though he told her he'd do them himself. He pointed to the places on the wall where Esther had ripped off the wallpaper. "Planning on redecorating the kitchen next?"

Esther's face got three shades redder. "You know perfectly well what happened to my wallpaper."

He cocked an eyebrow. "Couldn't find a pickleball paddle?"

"Mine are all broken, you know that. I wadded it up into a ball and chucked it as hard as I could. Rita said I have a *gute* arm." She pointed down the hall. "See for yourself. The paper is still there."

Levi glanced down the hall. "You do have a good arm. Did it make you feel better?"

"Not in the least."

Levi smoothed his hand over the wall where one patch of wallpaper used to be. "*Ach, vell.* At least you've got a start on the redecorating."

"Or maybe I'll leave it as a reminder to control my temper or face repainting my whole house."

Levi stopped drying the pan in his hand. "*Nae*, Esther. Don't do that. I like your temper just the way it is. If you didn't have your temper, you wouldn't be you. I couldn't bear it."

"My temper is very hard on the furniture."

He blew a puff of air between his lips and waved his hand in her direction. "Furniture and pickleball paddles are replaceable. There's only one Esther Zook, and she is irreplaceable."

Tears pooled in Esther's eyes. "Nanna said I would lose myself if I didn't stand up to Ivy."

He put down his pan and cupped his hand on her cheek. "Nanna is right. Much as I hate losing Winnie, I couldn't bear it if I lost Esther too." He leaned closer until their faces were mere inches apart and riveted his gaze to her mouth. "I just couldn't bear it," he whispered. Her blue-green eyes were warm and inviting, like a cool lake on the perfect summer day. The urge to kiss her seized him around the throat. He swallowed hard and, with supreme effort, dropped his hand to his side and stepped back. Much as he wanted to take her in his arms and kiss her to distraction, he wouldn't ever take advantage of her heartbreak like that. When he kissed her, he wanted it to be a joyful expression of their love, not some token of their shared grief that neither of them knew how to express.

Breathing heavily, Esther also stepped back. Her cheeks were a heightened color of pink, her lips more inviting than ever as they twisted in confusion. "Levi," she said. *Ach*, how he loved hearing his name on her lips. "Levi," she said again, as if saying it would give her time to gain her composure. She straightened her *kapp*, which had sat crooked on her head since he'd found her sitting in the bathroom. "If you need to go, don't let me keep you. I've already imposed on so much of your time."

He leaned his hand against the counter to the side of her but didn't touch her again. It was too dangerous. "There's nowhere I'd rather be than right here." He frowned. "Unless you want me to go. You're probably wishing I'd go away and leave you in peace."

"*Nae, nae,*" Esther blurted out. "I want you to stay. With Winnie gone, it's too quiet in this house." A tentative smile found its way onto her lips. "But it's not about the quiet or Winnie. I . . . I need you . . ." Her voice trailed off.

Levi held his breath. *I need you to . . . what?*

I need you to repair the grout in the bathroom?

I need you to prune the apricot tree?

I need you to mop my floor or cut my grass or take me to the gator farm?

Or had she said exactly what she wanted to say? I need you.

His heart beat a hundred miles a minute. "I'll stay as long as you want," he said.

He needed her too.

Like a man needs air.

Chapter Seventeen

"S-M-E-L-L-Y. Smelly," Mary Jane said. "That is a triple word score."

Mary Jane's husband, Tyler, groaned and wrote down her score on his yellow notepad. He glanced at Esther. "I told you that you didn't want to play Scrabble with Mary Jane. She always wins."

Esther hadn't been in the mood to laugh for weeks, but she grinned at Levi, and Levi winked at her. Tyler tried to hide it, but he was very competitive. He insisted on keeping the score, just to make sure it was done correctly, and he had to look every word up in the dictionary, even words like "smelly," before the game could continue.

Nanna was babysitting their children so Mary Jane and Tyler could come over and play games with Levi and Esther at Esther's house. "Mary Jane needs to get out of the house," Nanna had said, but what she really meant was, "We are doing everything we know how to cheer you up, Esther. Please humor us."

Esther sighed inwardly. What would she do without dear friends to watch out for her? What would she do without Levi, who had been to her house every day for the last week, making sure she didn't have to be alone and seeing that she ate at least one square meal a day?

Winnie had been gone for two weeks, and though life was still nearly unbearable, Esther could see that over time, things would start to feel like maybe they could get better, like maybe she would be able to breathe again if she gave it long enough.

"It's your turn, Tyler," Mary Jane said.

Tyler frowned in concentration. "I'm thinking."

Being so competitive, Tyler always took an extraordinary amount of time on his turn. He had to think through every letter and possible spelling and ways to come up with the highest possible score. The propane lantern hissed as he studied his letters. His expression suddenly brightened. "This is a *gute* one," he said, picking up his letters and arranging them on the board. "B-A-B-Y."

Baby. *Ach.* Winnie would be one year old in a few weeks. Would anybody give her a birthday party?

Glancing furtively at Esther, Mary Jane leaned forward and spoke from between clenched teeth. "Tyler, how could you be so insensitive?"

"What?" Tyler said.

Mary Jane inclined her head in Esther's direction. "Don't you think that's going to remind someone of someone who isn't here?"

Tyler caught his breath. "*Ach*, I'm sorry, Esther. I didn't mean no harm by it, but it's the most points I can do. The Y alone is worth four."

Esther waved away his apology. "Oh, please, Tyler, no apology necessary. There's no reason to tiptoe around me. Everything reminds me of Winnie. I'll be okay."

Mary Jane drew her brows together. "I suppose that's true. 'Smelly' is almost as bad as 'baby.'"

Levi laughed. "I changed enough diapers to know."

Leave it to Levi to make everyone feel better about it. If he acted as if there was nothing to be upset about, everybody else would do the same. She loved that he wanted to make things better for her, even if he wasn't sure how. And he *was* making things better, just by his being here. Esther loved him for that.

Someone knocked softly on Esther's door. Mary Jane lifted her head. "That's probably Caleb. Nanna said she'd have him fetch us if she had any trouble with *die kinner*."

Esther went to the door, opened it, and nearly fainted. Ivy stood on the porch with a pained expression on her face and Winnie in her arms.

"Mama," Winnie said, practically falling out of Ivy's arms reaching for Esther.

Esther gasped and squealed and snatched Winnie from Ivy's embrace without even asking permission. "Winnie, oh, Winnie, my sweetie." She gathered Winnie in her arms and hugged and kissed her dirty face and cooed and fussed and cried until Winnie took her chubby little hand and pushed Esther's face away. Esther laughed. Winnie was done with being kissed.

Levi, Mary Jane, and Tyler appeared in the entryway and huddled around Esther and Winnie as if they were sharing delightful secrets with one another. "Oh, Winnie," Mary Jane said, kissing the top of Winnie's little head. "You're home. We're so glad you're home."

"For sure and certain we missed you." Levi kissed Winnie on the cheek. Winnie made a face and turned away. She apparently didn't want excessive affection from anybody. Levi tried to take Winnie from Esther's arms, but Esther wouldn't let him. Winnie was back. Esther would never let her go again.

Esther turned to Ivy, who stood on the porch holding Winnie's diaper bag. Winnie's suitcase, car seat, and portable crib sat at Ivy's feet. "Thank you, thank you for bringing our Winnie back to us."

"Okay," Ivy said.

Levi pulled the car seat and the portable crib in off the porch. "You even brought her crib."

"Which is *gute*," said Mary Jane, wrapping her fingers around Winnie's arm, "because she looks bushed."

Esther formed her lips into a sympathetic O. "Poor thing. She does look tired. It's almost eight o'clock. We should get her to bed." She glanced at Ivy. "Is there a bottle in the diaper bag? How long ago did she eat?"

Ivy shifted her weight and stuffed her hands into the pockets of the oversized jacket she was wearing. "I fed her before we got here."

Mary Jane rummaged through the diaper bag. "Never mind. Here's the bottle, and there's still some formula in the can." She pulled them out and headed for the kitchen. "I'll make her a bottle."

Tyler followed her into the kitchen.

Levi laid a steady hand on Esther's shoulder. "Thank you, Ivy. This really means a lot to us."

Ivy nodded. Her dangly earrings tinkled softly. "Okay. See ya."

She turned and stepped off the porch. Levi shut the door and gave Esther a smile that knocked the air right out of her. He wrapped his arms around both Esther and Winnie, and they stood in the hall in a three-way hug, not moving, not saying anything, simply savoring the feel of each other. If Esther lived to be a thousand years old, she would never forget how happy she felt at this moment to have Winnie back in her life and Levi's arms around them both. She never wanted this feeling to end. Ever.

Winnie squirmed, and Levi relaxed his hold on both of them. She made a sour face and tapped Levi on the cheek as if to push him away. Levi threw back his head and laughed. "I recognize that look. You've given it to me a time or two."

Esther let her mouth fall open in mock indignation. "I have not."

"You have too. I think Winnie is going to have your temper."

Esther smiled at the thought that Winnie would inherit anything from her aunt who loved her like her own *dochter*. Esther gave Winnie another kiss on her grimy cheek. She seemed healthy enough, but she was filthy. She wore the same dress Ivy had taken her away in, and her matted hair looked as if she hadn't had a bath for two weeks. "I think I should give her a bath before a bottle. Then she can go right down after she eats."

Levi nodded. "I'll go set up her portable crib." He carried the crib into Winnie's room.

"Wait," Esther said, going into the spare bedroom. "I want her in my room tonight."

Something caught Levi's eye, and he peered out the window. "Look, Esther. Ivy's still here."

"What?" Esther got on her tiptoes and looked outside. Ivy was indeed sitting on Esther's porch step with her arms wrapped around her legs and her face buried in her knees. "I . . . don't understand," Esther murmured.

"She . . . I thought she was with Jordan. She just came to drop Winnie off, didn't she?"

"I don't know."

"Do you think she needs a place to sleep?"

"Maybe she's waiting for her boyfriend to pick her up."

Esther took a deep, painful breath as her heart sank. "Will you take Winnie? I guess I need to see what's going on. Maybe she has somewhere to go. Maybe she's waiting for someone to pick her up."

Esther knew better, even as the words came out of her mouth. The boyfriend wasn't coming. Ivy was waiting for nobody. Much as Esther wanted to be rid of Ivy, she couldn't just leave her out there. It was a chilly night, and Ivy's jeans were too holey to provide much warmth. Esther took a deep, resigned breath. *Ach*, she didn't want Ivy back in the house. She didn't want to see Ivy ever again. She wanted to be Winnie's mother and not spare another thought for her wayward sister. But as she knew all too well, things rarely turned out exactly the way she wanted them to. She certainly couldn't let Ivy freeze to death on her porch.

She handed Winnie to Levi. "It wonders me if you should give her a bath. I don't know how long I'll be."

"Okay." He pulled the quilt from the twin bed. "Here. Take this. It's cold out there."

With the quilt draped over her arm, Esther opened the front door and stepped out onto the porch. A chilly breeze greeted her as soon as she shut the door. "Ivy? Are you waiting for somebody?"

Ivy didn't look up. She didn't even move. It was as if she was made of stone. Or maybe she had turned to ice. Esther spread the quilt and laid one side of it over Ivy's shoulders, then sat down and wrapped the other half over her own shoulders. On cold winter nights when she was little, she and Ivy used to sit by the woodstove and share a blanket while Dat read stories from the Bible. On special nights, Mamm would pop popcorn or make scotcheroos, and they would huddle together in a blanket and make up silly songs together.

"Is somebody coming to pick you up?"

Ivy lifted her head and looked straight ahead. "If I died tomorrow, not one soul in the whole world would care." The despair in her voice was like a rip in the fabric of the sky.

Esther didn't know what to say. Of course she would care if Ivy died. She would even be sad. But things would be so much easier if Ivy left Winnie here and never came back. She felt wicked for having such thoughts, but there they were, and she could do nothing to stop them. Ivy had made her own bed, but lying in it was a bitter consequence indeed. "No one wishes for your death, Ivy."

"Oh, I'm sure you've wished it a time or two, like when Menno kissed me or when I took Winnie away."

"I have never wished it, Ivy." It was true, and Ivy needed to hear it. "Where is Jordan?"

Ivy spit air out of her lungs. "Who cares."

"Didn't he bring you here?"

"I left him in Fort Collins puking his guts out. He's always either drunk or hungover from being drunk. He blew through my four hundred dollars in about a week."

Esther wanted to point out that it was *her* four hundred dollars, but Ivy was low enough already. "How did you get here?"

Ivy eyed her as if she found the question confusing. "You told me to call Cathy, so I called Cathy."

Esther was momentarily speechless. "Cathy went and got you in Fort Collins?"

"I told her if we took a detour to the sand dunes, I'd break every window in her car."

Esther wouldn't have believed it. Cathy with her lumbago and gout and bladder problems and a bad hip had driven all the way to Fort Collins to pick up Esther's sister? But why?

"Cathy thinks the sun rises and sets with you," Ivy said. "I had to hear about how great you are all the way here. That and Cathy's migraines. She's thinking of getting her ears pierced by a doctor."

"Thank you for bringing Winnie back."

Ivy nodded, and her eyes pooled with tears.

It was obvious Ivy had done a lot of crying recently. "Why did you bring her back?"

"Because Jordan's a jerk. He won't get a job. He won't even take care of Winnie while I get a job, not that I'd want him to. He doesn't love me. He only loves himself and the money I can give him." She pressed her lips together. "He yelled at her yesterday."

"Winnie?"

"She was crying, and he was trying to sleep, and he yelled at her to shut up."

Esther pulled the blanket closer around her shoulders as a shiver traveled down her spine. "Did he hurt her?"

Ivy tossed her hair over her shoulder. "Hurt her feelings. But I could see it was only going to get worse because Jordan is a jerk and never thinks about anybody but himself. Even though you're Amish, I knew Winnie would be better off here with you."

Esther closed her eyes against the thought of what might have happened. "You're a good mother."

"You don't have to lie to me."

Was it a lie? Esther didn't even know. "You thought of Winnie first. That's what a good mother would do."

"You don't have to pretend with me anymore. I'll sign those adoption papers and then you won't have to pretend to like me. You won't have to be nice to me or call her Winter or give me a place to sleep. You won't have to pretend."

Ivy shuddered, and Esther slid her arm around her. "I'm not pretending. I do love you." She didn't like Ivy very much, but Ivy was her sister. She would always love her.

"Then why did you let me go? Why did you let me take Winnie and get in that truck with Jordan?"

"I couldn't stop you."

"You were willing to let Winnie go just to be rid of me, even after you told me I deserved better than Jordan."

"And you do," Esther said.

"But you didn't try to talk me out of leaving with him. You begged me to bring Winnie back. You said it didn't matter where I was, you would come and get Winnie any-where, anytime." Ivy turned her face away. "But you didn't care that I was going off with Jordan. Jordan! The guy who broke my collarbone. The guy who can't stay sober for more than a few hours. You wanted me gone, and you didn't care who I left with, even if it was the guy who beat me up. You didn't care what happened to me. You only care about Winnie. Don't try to deny it."

Esther expelled a deep breath. "I'm not going to lie. I

wanted you to go away. I wanted to keep Winnie and get rid of you."

Tears pooled in Ivy's eyes. She blinked them away. "Like throwing me in the trash."

Esther's temper flared. It was so unfair of Ivy to accuse her like that. "What should I have done? Even before Winnie, even before Jordan, you made my life miserable."

Ivy lifted her chin resentfully. "How can you say that about your own sister?"

Esther wasn't going to back down this time. Ivy had asked for the truth and she was going to get it. "How can you not see what you have done? Before you even turned sixteen, you were determined to ruin my life. You tried to steal every boy who was interested in me. You kissed my fiancé. Kissed. My. Fiancé. I cried for weeks. My heart was broken, and you just laughed about it."

"You didn't have to call off the wedding. Menno still wanted to marry you."

"Oh, yes, I was so eager to marry a boy who had been caught with my sister. Trust was completely shattered. Do you know how long it's taken me to trust another man?" Ivy would not look at her. Of course not. It was hard to come face-to-face with a lie you'd created for yourself. "And then you just left, without telling anyone. Mamm's heart was broken. I wouldn't have even considered marriage after you left, because Mamm didn't want me to leave her. I watched Mamm and Dat waste away with grief, all because of you. *Of course* I wasn't glad to see you when you came to Colorado. You dumped your baby on my doorstep, then came back thinking you could take her from me. Can you blame me for wanting to be rid of you?"

To her surprise, Ivy didn't throw off the quilt and storm

away. She didn't stomp her foot or punch Esther in the face. The light of the quarter moon illuminated her face enough for Esther to see that she was crying. Esther did the only thing she could think of. She nudged Ivy's head onto her shoulder, stroked her hair, and whispered, "Hush, hush, little dewdrop. Hush now."

She hadn't called Ivy "little dewdrop" for at least fifteen years. It sounded foreign on her tongue, yet natural and right at the same time.

"I wanted you to hurt," Ivy sobbed. "I wanted you to hurt as bad as I was hurting."

Esther frowned. Ivy couldn't have experienced any pain like what she had inflicted on Esther. The anger bubbled like bile in her throat. Ivy would never stop playing the victim. She nearly stood up and went inside, fed up with Ivy and her lies and her selfishness. Ivy could find another place to sleep tonight. Esther was done being hurt by her sister.

Faint sounds of Winnie giggling came from inside the house. Levi loved to toss Winnie up in the air and make her laugh. What would Esther do without him? Levi's words floated into her mind. *Can't you see how broken Ivy is?* Levi had always felt more pity for Ivy than Esther ever had, maybe because he didn't know Ivy as well as Esther did. Or maybe because he saw what Esther was not willing to see. Esther slid closer to Ivy and pulled the quilt tighter around them. Maybe she should look past her anger and just listen. Levi would want her to at least try to understand. "Why were you hurting, Ivy?"

"Because Mamm and Dat didn't love me."

"Of course they loved you."

"Not near as much as they loved you." She pitched her

voice higher. "'Ivy,' Mamm would say, 'why can't you be more like Esther? You can't sew and you can't cook and you won't help with your cousins. What a lazy child you are.' She wouldn't teach me how to cook because she said it was a waste of time. She said it was easier to let you help her because you already knew what to do."

Esther thought back to those years. It was true that Mamm had depended on Esther for help and rarely asked Ivy to do anything. Could it be that Mamm had been too tired or too impatient to teach Ivy when Esther could already do things so much better? She was four years older, and it was just easier for Mamm to get Esther to help than to try to teach Ivy how to do anything. Where Esther had thought Ivy was lazy, maybe Mamm had labeled her as incapable.

Ivy wrapped her arms around herself. "You were better than me at everything. You still are. Even at being a mother. Dat loved you. You helped him with the money and studied how to grow more corn."

"Dat loved you too."

Ivy shook her head. "He ignored me."

Esther couldn't believe it, didn't believe it. She'd seen the way Dat and Mamm had loved and cared for Ivy, but she could also see it from the eyes of a little girl who had trouble learning to read and a sister who could do everything better than she could. Of course Esther had been able to do everything better than Ivy. Ivy was four years younger.

"Every time I knew a boy was interested in you, I tried to get him to like me instead, just to prove I was better than you at something, anything. But it never worked out that way. You were prettier and more mature. The boys put up with me. They adored you."

Esther forced a small laugh. "I remember that differently."

Ivy curled her fingers around the quilt at her shoulders. "The trouble with Menno was all my fault. I'm sorry."

Esther tried not to show her surprise. She never would have dreamed that Ivy would apologize for that.

"I thought if I could get Menno to love me, Mamm and Dat would see that I wasn't worthless, and you would see that a boy could like me better than he liked you. I wanted you to be jealous. I was so jealous of you." She didn't look at Esther, but she wrapped her fingers around Esther's forearm and squeezed tight. "I'm sorry, Esther. I'm sorry I came between you and Menno."

"Menno made his own choices."

"But he never would have fallen if I hadn't tempted him."

Esther stroked her hand down Ivy's arm. "I was mad and deeply hurt over Menno, but you said it yourself—I should have been grateful. And I was, even if my pride didn't allow me to admit it." There was more than just uncovering Menno's unfaithful heart. If she had married Menno, she never would have met Levi. Levi was her true match.

"I wanted Menno to love me. I asked him to run away with me, but he wanted to stay in the community and try to make you love him again."

"That never would have happened."

Ivy nodded. "I know. Menno had lowered himself to kiss your sister. You didn't want him after that."

"He gave in to temptation. I didn't think he lowered himself. You were always prettier and more desirable."

"What a silly thing to say, and so untrue," Ivy said. "I tried to act like I didn't care, but I knew how much I had hurt you, Esther. I'm sorry. I'm truly sorry."

"I know," Esther said, even though she didn't know that she knew until that very moment. "I'm sorry too, for refusing to talk to you for a whole month. I wanted to punish you. I didn't mean to drive you away."

Ivy sat up straighter. "It's not your fault, Esther. After what happened with Menno, Dat told me I needed to go away, get out of the community. He said I'd done enough damage to the family and you were better off without me."

Esther's stomach dropped to her toes. "He . . . he told you that?"

"He gave me a thousand dollars to leave."

"But . . . but what about Mamm? She was heartbroken." Esther refused to believe it. Surely Dat wouldn't have done that to Mamm.

"He said Mamm would get over it. He said I would keep disappointing her every day if I stayed."

Esther opened her mouth to argue and promptly closed it again as memories of Dat's last days in the hospital came back to her. *I did what I thought was right by Ivy and your* mater, *Esther. I shouldn't have thrown off one of my children like that, and now Gotte is punishing me. I should have taken care of Ivy. Now it's in your hands.* At the time, Esther had thought Dat was missing Mamm and brokenhearted about Ivy leaving the family. But now those words sounded like remorse, remorse for something he'd done that he could never take back.

Maybe Ivy's leaving hadn't been completely Esther's fault.

"For eight years I tried to convince myself that you and

Mamm still loved me, even if Dat didn't, but I didn't dare come home for fear I'd find out you really didn't need me or love me or care for me at all. I never gave up hope that you would take me back and love me even though I was completely unlovable. But the day I took Winnie away, I saw the truth of everything in your eyes. Just like Dat had said, you didn't want me. You were better off without me. I'd caused too much heartache. You wished I'd never been born."

The tears trickled down Esther's cheeks like rain on a windowpane. "Oh, no, never, never say that." She clutched Ivy tightly to her, and loud, ugly sobs fell from her mouth. Poor Ivy. Poor, broken, frightened Ivy. Ivy truly didn't have a friend in the world, not even her sister. And she had lived with that burden for far too long.

Was this why Dat had left Esther all that money and asked her to look after Ivy? Did he feel guilty, profoundly guilty for what he had done, for words that couldn't be unsaid, for sins that couldn't be forgiven? Esther hadn't known that Dat had told Ivy to go away, but to her shame, she might have agreed with him, might have been happy to know Dat had stood up for her. But there was no pleasure in the thought that he had rejected one child for the sake of another. He shouldn't have done it, and Esther should have tried harder to find Ivy and bring her home. Hadn't Ivy said as much only a few weeks ago?

Esther caught her bottom lip between her teeth. She was torn between her dislike for Ivy and the need to take care of her sister and heal the relationship. How could she do anything but invite Ivy into her home again? Maybe they could start afresh. Maybe they could just be sisters. "I want you to stay, Ivy. I want you to stay here with us. There will always be a place for you."

"Now you just feel sorry for me. I saw your true feelings two weeks ago. You don't want me here."

Esther couldn't deny her misgivings. "Feeling sorry for you is a start, I guess."

Ivy turned away as if she couldn't bear the honesty in Esther's eyes. "I don't want pity, especially yours."

"What do you want me to say? I don't want to hurt your feelings, but you're very hard to live with. You seem determined to make everyone around you miserable."

"How else could I know that you'll love me no matter what?"

And there it was. The absolute and stark truth. Esther felt the heaviness of it like a fatal disease. "You're right, Ivy. I haven't loved you well. I haven't loved you as Jesus would love you."

Ivy groaned. "You're so pious, Esther. You think I want you to love me because it's your *duty* as a Christian? Don't bother."

"I should love you because you're my sister."

"Still sounds like duty." Ivy sighed, shook her head, and closed her eyes for a long minute. "It's not your fault you don't love me. Nobody loves me. Not even Jordan, and that's sinking pretty low. I'm not worthy of anybody's love, and I never will be. Even my own daughter doesn't love me. Jordan is all I deserve, and we both know it." She sounded so sad, so lost.

Esther had nothing to give, nothing to make her feel better. Lies and half-truths and declarations of love wouldn't convince Ivy of anything. Esther had been guilty of treating Ivy as a duty, and she didn't know how to treat her otherwise. But . . . Levi did. Levi always had. "Levi doesn't think you're unlovable. He likes you. He's told me before that he enjoys your company."

Ivy sneered. "Levi was being nice to me to get me to sign those papers."

"No, he wasn't. Remember the day under the apricot tree when you spilled lemonade on Winnie? He stood up for you and chastised me for being cross. I told him to go stick his head in the new toilet."

Ivy cracked a smile. The smile gave way to a giggle. "I bet that surprised him."

Esther grinned. "Oh, I've given him a setdown a time or two."

Ivy pressed her lips together. "It was Menno all over again."

"What do you mean?"

"The reason I started dressing Amish. It was easy to see that you loved Levi. Even easier to see Levi was in love with you. I wanted to steal him. I thought if I could make him fall in love with me, I would finally be worthy." She glanced at Esther. "He is the first man who has treated me well for a very long time. I was an idiot, but I truly thought he was going to ask me to marry him."

"I thought that too."

Ivy nodded. "I knew you did. The morning of the brunch, you were upset about Levi, and your sadness made me very happy, I'm ashamed to say. I was expecting a proposal, and when it didn't happen, I decided you were both in on a plan to lie to me and embarrass me. I knew then that you didn't love me. That you were only pretending so you could take Winter from me. I was wonderful angry."

"I know."

"I did my best to hurt you. I wanted to hurt you. It was a terrible thing to do, take Winter away. I guess I was hoping there was a small part of you that wanted me to stay—a small part of you that would love me for Winter's sake. But you were willing to lose Winnie to be rid of me. It cut right to my heart."

"I didn't want to let go of Winnie, but I couldn't let you treat me like that." Esther swallowed at the lump in her throat. "And you are Winnie's mother. I love her, but I have no right to keep her."

"I love Winnie. I want you to know I love her very much."

"I know that."

Ivy's voice shook with emotion. "I couldn't let myself love her. I didn't want it to hurt so much when I gave her up, and I knew I would give her up in the end. I can't be the kind of mother she needs, even though giving her up is just another sign of my failure as a person. Winter is better off with you."

"Giving her up is the greatest act of courage and un-selfishness I've ever seen."

Ivy snorted. "Yeah, right."

"You saw how Jordan treated her. She was hungry and cold and unhealthy. Whether you knew it or not, you brought her here because you wanted her to be safe. To have a better life."

"I brought her here because Jordan was going to dump me."

"It doesn't matter. You were desperate and frightened, and you had the good sense to come to me. It was very brave. Even though I was mad at you for weeks, Levi helped me see what a wonderful *gute* thing you did."

Ivy's lips curled upward slightly. "Levi is nice, I guess."

"And he wasn't just being nice to you because of the adoption papers."

She scrunched her lips to one side of her face. "He sure made a mess of it though."

Esther laughed. "He puts his foot in his mouth often enough."

"Has he asked you to marry him yet?"

Esther's heart jumped up and down at the very thought. "Do you . . . do you think he will?"

"For sure and certain. That boy is so in love with you, he can't see straight."

Esther giggled. "Either that or he needs glasses." She tugged Ivy closer to her. "Can we be sisters again, true, loyal, devoted sisters?"

The worry lines around Ivy's mouth deepened. "I want that very much, but I don't know how. I've lived for myself for so long, I don't know if I can be another way."

"It won't be easy." Esther grimaced. "And to be honest, I love you, but I can't live with you."

Ivy rolled her eyes even as she smiled widely. "At least I know you're not lying to me."

"Even in the best relationships, you have to set some rules."

"Jordan's stepmom called it 'setting boundaries,'" Ivy said, with just a tinge of bitterness in her voice. "That's why she kicked us out."

"I have a little money set aside," Esther said. She opted not to tell Ivy about Mamm and Dat's money just yet.

"What if we got you a little house or an apartment close by? You could get a job and earn enough to buy a car."

"Sounds pretty dull," Ivy said, but her eyes sparkled as if she was considering the possibilities.

Esther shrugged. "You have to start somewhere. Maybe you'll figure out what it is you really want to do, something that would make you happy, like my quilting does for me. You could go to school. Maybe you'll meet a guy, a good guy to date."

"I'm not dating ever again."

"Okay then. There is more to life than finding a husband."

Ivy laughed. "I tried to tell you that years ago." She pursed her lips. "Would you teach me how to cook? I could maybe even help you with your quilts."

"Of course. Remember how every year at Christmastime Mamm made chocolate Yule logs to give to neighbors? Christmas is coming up. We could make Yule logs together."

Ivy's smile was like a 100-watt light bulb. "I'd like that."

They hugged each other as if they would never hug each other again. "I love you, Ivy."

"I love you too, Esther."

Esther stood up and folded the blanket. "Come in. You can sleep in the spare room for a few weeks until we find you a place to live."

Ivy jumped to her feet, looking ten years younger than when she had arrived tonight. "I have one more question. What *have* you got behind your ear?"

Esther put her hand to the side of her head and slid whatever it was from behind her ear. She giggled. It was the red plastic rack that held Scrabble tiles. She must have tucked it behind her ear when she went to answer the door. She'd been completely unaware of even doing it. "You never know when you're going to want to play Scrabble."

Chapter Eighteen

Levi jumped from his buggy and ran to the house. The weather had turned cold, and an open-air buggy was no way to get around in the winter. Hopefully, Dat and Mamm would give him a buggy with a roof and a heater for his wedding. Levi's heart galloped down the road at the thought of a wedding. He'd bided his time long enough. Today was the day.

He pulled the collar of his coat closer around his neck with one hand and clutched the white paper bag tightly with the other. Lord willing, Esther didn't need anything to soften her up, but jelly-filled donuts certainly couldn't hurt.

Levi was as jumpy and eager as a racehorse at the starting gate. He'd been patient and long-suffering for weeks. He couldn't bear to wait any longer. They had found a little house for Ivy, not a ten-minute walk from Esther's house, and yesterday, Levi and Esther had helped Ivy move in. Not that she needed much help. She had a few clothes and all her earrings, and Esther had given her the twin bed from the spare bedroom. Ivy had also found a job, and today was her first day. It was Winnie's naptime, and Lord willing, Levi would finally have some time alone with Esther.

He hoped it was enough time to say what he had to say, eat a donut, and do a little kissing before Winnie woke up. Esther would never agree to kissing in front of Winnie. He wanted to kiss Esther so much, his throat ached and his lips were sore. He had to marry her before he keeled over dead.

Levi knocked on the door and let himself in, as was his habit. Maybe it was a bad habit, but Esther didn't seem to mind, and it made him feel like he was already an important and irreplaceable part of her life. He hoped and prayed that was true, because he could not, would not live without Esther.

As he walked into the house, a pillow sailed past his head, bounced against the door to Winnie's room, and fell silently to the floor on top of three or four other pillows already lying there. He glanced at the one that had almost hit him. It was the decorative pillow that usually sat on Esther's sofa. It was embroidered with the words, "As I have loved you, love one another."

He chuckled. Esther stood in the front room behind her quilt frames poised to throw another pillow in his direction. She lowered her arm and smiled. "*Ach.* I almost hit you. You should have knocked."

"I knocked. You didn't hear me."

Strands of chestnut hair stuck out from under the bandanna she was wearing, and a long, white ruler was tucked behind her ear. It could have been a weapon to keep anyone from getting too close to her. How did she manage to make something that long stay right there? And how did she manage to look beautiful no matter what was going on with her hair? She released the pillow, and it fell to the floor. "I didn't hear you because I have to grunt really loud when I throw something this heavy. It feels better if I really put some emotion into it."

Levi picked up the pillow with the Bible verse on it. "Having a bad day?"

"Maybe I'm redecorating."

He chuckled. "I guess that's why they call it a throw pillow."

She raised her eyebrows. "I never thought of that. I should have been throwing these for the last thirty years."

He couldn't keep a very wide smile from his face. She was just so adorable. "So what is all the pillow tossing about?"

Esther growled and plopped down on the sofa. "Look at this." She pointed to the quilt on the frames. "Just look at it."

Levi walked in the front room to get a closer look. "What's wrong with it?"

"*Ach*, look at the stitches. I went to pickleball this morning, and while I was gone, Ivy did a whole flower. She wanted to surprise me, and *ach*, was I surprised. Her stitches are wider than the Colorado River. The customer won't like that. Now Ivy has made unnecessary holes in my quilt, and she'll feel bad when I unpick her stitches."

"Why unpick them? I think it looks fine."

Esther's indignation seemed to explode. "No offense to you, but you don't know a thing about quilting, and I cannot in good conscience charge money for wide stitches. It's against the quilter's code."

"There's a code?"

She folded her arms. "Well, not really. But it's not up to my standards. I can't tell Ivy. She's trying so hard."

And she was. Esther had told Levi that Ivy insisted on making dinner every night for Esther and Winnie. She was getting better, but the two times Levi had been there for the evening meal, some things had gotten burned. Others had been undercooked or overseasoned. Still, the transformation in Ivy was quite stunning. It was amazing what could happen when you felt secure in someone's love.

"Maybe if you set up a sort of throwaway quilt when she comes over and then take it down when she leaves, she can put stitches in it to her heart's content, and she won't have to put unnecessary holes in any of the quilts you want to actually sell."

Esther thought about that for a minute. "That is a wonderful *gute* idea."

"Don't act so surprised."

Esther grinned. "I am surprised. You don't usually take a great interest in my quilting."

"That's not true. I take great interest in everything about you, Esther Zook." He saw his chance, a door in the conversation for him to walk through.

Her face turned a darker shade of pink. "You do?"

He cleared his throat. What if she still didn't want a husband? What if she was determined never to marry any man in general, and him specifically? She had told him right to his face that she would be better off alone, that she was as far from interested in him as she could get. Of course, that was several months ago, but still, when a man was about to propose, he wanted to be sure of the answer. It was time to distract her with sweets. He set the "love one another" pillow on the sofa and opened his white paper bag. "Would you like a donut? Jelly filled?"

Her lips twisted in amusement, probably at his sudden change of subject. "After crunchy rice pudding last night, a donut sounds like the most delicious thing in the world." She reached into his bag and pulled out a donut. She took a bite and moaned with pleasure. "This is like heaven in my mouth."

Gute. Now she was thinking happy thoughts. He set his bag on the sofa so his hands would be free to take her in his arms if he found the opportunity. "You know how I went to Ohio to find a *fraa*?"

She frowned. "*Jah.* I know."

"Well, I didn't."

"Find a wife?" she said.

"*Nae.* I didn't go to Ohio to find a wife. I went because I thought you were so mad at me about the adoption papers that you would never talk to me again. I went because I didn't want Ivy to take Winnie away from you. I went because the thought of losing you broke my heart."

She froze with the donut halfway to her lips and studied his face. "It did?"

"*Jah.*"

"The thought of losing you broke my heart too," she said softly.

Levi's heart was already racing like a river. Now it pounded on his ribs like a waterfall. "It did?"

She nodded. "Ivy wanted me to choose between you and Winnie. But I knew my happiness would never be complete or even worth having if I couldn't be with you."

"You chose me over Winnie?" His throat ached with

sharp longing. How could he be worthy of so much courage and sacrifice?

"I chose letting go over fear. I chose love over force. I chose you and me over a half happiness."

"*Ach*, Esther," he said. "I love you more than I will ever be able to say."

Her smile was as bright as a thousand sunrises, even with a dab of raspberry jelly smeared on her bottom lip. "Even though I throw apricots and pillows and have an unpredictable sister?"

He chuckled. "Even though."

"Even though I'm in a quilting group with your *mammi* and like to test the temperature of my bathwater?"

Levi raised an eyebrow. "*Your* bathwater? I thought you just did that for Winnie."

Esther sprouted a funny smile and looked out the window. "Umm, maybe. Maybe that's what I meant."

He wanted to kiss that jelly off her bottom lip so badly, he thought he might go crazy. His heart beat a wild rhythm as he stared at her mouth. She stopped breathing and stared at his. He curled his hands around her upper arms and lowered his face to hers.

And got a ruler right in the eyebrow.

Esther gasped and then giggled.

Levi pulled back and rubbed the spot on his eyebrow where Esther's ruler had gotten him. "Ow."

"Oh, dear," she said, pulling the ruler from behind her ear. "I'm sorry. I was measuring stitches and forgot it was even there."

"Am I bleeding?"

Esther couldn't stop laughing. "Move your hand," she said between giggles. Levi dropped his hand to his side.

He melted like a Popsicle when she brushed her fingers against his forehead. "There's a little scratch, but you won't have a scar."

"*Gute*, because I wouldn't want to tell our children about how I got it."

Her eyes glistened with hope and promise. "Our children?"

Levi wrapped his arms around Esther and pulled her close. "Will you marry me, my dear, darling quiltmaker? I love you more than you will ever know. I love you so much my bones ache and my head spins. Please say you'll marry me."

She caught her breath and looked down at her hand. He'd seized her so ardently, she hadn't had time to move her donut. There was glaze and raspberry jelly smeared all over the front of her apron and his shirt. "*Ach*. Hold on, Levi. I will get a towel."

He didn't relax his grip. "Can it wait? We're kind of in the middle of something here."

Esther's whole face spoke of happiness. "I was never fond of doing laundry." She slid her free hand around his neck and held the half-eaten donut between them like a baby. Winnie had often come between them like this. Levi didn't mind. "I once told you I didn't want to marry you, but it has come to my attention that I have since changed my mind. I love you, and I am the happiest girl in the whole world."

Levi couldn't help the tears that slipped down his cheeks. Esther loved him! He would never want for another thing in his entire life. This is what happiness felt like. He'd never set foot on solid ground again.

He gazed at Esther. She smiled at him.

Free from the threat of the ruler, he moved in for a long-awaited kiss.